OPERATION
SURVIVAL

R. "PETRA" BOHNET

MILTON & HUGO L.L.C.
4407 Park Ave., Suite 5
Union City, NJ 07087, USA

Website: *www. miltonandhugo.com*
Hotline: *1- 888-778-0033*
Email: *info@miltonandhugo.com*

Ordering Information:
Quantity sales. Special discounts are granted to corporations, associations, and other organizations. For more information on these discounts, please reach out to the publisher using the contact information provided above.

Library of Congress Control Number: 2024910088
ISBN-13:   979-8-89285-139-8   [Paperback Edition]
                 979-8-89285-140-4   [Digital Edition]

Rev. date: 11/25/2024

CONTENTS

Chapter One – The Infiltration 1
Chapter Two – The Discovery 14
Chapter Three – The Confrontation 27
Chapter Four – The Assignment Briefing 34
Chapter Five – The Preparation 41
Chapter Six – The Journey 52
Chapter Seven – The Encounter 67
Chapter Eight – Deepening the Web 82
Chapter Nine – The Trap and Execution 96
Chapter Ten – Hiding in Plain Sight 117
Chapter Eleven – Aftermath and Planning 126
Chapter Twelve – Dawn of Disguises 139
Chapter Thirteen – Shadows of the Plant 150
Chapter Fourteen – The Dance of Deception 164
Chapter Fifteen – Preparations in the Shadows 184
Chapter Sixteen – A Quiet Before the Storm 191
Chapter Seventeen – The Strike 197
Chapter Eighteen – Captured 219
Chapter Nineteen – Diverging Paths 232
Chapter Twenty – Shadows of Saint Petersburg 244
Chapter Twenty-One – The Covenant 258
Chapter Twenty-Two – Veil of Night 268
Chapter Twenty-Three – Bridge to Freedom 288
Chapter Twenty-Four – Chase Through Shadows 301
Chapter Twenty-Five – Dawn of a New Day 310
Chapter Twenty-Six – Epilogue 323

Operation Retribution (Sneak Peek) 339
Chapter One – Winter Cabin 341

CHAPTER

ONE

The Infiltration

Floodlights sliced through the forest as Liliya moved, her steps soft but sure. Engines rumbled, boots crunched—she pushed forward, shadows slipping past. She moved with precision, each step measured against the cold wind biting her skin.

Gravel crunched underfoot, each sound jarring. Campfire smoke drifted past, stirring memories. The smell tugged her back—a different night, the acrid bite of antiseptic and blood pooling on the floor, Mel'nyk's voice threatening as he came at her. Liliya forced the memory down. *Here. Now. Stay sharp.*

The squat building loomed, shadowed and hulking. Liliya focused on the thumb drive inside—the lifeline her people needed. She glanced once at the building, cataloging every detail: the slight tilt of the security camera above the entry, the narrow blind spot between the patrol's circuit and the guard's line of sight.

The commander's voice faded, lost in the hum of generators. Her jaw tightened. *Focus.* The drive, hope for the Ukrainian people after two years of conflict—nothing else mattered. His words didn't matter—she was already in the office. It would only take a second to grab it, then disappear back into the shadows. But each step closer made her chest tighten.

1

The guard snapped to attention. The commander gave a curt nod. "You're dismissed." The guard hesitated, then stepped aside, leaving them alone. The door groaned shut, smoke and leather filling the room as firelight danced over insignias on the wall.

Liliya's eyes fixed on the drive on his desk. Just a few steps. Her fingers reached out, her breathing shallow, closing in on the small metal shape among the papers. Her fingers grabbed it, slipping it into her pocket, steadying herself.

A weight settled on her shoulder—heavy, unyielding. She froze. Cold seeped through her. Her throat tightened`.

She couldn't move, couldn't breathe. *He's here*—Mel'nyk's voice, the fingers around her neck, her chest struggling for air.

It should have felt harmless. But to Liliya, it was a vise, cold and unyielding. The air froze in her chest. "Want a drink?" The commander's voice was light, as if the world hadn't just shifted. But Liliya couldn't hear him—not really. Her fingers twitched. Her body went rigid, the memory clawing at the edges of her mind.

The firelight twisted, shadows flickering across the walls, throwing distorted shapes over the commander's office. A memory clawed at her mind— *Fluorescent. Too bright. Mel'nyk's hand tightening. Squeezing.* Air cut off, her pulse hammering, wild. Her chest went tight, her vision narrowing on the flames, now dancing erratically, almost mocking. The walls of the office— shrinking now, tight like the lab.

The warmth should have grounded her, but her throat tightened as though she were back in that room. The air was too heavy, pressing down on her. The commander's voice droned, far away, his hand still on her shoulder. She couldn't tell if it was her heartbeat or his breathing filling the room, drowning everything out.

Instinct kicked in, and she twisted sharply, breaking his grip. The leather of his glove dragged across her skin, snapping her to the present. Her body created distance, muscle memory overriding her reeling mind.

Her left arm shot up, blocking without hesitation, her right hand dropping swiftly toward her knife. The cool hilt pressed into her palm—real, solid. The tactile sensation cut through the fog. In one fluid motion, her fingers closed tightly around it, the weight familiar, comforting.

One quick strike. Clean. No hesitation.

The blade sliced upward, swift and precise, piercing the commander's ribs. The fabric tore as the knife sank in, his body jerking briefly before slumping. Blood seeped through his uniform, grounding her in the stark reality of the moment. *This was real; this was now.*

Panic slipped away. Cold. Steady. She tightened her grip, establishing herself in the present, and twisted the blade deeper into his body.

The commander gasped, eyes wide with sudden shock. His body jerked involuntarily as his nervous system scrambled to respond to the wound. He staggered backward, his chest heaving as air struggled to escape his lungs. His hand instinctively reached toward her, more reflexive motion than deliberate.

She reacted instantly, her hand snapping to his wrist, twisting his arm across her body. Using his momentum, she pivoted sharply, throwing him off balance.

His breath became wet, each exhalation a strained gurgle as blood filled his mouth. For a fleeting moment, his body crashed against hers, heavy and desperate. She pulled back, her heartbeat steady now, and the weight of the knife felt right.

The commander's knees buckled, and with a dull thud, dropped to the floor. Liliya stood over him, her chest rising and falling with steady control, her grip on the knife unyielding. She watched the light fade from his eyes, his lips still parted in a futile gasp for air, expelling the bitter tang of vodka mixed with blood, swirled in the air and clawed at her senses. Her pulse pounded relentlessly in her ears, but she forced herself to stay focused, scanning the room for any lingering threats.

The room wavered. Liliya paused, attempting to shake the images of the lab from her mind, and focus back to the task at hand. She blinked—*no, not the lab. Not anymore.* Her fingers were still slick. She wiped the blade clean on his uniform. Time to move.

Drive. The door - no. The window - yes. Escape.

She sheathed the knife, straightened, eyes on the way out. This part was over. With one last glance at the room, she turned towards the window, her muscles taut and ready. The forest loomed beyond it, dark and quiet—a far cry from the noise screaming in her head.

She stripped off the Russian uniform, revealing the black covert gear beneath. The night air hit her skin like a cold slap, but she landed without a sound, crouching in the shadows. The thumb drive in her pocket felt like an anchor pulling her back to reality. No time to dwell. Each breath felt heavy, but she forced her body to move, slipping into the darkness.

Steeling herself, Liliya pressed deeper into the shadows, her body moving in sync with the night. The supply dump loomed ahead— its vague outline barely discernible in the cold darkness. She exhaled slowly, misting the frigid air, each inhale cutting through the fog in her mind like a sharp blade. Her fingers twitched, remembering the gentleness she once reserved for scalpel and suture—ironic, now, when it was the same precision that kept her alive. War had made her a different kind of surgeon, cutting away rot at the source. One hand on her knife, she slipped back into the shadows, her breath merging with the cold night air.

She drew the air in deeply, the cold sharp in her lungs. The acrid scent of diesel pricked at old memories, stirring something dark and buried, but she pushed it down, focusing on the crates stacked haphazardly in front of her. Each jagged shadow cast by the moonlight seemed to shift as she moved, her eyes never leaving the path ahead.

Her boots skimmed the ground, each step deliberate and firm. The wind whispered through the trees, carrying faint voices—soldiers, laughing, unaware of how close she was. The crunch of gravel beneath her feet sent a jolt of adrenaline through her limbs, heightening her senses. Every sound, every shift in the air, became a threat. Liliya's breath quickened as the supply dump loomed closer. She had to be faster than the fear.

She ducked low behind a stack of crates, pressing her back against the cold, rough metal. The acrid tang of gun oil filled her nose, cutting through the forest's earthy scent. *Ivan. Blood.* The copper tang sharp enough to taste. She swallowed hard, her fingers instinctively curling, feeling the warm wetness on her hands, only to snap her focus back. The forest was silent except for her quickening breaths. *Concentrate. Just get out.* She forced herself to steady, scanning for the next move, every muscle poised for flight.

The sentry was too close to her exit point, his outline clear in the dim light. She could see the rifle slung lazily over his shoulder, its metal glinting under a sliver of moonlight. His shoulders sagged with fatigue, and Liliya found herself unconsciously matching her breathing to his— slow, even breaths. A rhythm she recognized. For a second, her focus wavered. Her throat tightened—an old memory, sharp and suffocating. She blinked hard, forcing her body forward, her boots quiet on the ground.

A rustle nearby sent a jolt through her, muscles coiling in readiness. She forced her mind to stay sharp, eyes locked on the sentry. He yawned, the rifle slipping slightly in his grip. Sweat gathered at her temple, but she didn't move. She waited; every nerve focused on his posture. When he finally turned, she shifted her weight forward, moving with deliberate care. Her steps were slow and calculated. Each step felt like a risk, the night seeming to press in around her as she inched closer to her exit point. Shadows twisted around her. She tightened her grip on the thumb drive, focusing her senses forward. The ravine lay ahead, her way out.

Stop! A flashlight beam sliced through the dark, just missing her hiding spot. Her pulse quickened, but she stayed still, breath steady. The sentry muttered something in Russian, turning away as his light faded into the night. *Go!*

She hid behind a stack of crates, her mind racing. Each shadow pulsed with menace. Her eyes swept the dark perimeter as dread twisted in her stomach. Liliya glanced at the thumb drive, fingers curling protectively. She grasped a nearby branch, for balance as she made her soundless advance towards a tarp covered stack nearer to the sentry and the ravine entrance. *Ravine! Right there! Keep moving!*

She crouched in the shadows, eyes fixed on the sentry. His rifle leaned haphazardly against his shoulder as his head bobbed with drowsiness. Liliya held her breath as his eyelids fluttered, then snapped open before finally drooping into the deep rhythm of sleep. She picked up a small rock and threw it into the darkness away from her location.

Clack! The sound echoed in the stillness of the night, jolting the sentry awake. He stood with a start, his eyes wide and disoriented. For a moment, he seemed unsure of what to do, his brain struggling to process the sudden noise. Finally, he moved towards the sound. *Get to the ravine, get out.* Without hesitation, she darted towards the ravine's entrance, her heart pounding.

In the cover of the ravine, Liliya's pace slowed, her breath shallow as the cold air bit at her exposed skin. The earth beneath her feet grounded her, but the weight of the moment still clung like sweat on her skin. The shadows of the ravine closed around her, narrowing her focus. She stayed low, heart pounding as rushing water echoed. Her eyes swept the treeline—no movement. She tightened her grip and forced herself forward.

She crept down the ravine's slope, the darkness treacherous. A laugh echoed from the camp—close but unaware. Every step was calculated, pulling her further from the memories clawing at her. A low murmur of voices drifted through the trees. She stilled, eyes watching the path ahead. She could hear the voices now—closer than before. Her muscles tensed as three soldiers approached, rifles slung over their shoulders. The first gestured, and they paused, sweeping their flashlights across the trees. She lowered herself, her heart steady, waiting.

The patrol moved slowly, methodically, checking every dark corner. Liliya pressed herself deeper into the ravine's shadows, her breath controlled, her muscles taut. The soldiers drew closer, one of them stepping on a branch, the sharp snap cutting through the night.

For a moment, the patrol lingered, their flashlights hovering over the area. The bright light of a flashlight beam cut through the darkness, nearly exposing her. Her fingers gripped the knife, ready to strike, if necessary, but she stayed still, silent.

Then a soldier grumbled something in Russian—tired, irritated—and waved the others forward. For a tense moment, the soldiers exchanged a few words before turning back toward the camp, their footsteps retreating into the distance. The sound of their wading through the underbrush slowly faded, and Liliya allowed herself a slow exhale. They were gone. For now.

Branches snapped against her skin as she moved deeper, shadows curling around her. The extraction point was close, but danger clung to every corner. She pushed on, the thumb drive's weight settling her.

A dog barked in the distance—sharp and menacing. Liliya froze, her breath catching in her throat as it echoed through the trees. She squatted close to the ground, hiding in the shadows. The floodlights loomed in the distance, casting long, distorted images through the trees. She clenched her jaw and waited, every nerve on edge.

The moment stretched. Silence fell. She shifted her weight, preparing to move again. Each step toward the extraction point felt heavier, her past dragging at her like chains, wrapping tighter with every movement. The hum of the camp faded, replaced by a memory's cold grip.

But this mission—this fragile hope for her people—was all that mattered now. She couldn't let the past pull her under. She shook it off, eyes narrowing on the path ahead. She forced herself forward again, slipping deeper into the woods, drawing ragged and shallow gasps.

She spotted him through the trees, his shadow against the cold glow of the headlights. Her shoulders wanted to fall, her knees to give. Her fingers still felt the phantom slickness of blood. The clean lights of the operating room bleeding into the brutal reality of now. The knife in her hand felt foreign yet familiar, its weight pulling her senses into sharp focus. *Instinct.* She had relied on it in the past, stitching flesh with precision, now that same instinct had driven the blade deeper into the commander's ribs. A healer's hands turned to weapons.

Her fingers twitched involuntarily, as though still grasping a scalpel, and for a moment, she saw blood on the ground—dark stains that weren't there. She squeezed the hilt of her knife tighter, trying to shake the sensation, but it clung to her. The moisture on her wrists stirred another memory: warm blood, thick and clinging to her skin like an unshakable shadow. Her pulse echoed in her ears. *Not meant for this.* But she was. The healer and the killer. Both. There was no more dividing line between them.

She inhaled sharply, banishing the memory. Her gaze stayed on Davyd, taking a step forward, every nerve taut, pulse racing as though the shadows would swallow her before she reached him.

Davyd stepped forward, his hand reaching out. "Your okay?" His hand went to her shoulder instinctively, his hand steadying her without a word. Liliya nodded, but her voice caught in her throat. Her fingers twisted tighter into her sleeve. She shifted closer, not letting herself look at him fully. He held her shoulder, his touch steady. "It's over."

Her gaze dropped, a flicker of vulnerability she quickly shuttered. "Is it?" she replied, her voice barely audible. Her hand lingered on his jacket sleeve, fingers curling.

Liliya's hand fisted, knuckles paling as she braced herself. Davyd didn't move, his presence unwavering, waiting.

"You don't have to do this alone," he murmured, his voice barely a whisper against the silence.

Her jaw tightened, but she didn't pull away. "Don't I?"

His hand moved to her back, slow and deliberate. No words. Just steadying her as she stayed there, still. The weight of the mission, the danger, was in the silence between them.

Davyd nodded, his hand brushing her arm. "We keep going." She pressed closer to him, her gaze dropping. Her silence said everything. Davyd pulled her closer, his arm steady around her.

Her lips parted slightly. "I'm not sure..." Her voice was low, faltering, but she held his gaze for a second, then looked away, her pulse racing.

His hand reflexively tightened, though he left the silence undisturbed. "You're still here," he murmured. "That's enough."

She stayed silent, eyes distant. Davyd felt her tremor, faint but there. His hand moved to her hair in a steadying touch, and for a moment, she held on.

Davyd's gaze shifted to the dark forest; senses alert. Her breath stuttered against his chest, and his grip softened, reassuring her. He stayed close, silent but steady, his presence pressing against her with a quiet weight.

Her tears glistened in the dim light, and she buried her face in his chest. Liliya's fingers closed reflexively around the fabric, gripping tightly enough that she felt the worn fibers pressing into her skin. The pressure helped her steady herself, but the tremor remained, betraying the unease hidden beneath.

Her hand trembled slightly, grip loosening as her eyes darted away. Davyd noticed the shift, a fracture in her steady presence. He reached out, his hand settling on her shoulder, steadying her, grounding her. She blinked, jaw tightening, and held his gaze, barely nodding before looking past him again.

They moved toward the Land Rover, Liliya's grip on Davyd firm, her fingers digging into his arm as if anchoring herself to reality. Inside the vehicle, the silence was suffocating, thick with everything left unsaid. Davyd glanced at her from the corner of his eye—Liliya, always the one in control, now barely holding it together. Her breath was uneven, her gaze fixed on the dashboard, as though she couldn't bear to look at anything that might pull her back into the mission.

Without warning, her hand shifted on his arm, no longer seeking support but gripping with urgency. She leaned into him, her body rigid, movements sharp. Liliya pressed her lips to his, the touch almost mechanical. Davyd hesitated, feeling the coldness in her movements. His breath caught, but instead of pulling back, he cupped her face gently, his fingers tracing her jawline. He said nothing—just held her still, waiting for her to meet his eyes. Instead, she stared past him, hollow and distant. She clung to him, but there was nothing behind her gaze, just shadows.

Her fingers trembled, gripping him tightly, her face pressed into his chest, breaths shallow and uneven. He felt the weight of her fear and exhaustion settle against him, solid and heavy, an unspoken plea for steadiness as he held her closer, supporting her.

Liliya retreated and her body sank into the seat, muscles betraying her, no longer under her tight control. Her hands fumbled with the seatbelt, buckling it with a sharp click. The hum of the engine pulled her into a fog, her vision flickering— the memory of blood. She flexed her fingers instinctively, the phantom weight of a scalpel pressing down, but there was no relief in the motion.

Her breath caught for a moment, the present and past blurring at the edges. She forced herself to focus—this wasn't the time to lose control. Her fingers tightened around the thumb drive, knuckles white against the leather-worn seat.

The Land Rover jolted over the rough road, each bump making Liliya shift. Her fingers fidgeted with her jacket's frayed edge, her gaze fixed beyond the trees flashing by, lost somewhere Davyd couldn't reach.

"Liliya," Davyd murmured, his voice low, almost lost in the hum of the engine.

Her grip tightened on the armrest, knuckles paling. She didn't turn to him, didn't speak—just stared ahead, her silence coiled between them.

He shifted in his seat, the worry gnawing at him. Davyd's grip on the wheel tightened. "Anything." His voice came out low, a murmur carrying the weight of unasked questions.

Her breath hitched, her eyes narrowing as she turned to face him. "What are you looking for, Davyd?" Her voice was low, sharp-edged, challenging him to voice the concern he'd been holding back.

He met her gaze, his brow furrowing slightly, but he held steady. "Just... anything that tells me you're still here."

Her mouth pressed into a thin line, and for a beat, they simply stared at each other, the air thick with everything unspoken. She let out a short breath, her expression softening. "Don't worry about me," she said, looking away, voice barely a whisper.

He glanced over at her, his hand brushing hers as he turned his eyes back to the road. 'You're here,' he said quietly, grip tightening on the wheel as he drove on.

For a long moment, she said nothing. Her eyes locked with his, distant and aching. "Am I?"

The hum of the engine filled the silence, broken only by the occasional creak of the road beneath the tires. Davyd's hands gripped the steering wheel, his fingers tapping against it, restless. He glanced at Liliya—still staring out the window, her body rigid, her hand close to her side as if she hadn't left the mission behind.

He tightened his jaw. He shifted in his seat, eyes flicking back to the road. *She's fine*, he told himself, but the thought rang hollow.

His hands flexed around the wheel.

She wasn't fine.

The night felt heavier than usual. The low hum of the engine did little to drown out the memory of her hands trembling back at the briefing. He should've seen it then—pulled her back, asked her something— anything—but the mission had been clear, and Liliya? She didn't pull back. Not for anything.

A flicker of movement—her fingers twitching against her leg—caught his eye. He almost said something, but his throat tightened. What was there to say?

He kept his eyes on the road, but his thoughts wouldn't settle. Every crack in her composure gnawed at him. She was slipping, and he was watching it happen. His fingers drummed harder on the wheel. *Goddamn it.*

He cut a glance at her again, her shoulders still stiff, her breathing too controlled. She was wound up tight, and he was the one asking her to keep going. *How much longer could she keep this up?* He let out a breath, long and slow. He wasn't sure anymore.

Davyd's fingers stilled, a tremor betraying the tension he held back. He glanced sideways at her, eyes catching the faint tremor in her hands as she held the armrest. His gaze lingered a beat too long, his jaw tightening. "You're pushing yourself hard," he murmured, voice low, almost a question.

Liliya's grip tightened in response, her fingers digging into the fabric as she fixed her gaze out the window. "And?" she whispered, the single word clipped, defensive. Her gaze flicked briefly to meet his before snapping away, as though the directness was too much to bear.

A beat of silence fell between them, thick and palpable. Davyd released the wheel slightly, his shoulders sagging. "Just... be careful." He paused, catching her in his peripheral vision. "We need you intact, Liliya."

She scoffed softly but said nothing, her fingers loosening on the armrest as she stared into the darkening road ahead.

Davyd glanced sideways at her, the quiet in the car pressing down as heavily as his own memories. She was staring out the window, her posture tight, her gaze far beyond the shadows passing them by. The silence between them should've felt like a relief. Instead, it sank deeper, stirring something he'd buried a long time ago.

A quiet night in the Carpathians, lying in a trench beside Sergei, came to mind. They'd barely made it through a skirmish, the snow masking the blood until the stench hit. Sergei had whispered then, voice broken, "You'll make it home, Dee." Davyd had made it, just not whole.

He pulled his gaze back to the road, fingers tightening around the wheel as he fought the urge to reach for her hand. It wasn't Sergei in that trench this time—it was Liliya. And damn it if he wasn't going to pull her out of this. Not this time.

CHAPTER

TWO

The Discovery

Cold air pressed against Davyd's skin as he leaned on the Land Rover, breath coming fast. The mission's adrenaline hadn't faded; his heart still hammered; each beat a pulse of urgency. He ran a hand through his hair, fingers trembling from the night's intensity.

Liliya's image flashed before him—her face pale and drawn, eyes haunted by something beyond the mission. She had looked right through him, as though the present was too thin a veil to hold back the nightmares clawing at her mind. Davyd squeezed his eyes shut, trying to block out the memory. But the weight of her vulnerability still hung on him like a heavy coat, suffocating in its familiarity.

The drive back had been thick with silence, his knuckles tight on the wheel. He couldn't shake the images replaying in his mind—Liliya's sharp movements, the blood on her hands, the emptiness in her eyes. His grip tightened, but nothing could shake the weight settling in his chest.

Standing outside headquarters, Davyd inhaled deeply, but the city's faint hum did little to quiet the tension crackling within him. Every shadow in his periphery felt like a threat, each footstep from passing agents jarring.

14

He rubbed a hand over his face, memories of Liliya's trembling hands flashing in his mind. She'd never faltered—until now. His fist clenched reflexively as he pushed the thought away, steadying himself. He couldn't afford doubt. Not now, not with her survival—and possibly the mission—hanging in the balance.

Davyd took a breath, stepped back, and stretched his shoulders, trying to release the knots of tension. Exhaustion pulled at him, but his mind wouldn't rest. Liliya's face hovered in his thoughts—strong yet cracking under the pressure. He shook his head, forcing the distraction aside. *Focus.*

The Security Service of Ukraine headquarters loomed, its sharp edges cutting into the morning light. Davyd straightened his posture, bracing himself. He had to focus, stay on task, but the tension from last night refused to let go.

Inside, the command center buzzed with life—voices, tapping keys, and the hum of machines merging into background noise. Davyd took a steadying breath, but adrenaline still coursed under his skin, restless. His eyes scanned the room, every corner, every movement. The sense of lurking danger wouldn't ease, each footstep too loud, each creak too sharp. Muscles tense, his mind spun with what-ifs.

Davyd stepped into Commander Sanenko's office, flexing his hands to dispel the tension. Adrenaline had left a hollow ache in its place. Sanenko nodded, but Davyd's mind replayed last night, each detail sharpening in his memory.

"Any problems?" Sanenko asked, his voice cutting through the haze in Davyd's mind.

Davyd blinked hard, refocusing on the present. He forced his body to relax, but it felt unnatural. "Liliya's not herself after last night," he said, his voice betraying the tightness he had tried to suppress. "Something's wrong."

15

Sanenko's stern gaze softened, his shoulders relaxing. He placed a reassuring hand on Davyd's arm. "You know her best, Davyd. We'll ensure she gets the support she needs."

Davyd got up and put his hand in his pocket where the thumb drive rested. Just then Lead Tech Specialist Yankovic opened the door, "Commander, the team's ready in the Tech Ops room," he announced.

"Let's get to it," Sanenko said, as he and Davyd followed Yankovic to the specially shielded room where the tech team worked their magic.

As they entered, Davyd's eyes scanned the busy tech team, their fingers dancing over keyboards with a familiar intensity. He pulled the drive from his pocket, "I hope this helps us find a weak spot," he said, his mind still on Liliya.

While Davyd handed the drive to Yankovic, Sanenko pointed to it. "Scour that for every detail. Time is critical," he commanded.

The commander's words sparked a memory, and for a moment, Davyd was back in that cold, sterile courtroom, the gavel's echo reverberating in his mind. The accusations had been a blow to his career, but it was the weight of his own choices that lingered.

With the thumb drive now in play, the weight of his current worries pressed down on him. Davyd's breath caught, his jaw clenched as the tech team turned their focus to the drive, their precise movements reminding him of his own dedication and what it cost him. It was the same resolve that had carried him through his court-martial gripping him now. The fight hadn't ended there—it was just another chapter. The loss of his insignia still stung, but it had only sharpened his purpose. He shook off the memory and focused on the action in front of him. This mission wasn't any different.

Davyd's eyes followed the tech team as they worked on the drive, their focus sharp. The energy in the room was palpable, but his thoughts drifted back to Liliya. He needed to be there for her. With a final glance at the team, he slipped out of the room, dread settling in his chest as he moved to complete a task, he wished he could avoid.

After Davyd's departure, the room continued to thrum with urgency, all those involved knowing the stakes were high. They were racing against time to uncover the hidden missile schedules and troop movements.

"Yankovic, look at this," Specialist Ivanko called urgently.

Yankovic hurried over, curiosity piqued. "What is it?"

"A hidden, encrypted file. It'll take time to crack," Ivanko said, already starting the decryption process.

"Can you get the data?" Yankovic asked.

"Not yet, I need more time." Ivanko replied.

"Get to it. We need everything we can find," Yankovic ordered.

Ivanko nodded and dove back into his work, his resolve only strengthened by the challenge. Each complex line of code deepened his resolve. "I'll crack this." he muttered under his breath.

After what seemed like hours of work, Ivanko's eyes burned, and his back ached. Still, he pressed on. "Come on, come on," he muttered. The room buzzed with tense energy.

"I'm getting close," Ivanko called out.

"How much longer?" Yankovic asked.

"Thirty minutes, maybe less," Ivanko replied.

Suddenly, the screen flickered, and a new line of code appeared. "Yes!" Ivanko whispered. Minutes later, the decryption tool beeped in success. "Got it. We're in."

Exhaustion evident but satisfaction gleaming in his eyes, Ivanko leaned back. "Told you I'd get it," he said with a tired smile.

As Ivanko examined the file, his smile disappeared with each passing line. A new biological weapon with specialized missile deployment and radar evasion systems. The information was significant, the implications dire. With each revelation, his heart sank further, the seriousness of the situation becoming starkly apparent.

Unable to find the words, Ivanko pointed at the screen. "Sir, this is...," was all he managed to say.

Seeing Ivanko's shift in demeanor, Yankovic approached, concern etched on his face. "What's going on, Boris? What did you find?" he asked, apprehensively. His face paled as he read the contents, "This changes everything," he murmured.

Their discovery meant disaster. The stakes were higher than ever; the future of their nation was on the line.

As the tech team sprang into action, Davyd moved with purpose. He entered his office and shut the door, taking a deep breath to steady himself. The weight of his job pressed hard on his shoulders. There was no room for mistakes—not now.

He settled into his chair, eyes scanning the room briefly. The scent of leather-bound reports and the hum of the computer barely registered. His gaze flicked to the wall of medals—each a symbol of sacrifices made. But that past didn't matter now. What mattered was the next move.

Davyd's finger hit each key with a precise force, printing his recommendation. The weight of it didn't slow him. Liliya's exhaustion flashed in his mind, but he pressed the feeling aside and printed the report without hesitation. The mission couldn't wait. He'd been careful with every word, framing his recommendation as tactical, not weakness. *She'll understand*, he told himself. *She has to.*

Without another glance at the medals, he grabbed the document and slid it into a folder. His steps quickened as he left the office, each one more decisive than the last. Their missions demanded everything, and he couldn't let emotions cloud the path ahead.

Davyd moved toward Sanenko's office, his pulse steadying into the rhythm of footsteps on the cold floor. His hands flexed—ready, as if for action. Liliya's strained face lingered in his thoughts, but he pushed ahead, each step solidifying his resolve. The thought of her, lost and distant, refusing to fade from his memory, made his chest tighten. *She always held the line—until now. Could she still?*

Davyd hesitated at the door for just a moment, his fingers tightening on the cold knob, jaw clenching. He could picture her sharp eyes, calculating yet wounded—she was no stranger to isolation, nor was he. She'd survived worse than anyone knew. Maybe that's why he felt the pulse of responsibility every time her name crossed his mind, his knuckles whitening on the handle. He took a breath to steady himself, then knocked firmly.

"Commander," Davyd said, his voice steady, though his jaw clenched tightly as he handed over the report. His fingers lingered on the document for a beat longer than necessary, as if letting it go was an admission of everything that weighed on him. "I've noted some concerns from the last mission. Bottom line, Liliya needs to be shut down."

His eyes darted to Sanenko's face, searching for some hint of agreement, some recognition of the danger Liliya was in—not just from being on missions, but from herself. His heart hammered in his chest; each beat a reminder of the urgency of the situation. His muscles were taut, his posture rigid, the tightness creeping up his spine.

Commander Sanenko took the document, his brow furrowed as he scanned the report. He nodded thoughtfully, but the tightness in his expression didn't ease. "I hear you, Davyd," he said, his voice calm, though there was a hint of something unspoken in his tone. "We can't afford to lose her, not in the long run."

Davyd leaned in, one hand gripping the edge of Sanenko's desk, knuckles pressed white. His voice was low, controlled, but the memory of Liliya's blank stare last night cut through his words, filling him with an instinctual pull he couldn't shake. He had to push back, to demand her safety, but how much would they listen? "Any updates on the thumb drive?" His voice was lower now, a whisper, as if the strain constricting his throat made it difficult to speak. "Some good news might help Liliya with my recommendation."

He shifted his weight, feeling the cramping in his legs from standing too rigidly for too long. The pressure in his chest didn't ease, and a tightness began creeping up his neck as he waited for Sanenko's response. He didn't know if he could face her without something positive—he needed something concrete, something to cling to.

Sanenko sighed, his shoulders sagging slightly as he leaned back in his chair. "Nothing yet," he said, rubbing the back of his neck as if trying to shake off the weight of the situation. "But I'll inform you as soon as we hear something."

Davyd forced himself to nod, but his jaw was still set, his teeth grinding together. He could feel the frustration rising in him, a bitter knot forming in his gut. "Sounds good," he said, though the words felt like gravel in his throat. He took a step back, feeling his body tense again as if he was preparing for a fight that hadn't happened yet. "I'll be in my office, finishing some reports. Let me know."

As he left the office, Davyd exhaled slowly, his shoulders slumping as he walked down the hallway. He rolled his neck, trying to loosen the knots that had settled there, but they refused to leave. He couldn't shake the gnawing feeling of dread, the weight of the unknown pressing down on him. Liliya wasn't just another agent—she was the backbone of their operations, and her unraveling threatened to bring everything down with her. His hands clenched and unclenched at his sides as he walked, his body still humming with the remnants of adrenaline, waiting for something—anything—to break.

A few minutes later, Yankovic burst into the commander's office. "Sir, we found something very important on the thumb drive," he stated urgently.

Sanenko picked up the phone and hit a button. "Davyd, stick around; we might have some new developments."

"I'll be in my office," Davyd replied from the other end. "Let me know."

After hanging up, Yankovic turned to Sanenko. "Sir, the drive had the usual info, but there was a deeply buried encrypted file. We decrypted it, and it's bad."

The National Security and Defense Council (NSDC), comprised of the President, the Secretary of the NSDC, Minister of Defense, Minister of Foreign Affairs, and the heads of SBU and the Foreign Intelligence Service (SZRU), gathered around the digital map depicting the current state of the war front. The map, marked with the recent lines of engagement and key battle zones from the 2022 Russian invasion and subsequent skirmishes. These represented the ongoing struggle for Ukrainian sovereignty. The map detailed the movements of Russian forces, including missile attacks, as well as the positioning of Ukrainian forces in opposition. Utilizing the voice command system, the council accessed the data from the thumb drive procured by Liliya.

The atmosphere in the war room was heavy with stress, exacerbated by the recent missile strikes on Kyiv, Mykolayiv, and Odessa. The barbaric actions of the Russians, resulting in civilian casualties, had deeply affected the council members, whose frustration was palpable. The Russians' blatant disregard for the Geneva Convention, particularly regarding the sanctity of civilian life, was difficult to comprehend. It was evident that the Russians aimed to use the targeting of civilians to undermine the morale of the Ukrainian nation.

Putin's resolve to restore Russia to its former state, disregarding the value of the Ukrainian nation and its citizens, was evident in the contents of the thumb drive. The information revealing Russian military movements and missile schedules, crucial insights for preventing and countering Russian aggression. But the newfound intelligence became the nation's top priority, emphasizing the gravity of the situation, Ukraine's complete demise.

"We cannot let these missiles be produced; we have no defense for them!" Minister of Foreign Affairs Davidenko exclaimed urgently. "The plant is too deep in Russian territory for a precise strike. Any ideas?"

Commander Sanenko assessed the situation. "We have three critical tasks. First, find and destroy the bioweapon," he said, displaying a photograph. "This individual developed both the bioweapon and deployment system. We need to extract information from him."

"Once we know where the weapon and data are, we will need to remove it and all the data associated with it for destruction," he emphasized. "Also, he either has the plans for the deployment system or knows where they are. Once we know that, we can determine how to retrieve them."

"Then, he must be exterminated," Sanenko stated with finality. "We can't allow him to survive and continue to develop weapons that can be used against us."

He continued, "Next, we must neutralize the plant before missile production begins. They're set to start in two weeks." He pointed at the map to the location the plant was located.

Opening three more files, he produced a photo from each one and placed them beside the first one. "Lastly, we have to eliminate the brain trust behind the radar cloaking system design for the missiles and remove all their research and data."

He paused, the weight of the task at hand clear in his expression. "The agent who retrieved the thumb drive for us is the only one capable of completing this task. As an intern, she worked with Mel'nyk and has the expertise to identify and handle biohazardous materials. Also, her past missions have allowed her to be a known fixture in the region where the missile plant is located. There will be far less scrutiny on her, allowing her better access to the plant. Anyone else would be considered an outsider, making the task of getting inside far more complicated."

Valeriy Dmitrienko, the Minister of Defense, interjected with a pertinent question. "Based on the report that just appeared on my desk, wasn't there concern regarding psychological stress at the end of her last mission?"

Commander Sanenko acknowledged the concern with a solemn nod. "There was indeed a note of an issue. However, she possesses the necessary skill set and has valuable contacts in the vicinity of the plant. During this last mission, she proved her mettle by infiltrating enemy lines and gathering critical intelligence. This mission cannot afford delays. If even one of those missiles is launched, it spells disaster for our nation. She will have to confront her challenges and ensure the job gets done," he declared resolutely. "Our nation's security is at stake."

The phone rang and Davyd instinctively picked it up, "Yes, this is Davyd, who is this?"

"This is Doctor Adamovich. I understand that you placed a request for your agent to begin therapy for stress-related issues. Is that correct?" Came the reply from the other end.

"Yes, Doctor, I want her to get the best care as promptly as possible."

"Well, sir, I've already contacted her to begin the process, but now there is a problem. When I attempted to enter her in the system, I was informed that she will be back out on mission ASAP."

"That can't be, I made it clear that she needed to be shut down for the extended future."

"Sorry to tell you this, but the order came from the highest level. My hands are tied."

Davyd slammed the receiver down, the sharp sound reverberating through his office. His breath was quick, shallow, and he could feel his pulse thrumming in his neck. Without a second thought, he stormed toward Sanenko's office, each step heavy with frustration. His fists clenched tightly, and the strain coiled in his chest, like a spring wound too tight.

His hand rapped once on the door before he shoved it open, the force of his movement betraying the restraint he was barely holding onto. "Liliya needs a break," he snapped, his voice tight, frayed at the edges. "Sending her back out is a mistake."

The commander looked up sharply, his brows knitting together at the force of Davyd's entrance. He rose slowly, his eyes tracking Davyd's tense movements. Then stepped around his desk, placing a firm hand on Davyd's shoulder. The gesture was meant to steady him, to pull him back from the edge. Davyd's muscles stiffened under the commander's grip, but he stayed rooted in place, his chest heaving with the effort to keep his emotions in check.

"Dee, I get it," Sanenko said, his voice low, measured. He squeezed Davyd's shoulder, his gaze softening slightly. "If this wasn't such a critical mission, and if Liliya wasn't the only one who could pull it off, I'd send her home."

Davyd stepped back, jaw tight. For a moment, he held his breath, the weight of the situation settling over him. He dropped into the chair opposite Sanenko, fists still clenched, searching for words that might sway him. "Why her? Send me instead." Davyd's voice cracked, and he tightened his grip on the chair, struggling to hold back the anger, and fear, rising in his chest.

Sanenko moved toward the window, watching the city below. "Davyd, this new missile—X-103—could bypass every radar we have," he added, each word dropping like a stone. Returning to his desk, he scanned the decrypted files on his screen, his fingers clenched on the table's edge. "Missile plant is in Dmitryashevka," he said, voice low, grim. "Production capacity shows they're aiming for mass deployment."

Davyd's jaw tightened. "Biological payloads?" he asked, already knowing the answer.

Sanenko nodded, his gaze steely. "They're not just targeting soldiers. Civilian casualties are almost guaranteed, designed to break morale and force our borders. They'll push Ukraine to its knees if we don't act."

Davyd's mind raced. "Then we need to neutralize the plant, hit their scientists. We can't let them get these weapons in the air."

"We have to send Liliya," Sanenko replied, his voice as hard as granite. "She's familiar with bio labs, and if anyone can slip past their security, it's her. Make no mistake—failure isn't an option."

Davyd exhaled sharply, running a hand over his face. "And if she can't handle it?"

"Then we'll deal with that when we get there," Sanenko replied, finality in his tone. "She knew the risks, Davyd. So do you."

Davyd nodded, his head bobbing mechanically. He understood, intellectually at least, but his body tightened at the thought of Liliya alone in the field again. The image of her haunted expression from the night before flashed in his mind, and he had to blink hard to push it away. His hands flexed and tightened again, the skin pulling taut over his knuckles as if he could squeeze the fear out of his body.

"I need to be close," Davyd insisted, his voice trembling now with a different kind of strain—one born of fear. "I need to be ready to get her out if something goes wrong. She's not stable." His breath hitched slightly, and he swallowed hard against the lump forming in his throat. He looked up at Sanenko, his eyes pleading now, searching for some way to make the commander understand.

Sanenko met his gaze steadily, the lines around his mouth tightening. For a moment, he said nothing, letting the silence between them stretch out—heavy, oppressive. Finally, he spoke, his voice firm but kind. "You'll be there when you can, Davyd. But the village is small. Strangers stand out." His eyes softened, just for a moment, as if acknowledging Davyd's unspoken fears. "Liliya has people there. She won't attract attention, but you will. Understand?"

Davyd's shoulders sagged, but his eyes remained steady. "Then give me one thing, Commander. If she falters, I pull her. No questions asked."

Sanenko met his gaze, giving a small, tight nod. "Agreed." His voice softened. "You'll be her backup if anything changes."

Davyd nodded, feeling the tension simmering just below the surface. He couldn't shake the memory of Liliya's vacant stare. This was as close to control as he was going to get. He rose, glancing back one last time. "Thank you."

Davyd left Sanenko's office, fists clenched. She's strong, he told himself, but a thread of doubt remained. Everyone has a breaking point.

As he strode down the hallway, a gust of cold air from an open window brought him back to the mountains, the biting wind cutting through his fatigues like glass. He had seen that raw fear in Liliya's eyes last night—the same vulnerability that had haunted him before. A vulnerability that cut deep. It mirrored the look his comrades had given him in the mountains, when every step through the snow had felt like a gamble with death. He wasn't in the Carpathians anymore—but the stakes felt just as high. He swallowed the memory down and kept his stride steady—Liliya needed him to be strong now. With each step, the weight of her vulnerability bore down on him. She wasn't invincible, no matter how much he wanted her to be. He had to be ready for whatever came next.

CHAPTER

THREE

The Confrontation

After Davyd dropped her off, Liliya navigated the familiar but now alien corridors of her apartment building. They were scarred by two years of conflict. The elevator's slow ascent felt like a climb towards judgment.

Stepping into her apartment, Liliya felt her nerves tighten. The mission had pushed her to a breaking point. Months of tension and sleepless nights had eroded her edge, her mind now tangled in fear and doubt.

Liliya stepped into the shower, twisting the knob until the water scalded, pushing through the heat that raised angry patches on her skin. Her fingers twitched as steam filled the small, enclosed bathroom, the space tightening around her. Fog clawed its way up, thickening the air, pressing down. She focused on the water drumming against her skin, but her chest tightened.

Her fingers pressed into the tile, the ceramic cold beneath the heat of the water. She blinked hard, pulling in a sharp breath—steam filling the air, thick like smoke. Liliya clenched her fists, her heartbeat slowing as she focused on the icy bite of the wall against her shoulder. She drew in a breath, the memory loosening its grip as she steadied herself.

With a sharp twist, she shut the water off, a bead trailing down her neck like a scalpel's edge. She gripped the faucet tight, metal cutting into her palm. She didn't let go until her breathing slowed, until all she felt was the cold metal.

Liliya dried off and moved into the living room. The dim light felt sharper, shadows pulling at her senses. She glanced at the door, locked with an iron bolt, then back to the thin slice of city light slipping through the curtains. Her skin prickled—like something was in the room, lurking just beyond the reach of light.

Get it together.

She forced herself to the go-bag by the door. Her hand slipped on the strap before she tightened her grip, but the walls felt too close, the darkness too thick, pressing in, swallowing corners of the room. Her pulse quickened. Shadows pulled her back to the alley. *Dark. Cold. Steam. Ivan.* She pulled her knife out from the bag.

A faint creak—the old apartment settling. Her spine jolted. She whipped her head toward the sound, her breath tight, fingers brushing her knife's edge. *Focus.* It's just you, she reminded herself, forcing her grip to loosen. Her own space, her own shadows. But the hum of the city felt distant, slipping away as she stayed in the silence, waiting for something to move.

She lay motionless, her gaze locked on the ceiling as shadows flickered above, closing in. Her hand tightened on the blanket, its rough edge biting into her fingers—a tether holding her steady in the darkness. Each breath was a fight to keep still, to outlast the quiet pressing in on her.

Another creak outside. Her chest tightened. She turned, pressing her palm to the wall, cold and solid. She stayed there, breath shallow. Waiting. She couldn't shake the echo of footsteps, too close, too familiar. *They weren't real*, she told herself. It's over. But the silence didn't loosen.

Liliya's grip tightened around the bag's worn strap, her thumb tracing the frayed edge as if testing its endurance. Until sleep overcame her.

A sharp buzz broke through the static—a sound too loud, too close. She jolted upright, her senses on alert, room sharpening as her pulse steadied. Her phone. The vibrations rattled on the table, clinking like metal trays in the lab. She flinched, the muscles in her neck tightening.

With a shaky hand, she grabbed the phone. "Hello?" Her voice came out strained, hoarse. She swallowed, forcing steadiness. "Yes, this is Liliya… Counseling? On whose authority?" Her grip tightened as she listened to the doctor's explanation, jaw set. She kept her tone steady, controlled. "Thank you, doctor. Let me know when I need to come in."

She hung up and stayed still, her eyes fixed on the ceiling. The weight of exhaustion pressed down on her body, but her mind refused to quiet.

The missions had always kept the memories at bay, her mind forced into sharp focus. But here, in the quiet, the ghosts slipped through the cracks. How much longer could she keep going like this? Could she finally confront the shadows she'd been running from? Or would facing them be the thing that finally broke her?

Deciding she needed to clear her mind, Liliya again attempted a hot shower, hoping to let the water wash away the ever-present fatigue and the haunting memories. Liliya lingered in the steam, letting the heat press down on her until the stress faded, just slightly. She realized she needed to talk to Davyd, to share her burden and find strength in their shared mission.

As Davyd navigated the dimly lit streets away from the command center, his mind wandered back to when Liliya entered his life. Her infiltration of the bioweapon's lab and the subsequent killing of Mel'nyk had initially marked her as a promising operative, yet her transformation from a dedicated doctor to a skilled agent had always left Davyd conflicted. He admired her resilience, her intelligence, her ability to adapt to any situation. But with that admiration came a growing personal attachment that complicated his professional judgment.

Davyd paused outside her door, fingers just brushing the cool metal of the knob. His hand hovered, frozen, the air around him thick with indecision. He flexed his fingers. *Just knock. Get it over with.* But he stayed rooted to the spot, the weight of the last mission pressing hard against his chest.

He should've pulled her back. Should've seen the way her hand trembled, how her eyes didn't quite focus when she looked at him. But he hadn't. He'd sent her anyway. The guilt gnawed at him, low and constant, the same thing every time. He needed her in the field—she was the best they had. But it was getting harder to ignore the cracks. Harder to pretend that she wasn't unraveling, piece by piece, right in front of him. He clenched his jaw, resisting the urge to punch the door in frustration. *How much longer could she hold up?* His hand dropped to his side. *Damn it.*

No more second-guessing, he thought, tightening his jaw. With a sharp breath, he finally turned the handle and stepped into her apartment.

Humidity lingered, carrying a faint trace of her shampoo, and he moved down the hall, past the neat kitchen and into the living room, each step weighed with apprehension. The steady drip of water, the dim glow from the bathroom—it cast the whole place in a surreal haze.

At her bedroom door, Davyd paused, shoulders tense. The light spilled in just enough to reveal her room, a stark mix of past and present. A worn sweater lay draped over a chair, the softness in contrast to the gear piled in the corner. A stack of books sat beside the bed, an old stethoscope coiled on the dresser. Little pieces of who she'd been, half-preserved, almost forgotten.

Then he saw her, silhouetted against the window, the city lights catching the edges of her face. He opened his mouth to speak but stopped. She was standing there, wrapped in shadows and quiet, and in that heavy silence, words didn't feel like enough.

He hesitated, his eyes tracing the droplets that clung to her skin, the damp tendrils of her hair sticking to her neck. His mind flashed back to their first mission together. The initial uncertainty had given way to a powerful, unspoken bond forged in the crucible of danger. He remembered the nights spent strategizing and the quiet moments where their professional facades slipped, revealing the deeper connection they shared. The sight of her now, vulnerable and exposed, brought a surge of protectiveness and fear.

Yet, with every step he took towards her, the weight of his responsibilities pressed down harder. He was her superior, her handler, tasked with ensuring the success of their missions and the safety of his operatives. Allowing personal feelings to cloud his judgment was a risk he couldn't afford, especially now.

Davyd took a breath. "We need to talk," he said, the silence stretching long between them.

Liliya turned to face him, her eyes narrowed, her stance bristling. She stepped closer, her voice quiet, clipped. "The doctor called." Her fists clenched at her sides, her gaze cold. "You didn't tell me."

Davyd let out a breath, shoulders slumping slightly. He didn't answer right away, his gaze dropping to the floor as his fingers twitched. When he finally looked up, his expression was guarded. "It isn't about you."

A flicker of something softened in her eyes, though her jaw remained set. She crossed her arms more loosely now, hands finally dropping to her sides. She exhaled, a faint sigh. "Then... what is it, Davyd?"

He clenched his jaw, stepping closer, his hand flexing unconsciously by his side. "It's getting worse," he said, voice barely audible. "We don't have time..."

Her gaze shifted, breaking slightly, and he could see her defenses weakening. She looked away, her voice quiet, uncertain. "Another one?"

He noticed the tremor in her fingers before she could hide it. Instinctively, his hand rose, hesitating just above her shoulder, caught between reaching out and holding back. After a beat, he settled his hand lightly, gently, on her arm. She didn't pull away.

The mission loomed between them, thick and unspoken. Davyd's hand lingered on her back, his touch a quiet reminder that she wasn't alone. Her fingers brushed his jacket, curling into the fabric, just briefly, before slipping away. Neither spoke; the silence held more than words ever could. His hand traced slow circles on her back, offering comfort words couldn't capture. She stayed there, letting the quiet carry what neither dared to say.

Finally, she straightened, her breath evening out as her shoulders relaxed, tension giving way to a shaky steadiness. She pulled away, but a faint tremor lingered in her hand, her movements sharp, as if she'd already said all she couldn't put into words.

Davyd's fingers brushed her arm once more, firmer this time, a silent reassurance. "We'll keep going," he murmured, each word measured. His grip tightened briefly before releasing, an anchor holding them to the present.

She exhaled, her body settling into a stance of quiet resolve. When she turned, her shoulder barely brushed his arm, grounding her just for an instant. She stepped back, tension easing from her shoulders as she squared them once more. He'd always been there, reliable as steel—a force she could lean on in silence. She didn't need his words, only his presence. Without another glance, she nodded and moved forward. Only the mission remained—and the promise they'd see it through, no matter the cost.

Early the next morning, Davyd sat alone at the kitchen table, the hall light casting shadows on the walls. The weight of his responsibilities pressed heavily on his shoulders as he considered the next operation. His mind wandered back to the day he first felt the call to serve his country.

The fall of the Berlin Wall had ignited a spark within him, a glimpse of what freedom could look like for eastern Europe. When Ukraine proclaimed its independence, that spark became a fire. Davyd had been just a young man then, filled with resolve and resolve to see his homeland free from the shadows of foreign oppression. He joined the military, driven by a desire to protect and build his nation.

With his desire to serve came fears that gnawed at him—the fear of failing, of losing those he cared about, of watching his country fall back into foreign hands. These thoughts lurked constantly in the corners of his mind, but now they pressed closer as he prepared to send Liliya on another perilous mission.

Davyd stood beside her, close enough to feel the tension radiating from her. She shifted, reaching for the door, but he laid a hand on her shoulder—a quick, supporting touch. Her body stilled, breath caught, yet she didn't pull away.

For a second, it felt like helping fallen comrades off the snow-bitten ground, bracing himself for another mile. That old, gut-deep tightness twisted in his chest, fierce and unforgiving. His hand fell away as her gaze hardened, fixed on the mission ahead. He kept his face impassive, but a trace of that unshakable fear lingered as she opened the door.

CHAPTER

FOUR

The Assignment Briefing

Davyd and Liliya arrived at headquarters, their steps echoing off the concrete floors of the sterile hallway. A sharp scent of bleach filled the air, bringing them back into the its calculated calm. Davyd's eyes tracked the familiar path to the high-tech missions briefing room, a place he knew held the weight of life-or-death decisions. At the iris scanner, he hesitated for just a second, then steadied his breathing, leaned in, and watched as the door unlocked with a soft click. 'Time to focus,' he muttered, feeling Liliya's gaze steady beside him.

The briefing room buzzed with tension, high-definition screens lining the forward wall. Two agents at their stations worked swiftly, preparing data. In a semicircle sat the President and NSDC members, with Commander Sanenko at the end, two empty seats beside him.

Sanenko, seeing Davyd and Liliya enter the room, beckoned them over. "The data input for the briefing is almost complete. We will start in a moment," he said as they approached. They had no sooner taken their seats when the lights began to dim, and the screen flickered to life.

Lead Tech Specialist Yankovic stood at the front, "the KH-101 and KH-102 missiles pose a direct threat ...," his voice droned over the image of the Russian missiles projected behind him. Liliya's fingers twitched at the mention of nuclear payloads. However, the words, "New biological weapon...," cut through the haze, causing her jaw to tighten and brought her focus fully back to the briefing. Liliya's gaze flicked to Davyd, catching the tension in his grip on the dossier. She felt it too—pressure building, mission urgency tightening every muscle.

As the Yankovic continued, Davyd's facade tightened the strain visible in his jaw. Beside him, Liliya's fingers twitched against the table, as the hum of the briefing room projector carried a familiar rhythm. *BSC. Lab. Vials.* Her pulse quickened. She forced herself to keep her gaze on the screen, tracing each movement of Yankovic's pointer as he spoke. *Focus.*

The screen projected missile schematics, grim details of Russia's newest arsenal. Ivanko's voice was level, but the urgency crackled beneath. "Dmitryashevka's missile production will churn out biological weapons, undetectable to us and capable to strike cities without warning."

Davyd's voice held tight control; tension evident in his clenched fists. Liliya's fingers tapped against the dossier, a grounding rhythm. A single hit, she knew, and Ukraine's defenses would be overwhelmed.

Yankovic returned to the front and pointed at the screen., the low hum of the projector clicking in rhythm with Liliya's tapping foot. She pressed her fingertips into her jacket sleeve, feeling the fabric between her fingers. "This is Vladimir Aleekseev ... perfected Mel'nyk's bioweapon." Liliya's jaw clenched. *Mel'nyk, Hands. Squeezing throat. Air—thick. Choking.* She exhaled slowly, the room's hum vibrating in her chest. *Concentrate. Not now.* Her fingers twitched as she shifted in her seat, nails biting into her palms, the sting sharp, grounding her.

As Yankovic continued, Davyd's attention flicked between the screen and Liliya. watching her tense, fidget, her breath growing shallow as they reviewed Aleekseev's photo. His gut twisted with the gnawing worry that she was fraying more each day, slipping through his fingers. He wanted to reach out, a small, supportive touch on her arm, but he stopped himself. She would only steel herself further if she knew he'd noticed.

His chest tightened with the pressure of what was left unspoken. But this wasn't the time for emotions. If she slipped now, with Aleekseev's weapon so close to deployment, there would not be time to pull her out. He needed her sharp, present, and unshaken.

He nodded to Yankovic, signaling his understanding. Still, his gaze remained on Liliya, watching as she fought to hold herself together. He couldn't afford to lose her now—not when they were so close.

Liliya's eyes narrowed, locking onto the mission map. She pushed her focus to the strategy, fighting back the weight of memories pressing in. Each mission tugged harder at the fraying edges of her mind, cracks widening, shadows of the lost inching closer. How much longer before something inside her gave way? She got Davyd glance at her, a flicker of concern in his eyes, but he stayed silent. They both knew what was at stake—and that hesitation wasn't an option.

Sanenko turned to Liliya, his gaze steady but his tone softening just a touch. "Your expertise with Mel'nyk's work makes you the only one who can secure this bioweapon quietly." His eyes flicked over her, a brief pause that was barely noticeable, but she caught it—the subtle dip in his voice that hinted at something more than duty. ""You're our best option." The words hung in the air, heavier than the dossiers piled around them. Liliya swallowed hard, catching Davyd's eyes for a fraction of a second. His nod was subtle, but the weight behind it wasn't.

Liliya clenched her jaw. Her hands flexed, a tremor barely noticeable, but Davyd's gaze found it instantly. She pressed her fingers down harder. She wanted to say yes, to be certain, but her throat felt like it was closing. Her hands trembled, eyes unfocused for a beat too long. Her fingers worked the fabric of her jacket, squeezing it tight as her knuckles whitened. Her voice, when it came, was low, clipped—nothing more than a quiet affirmation.

Sanenko held her gaze for a beat longer, his expression neutral, but there was a tension in his posture that wasn't there before. "Good," he said, the formality creeping back into his voice. "We need to neutralize these weapons before they're deployed. We're counting on you." His tone was firm, but it carried a note of something unspoken, a trace of concern that lingered just beneath the surface.

Liliya nodded, her throat still tight but her resolve returning. "I can control it," she said, more forcefully this time, though her voice wavered. She straightened her shoulders, locking eyes with Sanenko again, forcing herself to hold steady. She wouldn't let this break her—not now.

Sanenko nodded in response, his gaze flicking between her and Davyd before settling back on her. Sanenko's voice was steady, but Liliya barely heard it. Her pulse pounded in her ears. Right... as if anything about this could feel right. She nodded, her gaze fixed on the mission map, trying to drown out the roar of uncertainty.

Davyd leaned in, his words low. "Don't let him get to you."

Liliya's eyes flashed, a mix of resentment and something sharper. "He doesn't. Not anymore." She gripped the edge of the table.

His hand hovered near hers, almost touching but never quite closing the gap. He shifted closer. "You ready?" he murmured, barely a question.

Liliya stilled, her gaze straight ahead. "Yes," she replied, clipped, her fingers pressing down harder.

Davyd pressed his fingers against the table, focusing himself on the mission, but the concern was there, an itch just beneath his skin. He held her gaze a moment longer, but she didn't turn. He hesitated, then nodded, fingers tapping once on the table. "Just stay with me," he said quietly.

She nodded, her breath shallow, and tapped the table twice in response, her jaw set.

Sanenko turned, nodded and Ivanko stood up. On the screen, Aleekseev's image was replaced by another man: Ilya Belyeyev, Primary Detection and Anti-Radar Scientist.

Ivanko began his briefing, "Ilya Belyeyev has refined the radar-cloaking systems for missile deployment, making the bioweapon nearly undetectable—posing an unprecedented threat to Ukrainian forces and civilian areas alike if it reaches full operational status. Eliminate him and his team, if possible, but Aleekseev and the bioweapon take priority. Disrupt Belyeyev if possible, but our main focus is preventing that bioweapon from being deployed."

The screen then displayed images of Belyeyev's assistants, Mikhail Ilyia and Matvey Smirnov, both given the title Assistant Detection and Anti-Radar Scientist. "His assistants, also capable of reproducing his work, must be dealt with if Belyeyev is eliminated. Complete dossiers are available in the file folders."

Ivanko finished his briefing, and the lights brightened. Sanenko's gaze fell on Liliya. "This isn't just recon, it's a takedown. Get in, secure their research data, and dismantle their operation from the inside."

Liliya nodded, gripping the dossier tight. She wouldn't just be infiltrating a lab—she'd be dismantling the enemy's very strategy for annihilation. Failure meant more than just bodies; it meant Ukraine on its knees.

In that moment, Davyd's eyes shifted subtly to Liliya's hands, noticing the rhythmic tapping of her fingers on the dossier. He kept his gaze trained, hoping she'd look up. When she finally did, their eyes locked— her nod was barely perceptible, the kind of acknowledgment that spoke more of routine than reassurance. For a moment, he held her gaze, as if searching for something more. She blinked first, dropping her gaze back to the dossier, leaving his question unspoken in the space between them.

Without another word, they gathered the rest of the dossiers to move toward Davyd's office. As they were about to leave, Liliya hesitated, her gaze flicking back to the screen where Aleekseev's face lingered in a grainy projection. Liliya's voice dropped, barely above a murmur. "Give me a minute." Her eyes lingered on the screen for a moment too long, before she waved him away. "I'll be right behind you."

Davyd paused for a moment, concern flashing across his face, but he nodded and continued, leaving her alone in the briefing room.

Liliya's breath quickened as Aleekseev's image flickered on the screen, but it wasn't his face she saw—it was Mel'nyk's. Her pulse thundered, rage flashing through her. Too late. She'd been too late, and now they were on the edge of something far worse. She forced a sharp exhale, locking her focus. *She had to stop this. Now.* Her hands trembled as she turned away, resolve wrestling with the doubt gnawing at her mind.

With a sharp inhale, Liliya pushed the door open and stepped into the hallway. She had to get back to Davyd. She couldn't afford to lose focus now. The mission was all that mattered.

The hallway felt longer than usual, the echoes of her footsteps unnervingly loud in the quiet. As she approached the office, she spotted Davyd standing by the door, his brow furrowed in concern.

"You okay?" he asked, his voice low but steady.

As Liliya brushed past Davyd, he caught her shoulder—firm but gentle. She tensed, a flicker of resistance in her stance. He didn't release her.

"I don't need this," she muttered, a barely audible edge in her voice.

Davyd's hand lingered a beat longer. "You're still shaking." The words landed, clipped, as he pulled back.

Davyd felt the fabric of their silence shift. Liliya pressed her fingertip into the map, tracing their route with an intensity he recognized. Her focus was impressive—unyielding, even. But it was fragile, her mind holding back a torrent he was certain would break free if pushed too hard.

Liliya leaned forward, studying the maps. As she traced a route, a flash of memories from Kursk rose unbidden, carrying the sickly, metallic tang of gun oil and blood. The smell clung to her senses as her fingers pressed down harder on the map, feeling the roughness of the paper.

Davyd caught it out of the corner of his eye. He kept his voice steady, a soft encouragement, but the knot in his chest told him she was pulling away, inch by inch, becoming something unrecognizable even to herself. How long had he known she needed help? He bit back the thoughts, each one an accusation. He'd insisted she could keep going. She had to keep going. And yet, watching her now, he feared she'd be gone, lost to herself or the mission, before he could pull her back. If he even could.

Davyd's eyes skimmed the map, fingers tracing a line that stopped at a cluster of faint markings. His brow furrowed.

"We need a way in. We can't afford a mistake," he murmured, barely audible, more to himself than to her.

Liliya shifted beside him, her gaze sharp. She tapped the map, just below where his fingers rested, a small smirk tugging at the corner of her lips. "We'll blend in," she said quietly, almost to herself.

Davyd's eyes narrowed. He looked at her, then back at the map. "You're sure?"

She ran a fingertip along the map, her voice steady but low. "We've done it before."

Davyd frowned, his hand tightening on the dossier. "That was before... before everything that happened."

Her finger paused, pressing against the map. She didn't look at him but replied in a clipped tone. "I know what I'm doing, Davyd." There was a fragility under her words, a vulnerability she wasn't ready to show. His jaw tightened, wanting to push, but instead, he nodded, choosing silence over an argument he couldn't win.

CHAPTER

FIVE

The Preparation

Night deepened over Kyiv, its streets heavy with history and war. In his office, walls lined with maps and screens, Davyd and Liliya stood shoulder to shoulder, studying the documents that mapped their entry into Russia.

When the door groaned open, Liliya's body reacted instinctively—muscles tensing, her hand brushing the concealed weapon at her side. But she hesitated, fingers tightening on the grip, her eyes darting towards Davyd as if unsure.

"Relax." The word came out with practiced ease, his tone light. But beneath his calm exterior, Davyd's mind raced. He knew her instincts were necessary, the sharp edges honed by past scars. Still, part of him hated how her vigilance left her coiled, every creak and shadow another potential threat. Would he ever be enough to let her truly relax? His hand brushed the edge of the table, a steadying gesture—his own silent promise that he'd watch her back, even if she'd never ask him to.

A flush of heat rose in her cheeks as she released her grip, exhaling slowly. It was just a door creaking, a routine entrance. She let her gaze drift to Davyd, who spread the map over the desk. "Satellite intel shows heightened Russian troop movements in Kursk. Their border defenses are tighter than ever."

Liliya leaned in, her eyes scanning the marks he'd made. "They know we're watching. They've ramped up security, diverting resources to guard the plants." She hesitated, then continued, "If we're compromised, they'll escalate immediately. Those missiles could hit our cities within days."

Davyd's hand clenched. "And Moscow's counting on it. Their strategy relies on overwhelming our defenses before we can respond."

"We won't give them that chance," Liliya replied, her gaze hardening. The risks were high, but she'd trained for this—trained to bring down the very machinery threatening her homeland.

The scent of coffee wafted through the room, rich and warm, but as it filled her senses, something darker crept in. The coffee's warmth soured, twisting into the sharp metallic tang of blood, fresh and unmistakable. The flash came fast—her hands, slick and shaking, pressing against Ivan's wound. The stark red against his shirt, his breath shallow and uneven. She'd felt her control slip, cold fear spreading as his life ebbed beneath her fingers.

A shiver ran through her, and she forced herself back, her fingers instinctively gripping the table as she blinked hard, pushing the memory down. Her throat tightened, the phantom taste lingering, bitter and relentless.

Davyd traced a route on the map with his finger, his voice steady. "We step wrong..." He paused, glancing at her, then back to the map. "And we're swarmed." He waited, as though he expected her to nod, to reassure him. But her hand stayed rooted to the table, fingers pressing into the wood.

His eyes flicked back to her, lingering on her expression. "Liliya?"

She blinked, realizing he'd noticed her lapse, and she quickly looked back at the map, forcing a small nod. "We've seen worse," she muttered, but the weight in her chest lingered, her fingers clinging to the table's edge.

As they continued, Davyd pointed to the thick lines marking their route. "This is the best place for entry. Closest to the border with enough cover."

Liliya traced the path with her finger, nodding. "The forest provides concealment," she replied. However, the sour scent persisted. Her nails bit into her palm. *Cold. Metal.* Her pulse spiked, a memory flickering— the sound of footsteps and the smell of blood mingling with gunpowder, pulling her back before she could stop it.

"But getting there..." Davyd paused, eyes narrowing. "Patrols are tighter here."

She snapped her gaze to him. "Forget the 'what ifs,'" she cut in, though her voice caught at the end. The words hung between them, the silence stretching as Davyd's gaze slid to her, a brief pause in his usual focus. He continued, but his voice was softer, as though he were weighing her words, perhaps sensing the shadow of hesitation she was trying to bury.

She forced herself to exhale slowly. She tapped her fingers, aligning her breath with the rhythm of his voice until her focus sharpened. These were her hands now, steady, composed, made for the task ahead.

He continued, "We'll need to stay low until we reach cover. Quick movements, no lingering."

"Got it," she replied, her gaze locked on the map. "We'll watch from here first and make our move. Agreed," she said, her voice clipped but steady.

"Yes," Davyd said, turning to look at her with a brief nod.

Shaking her head slightly, she refocused on the map as a familiar tension tugged at her chest. "Low profile till the forest," Liliya muttered. "Then, we disappear."

Davyd met her gaze, a flicker of something unreadable crossing his face before settling into steely determination. "Agreed." His voice was steady, but his fingers tapped restlessly against the map, betraying his nerves. His eyes softened, just for a moment, before the hardness returned, giving her a quick nod as if to steady them both.

They moved to Aleekseev's dossier. "Embedded deep," Davyd muttered. "A clean shot would be easiest, but it'll trigger a lockdown. We need subtlety."

Liliya scanned the dossier. "His weakness—the club. Risky, but if we play it right, he'll see us as just another night out."

Davyd rubbed his chin, his thumb tracing the faint line of a scar as he mulled over her suggestion. He looked up, catching her eye, his gaze holding a quiet, unspoken concern. "He'll be watching," he said, voice dropping low. "You think he'll take the bait?" A pause, and then his gaze drifted just past her, his jaw clenched tightly, as if holding back a dozen other questions.

Liliya's eyes narrowed, watching him closely. "He'll be too distracted by what he wants to see," she replied, barely a whisper. A flicker of doubt crossed his face, but she kept her tone firm. "I'll play to his tastes," she continued, her gaze steady, daring him to challenge her plan. She forced a small smile that didn't quite reach her eyes. "I've handled worse situations."

His jaw eased, but his eyes lingered on her, a slight frown betraying his worry. He nodded, accepting her plan without words, though his gaze remained troubled.

Davyd nodded, but his eyes remained on the notes.

Liliya's fingers skimmed the dossier—paper, but colder. *Blood. Ivan's lifeless weight.*

"Liliya?" Davyd's voice cut through. Her hand jerked back; the dossier colder than it should have been. She blinked, forcing herself to respond. "I'm fine," she said, though her pulse hammered beneath her voice.

Davyd didn't push, his attention back on the map. She straightened and picked up the dossier again. "Let's finish this," she said, tone sharp. Mistakes weren't an option, not with everything at stake. Aleekseev's vulnerabilities wouldn't wait for her memories to settle. There was no room for doubt now. Only action.

Davyd nodded, satisfied with the plan and began the process of dealing with logistics, discussing disguises and cover stories for the club. Each detail was meticulously planned, but as they moved forward, the tightness in Liliya's chest remained—a quiet reminder that the past was never far behind.

Davyd outlined their encrypted communication, his voice steady, urgent, the air conditioner's low drone filling the room. She nodded, clenching her fingers against the sensation pressing in around her.

Davyd looked up, meeting her gaze, but for a split second, his face blurred. His features shifted. *Mel'nyk. Cold, detached.* Liliya exhaled slowly and closed her eyes, forcing the ghost of the lab to recede. She ran her thumb along the table's edge, the roughness snapping her focus back.

He paused, and Liliya moved her pen swiftly over the scattered maps and dossier attempting to mask the tremor in her hand before setting the pen down carefully. The air conditioner's hum receded, but her pulse lingered, steadying with effort.

Davyd frowned. "We need a specialist. Someone local who can improvise."

Liliya thought for a moment, then an idea came to her. "There's someone in the resistance network, a specialist. I've heard about him, but we've never met. He's a phantom. My contact might be able to get in touch with him for us."

"A phantom?" Davyd repeated, considering the idea. "Can we trust him?"

"We don't have a choice," Liliya said, purpose hardening her voice. "Father trusts him, and that's good enough for me."

With that Liliya set up the secure line, her fingers moving swiftly over the keyboard. The screen glowed softly, its hum steady in the quiet room. As the light flickered, it suddenly felt too bright. A brief flash: *Harsh. Sterile. Lab. Mel'nyk.* Her jaw clenched, breath shallow. A sharp beep snapped her back. The connection was live.

"Father," she typed, "we need your help."

"Liliya, what's going on?" the text response came through the connection.

"We need technical expertise on the ground, you know who I'm referring to. Can you reach him and make the arrangements?"

Father didn't hesitate. "Give me the details. Where and when do you need him?"

"We'll be crossing the border into Suzemka. We need him to meet us there with a car," Liliya quickly briefed Father on the updated plans. "Prep go bags. I'll send the details later."

"Understood. I'll get in touch with him to inform. It's done," the confident text response replied. As the connection ended, Liliya felt a surge of hope. She glanced at Davyd, already adjusting their plans.

With Father reaching out, the team was set to be complete. "We have a good team," she said softly. "We can do this." They both knew the road ahead was perilous, but with the phantom specialist, their plan was almost complete. Suzemka waited.

The chime of the secure line jolted Davyd, but he hesitated, his thumb hovering above the keypad. A single thought echoed: *what if they missed something?* Just a flicker of doubt, but it shook him. His eyes darted to Liliya; her focus razor-sharp. He envied her clarity, her single-minded drive, but he also felt the strain pulling at her. For a moment, he wanted to voice his unease, to share the burden of his doubt, but he swallowed it back. They couldn't afford any distractions, least of all his own.

Davyd answered, his expression darkening as he listened. "The mission's moved up," Davyd answered Liliya's questioning look.

"Then we move faster," Liliya said quietly, "We adapt," her voice becoming steadier. She glanced at Davyd, then locked her gaze on the map. The cold focus returned, her hold on the present firming as she straightened, ready for the next move. Davyd, oblivious to her inner struggle, continued outlining their next steps. His voice was calm, anchoring her further in the moment.

The night passed in a blur of refining strategies, double-checking gear, and rehearsing cover stories until every detail felt natural. With the first light of dawn on the horizon, casting a soft light through the blinds, Liliya and Davyd shared a quiet moment of reflection. Davyd stood beside her, their shoulders brushing. "Not a walk in the park," he muttered.

Davyd looked at her, his gaze intent, his lips parting slightly as though a thousand words were on the verge of spilling out. But then he stopped, a shadow of doubt flickering in his eyes. He reached out, his hand resting on her shoulder, his touch warm and caring. His fingers lingered, the silent weight of everything he couldn't say pressing through that single point of contact. She glanced down, inhaling slowly, absorbing the unspoken reassurance. No words were needed. In that small, quiet moment, everything between them was understood.

As the door to Davyd's office clicked shut behind them, a quiet resolve settled over the pair. Their steps were measured, matching the rhythm of their thoughts. In a few hours, their carefully laid plans would come to life. But for now, they allowed themselves a moment of stillness, knowing that soon, rest would be a distant memory.

The briefing room hummed with quiet energy as Davyd moved to the front, his posture steady and commanding. Around the table, the team shifted slightly, eyes intent on the large digital map casting a faint blue glow over their faces.

Davyd's voice broke the silence, steady and precise. "We all know what's at stake here. Each of you has a role, and every step has been planned down to the last second." He swept his gaze over the team, each member straightening under his scrutiny.

Artem, usually calm and unshakable, adjusted the strap on his gear, fingers lingering a bit longer than usual before he stilled. Across from him, Boris tapped a pencil against his knee, his gaze flicking between the map and Davyd, brows drawn in concentration. When Davyd's eyes landed on him, he held his gaze, chin lifted in silent resolve.

As Davyd outlined the infiltration points, his tone sharpened, cutting through the tension. Another analyst, stationed near the door, exhaled slowly, the faintest twitch of his jaw betraying the anticipation building under his composure. His fingers grazed the radio at his side, as if confirming its presence.

"We'll have local support as needed," Davyd continued, eyes narrowing slightly as he traced their planned route on the map. "But don't expect miracles. This relies on precision. No room for error."

A murmur swept through the room—soft, nearly imperceptible. Each team member seemed to tense, backs straightening, breaths steadying. Artem shifted again, his grip firm on the table's edge. Even Boris's fingers stilled, his focus homing in as she absorbed every detail.

Davyd took a final, sweeping look at his team. "Stay sharp. Move fast. Focus." The room absorbed the command, silent but charged, as each member instinctively checked their gear, ready.

With a final nod, Davyd stepped back, allowing a beat of silence to cement his orders. One by one, the team members gave brief, decisive nods in return, hands instinctively moving to check their gear. As the lights dimmed, a collective resolve hardened in the room—a quiet pact sealed without a single word.

As the briefing was in progress, Aleekseev's grainy image appeared on the screen. Liliya's gaze caught on his face, her breath slowing, then stuttering. Shadows shifted, twisting the image, the sharp features of his face softened into the familiar contours - of Mel'nyk. She swallowed, the memory pressing down with an eerie weight, and forced herself to focus on the present. The room around her faded, and her chest tightened.

She blinked, trying to lock herself back in the briefing room. *Keep up. Don't fall behind.* But it wouldn't stop. Clinking glass vials, the hum of machines in the lab, and Mel'nyk's voice, "What are you doing here?" became all she could hear.

Davyd's voice cut through. "Stay sharp," he said, meeting her eyes.

She forced herself to nod, fingers trembling but mind beginning to clear. "I'm fine."

As the room cleared and the door clicked shut behind Davyd, Liliya remained still. She pressed her nails into the fabric of the chair, forcing herself to stay grounded, though the pressure on her palms pushed back. Something slipping, clawing at the edges. *Not now.* But the sensation that came to her wasn't the roughness of the cloth—it was the heat of blood. Ivan's, the commander's blood. Hot and slick, slipping through her fingers.

Mel'nyk's face shifted, transforming into Ivan's blank stare, his body collapsing in a haze of gunfire. Ivan's weight—crushing. Gasping breaths. His last. Mel'nyk's grip on her throat tightened.

Not again. Please, not again.

Her fingers trembled, the past's grip refusing to let go. The metallic scent of blood overwhelmed her senses, mingling with the scent of diesel, pulling her deeper into the memory until the line between past and present began to blur entirely.

Lights flickered—*no, not here. Lab. Mel'nyk. Cold, sterile.* She blinked, banishing the image, weakness creeping into her legs. Her fingers grazed the table's edge, steadying her.

Focus. Stay here.

She bit down, tasting blood, and took a sharp breath, bringing herself into the present—the hum of the room, the weight of the dossier, the quiet voices beyond the door.

Aleekseev's face cleared on the screen. Cold. Familiar. But only him now. The projector's hum growing distant as the room sank into darkness. The sensation retreated but stayed. Lingering. She exhaled again, slower, chest tight. Not yet steady, but present. But as the darkness settled, the weight in her chest remained—a ghost, unshakable.

Taking a moment to compose herself, she pressed her hands to her face, the coolness helping to steady her breath as Ivan's shadow hovered nearby. With a final breath, she forced herself to stand.

The door opened, and Davyd appeared in the doorway, his brow furrowing when he saw her pale face. "You ready?" he asked softly, his voice pulling her further back to the present.

Liliya straightened her jacket with hands that felt heavier than usual, her fingers trembling before she forced them still. She met his gaze, the shadows of doubt flickering in her eyes before she masked them, managing a small, firm nod. Davyd's eyes lingered, a momentary softness crossing his face before he returned the nod, his mouth a thin line.

Upon arriving home, they wasted no time in getting to work. They showered and repacked their go bags, taking a moment to rest. During this moment of respite, they could not help but feel a sense of anticipation mingled with apprehension. The journey ahead would be fraught with danger and uncertainty, but they were prepared to confront it head-on. With their minds set, they were ready to embark on their mission into the lion's den.

CHAPTER

SIX

The Journey

As Liliya prepared for their perilous journey, her resolve was bolstered by the previous generations experiencing oppression and the desire to remove it. To her, Moscow symbolized the epitome of oppression, inhumanity, and destruction perpetrated by both the former Soviet regime and the regime under Putin. Memories of Russian oppression fueled her resentment. This mission was for the countless Ukrainians yearning for true independence. Darkness shadowed her heart, but her mission was clear: stop the regime.

Davyd and Liliya packed their go-bags in the car and embarked on the first leg to the Service's secret engineering facility. Their objective was to have one of the buses specially fitted with a secret compartment where they could hide during their travel through the Russian-occupied areas.

The journey from Kyiv to Moscow was fraught with danger, but Liliya and Davyd were meticulously prepared. Leaving Kyiv, the cityscape melted into sprawling suburbs as they travel Northwest to the facility. Checkpoints and barricades flashed by, ghosts of a conflict still burning. They pressed on, unease growing with every mile. Davyd gripped the wheel, his eyes locked on the road. Silence hung heavy, thick with unspoken fears.

Liliya glanced at him, breaking the silence. "You're quiet."

His jaw tightened, and his knuckles whitened as he gripped the wheel. Without looking at her, he replied, "Just thinking about the crossings… the green zones… it's a lot." His voice was low, the tension sharpening each word.

She nodded, her fingers tapping a steady rhythm on her thigh—each tap in sync with the hum of the engine.

To navigate the dangers, they were relying on the green humanitarian corridors set up in the Sumy Oblast. These corridors, coordinated by humanitarian agencies and supported by NATO, involved negotiations with Russian authorities to allow the passage of buses and other vehicles into the region for evacuation purposes. One of the cities where this evacuation effort was permitted was Serindina-Buda, located in the most northern region bordering Russia. This arrangement allowed civilians in the affected areas to escape the dangers of conflict and seek refuge in safer locations. This would be Liliya and Davyd's way into Russia.

Liliya nodded, understanding his worry. As she adjusted her seatbelt, her eyes flicked to the folded map tucked in her go bag. "We know the way." Her fingers tapped a rhythm against her thigh, but her voice remained steady. "Stick to the plan. No deviations."

His knuckles whitened on the wheel. "They say it's safe…" His jaw tightened. "But we both know better. If we get caught…" Davyd's voice trailed off, the unspoken consequences hanging in the air.

"We won't get caught." Liliya's voice was steady, but the rhythmic tapping of her fingers against her thigh betrayed the worry simmering beneath the surface. Each tap felt like a countdown, the mission pressing on her chest. "We can't afford to fail—not now."

"And once we're inside?" Davyd's words were clipped, but Liliya caught the flicker of doubt in his eyes. The question cut through the silence, pulling her thoughts into a spiral of what-ifs. She met his gaze, even if just for a moment.

"We finish it," she murmured, her voice barely above a whisper, as if saying it too loud would shatter the fragile resolve she clung to. Davyd glanced at her, then back to the road, his hand brushing her shoulder. The car fell silent again, but the atmosphere was lighter, charged with renewed determination. They knew the risks—and the stakes.

The desolate stretch of Bucha swept by, buildings crumbling like faded memories of resistance. Liliya's jaw tightened as she traced the scars etched into the town's frame, each bullet hole a reminder of the fight she'd inherited. She glanced at Davyd, his grip white-knuckled on the wheel, unspoken resolve hardening his gaze. They were close now. She let her hand rest on the map in her lap, fingers brushing over it. 'For them,' she whispered, as if the ghosts of Bucha could hear her, and straightened, the facility's silhouette rising like a challenge on the horizon.

Their resolve hardened as they met the engineers—quick handshakes and nods before Fedir introduced himself and revealed the hidden compartment. Oxygen tanks and surveillance monitors lined the walls. This small space, suffocating yet vital, would be their only shield against detection.

"Don't worry about the oxygen," Fedir reassured them. "We've got enough to keep you safe during the trip."

Liliya and Davyd stowed their go bags in the container and then expressed their gratitude to the engineering team for their hard work. Another agent, their driver for this leg of the mission, stepped forward. His enthusiasm and pride in assisting them was palpable, highlighting the importance of their mission and the dedication of everyone involved.

Rostyslav introduced himself with a firm handshake and his confidence was reassuring. "I'll be your driver," he said, taking the driver's seat and starting up the engine.

An hour from the real departure point, it was time for Davyd and Liliya to board. They stepped onto the bus, Davyd looked at Liliya. He said, more to himself than to her, "You ready?" his voice barely above a whisper.

Liliya nodded, there was no need for more. The hum of the engine filled the silence as they both stared ahead, the weight of the mission pressing down.

The bus jolted over the uneven streets, weaving through Kyiv's maze-like alleys. Crumbling facades and charred buildings loomed overhead; the aftermath of recent missile attacks etched into every corner. Tension mounting as the city's wounds closed in around them. As they retraced their route, Liliya's mind lingered on the image of a mother and child escorted by Ukrainian tanks outside Bucha.

The journey served as a stark reminder of the recent turmoil. The destruction along the way highlighted the imminent threat posed by Russian forces. Liliya glanced at Davyd, who gave her a reassuring nod. They both understood the gravity of their mission.

There's no time for tears now, Liliya thought, steeling herself.

The wooded stretches along E373 offered a brief respite, the dense canopy casting dappled light on the road. The smell of pine and earth was a stark contrast to the urban landscape they had just left. They turned onto Velyka Kiltseva, skirting the city's edge. Residential blocks blurred past—normal life teetering on the brink of chaos, but none of it reached them inside the bus.

As bus rolled onto cracked asphalt, where other buses idled, the other drivers paced, tense with the dangers ahead. After parking, Rostyslav joined them, his face serious. "Everyone ready?" he asked, his eyes scanning the area.

They quickly changed into their disguises, the rustling of fabric the only sound breaking the tense silence. They donned jackets and identification to blend in as humanitarian workers for the initial part of their journey, maintaining the secrecy of their mission.

"Let's make some friends," Rostyslav suggested as he adjusted his jacket, the sound of his zipper being pulled up filling the quiet.

After a few minutes of interacting with the humanitarian workers, they returned to the bus and waited for the caravan to depart. The time used to review their plan in hushed tones.

The hum of engines filled the air as they joined the convoy as the last bus. Silence settled over them, the weight of their mission pressing down as the city faded in the rearview mirror. The bus's interior was dimly lit, the sharp smell of diesel hanging heavy in the air. Liliya's breath caught. *Diesel. Smoke. Burning wood.* Her chest tightening as the memory gripped her. The memory of icy wind chilled her skin, the scent choking her. *Blood on hands. Ivan.* She blinked, forcing the hazy memory aside. *Not now.* Liliya forced a steady breath, her focus locking onto the mission ahead. *No time for ghosts. Ivan was gone. Kursk was behind her. All that mattered was now.*

Just as the they approached the highway beyond Perova Boulevard, Liliya glanced out the window at the convoy ahead. She leaned forward, her thoughts sharpening into a single directive: speed and silence. She broke the silence, her voice unsteady. "Once we're on the E101, we'll be in Sumy Oblast. That's where things get tricky. We need to be prepared for any unexpected checkpoints or patrols."

Davyd nodded. "We've got a solid plan for Dubovichi. We'll get in the compartment there. But we need to be precise. Timing is everything."

Rostyslav's eyes scanned the landscape, his grip firm on the steering wheel. "We're making good time," he said, glancing at the road ahead. " We'll reach Dubovichi as planned. Let's stay focused." The plan was simple: slip into the container unnoticed before crossing into Russian-occupied territory. Rostyslav scanned ahead, making sure the convoy held. "The forest is thick there and I'll find a spot just off E101. You'll disappear there."

Miles slipped away, each inch drawing them closer to E101. As they neared Dubovichi, thick forest closed in around them, the trees standing like sentinels. Liliya tensed, the silence tightening around her like a noose. Liliya's pulse quickened, a cold sweat breaking out along her spine. The forest pressed in—*cold, suffocating. Lab walls, metal clanging. Blood. Breathe. Stay here.* Her vision tunneled, narrowing to a single point of focus—the jagged edge of a set of keys in her hand. She pressed her palm against it, the sharp pain pulling her back from the brink. Slowly, the forest returned to its natural state, and Liliya exhaled, her grip on reality restored.

Davyd checked his watch, his gaze sharp and unyielding. "We're getting close," he murmured, voice dropping to a near whisper. He glanced sideways at Liliya, his brow furrowing as if gauging her readiness. "We'll need to move fast."

She inclined her head in response, jaw set, her fingers clenching briefly around the edge of her seat.

Rostyslav's grip tightened on the wheel. "I'll find the right spot," he said, his tone an unspoken promise. His eyes darted to the shadows along the treeline, his posture rigid with focus.

The bus crept off the road, finding refuge in the dense underbrush where they would make their move—hidden and breathless. Liliya exhaled, steadying herself. No time for anything else—they had work to do.

Rostyslav unlocked the container, and Davyd activated the monitor, while Liliya opened the oxygen tanks. The air thickened, but her hands stayed steady. *One step at a time.*

"Remember, once we're inside, minimal noise and talking," Liliya reminded them. "We need to be invisible."

Rostyslav checked his watch again. "We need to go and catch up."

Liliya nodded, her heart pounding in her chest. "Let's hope this works."

The container door clicked shut. In the dark, their breaths synced with the oxygen's steady hiss, the world outside fading to silence. With the compartment secured Rostyslav slid into the driver's seat, started the engine, and steered back onto the road, accelerating to catch up with the convoy. Determined to rejoin the convoy before the first checkpoint.

Time blurred and the convoy came into view as they neared the checkpoint, its harsh lights blaring on their monitors. Liliya's breath caught as she whispered, "Here we go." She felt Davyd's steady hand on her knee, grounding her, a silent pact between them.

The bus jerked to a halt. Outside, sandbags and barbed wire framed the Russian soldiers, their eyes scanning, sharp and unforgiving. Davyd leaned closer. "Perfect timing," he muttered, his voice barely audible. "Any later…"

Liliya didn't respond, focused on the image of Rostyslav exiting the bus, his face calm as he stepped into the glare of inspection lights. The guards' voices, muffled but tense, filled the compartment.

"Just me. Had to catch up," Rostyslav said, words clipped, deliberate.

The officers scrutinized him. "Unusual… an empty bus."

Rostyslav remained impassive, offering his papers with steady hands. Liliya's pulse hammered as the guards lingered, flipping through the documents. She imagined each second stretching, each breath a probe for weakness.

Then, after what felt like an eternity, one officer spoke. "You may pass."

Rostyslav's shoulders eased, just barely, as he re-entered the bus. When it rumbled forward, he muttered, "All clear," through the compartment's speaker.

In the dark, Liliya and Davyd let out shallow breaths, exchanging a glance filled with quiet relief and renewed focus. One checkpoint down—but the journey was far from over.

"That was way too close," Liliya whispered.

"Too close," Davyd replied. "Yeah, but Rostyslav nailed it. The remaining checkpoints need to go as smoothly."

Liliya smiled, though the tension still lingered. "One down, more to go. We just need to stay on track."

"We'll get there," Davyd said, his voice steady, but Liliya heard the undercurrent of desperation in his tone. She met his gaze, searching for the resolve she needed to keep going.

"Together," she echoed, but even as she spoke, the word felt heavy, burdened by the ghosts of those she had already lost.

The checkpoint's picket line faded into the distance as the convoy divided, leaving their bus with fewer companions. Liliya's gaze swept the surrounding countryside, now stripped bare by the season.

In the thinning convoy, each engine rumble felt louder, like a heartbeat amplified by silence. She clenched her fists, forcing herself to breathe with the road's rhythm, the path forward looming like a silent promise. Davyd adjusted his position in the compartment, his movements deliberate and precise, every muscle tensed with readiness.

Rostyslav's gaze remained fixed on the road. "Thirty minutes to Yampil," he noted, more to himself than anyone else. "Then we push straight through to Doroshivka."

As they passed through Yampil, Rostyslav provided his hidden passengers with a timeline for the remaining trip. The bus rumbled over cracked asphalt, Rostyslav's focus unwavering as he calculated their progress. "Two hours to Doroshivka," he muttered, the names of towns blurring together as the route etched itself into his mind.

At each checkpoint, the process repeated—passengers disembarked, questioned, then moved on. Rostyslav, driving alone, was soon recognized and waved through. The convoy thinned as buses reached their destinations. Liliya and Davyd's bus continued to Seredina-Buda, the final stop. There, they would cross the border on foot, heading northwest to Suzemka.

Davyd whispered, "Once we get past Kam'yanka, we're almost there. Keep your head in the game."

Rostyslav's voice was steady as he navigated the bus through the winding roads. "We'll make it. Just follow the plan."

They pressed onward through war-torn streets, the acrid stench of smoke and decay choking the air. The ruined cities they passed, heavy with despair, mirrored the devastation of the people lining the streets. Each ruined building was another reminder of what waited for them on the other side.

"Everywhere we look, it's just destruction," Liliya murmured, her voice heavy with sorrow. "So many lives, gone."

Davyd nodded solemnly. "That's why we've got to keep going. We have to stop this."

"These people never stood a chance," Liliya said, her eyes scanning the remnants of the city. "It's heartbreaking."

Davyd reached for her hand, their fingers intertwining for a moment. "We're doing this for them," he said quietly. "We can't let their suffering be in vain."

The sharp scent of burning wood and metal filled the air. Liliya's pulse quickened. Her grandparents had fought the Nazis and Soviets in streets like these. She couldn't fail them now.

They approached Seredina-Buda, devastation clawing at every corner. But there was no time to dwell on the ruins. They needed to focus on preparing for their escape from their concealed compartment.

"Almost there," Davyd murmured, the tension in his voice mirroring the tightness in Liliya's chest. The closer they got, the more her thoughts fragmented, darting between the past and the looming danger ahead. She clenched her fists, trying to anchor herself in the moment.

"Stay sharp," she whispered back, but the words felt fragile, like they could shatter under the weight of her fear. "Once we're out, we stick to the plan. Head towards the forest, find cover, and then make our way to Suzemka."

Davyd nodded; his eyes sharp with focus. "We move quickly and quietly. No unnecessary risks."

Liliya nodded, readying herself. "We'll wait for the right moment. Stay alert."

As the bus entered the city, they aimed away from the hospital, where patrols thickened, and civilians clustered in desperate anticipation, and towards it's southern flank. They needed shadows—just enough cover to slip through unnoticed and press north.

The bus crawled to a stop behind a dense stand of trees, Rostyslav looking toward their next refuge. "There," he whispered to himself. "Close enough to move quickly, hidden enough to survive."

Rostyslav pulled into the location and as the bus came to a stop, Davyd turned to Liliya. "This is it. We emerge, we move, and we don't look back."

Rostyslav then tapped the predetermined signal on the side of the bus, letting Liliya and Davyd know that it was time to disembark. However, just before they could execute their plan, a rapid succession of taps filled their ears, signaling that something was amiss.

Rostyslav had noticed a vehicle approaching from the south and used their predetermined signal to instruct Liliya and Davyd to remain hidden for the time being. Concerned that it might discover the bus and investigate, he took out his pack of cigarettes and casually strolled to the front of the bus, ensuring that he was clearly visible to anyone in the approaching vehicle.

Rostyslav approached the Russian patrol vehicle cautiously, his hands raised in a gesture of non-aggression, and his burning cigarette in hand.

"Afternoon," he greeted them calmly, though an almost imperceptive tremor coursed through his fingers. "I'm the driver of the bus for the hospital. Hope it's alright that I took a quick smoke break before heading there for the passengers." His demeanor was composed, but inside, Rostyslav's heart raced with the knowledge that any suspicion could jeopardize their mission.

"You're lucky we have a ceasefire deal. Otherwise, things would be different. Don't stay too long; the next patrol might not be as friendly.," the driver and the senior officer remarked.

"Thanks for understanding," Rostyslav replied with a nod, acknowledging the officer's warning. The Russian officer then reversed the vehicle, left the enclosure, and turned in the direction of the hospital.

As the patrol vehicle departed, Rostyslav tapped the pre-determined signal once more and waited. With a hydraulic hiss, the compartment door slid open. Liliya and Davyd emerged, their bodies stiff and cramped from hours of confinement. As they stretched and regained their bearings, the weight of their mission pressed heavily upon them.

Once they were steady, they retrieved their go bags, leaving the jackets and IDs inside the container. Pulling out their map of the city, Rostyslav pointed out their current location, and together they planned their route to the area north of the hospital, where they could breach the Russian border under the cover of darkness.

With gratitude to Rostyslav, for his assistance and quick thinking, Liliya and Davyd prepared to move towards the next waypoint in their plan. Rostyslav returned to the bus, drove away from the area, and silently prayed for the success of his comrades and the mission they were undertaking.

Liliya and Davyd watched as the bus departed from the tree grove and turn towards the hospital. Instead of following, they went in the opposite direction, heading northeast along residential streets. After a couple blocks, they veered westward and continued until they reached Vokzak'na Street, which ran northward, parallel to the main road leading to the border crossing.

They knew this route would be heavily patrolled and moved with caution. Daylight gave little cover. Instead, they blended in with the surroundings, ensuring that their movements appeared natural and unassuming. Simple residents going about their daily activities rather than individuals with a specific destination in mind.

Staying inconspicuous, they followed Vokzak'na as it transitioned into several different streets, maintaining their course northward towards the border. As they progressed, they anticipated reaching a crossroad that would lead northwest towards the main road and bordered their entry point.

As dusk settled, Liliya and Davyd approached the large stand of trees marking the neutral zone's beginning. Guided by their satellite images, they crossed over and entered a property leading to the observation point, a shack looking out towards the forest.

They located the shed that Liliya had noted, during their planning. As they carefully attempted to open the door, they found it thankfully ajar. They slipped inside, closing the door behind them. Secure in the shed, a sense of relief washed over them. Yet their nerves were still energized, aware that the most perilous part of their mission still lay ahead.

Now concealed they each opened their go-bags and pulled out their black outwear to replace the civilian clothing they had started the journey with. Once changed, they stowed the bags inside the shed, choosing to travel light and only taking the necessary items: wire cutter, compass, rations, water bottles, knives and pistols.

Davyd checked his weapon, each movement measured. Years ago, he'd gone through these same motions with men who shared his vision—a free, unbroken Ukraine. Every piece of gear felt like a vow renewed. He secured his weapon, a reminder of every friend and mentor he'd lost to this cause. Today, as always, he'd walk into the shadows with their voices guiding him. Peering out the window, they surveyed the landscape before them, carefully timing the movements of the Russian soldiers on foot patrol.

The silence pressed down like a weight, filling the small space with a tension that hummed just below the surface. Liliya's father had spoken of similar moments—long stretches of waiting in silence before the protests broke out, every breath charged with unspoken fear and defiance. This was no different. Liliya closed her eyes briefly, summoning that same quiet strength her father once had. The waiting was the hardest part— but it was also what made the fight worth winning.

Over the course of watching the patrols the optimal path and timing for their movements into the forest crystalized. They pinpointed two blind spots in the patrol's route and devised their route accordingly.

Under the cover of nightfall, Liliya and Davyd began their plan. The second patrol just completing its route and returning to its starting point, gave them a 45 second window to reach the first blind spot. The smooth terrain allowed them to swiftly cover the necessary distance and find refuge behind a cluster of bushes.

With a few moments before their next maneuver, they took the opportunity to compose themselves, keeping a vigilant watch on the sentries.

As the first group of sentries completed their rotation, Liliya and Davyd moved swiftly but cautiously, crouching low as they slipped into a small ditch just meters from the forest's edge. From this concealed position, they observed a third sentry group pacing along the perimeter, forcing them to adjust their approach.

They waited, muscles tense, as the sentries completed their route. Every movement was calculated, their eyes tracking the patrols' progress, measuring the narrow window they had to reach the cover of the forest.

When the moment came, they acted in unison. Liliya pushed off first, her body low to the ground as she darted forward. Davyd followed, matching her pace, his breath steady but his heart racing. The uneven terrain threatened their balance, and as Davyd's foot caught on a hidden root, he stumbled. Liliya reacted instantly, her hand shooting out to grab his arm, pulling him upright without breaking stride.

They sprinted, the forest's shadows creeping closer with each pounding step. Reaching the tree line, they dropped into the underbrush, their breaths shallow but steady. They crouched low, pressing themselves into the earth, scanning the area for any sign of pursuit.

Once sure they were unseen, they moved deeper into the forest, their footsteps nearly silent on the soft earth. Every rustle of leaves, every distant sound put them on high alert, forcing them to adjust their course multiple times to avoid detection. The forest was a maze of shadows and faint noises, each step bringing them closer to their objective and further from the dangers behind.

Finally, they emerged near the border patrol station, separated only by a narrow road and a chain-link fence. Crouching in the thick shadows, they assessed the situation, their eyes locked on the checkpoint ahead. The timing had to be perfect. They exchanged a brief nod, readying themselves to cross the road and breach the fence in one fluid motion.

With nerves taut and hearts pounding, they seized the moment, scrambling across the road and swiftly cutting through the fence.

Emerging on the other side, they quickly sought cover among the trees, ensuring they remained hidden from any prying eyes. Now, with the border behind them, they pressed onward, venturing deeper into Russian territory.

SEVEN

The Encounter

In the dense Russian woods, evening's chill settled on Liliya's skin, stark against the warmth they'd left behind. Towering pines loomed, branches swaying with each gust that slithered through the underbrush. She ignored the bite of cold, the damp earth seeping into her gloves with every step.

Ahead, Davyd moved with unnatural precision, a shadow against the dark forest.

A sudden rustle.

She froze, hand drifting to her sidearm, her pulse spiking as she held her breath. A gust swept through, brittle branches cracking above. She strained, listening past the wind, her heartbeat slowing, blending with the forest's rhythm.

The dirt road lay just ahead.

Their cover thinned, shadows darkening with each step. Her boots pressed into damp soil, each crunch echoing louder than it should.

Liliya caught the scent of smoke —maybe from Suzemka. A reminder of how close they were, the air thick with fear. She glanced at Davyd; his gaze sliced through the dark, sharp, searching for any hint of movement.

Then—a branch snapped behind them.

Her hand shot to Davyd's shoulder, signaling stillness. They held their breath, pressing against the rough bark, skin prickling. The forest fell silent again, only the leaves rustling in the icy breeze.

Another exhale. Her breath clouded, dissolving into the dark.

They continued, slipping from tree to tree, until the waiting car came into view. It sat half-hidden under a large oak, shadows cloaking all but the pulsing glow of the driver's cigarette, the smoke spiraling up. Liliya paused and remembered a different kind of signal. A different mission. *Ivan. Betrayal. Escape.*

She tightened her grip on her knife, eyes narrowing as she scanned the area, unwilling to trust even a small sign. Davyd moved closer, each step silent as they neared the vehicle, tension radiating from him in waves.

The driver's low voice broke the silence, barely audible. "Quick. Get in."

She met Davyd's eyes. This time, she was ready.

They slipped across the clearing, each muscle braced for the shattering beam of a flashlight or a shout. But there was only silence, the soft purr of the engine welcoming them as they slid inside.

Inside, the warmth felt stifling against the cold. Liliya's fingers tingled as they thawed, her senses sharp. The scent of tobacco and gasoline filled the space, the seats worn and cracked with years of use.

"We're ready," she said, tapping the driver's shoulder, her voice steady.

Davyd didn't respond right away. His eyes fixed on the street, fingers tapping unevenly against the worn armrest, his breath slow. His jaw tightened, eyes flicking toward the shadows beyond the car, his hand brushing his pocket, feeling the weight of his weapon.

Silence thickened inside the car, filled only by the hum of the engine as they waited. A single nod. Barely noticeable.

The driver's hands held steady on the wheel as he guided the Lada through Suzemka's narrow streets. In the rearview mirror, Liliya caught a final glimpse of the forest retreating, the twisted branches reaching back, like dark claws pulling her into the shadows.

They passed Soviet-era buildings, their paint peeling and facades crumbling, the car rattled over a bridge spanning a sluggish, algae-covered stream. Liliya sifted through the go bags on the floorboard, retrieving the false IDs and other supplies they would need for their mission. They passed a market square where a few late-night vendors were packing up their stalls, the faint hum of a distant generator adding to the background noise of the town. "False IDs are in the bag. Here's yours," Liliya said as she handed Davyd his IDs. *Just another face in the crowd.*

Davyd followed suit and grabbed his travel clothes from the back. "Let's go over our cover stories to make sure we've got them."

As they peeled off their black sweatsuits, Liliya adjusted the medical researcher's badge now pinned to her chest. "Natalia Ivanova," she muttered, glancing at her reflection in the side mirror. "Medical researcher. Moscow conference on infectious diseases. I met Anton on research trips and Ivan at past workshops."

Davyd pulled on his jacket, smoothing the creases before nodding. "Ivan Petrov," he said quietly, slipping his forged ID into his pocket. "Logistics manager. Been working with Natalia for years, know Anton from the trade." He glanced at Liliya, waiting for her approval.

Liliya nodded back, satisfied.

Anatoli, adjusting the driver's cap snugly on his head, let out a low chuckle. "Anton Federov," he said, his tone more somber now. "Truck driver. Lost my boys to the war..." His voice trailed off, jaw tightening as his grip on the steering wheel firmed. "I'm here to drive you."

Anatoli's fingers grazed the worn photo on the visor. "Aleksandr and Ivan," he murmured, his voice tightening. He flipped the visor back up, eyes sharp. "Time to focus and get out of this region."

Liliya met Davyd's eyes, then turned to Anatoli. "We know what it's like," she said quietly. "We won't let them down."

Anatoli gave them a resolute nod and took a deep breath. "We have to stay sharp and stick to our stories. If anyone asks, we've known each other for years through our respective professions. Our connections are believable, and our stories align perfectly."

Liliya nodded. "Agreed. We need to remember the details and be ready to back each other up if questioned. We can't afford any slip-ups."

Davyd's eyes flicked between them. "We stick to the plan. No matter what."

With their cover stories solidified and their resolve strengthened, the trio prepared to navigate the dangerous path ahead, each carrying the weight of their past and the hope for their nation's future.

Despite the tragic circumstances that brought them together, they found solace in their shared commitment to their mission. As they sped towards Moscow on the M3 highway, Anatoli's words lingered, a stark reminder of the war's toll.

Soon the discussion shifted to the mission specifics. Anatoli listened intently as Liliya and Davyd briefed him on the plan to assassinate Aleekseev. His role as an extra surveillance eye and backup was crucial in ensuring Liliya's safety and facilitating her movements during each phase of the operation.

Anatoli absorbed the details of the plan with focused attention. He could not help but feel a sense of awe at Liliya's unwavering dedication and resolve. Her willingness to sacrifice herself for the cause left him speechless, highlighting the depth of her commitment to protecting Ukraine's borders and ensuring justice for her people.

He had just one question: "What do I do if Liliya gets caught?" Liliya pulled out a DX1-5 pistol and two clips. "You put a bullet in their heads, and if you can't stop them from taking me, you put one in my head."

Anatoli admired her selflessness and strength. Her turned his attention back to the road, his hands steady on the wheel. Liliya sat in the back, her gaze fixed out the window.

The hum of the tires on gravel blended into something else—the low whine of an air filter, sterile walls creeping into her peripheral vision. She blinked hard, trying to focus on the passing fields. Then the scent of diesel hit her. *Smoke, Thumb drive. Shoulder.* Her fingers twitched. For a second, she wasn't in the car.

"Almost there," Anatoli's voice cut through, pulling her back. Moscow's distant lights flickered on the horizon. She nodded, gripping her seatbelt.

They entered Moscow and merged onto the Third Ring Road, navigating the crowded artery lined with flickering neon signs and towering buildings. The glow of the city blurred, then sharpened. Traffic swelled, horns blaring, engines rumbling. Her pulse matched the rhythm—too fast. Too loud.

Anatoli glanced at her through the rearview mirror. She forced a nod, her hands trembling. *Focus. Stay here.*

Ahead, the Russian Academy of Sciences loomed, but the hum of the generators still lingered in her ears, just beneath the surface, waiting.

Their hotel, strategically nestled in the Presnensky district, mirrored the city's blend of old and new with its sleek glass facade reflecting the

Moscow skyline. Aleekseev's residence was only minutes away, allowing them to closely monitor his movements and verify the accuracy of their contact plan. Additionally, being situated near the Loft Men's Club provided them with an opportunity to gain access to Aleekseev's weekly activities as potential operation targets.

While they would not be taking advantage of the hotel's lavish amenities, they appreciated the spacious rooms that would serve as their well-equipped command center throughout the operation. From there, they would plan their moves to ensure seamless and constant communication.

A bonus was its location was the known landmarks like the State Museum of Oriental Art and tranquil parks like Patriarch's Ponds, Davyd and Liliya saw the potential for much-needed relaxation and debriefing after the intense surveillance operations ahead. They agreed that these amenities would offer a reprieve from the stress of their mission, allowing them to recharge and strategize effectively.

The car eased to a stop, the hotel's opulent lights casting long shadows across the street. Liliya adjusted her grip on her bag, feeling the reassuring weight of the gear inside. She took a breath, her mind slipping into her cover story's cadence. As she stepped inside, the lobby's warmth wrapped around her, but she kept her gaze cool and unreadable. Just another traveler, just another night. She caught Davyd's eye—his nod was subtle but clear. *Blend in. Don't linger,* she reminded herself, melting into the crowd with practiced ease.

"Check in. I'll handle recon," he said, voice low.

She caught the familiar look in his eyes—one they'd shared countless times before the mission. "We've done this before, Davyd," she murmured, forcing a small smile. He returned it, just barely, the tension still crackling between them, but he nodded, his gaze softening. This was just another mission, another disguise, but the weight of past failures lingered, shadowing their resolve

Liliya walked to the reservation desk, her steps deliberate. Each move controlled. Measured. When the key was finally in her hand, she exhaled slowly, forcing her heartbeat to slow. She couldn't afford to slip up now.

Davyd returned to the Lada, and Anatoli pulled it onto the street toward the Men's Loft Club. Davyd wanted to get a first-hand look at the location in preparation for completing the plan.

Liliya stood motionless by the window, her silhouette framed against the opulent backdrop of the Moscow skyline. The golden hues of the sunset bathed the room in a soft, misleading warmth, contrasting sharply with the cold fury in her eyes. As she stared out at the Red Square, her breaths became shallow, each inhale sharp as the blades of ice that seemed to pierce her heart at the sight of the Kremlin. Her hands, balled into fists at her sides, trembled slightly with the force of her anger.

She pressed a hand to the cool glass, her fingertips tracing the edges of the distant buildings. Her jaw tightened; breath shallow as she stared out at the city below. The weight of it all settled in her chest, silent but heavy. Her fingers curled slightly against the window, leaving faint marks in the condensation. "We'll bring them down," she murmured, the words barely audible as her gaze remained fixed on the skyline.

Liliya turned from the window, pacing in measured steps, her thoughts heavy with determination. She paused, catching her reflection in the mirror, studying the set of her jaw, the tension in her shoulders. For a moment, her gaze lingered, the silence around her sharper than any words. She drew in a slow breath, her fingers flexing at her sides. No need for promises—her resolve was written in every controlled movement, every tightened muscle.

After returning from their reconnaissance mission, Davyd and Anatoli gathered their belongings and checked into their adjoining room. After freshening up, Davyd made his way to Liliya's door and found it unlocked. Without hesitation, he entered the room and saw Liliya standing by the window. He recognized the familiar signs of her mental preparation, that focused state essential to their objectives. Yet, he also sensed the longing and frustration that had built up during their time confined in the Lada. "Lost in thought?" he asked.

Liliya turned to him, "Just thinking about what's at stake."

Davyd pulled her in, tight. Her body softened against his. He whispered, "We'll get them."

Liliya gripped his arms. "We will," for she said, her voice low, steady.

The next morning, they were on recon as they began to ensure that the information on Aleekseev was still reliable enough to activate their plan. To bait the hook with an inadvertent contact between Liliya and Aleekseev or if they would need to adapt it.

The team positioned themselves strategically outside Aleekseev's apartment building, ready to begin their surveillance. With Liliya orchestrating their movements from a distance, Davyd and Anatoli took up their positions to track Aleekseev's movements. Liliya voice came over the earbuds, "Positions ready. Let's stick to the plan." In response Davyd responded, "We've got this. Stay focused."

Aleekseev's apartment, located in a sleek, modern 20-story complex on Anuchina Street, was a prime location for their surveillance operation. The building's exterior was a mix of glass and steel, with a minimalist design that stood out amidst the more traditional structures in the area. From their observation point across the street, the team could see the well-manicured gardens and the lobby entrance, where a doorman in a crisp uniform greeted residents. The surrounding area was a blend of residential and commercial spaces, with a small park and a few local shops providing cover for their movements.

As their surveillance notes indicated his usual departure time of 8:00 AM, they ensured that all members of the team were in position well in advance. Davyd stationed himself across from the apartment building, while Anatoli positioned himself a block north along the anticipated route to the Academy. This arrangement allowed them to cover multiple points along Aleekseev's route without alerting him to their presence.

Liliya's voice crackled through the earpiece, "Stay sharp, he's on the move." Davyd's muscles tensed as he readied himself. The team's preparation paid off; each member perfectly positioned.

With Aleekseev in their sights, the team moved with practiced precision, slipping into the flow of pedestrians like ghosts. The city's morning hum wrapped around them, masking their presence as they fell into step behind their target. Every glance, every move was calculated, the mission now in motion.

Aleekseev veered northeast. Anatoli's pulse quickened as he slipped behind parked cars, threading through the morning crowd, shadowing his every step. Each step was deliberate, every movement calculated to stay within sight but out of Aleekseev's line of vision. Once Aleekseev turned north, Davyd received instructions from Liliya to move north and observe the intersection where Aleekseev would cross Kostgina Street.

Aleekseev crossed the street, and Anatoli matched his pace, slipping into the flow of foot traffic. He found the footpath, a narrow, shadowy lane that twisted north then west, running parallel to Kostgina Street. Recognizing that Aleekseev was heading towards Davyd's location, Anatoli alerted Liliya, who directed him to a suitable observation point near the mini zoo across the street.

Meanwhile, Davyd monitored the intersection as Aleekseev turned north and then back east, maintaining a safe distance to avoid detection. After half a kilometer, Aleekseev turned northeast towards the mini zoo, where Anatoli was positioned to observe him. "He's headed your way," Davyd murmured into the mic, his eyes never leaving Aleekseev. He jogged back to the waiting Lada, where Liliya sat, her fingers drumming a tense rhythm on the steering wheel.

"Let's move," she said, her voice steady but eyes blazing with focus. Together, they proceeded to the next intersection point, Andreyevskaya Naberezhnaya, ready to continue their surveillance along the Moshka walkway.

Anatoli now picked up Aleekseev's trial as he crossed through the mini zoo. He did so discreetly, aware of his surroundings and watched as Aleekseev proceeded towards Andreyevskaya Naberezhnaya. Upon confirming that he was within line of sight of Davyd, he concluded his reconnaissance and contacted Liliya for further directions. Liliya directed him to Andreyevsky Ponds, Aleekseev's destination before reaching the Academy.

Davyd then intercepted Aleekseev as he turned down the river walkway towards the ponds. Davyd observed Aleekseev until he was close to the ponds, at which point he handed off the surveillance to Anatoli. Anatoli then followed Aleekseev from the ponds to the Academy, maintaining discreet observation throughout the journey.

For three days, they tracked Aleekseev, his movements precise and unchanging. Each morning, their team took positions, shadowing him along his route. Each night, they regrouped, dissecting every moment.

"No change in departure," Liliya said, glancing over her notes. "We know that our timing is in place."

"Okay, so tomorrow I take over the observational role," Davyd replied, tapping his route on the map. "I'll follow him from the apartment until he turns onto Kostgina, then Anatoli you'll position yourself across the street to follow him to the riverway."

Anatoli nodded. "I'll pick him up near the mini zoo, keep him in sight until you can pick him and Liliya is in place."

"Stay close, but don't shadow him too tight," Liliya reminded them, her eyes sharp. "He can't suspect a thing."

Each gave a nod, knowing their roles were set. This was it—the plan would either unfold with flawless precision, or fall apart in a single misstep.

Davyd lingered by the table, his fingers tracing the frayed edge of a discarded map. The silence stretched after Anatoli left, thick with unspoken words. In the kitchen, Liliya moved with quiet precision, the clatter of dishes too loud in the stillness.

"You okay?" she asked, her back to him, voice distant.

Davyd nodded, though she couldn't see. "Yeah. Just tired."

But the air between them felt strained, heavy. Not just from exhaustion. Each decision weighed them down, pulling them toward a point of no return.

Liliya stirred the pot, her fingers steady as steam curled upward. The room's warmth mingled with a sharp hint of iron at the edge of her senses. *Ivan. Alley.* She blinked hard, fixing her gaze on the rising steam, grounding herself in the present.

After supper, they walked around Patriarch's Ponds, the cool air easing the tension. Conversation floated between them, light, but beneath it, the mission loomed. Every word felt cautious, every step deliberate. Even then, Davyd noticed how Liliya's gaze drifted, her mind somewhere darker.

Back at the hotel, silence fell again as she stood by the window, staring out at the faint lights of the Kremlin. Her fists clenched. The city lights blurred. *The alley. Cold. Ivan's body. Heavier. Colder. Footsteps fading.* The sting of betrayal wrapping tighter around her chest.

"Liliya," Davyd's voice was soft, caring. She didn't turn, her reflection still against the glass.

"I'm fine," she whispered, her fingers pressing into the cool glass, but her breath stayed shallow. The memory clung to her skin like the weight of Ivan's lifeless body, refusing to let go.

Davyd didn't push. He knew the fight wasn't just the mission—it was inside her. His presence, quiet and steady, was all he could offer. For now, that would have to be enough.

On the fourth day, Davyd took on the role of communication officer, while Liliya prepared to activate the next phase of their plan. She stood before the mirror, her decision firm, mentally running through each step.

She would position herself near the river walkway, casual yet deliberate. The summer dress—simple, alluring—was chosen to catch Aleekseev's attention. The wig, the low neckline, the handbag—everything was designed to make her seem vulnerable, approachable. He'd have no reason to suspect her, no hint of the trap waiting to spring.

Make him believe she was harmless. *Get close. Reel him in.* Davyd would be watching from a distance, ready to intervene if needed. But this part—this first confrontation—was hers to execute.

She adjusted the black bob-cut wig, ensuring not a single trace of her real identity was visible. The light dress clung just right, and with a final glance in the mirror, she hardened her gaze.

He won't be able to resist. This will work.

She rehearsed her approach once more, her reflection staring back with cold determination, her role perfected. All she had to do now was play it out.

Following their established routine, Davyd assumed his position across from Aleekseev's apartment, while Liliya prepared for her part. As Aleekseev crossed the intersection on Kostgina Street, Davyd shifted into the driver's seat, ready to transport Liliya to Andreyevskaya Naberezhnaya.

Arriving at the designated location, Liliya disembarked and began walking east along the river walkway, positioning herself beyond Aleekseev's usual entry point after passing through the zoo. With a slight breeze causing her dress to billow, Liliya waited patiently, poised to execute her plan when Aleekseev appeared.

As Aleekseev stepped onto the cobblestone walkway, his eyes adjusting to the early morning light, Liliya, already in motion, felt her heart rate pick up. Her stride confident yet unhurried, weaving through the early risers with practiced ease. Her gaze flickered across the landscape, noting each passerby with a swift, discreet sweep—an ingrained habit from countless surveillance missions.

The path, flanked by ornately designed lampposts that cast long shadows in the morning light, led her closer to the rendezvous point. She found the designated bench, its wood worn smooth by time, nestled under the expansive branches of a cherry tree in full bloom. The delicate petals, stirred by a gentle breeze, fluttered around her like a natural veil, masking her true intent.

Davyd's words echoed in her mind, "Stay sharp, observe, then approach." With Aleekseev's silhouette now in view, her fingers brushed against the small transmitter in her ear, a subtle reassurance of backup at a touch. She seated herself, her posture relaxed but alert, her senses attuned to the surrounding rustle of leaves and distant chatter, a stark contrast to the turmoil brewing within.

As Liliya waited, she closed her eyes for a moment, the sunshine casting warmth over the scene. It felt distant, not quite real. The breeze carried the scent of the river—earthy, familiar. She inhaled slowly, trying to let it ground her, but her pulse still quickened.

Footsteps. *Too loud. Too sharp.* Her chest tightened.

A flicker of light—too harsh. The alley. Damp air. Cold metal. She blinked. *Concentrate. Blend into the scenery, part of the morning.*

Aleekseev a few steps closer now.

Her breath caught, the weight pressing harder.

Her throat constricted. *No.* She blinked, but her vision kept shifting, shadows stretching unnaturally across the pavement. The wind rattled a nearby branch, the snap of wood too much like bone breaking. Her pulse spiked.

The streetlamp flickered overhead. On then off. Her breath hitched with each blink of the lamp, her pulse refusing to settle. The hum of the city felt off—too low, too steady. Like murmurs. Whispered voices she couldn't quite catch.

Aleekseev was close. Chest tightens. His cologne—spice and leather— warped into something else. *Damp earth. Rot.* Her skin prickled, as if eyes were crawling over her. She turned, scanning the street—empty. Still, the feeling clung to her like damp fog. Her chest tightened. *Focus.*

The wind stirred again. The rustling leaves became whispers. Faint. Persistent. She moved before they grew louder, stepping into Aleekseev's path.

They collided, the impact jolting through her. Her vision tilted. For a second, the street vanished, replaced by cold damp alley. She blinked hard, her breath shallow, the ground unsteady beneath her feet.

Aleekseev mumbled an apology, his eyes darting away. "I'm sorry."

Liliya forced her breathing steady, eyes locking on his. "You should be," she said, though the edges of her vision trembled, flickering like a dying bulb.

He muttered another apology, already distracted. As she walked past, her mind spun. The streetlamp flickered again. The shadows stretched further. She kept walking, but the whispers in the wind followed, faint, insistent.

She glanced back. Aleekseev stood there, watching. He'd taken the bait. But her pulse still pounded, her fingers trembling. Somewhere, a dog howled, long and low, the sound cutting through her like a blade.

CHAPTER

EIGHT

Deepening the Web

They returned to the Lada and headed back to the hotel. Sunlight streamed through the windows as Liliya broke the silence, her tone focused. "Aleekseev took the bait. He'll step into our trap." Her fingers gripped the armrest, then relaxed. *Focus. Stick to the plan.*

The hotel lobby buzzed with morning energy. After a brief lunch, they returned to planning, setting tasks, refining steps.

Davyd spread the Academy's map across the table. "Priority one is the bioweapon lab. Then we find the data."

Liliya nodded, her expression serious. "Agreed. Aleekseev's at the Academy daily. We track him to the lab."

Anatoli leaned forward, his voice low and intense. He leaned back, rubbing his temples. "We need the plans." His eyes flickered with something darker. "Aleekseev... he won't talk. Not unless we... push him."

Davyd completed the thought, "Our plan makes it look accidental. Any extra force will expose us."

"What if..." Liliya's fingers tapped the edge of the map. "We dose him. Just enough to loosen his tongue. He won't see it coming."

Davyd considered, then nodded slowly. "You'll need time for that—no interruptions."

"I'll handle it. I'll make sure of that…" Liliya replied, her fingers grasping the back of a chair, tension rippling between them.

Anatoli, arms crossed, added quietly, "And if it goes south?"

"We improvise," Liliya replied, her voice cold. The tension between them thickened, neither needing to spell it out further.

"We'll plan for the club once you're inside," Davyd replied. "Let's get back to the Academy. I'll initially shadow him and then we rotate."

Liliya's finger hovered over the map. "I'll make contact," Liliya said, gaze sharp. "Stay back."

Davyd nodded. Jaw clenched, "I'll be ready."

Liliya's gaze shifted to Anatoli. "Backup. Watch the exits."

Anatoli's jaw clenched. "And if… things go sideways?"

Liliya's grip tightened on the edge of the map. "They won't. Stick to your post, Anatoli."

He nodded, but his eyes lingered on her, as if waiting for another reassurance.

Davyd glanced at the clock. "Surveillance is set. Now… what else do we need from the resistance for tomorrow. We'll need a tracking device, jammer, and emergency transmitter."

"A dress," Liliya replied, her gaze already shifting back to the map. "Something for the Loft, too. I need to… stand out."

Davyd's brow lifted, but he nodded. "Alright. Noted."

Liliya continued, "We'll need Sodium Pentothal with a syringe."

Davyd nodded, mentally adding them to his list, "I need to get the message into the pipeline this evening so Anatoli can make the pickup later tonight."

They all nodded in agreement, the weight of the mission pressing down on them. Each knew their role and the importance of their tasks. The stakes were high, but they were determined.

As they temporarily disbanded, Liliya's mind was already planning about the next day and how she would approach Aleekseev. She thought to herself, *He won't know what hit him.* As she considered how he would respond to the second unexpected contact.

As each completed their tasks, they reconvened, the tension in the room palpable. Liliya started, "Communications have checked out."

"The message is coded," replied Davyd, as he tossed the small metal dead drop container, holding the message, up in the air.

Anatoli nodded. "The car is ready for tonight's pick-up and tomorrow. I've mapped three escape routes. We'll be ready for anything."

Davyd's voice lowered as he leaned in. "After the walk tonight... I'll get Anatoli to drop me at the Academy. I'll do a quick recon. We need as much intel as we can get."

Liliya nodded, eyes sharp. "Good. We move forward—caution, precision... and we make this happen."

Davyd's gaze held hers, a flicker of worry crossing his face before he masked it. "Let's keep it clean."

Later that evening, Liliya and Davyd strolled through Patriarch's Pond, but this time with a dual purpose. As they passed the second bench, Davyd swiftly marked an 'X'—the signal to the resistance. At that precise moment, a member of the resistance watched from a distance as Davyd made the mark. Their next supply drop was set.

The pond's calm surface mirrored the star-studded sky as Liliya and Davyd strolled back, their steps timed with a quiet tension. She glanced at the benches, each one a possible drop point, and caught sight of the second bench—the drop for tonight's mission. Davyd's fingers brushed hers as they settled on the bench, a subtle exchange of readiness. They sat close, their movements casual, blending into the park's late evening quiet.

Keep calm, Davyd thought, ensuring his actions were smooth and natural. As he secured the drop beneath the bench, Liliya felt the weight lift slightly. One task down. She exhaled, her fingers finding rhythm on her lap, as if coaxing her pulse back to normal.

He and Liliya got up and completed their stroll. Within a few minutes, the resistance member sat at the same location and took possession of the encoded message inside the container and left the scene.

Back at the suite, Davyd methodically packed his gear—binoculars, comms, black outerwear. His movements were precise, but his jaw was tight.

Liliya watched him from the corner of the room, arms crossed. "You'll need eyes on every exit."

"I know," Davyd replied, adjusting the binoculars. His expression unreadable.

Anatoli stood by the door. "Ready?"

Davyd nodded once, wordlessly. The tension in the room crackled as they headed for the door.

Anatoli stopped briefly at the Academy perimeter, letting Davyd out before heading toward the coffee shop on Bolshaya Polyanka. With

90 minutes to recon, Davyd circled the complex, binoculars in hand, feeding intel back to Liliya at the hotel.

Stay sharp, Davyd reminded himself. *Every detail counts.*

While Davyd scoped out the site, Anatoli arrived at Kofeynya Erna just after closing. He flashed his lights at the front windows, then parked by the back alley, waiting for the signal. Minutes later, a young man emerged from the alley, lit a cigarette, and disappeared again. Anatoli got out, flashlight in hand, and approached the small dumpster behind the shop. Inside, a brown paper-wrapped box sat in the darkness. He grabbed it, stashed it in the backseat, and drove off, heading back to pick up Davyd.

Anatoli tapped his earwig as he drove. "Pick-up was successful. On my way back now," he informed Liliya.

Liliya, in turn, passed the information onto Davyd. "Anatoli got the package and is on his way back," she relayed.

As soon as Anatoli turned onto the street towards the Academy, Davyd was waiting for him. Jumping in before the car came to a complete stop.

"What did you discover?" Anatoli inquired.

"The front's administrative. No sign of the lab. We'll stick close to Aleekseev tomorrow. How about you?" Davyd replied.

Anatoli jerked his thumb towards the back. "Got the package. Let's check it upstairs."

Davyd nodded. "Let's hope it's everything we need. Tomorrow is going to be crucial."

After arriving at the hotel, Davyd grabbed the package, and they crossed the lobby to the elevator. The ride up was silent, each of them lost in their thoughts, the weight of the mission pressing down on them. As they stepped into the suite, Liliya was already waiting for them, her eyes reflecting both relief and determination.

"Did you get everything?" Liliya asked, her voice steady but with a hint of underlying tension.

Davyd nodded, setting the package on the kitchen table. "Not sure, we haven't checked the contents yet. Let's see what we've got."

He unwrapped the package and opened the top. Inside were three disguises for Liliya and a brown paper bag with an unmarked vial of clear liquid, a syringe, and the electronics. Davyd carefully laid each item out on the table, ensuring nothing was missing.

Liliya's eyes scanned the contents, finally resting on the disguises. "Perfect. These are exactly what I asked for," she said, lifting the outfits and inspecting them. As she examined the last outfit she noted, "This will work perfectly for my meeting with Aleekseev at the Loft."

Anatoli, who had been quietly observing, stepped closer. "The plan's solid. Stick to your cover. Aleekseev's sharp—one slip, and we're done."

Davyd's gaze held hers, steady and firm. "One more run-through. No mistakes."

Liliya's fingers dug into the map's edge. "I've got this."

He nodded, a shadow of doubt crossing his face as his eyes flicked to her clenched hand.

They gathered around the table, reviewing the plan. Each step was meticulously discussed, ensuring everyone knew their role, coordinated movements and contingencies. The conversation was intense but necessary, each of them contributing insights.

After an hour of discussion, Davyd finally leaned back. "Alright, I think we're as ready as we'll ever be. Get some rest. Tomorrow is going to be a long day."

Liliya and Anatoli nodded, the fatigue of the day catching up with them. They knew the importance of being rested for the mission ahead. As they prepared for bed, the gravity of their task hung in the air, a silent reminder of the stakes involved.

Anatoli left the suite through the connecting entrance, while Davyd and Liliya moved towards the bedroom. Before turning in, Davyd caught Liliya's eye. "We've got this," he said quietly. "Just remember your training and trust your instincts."

Liliya gave him a small, determined smile. "I will. And we'll make it through this, together."

With that, they each rolled on their sides, the suite falling into a tense but necessary quiet. The next day would test their skills and resolve, but for now, they needed rest.

Liliya stood before dawn, staring at the skyline as the sun broke over Red Square. Her fists clenched. Mel'nyk's research—still out there. She should've stopped it. This mission wasn't just another assignment; it was personal.

The memory of Mel'nyk in the darkened alley with his handler surfaced, *"The Kremlin doesn't take kindly to those that disappoint us."* She shook it off, forcing her focus back.

Find Aleekseev's lab—hidden within the Academy. Remove everything: bioweapon samples, data, research. Nothing could be left behind.

Dressed in the summer outfit from the resistance, she joined Anatoli and Davyd in the car. "Today, we find the lab," she said, voice steady. "Everything hinges on this."

Davyd nodded, his eyes meeting hers with a mix of determination and concern. "We're ready, Liliya. Just stay sharp," he said, offering a reassuring smile.

Anatoli drove, the car silent with tension. He parked a block from Aleekseev's apartment, each preparing for his usual routine. At exactly 8:00 AM, Aleekseev emerged, following his predictable route. Following the same pattern of observation from the previous day, they followed Aleekseev as he moved through his normal routine.

At the parking area near the Academy, Liliya steadied her breathing, mentally reviewing the plan. "He's passing the ponds. You should have eyes on him in a minute," Anatoli reported.

Moments later, Aleekseev came into view, walking toward the front entrance. Anatoli followed a few paces behind, careful not to attract attention. As they neared the building, Liliya stepped out of the car, her gaze briefly meeting Davyd's before turning back to Aleekseev.

"I'll be watching you the whole time," Davyd said, his gaze firm as he also got out.

Anatoli added, "You know what to do if things go sideways."

Liliya nodded, appreciating their support. However, as she approached the Academy, she felt her stomach knot up. *Let's get this done,* she thought to herself, attempting to quelch the rising apprehension.

The Russian Academy of Sciences stood before her, an imposing structure founded in 1724 by Peter the Great, embodying centuries of Russian scientific advancement. Its manicured lawns and impressive architecture reflected its storied history, surviving through Tsarist, Soviet, and modern eras.

Liliya's eyes scanned the imposing structure of the academy, her thoughts sharp and precise. The team's meticulous investigation had painted a detailed picture of Aleekseev, pointing to the academy as the repository for his research. Her heartbeat quickened.

The building was comprised of a three-story fronting structure with two white 20 story office towers further to the back. As she ascended the steps to the front entrance, she could not help but notice the bronze sculptures adorning the rooftop, evoking the grandeur of the Tsarist era and the Soviet Union's ambition to showcase intellectual might. These statues, untouched by the passage of time, stood as silent witnesses to Russia's turbulent history.

Liliya paused at the Academy's entrance, heart pounding. A flicker of a fallen comrade flashed in her mind. She clenched her fists. *Focus.* She glanced back at Davyd and Anatoli, both in position. *The mission depends on you.* She straightened and pushed through the doors.

Inside, Liliya scanned the foyer—no sign of Aleekseev. Her composure faltered. Davyd stepped in behind her, reading the concern on her face. He moved closer. "What's wrong?"

"No Aleekseev. We missed him," she whispered, panic creeping in.

Davyd's hand rested on her shoulder. "Stay calm. We'll split up—search both wings."

Anatoli stepped in, sensing something off. "Aleekseev isn't here," Davyd told him. "Stay in the foyer and keep watch."

Anatoli nodded. "Got it."

Liliya took the left wing, quickening her pace as she passed closed office doors. Her mind raced with possibilities, each more dire than the last. At the end of the corridor, she turned back, moving faster.

Davyd swept through the right wing, checking each room efficiently, his mind focused on the task. Reaching the last room, he paused, listened, then headed back to the foyer.

They regrouped with Anatoli, each slightly winded. "Anything?" Liliya asked, eyes sharp with worry.

"Nothing," Davyd replied, shaking his head. "Anatoli, any sign of him?"

Anatoli shook his head. "Not yet."

"He's got to be in one of the towers," Liliya murmured, her nerves tightening as they moved out in staggered positions. With they again took their staggered position and pushed on to the toweres.

Liliya's pulse quickened, her anxiety heightening with every step, a silent reminder of their near-failure. Davyd's voice crackled in her ear. "Stay alert."

As they approached the tower, she spotted Aleekseev. His figure—unmistakable. "I see him," she whispered, her voice barely steady.

"Remember the plan," Davyd's voice came, calm and composed. "Make contact, keep moving. I'll follow. Stay unnoticed."

Liliya positioned herself in Aleekseev's path, forcing a small smile. "Good morning." Aleekseev hesitated, holding the door for her. Their eyes met—he was hooked. She brushed past him, confidence surging.

The brief interaction confirmed it—Aleekseev's lab was here. As she moved further down the hallway, her mind raced. Is this the moment? She observed him exchange brief words with colleagues, while Davyd tracked him from a distance. Liliya caught Anatoli's eye at the corner. They were in sync.

"He's heading to the elevator," Davyd's voice broke the tension, "Get to the stairs and I'll let you know what floor." Liliya's muscles tightened as she slipped toward the stairs, Anatoli close behind. The mission hanging by a thread.

Davyd's voice came over the comms, "I see you're going to three, could you press four for me ... Thank you." With the information they picked up the pace to beat the elevator's arrival. They reached the third floor, taking positions on either side of the elevator. Liliya's breath quickened. *Stay calm.*

The doors pinged open. Aleekseev stepped out, oblivious, his back to her. Liliya followed, each step deliberate, her nerves a live wire. As he turned into a room, her eyes caught sight of the lab beyond. Her heart stopped. *Disinfectant.* The smell flooded her, acid sharp. *Mel'nyk's lab. Blood, thick on the floor.* Her hand trembled, nails cutting into her palms. *Stay here, stay present. Don't fall back there.* But the fluorescent lights above buzzed, needles in her skull. She edged closer. "Full...full setup," she whispered. The words barely made it out, her voice tight with tension.

Her fingers shook. *Control.* She repeated it like a mantra, steadying her breath. She braced herself, forcing her mind into the moment. The mission. *Now. Not then.* This time, she was here to destroy everything he'd left behind.

She edged forward, her breath catching. *I need to see more.* The tension in her chest tightened, each second amplifying the pressure. Every movement was sharp, deliberate—yet she teetered on the edge. *Cold. White. Too much light.* She swallowed hard, shoving the memory down. But the metallic tang clung to the air, choking her. The hum of the bio-cabinet vibrated through her bones, rattling fragments of buried moments.

"Keep your distance," Davyd's voice grounded her. She nodded, fighting the urge to move. Her mind struggled to stay in the present, her gaze darting across the room, trying to note the details.

Aleekseev's voice blended with the machinery, distant. Bright lights flickered overhead, stabbing at her focus. *Not now.* She blinked, forcing herself back. Glass vials. Cluttered counters. The buzzing sank into her skull, pulling her apart. Blink. *Stay here.* The ventilation hissed. *Too close to before.* Her breath quickened, hands trembling, fingers twitching.

Noise. Lights. People. All crashing down. *Stay. Now.*

A flicker—Aleekseev's sleeve. The clink of glass. It hit her. Her fingers curled into her palms, a tremor shaking its way up her arm. *Hold steady.*

Then she saw it—a door. Sealed tight. *That's it. The samples.* A quick surge of relief shot through her, but it was chased by the cold edge of danger creeping up her spine.

Footsteps. Heavy. Slow. Aleekseev. He was coming closer. Liliya pressed herself into the wall, breath catching in her throat. *Too close.* Her pulse thudded in her ears, loud and insistent. Her body seized, muscles locking in place. The sterile air burned her lungs, bitter and suffocating.

"He's coming," she whispered, voice barely there. "I—can't move."

Aleekseev's hand hovered near the door handle. She dug her nails into her palms, bracing, waiting for the unraveling. His shadow stretched, long and suffocating, tightening around her like a noose.

Then, a voice called from within the room. Aleekseev paused. His shadow shifted, and she exhaled, the breath breaking free in ragged bursts as her body sagged against the wall. The conversation buzzed back to life, pulling her back into the present. "Clear," she whispered, voice shaky but firm.

With the situation escalating, Davyd and Anatoli moved into position to extract her. However, with the all clear signal they relaxed. Davyd came over her comms, "Liliya, you okay?" Davyd whispered, concern evident in his voice.

She nodded, though her heart was still racing. "I'm fine. Aleekseev almost saw me, but he got distracted. I saw a sealed door at the back of the room. I think that's where they're storing the samples."

Davyd's eyes lit up with interest. "Good job. Now, we need to ensure you stay safe while we keep an eye on him. Move down the hallway and take cover behind those supply cabinets. Just before the hallway of offices we walked past. We'll coordinate from there."

With his whispered guidance, Liliya moved cautiously down the hallway, her senses attuned to any potential movements of their target. Davyd was approaching her and continued walking down the hall. "I'm going to past the lab and observe from further down the hallway." Davyd informed the team, "When he comes out, I'll follow if he goes your way. Liliya you follow if he comes my way."

From her vantage point, Liliya remained concealed, her gaze fixed on the door of Aleekseev's laboratory, ready to react to any sign of his departure. She checked for unlocked doors, finding a broom closet to hid in.

Meanwhile, Davyd now past the lab, maintained a watchful eye on their target's location. Anatoli reestablish his role as backup and moved past Liliya to the elevator corridor, where he could watch for anyone coming and keep his eyes of her.

As moments passed, tension hung heavy in the air, each second stretching into an eternity as they waited for Aleekseev's next move. Aleekseev exited the room and turned away from Davyd, moving back up the hallway. With his movement towards her, Liliya made her move. "I'm in the closet two doors down on the right," Liliya whispered.

Aleekseev moved past the closet, and then hesitated for a second as he fumbled with something in his pocket. As he paused in the hallway, Liliya observed his movements with heightened attention. Liliya, held her breath, her heart pounding in her chest as she waited for Aleekseev to move on. Davyd, trailing from behind, and Anatoli also noted the pause. Each followed his gaze as he proceeded to a door further down the hallway.

Aleekseev took out his key, unlocked the door and stepped inside, Liliya came out of the closet. Both she and Davyd remained vigilant and moved towards his door, taking note of Aleekseev's actions inside. As they watched, they observed him bending down in front of the safe, his fingers punching in a code. As the final tumbler fell in place a metallic clunk was audible. Alekseev then stepped back, pulled open the steel door and placed something into the box. This confirmed their suspicions and with this crucial discovery, they knew that their reconnaissance mission had been successful.

"Okay, I think we have everything. Let's get out of here," Davyd advised and the three, feeling confident in their findings, swiftly retreated from their vantage points. As they separately made their way back to the car, Liliya glanced at Davyd, a slight smile playing on her lips. "We've got what we need," she said.

Davyd nodded, "I think we do." Once in the car, Anatoli turned to them, his eyes questioning. "Okay, exactly what are we looking at?"

Davyd replied, "We have the lab. Now, next move."

Liliya added, "And he's got a steel box in his office—probably where he keeps his notes and data." The three exchanged determined looks, their next steps clear in their minds.

The clock was ticking, and every second brought them closer to a crucial window of opportunity.

CHAPTER

NINE

The Trap and Execution

That early afternoon, in their temporary headquarters, Liliya and Davyd refined the plan. They needed to get close to Aleekseev, extract the information, and eliminate him. His regular visits to the Loft made him vulnerable. The first part of the plan was already in motion—Liliya's image was planted in his mind. Now came the execution, the critical moment.

Liliya, knowing his submissive tendencies, had already crafted her approach. Convincing the Loft's staff was the next step, and discretion was key. Advanced monitoring was likely, so precautions needed to be in place.

Liliya pointed to the hallway near the emergency exit. "I'll take one of these rooms."

Switching maps, Liliya's finger flicked over the map. "Emergency exit, third floor lab. One shot at timing."

Davyd gave a curt nod. "Military cover. We're in, grab the files, and out."

"I'll secure uniforms, IDs—everything for transport," Anatoli added, shifting to his phone without waiting for approval.

She moved the map aside, mentally etching each exit and timing. "No delays. We're on."

Davyd met her eyes. 'If anything throws us off, we'll improvise.'

Liliya's expression softened for a beat, her lips almost forming a smile. 'Always do,' she replied, her confidence masking the tension beneath. "Aleekseev first. Anatoli, call in your contacts; Davyd, we handle the rest."

Their eyes met, tension settling between them. Davyd's jaw tightened. "We stick to the plan."

Liliya's eyes returned to the map. "Exits?"

"Main exit here," Davyd pointed. "And backups here and here."

"Noted," Liliya said, memorizing them.

Davyd pressed the watch into her hand, his jaw tightening. "Tracker's inside. Jammer's live."

She slipped it on, eyes already on the exit plans. "Backup routes?"

"Maintenance exit if it heats up." He was all business, barely a flicker of hesitation as they reviewed the contingencies, each step etched from muscle memory. They'd faced worse.

"If there's a sweep, blend in. Worst case, use the maintenance exit," Davyd added.

Liliya nodded, not needing to respond. The steps were clear.

"If Aleekseev gets suspicious?" she asked.

"Distract with science talk. Use the safe word if it escalates," Davyd replied. "If blown, take the service door. We'll be ready."

Liliya's breath steadied as she nodded. No more details were needed. The plan was solid. Risks accounted for.

"If it gets too dangerous..." Davyd hesitated, voice softer. "Call it off."

Liliya locked eyes with him. "Understood."

The room fell quiet, their unspoken fears hanging in the air. Liliya's gaze fixed on the map, eyes sharp, each detail burned into her memory. Her fingers tightened over the metal device. *No time for hesitation.* She tucked it away, shoulders squared, her face unreadable as she prepared for the role ahead. She stood, her movement fluid, deliberate, as though each step toward the bedroom brought her closer to the role she would soon assume.

Liliya secured the wig, her hands steady, gaze catching on her reflection. A stranger stared back—cold, untouchable. She adjusted a strand, slipping seamlessly into the persona Aleekseev would find irresistible. It was time. A flicker of something dark and heavy glinted in her eyes, but she pushed it down. *No room for that now.* Makeup followed; each move as mechanical as her heartbeat.

A trace of perfume, a final look in the mirror. She met her gaze in the mirror. The transformation was complete. Time to become the woman Aleekseev couldn't resist. Calm, controlled, unstoppable.

To those in the club she would appear as a black haired, sensual, and commanding woman. However, with her two encounters with Aleekseev, he would see beyond the wig and recognize his fantasy come to fruition. The woman he desired in the role he most wanted her to be in.

With her appearance perfected, Liliya was ready to venture into the world of the sex club frequented by Aleekseev. Bracing for the challenges ahead, she ran through their plan one last time in her mind.

Davyd quietly entered the room just as Liliya completed her transformation. She caught sight of him in the mirror's reflection, his expression one of admiration and quiet approval. She turned, offering a small smile. "You startled me."

Davyd's gaze lingered a moment too long. "You're going to turn heads in there," he said, keeping his tone light but serious, as if testing her reaction. "You look... perfect for this. Exactly what we need."

Liliya held his gaze a second longer than necessary. "Good. That's the goal," she said, her tone steady but with an edge, one that warned him not to go further. She adjusted the clasp on her bag, double-checking her gear. "No room for distractions."

Davyd's mouth tightened into a thin line, his voice dropping. "Just don't—" He paused, swallowing whatever he meant to say, his focus snapping back to the map. "Just signal if you need extraction.

Dusk was just falling, and the rain clung to the air, thick and heavy. Anatoli and Davyd waited in the car, watching as Liliya walked toward the club, her steps echoing against the tension. She adjusted her posture, slipping into her role.

With the Loft's cliental came a degree of extra security, and as Liliya entered, two individuals, both lacking necks, approached her. Their imposing presence was undeniable, and Liliya's pulse quickened, though she kept her composure.

"Evening, gentlemen. I'm here to speak with the manager about a job opportunity," she said with a smile, her voice steady and confident.

The first guard, a mountain of muscle, eyed her suspiciously. "Name?" he grunted, his tone flat and uninterested.

"Sarah," Liliya replied smoothly, using her cover name.

The second guard, slightly shorter but just as broad, looked her up and down, his gaze lingering on her shapely legs disappearing into her mini-skirt and her ample bosom pouring out of her top. "And what kind of job are you looking for, Sarah?" he asked, his tone carrying a hint of curiosity.

Liliya held his gaze, her smile unwavering, the practiced ease of a woman who'd taught herself not to flinch. "I'm a dominatrix. I heard the Loft is looking for someone with my... skills." Beneath her confidence, her fingers pressed just a bit too hard into her own palm, a tiny anchor she released as soon as she felt her nerves settle.

The first guard raised an eyebrow, his expression shifting from suspicion to mild interest. "Dominatrix, huh? We've had a few inquiries about that recently. Wait here."

He turned and walked away, leaving Liliya with the second guard. She could feel his eyes on her, assessing her every move. She fought to keep her breathing steady, her mind racing through possible scenarios and escape routes.

Just stay calm, she thought to herself. *You've got this.*

The first guard returned a moment later, nodding towards the curtain that separated the entrance from the main lounge and bar. "Follow me."

The guard pulled back the curtain, letting Liliya slip through. Stepping through the threshold, the ambiance of the Loft hit her instantly: a harsh green neon glow leaked over the bar, casting long, fractured shadows across the smoky room. The light flickered, catching on glassy eyes that watched her from half-hidden corners. Every face seemed to turn her way before vanishing back into the haze, their whispers folding into the murmur of low music. Liliya moved deliberately, letting her eyes skim the room without lingering. Around her, the shadows felt restless, like something half-awake.

100

The hallway walls were lined with photographs—women posed in half-lit frames, their eyes staring out blankly or with faint, unsettling smiles. Each image seemed to watch her as she passed, the glossy surfaces reflecting brief glimmers from the dim lights overhead. She caught the guard's eye for a moment, but he quickly looked away, focusing ahead with practiced indifference. Liliya kept her stride measured, but the cold knot in her stomach tightened with each step, the narrow corridor pressing closer around her.

The guard led her to a door at the back of the lounge and knocked twice before opening it. Inside, a sharp-eyed man sat behind a desk. The guard gestured for Liliya to enter, "Boss, this is Sarah."

Liliya wasted no time. "Here to offer my services."

Dmitri dismissed his companion with a glance, his gaze assessing her.

"Sarah, is it? I'm Dmitri. Have a seat."

Liliya took her seat, crossing her legs deliberately, letting the hem of her skirt rise slightly. The subtle move wasn't lost on him, as his eyes faltered for a second before he regained composure.

"So, Sarah, what makes you think you're a fit for the Loft?" Dmitri asked, but the power was already shifting.

Liliya met his gaze, her voice steady. "I have years of experience and a list of satisfied clients who can vouch for my skills. I understand discretion is key in this line of work, and I know how to handle myself in any situation."

She continued, "I collect direct and give you a kick back of 10%. In the end, it's a win-win. Also, I need a private room where I can conduct my sessions without interruptions. This room access should be restricted, no one enters under any circumstances. In return, I assure you that my services will attract a high-profile clientele, increasing your revenue significantly. What do you think?"

Dmitri considered her words, his expression thoughtful. "Privacy is a luxury, Sarah. It comes at a cost."

Liliya smiled, sensing she had his attention. "Of course. I'm willing to share a percentage of my earnings with the club. Let's say... and additional 10% of my take. I believe that's a fair trade for the privacy and discretion I require."

He nodded, caught up in the moment. "Fine. You'll have your private room—room eleven. No one will disturb you."

"Perfect." Liliya smiled, the deal secured. "I won't disappoint."

Dmitri, visibly intrigued, leaned back. "When can you start?"

"Tomorrow, Tuesday, at 7:00 PM."

Liliya got up, excused herself, and left the office before Dmitri had time to think about what he had just done. He had just agreed to let an enemy agent work at his establishment without doing the normal vetting procedure. Liliya would be an enigma that would appear one day and be gone the next.

She walked back down the hallway towards the bar and was met by the smaller musclemen. He escorted her to the back side of the complex to a hall that was lined with doors, each marked for who was using it that night. They proceeded down the hall and Liliya occasionally could make out voices and sounds coming from behind the doors. It was clear what was happening in each of them.

They stopped at the end of the hallway at the door marked 11 and the flunky unlocked the door and opened it for her. Inside she found a sparsely furnished room with a king size bed, and a bathroom and nothing else. She gave it a brief inspection and put out her palm to accept the key. With it safely secured, she moved back down the hall. and towards the entrance. Her thoughts briefly turned to Davyd and

Anatoli, waiting for her outside. *Stay sharp*, she reminded herself. *This is just the beginning.*

Outside, the chill wrapped around her, snapping her focus sharp. The room key pressed into her palm, a simple reminder: no room for error. She adjusted her stance and strode forward, each step marking her path into the unknown. She took one steadying breath before slipping into the back seat of the car, her mind sharpening as she met Davyd's gaze. 'We're in,' she said quietly, her voice carrying the unspoken tension between them.

That evening light fading, Anatoli left to pick up the remaining items that Davyd requested though encoded message and the dead drop. He returned just before 11:00 PM and strode in, a rare smile breaking his usual stoic demeanor. He deposited another medium size box on the table and presented two wardrobe bags with a flourish. Davyd and Liliya peeked inside, their eyes lighting up at the sight of the perfectly tailored Russian military uniforms, the fabric still crisp and the insignia meticulously stitched. They went back into the room and changed and then returned to Anatoli.

As they approached, Anatoli handed over their ID badges. "Passable, but steer clear of military."

Davyd's slight smile matched Liliya's as he glanced at her. "Just like Minsk."

She gave a quick nod, her mind already on the mission ahead.

"Liliya, you will want to check the contents to ensure it will do the job," Anatoli said, pointing at the box on the table.

Liliya moved swiftly to the box, tearing away the paper in a few quick motions. The metal case inside was compact, sturdy, its seal tight. She unclipped the tabs, the soft click of metal releasing echoing in the room. Inside, a small cylinder labeled "Liquid Nitrogen" nestled against three protective layers.

Without hesitation, Liliya inspected the compartments—the sealed outer layer, the buffer zone, and the two metal cylinders for the bioweapon samples. She snapped the lid back into place with a sense of finality. "Perfect. Right size, right model," she said, her tone brisk as she pushed the box aside, ready for the next phase.

As they completed their review, the clock struck midnight, moonlight through the patio window cast sharp lines across the table strewn with maps and gear. With a quick exchange of nods, each retreated to snatch whatever rest they could, knowing they'd be back here by first light, ready to set their plan in motion.

A couple of hours before Liliya was to arrive at the Loft on Tuesday evening, she sequestered herself in her room to prepare for the role she was about to play. She again put on the wig and did her makeup the same way. However, she changed her wardrobe. Instead of a mini skirt, she would be wearing skin-tight black leather pants, with the sides held together by black laces, exposing most of her outer leg. Her top would be a backless and sleeveless black leather top, which also had lacing at the back. To finish her ensemble, she wore a pair of 4-inch stilettos.

After getting herself ready for her role, Liliya packed her go-bag with meticulous care. The second outfit, makeup, and shoes were neatly packed inside—her escape plan. The capped syringe sat alongside the small leather strap. She paused, her fingers grazing the strap's worn surface. Its texture was rough, familiar—like a tether to what had to be done. The backup. Her mind flashed briefly—*her neck, skin under his hands, grip tightening.*

She zipped the bag and paused again. The air felt too thick, her breath catching.

Liliya stepped out of the room, her grip on the bag tightening as the strap's texture burned into her palm. *Eyes forward. Breathe.* The hallway seemed longer, each step echoing too loudly, the strap heavy on her mind, tethering her to the reality of the mission.

Early evening in Moscow, under the darkening sky... Liliya exited the apartment, her heels clicking against the pavement as she approached the waiting car. Anatoli glanced at her, nodding once before settling back, while Davyd's gaze lingered a second longer, a flicker of acknowledgment passing between them. They slipped into the shadows, the city's pulse growing faint behind them as they neared the Loft. The mission was live.

"Review the secondary exit points again," Davyd said, sensing her anxiety. "It's crucial you know them inside out."

Liliya's mind flicked to the map's image. The exits were already etched in her mind, and she noted them for him.

"Good," Davyd affirmed. "And remember, your main objective is to get close to Aleekseev. If anything feels off, abort the mission. We can always find another way."

Liliya glanced at the map again, eyes narrowing on the key entry points. She mentally filed Aleekseev's predictable routine, her hand tracing a path along the room layout. "I'll get him to the back rooms," she murmured, tapping her foot impatiently as if already feeling the seconds ticking by.

Liliya clenched her hands, fighting to conceal the faint tremor. *Don't let him see.* The leather strap in her bag pressed against her palm. It was too heavy, too real. She blinked hard, forcing the memories back. Davyd glanced at her briefly, and she forced her expression into calm. They couldn't afford any weakness, not now.

The car rolled to a stop, the sudden shift in momentum jarring her back into the moment. Her pulse quickened as the cold evening air hit her face. She stepped onto the pavement, her heels clicking against the concrete. A flash of another sound—a different place—her boots hitting the sterile floor of the lab. *Focus.*

The bite of the wind against her skin grounded her, the sharp sting dissolving the memory. *Keep moving.* Her fingers brushed the strap again, pulling her thoughts back to what was coming. There was no time to dwell, no space for hesitation. The mission demanded precision.

Ascending the stairs to the Loft, Liliya felt a surge of anticipation. The plan was timed perfectly to ensure Aleekseev was settled and engrossed in his surroundings, making him more susceptible to her influence.

As Liliya entered the Loft, she was greeted by the same imposing figures at the doorway, now adorned in tailored suits that did little to disguise their intimidating presence. Their gaze lingered on her form as they ushered her into the club, parting the curtain with a silent nod.

Stepping into the dimly lit interior, Liliya was immediately greeted by the steady pulse of bass-heavy music, each beat vibrating through the floor beneath her feet. The air was thick with the mingling scents of leather, sweat, and expensive cologne, the low hum of conversation blending into the rhythmic sound of clinking glasses. The atmosphere buzzed with an undercurrent of tension, the kind that thrived on secrecy and desire.

Her gaze swept the room, sharp and deliberate, taking in the shadowy figures draped in plush green leather booths along the edges of the space. The pole dancers moved in hypnotic, practiced rhythms, their swaying bodies capturing the attention of the patrons, but Liliya's focus never wavered.

She moved through the haze, her heels silent as her eyes scanned the room. Bodies shifted in the dim light, but her focus locked on the bar, where Aleekseev would linger. Each second counted. She slipped into view, exuding confidence—a lure designed to draw him closer.

Aleekseev was already watching, his gaze heavy. *Perfect.* She moved to the bar without glancing his way, playing her role with practiced ease.

She trusted in her training and instincts, knowing that once their eyes met, she would be able to gauge the success of their encounter. All she had to do now was wait, allowing Aleekseev to come to her in his own time, like the condemned man seduced through his dreams to a succubus.

At the bar, illuminated by the soft glow of a neon sign, she spotted Aleekseev seated among the crowd of patrons. His eyes were locked on her, intense and unwavering, but he was not alone in his scrutiny. Every pair of eyes in the room was now trained on her, captivated by her presence and intrigued by the aura of mystery that surrounded her.

With a calm resolve, she continued to move from the entrance and made her way to the bar, her steps purposeful and measured. She knew that this encounter would set the stage for the events to come, and she was prepared to play her part with precision and finesse.

She slipped past Aleekseev, close enough to catch the faint scent of his cologne—something sharp, mingling with the club's haze. She could feel his eyes follow her as she slid onto a barstool, her hands resting easily on the polished counter. A slight nod to the bartender, a quick smile. "I'll head off to drop this off in my room," she murmured, her tone so casual it was almost dismissive, yet her words carried enough force to shift his focus. "Pour that gentleman at the end of the bar another glass of whatever he is having and put it on my tab."

Behind her, Aleekseev's attention didn't waver, his gaze palpable even as she rose from her seat, every move timed, calibrated. She could almost sense the moment his interest sharpened, his silent approach bringing him into her orbit as if drawn by an invisible line.

Liliya then walked to the room and pulling out the key, she unlocked it and went inside. She deposited her bag on the bed, went to the bathroom to freshen up and then went back to the bar.

At the bar, the bartender gestured toward Aleekseev. "Know him?"

"No," Liliya replied.

"He's been watching since you walked in," the bartender said. "Asked how to approach you."

As Liliya listened to the bartender's explanation, she glanced discreetly towards the end of the bar, where Aleekseev sat. His gaze was fixed intently, clear recognition and hunger apparent in his eyes.

With a knowing smile, Liliya turned back to the bartender. "Send him another and bring me a club soda," Liliya instructed, moving gracefully towards the empty seat next to Aleekseev. She kept her eyes locked on his, a seductive smile on her lips.

She slid into the seat next to him, silent. The bartender set their drinks down, and Liliya lifted her glass without looking at Aleekseev. The pause lingered between them. When she finally turned, her eyes met his—a flicker of recognition, followed by something darker.

She leaned in close, her gaze steady, an almost predatory calm in her voice as she said, "I'm Sarah." Her words slipped out quietly, barely audible beneath the hum of the club, but Aleekseev's posture shifted, his eyes widening just enough to reveal a flicker of something darker than surprise.

Silence stretched between them, thick with unspoken understanding, each second weighted. Her eyes held his, unwavering, and as he swallowed, she caught the hint of a nervous pulse quickening at his throat. When she pulled back, her movements were measured, leaving just a trace of her perfume lingering in the air as she moved down the hallway.

Aleekseev followed without a word, his breath ragged, the pull of her presence too strong to resist. As he caught up, his breath came in uneven gasps, but she never turned back.

At the door, she stopped, her gaze sharp and unreadable. Without a word, she tilted her chin, a barely perceptible motion that sent an unmistakable command. The silence between them was heavy, and

Aleekseev hesitated for a moment, feeling its weight press down on him. Slowly, he sank to his knees, his breath shallow, the tension thickening with every second that passed.

Inside the dim room, Liliya gestured to the chair with a flick of her hand. "Strip," she said simply, not watching as he fumbled with his clothes. Her focus was elsewhere, her mind already a step ahead.

When he finally sat, his nerves apparent in the jerky movements, Liliya looked at him, her expression unreadable. "You were always watching me at the Academy, weren't you?" Her words barely needed to be spoken—he knew what she meant.

Aleekseev flinched under her gaze, his hands trembling as he fought to maintain composure.

She stepped back, slow, deliberate. "Take off the rest. Then come here." Her tone was flat, indifferent. Each word was a test, and she knew he would pass.

Aleekseev stumbled through the motions, eager to please. When he reached her feet, his breath hitched as he placed his lips against the leather of her shoes, worshiping with frantic devotion. Liliya watched, her face unreadable, as his desperation deepened the control she held over him.

She stayed silent, her gaze flicking over his every move, offering no approval—just a steady, cold observation. His every action thickened the tension in the air.

While he worked, she calmly opened her bag, her fingers brushing the syringe inside. Her eyes never left him as she laid the scarves on the bed. The preparation was clinical, detached, as if she were performing a procedure, not orchestrating a death.

"Almost there," she murmured, her voice low. Aleekseev flinched at the sound but didn't dare speak. She lifted his head, gripping his chin with a firm hand. "You've done well. Look at me."

His gaze snapped up, desperate for any sign of approval, but Liliya gave him none.

"Enough," she said, voice sharp again. "Stand." She tossed him the scarves. "Tie yourself." As Aleekseev fumbled with the knots, his hands betraying an arrogance too comfortable with power, Liliya's jaw tightened. The familiar burn of regret stirred as she remembered Mel'nyk's vials—a failure she couldn't erase. Aleekseev's survival would mean the same mistakes, multiplied.

Darkness swallowed him as she tied the final scarf and then a blindfold around his eyes, tightening it with the flick of her wrist. His breathing grew shallow, betraying his excitement—and fear. Liliya stepped back, her expression cold, calculating.

Her footsteps circled him slowly, each step precise, her gaze never leaving his vulnerable form. "Let's see if you can follow orders," she whispered, watching him twitch at the sound of her voice. He could only wait, trapped in the darkness she'd created.

Her control over him was absolute now, but as she prepared the syringe. Her hands stayed steady, but a flicker of something darker threatened to rise, the hatred simmering quietly. She forced her grip firmer on the syringe, her pulse falling into line. For a brief, disorienting moment, it was almost too easy. Her voice, low and detached, echoed back to her. *Calm, steady.* As though this were all routine, her own feelings tucked away.

The syringe in hand, she uncapped it with a slow, deliberate movement, the sound of the plunger echoing in the quiet room. "Oh, I have something special for you," she whispered, each word laced with dark promise. She knelt at his feet, her fingers separating his toes as if she were simply examining them.

Aleekseev's confusion rippled through the silence. "What... what is this?"

Liliya's gaze hardened, her voice dropping to a whisper. "Doctor Aleekseev," she said, the words cutting through the air. "All that brilliance... and yet here you are. You were always so easy to read." She paused, watching the fear flicker across his face.

"I'm here to erase everything you've done," she whispered, leaning closer. "You should have seen this coming." Liliya leaned closer, her voice low. "This isn't about your habits or the club. It's your work, Aleekseev. That's what makes you dangerous—and why you'll regret crossing us." Without waiting for a reply, she injected the serum. Her eyes never left his face as the fear rooted itself deep inside him. His body slumped, and she calmly watched the fight drain from him.

Liliya observed him carefully, calculating her next move. "Your data," she began, her tone cool, "is it in the office? Or is it in the lab?"

Aleekseev's head continued to lull, and he replied, "What notes? I'm working on many projects."

Impatiently Liliya clarified her question, "Is your data and notes in your office safe?" Liliya asked, her voice cutting through the silence like a knife. Aleekseev's head wobbled as he tried to focus. "Yes, I wouldn't leave my data in the lab," he slurred.

"What about the bioweapon samples, what is the code to the storage area?" She inquired.

"Alexei. is in charge of changing the code every morning. Even I don't know until I arrive, and he informs me of it."

"Will Alexei be in the lab tomorrow morning?"

"Oh, yeah, he is always there early, 0600. Yes, he will be there. He never misses a day of work. He's a little dense when it comes to the work, but he is reliable."

"This Alexei, what does he look like?"

"Oh, about 185 centimeters, thin, blonde hair, black glasses with thick lenses." As he described his assistant, she remembered seeing him among the other sycophants that had been around Aleekseev the day before.

"The safe. What's the combination?" Liliya's voice was steady, unyielding.

"1917," Aleekseev muttered, "the October Revolution." His answer was met with silence, and in that pause, the weight of his mistake seemed to settle over him like a noose. Liliya's gaze hardened, but she remained in control, letting the gravity of his situation sink in.

She returned to questioning him, "Where are the plans for the missile? And are there more than one?"

Aleekseev, with his head still lulling, responded, "There's only one set of plans and they're at the plant under guard in the commander's office."

Liliya continued, "Last question. Besides guards, what other security measures are in place?"

"The plans are in a biometric sealed safe which can only be opened with the commander's handprint," was the answer she received.

The silence that followed his final admission felt heavy. Liliya stood, leaving him blindfolded and bound. She surveyed him, a predator watching its prey.

She removed the blindfold and untied his hands, knowing the drugs had dulled his resistance. "Untie yourself," she ordered, her voice flat again. His sluggish movements mirrored the drug's effects as he struggled with the knots.

R. "Petra" Bohnet

When he was free, she moved toward his discarded pants and removed the belt with a practiced motion, the sound of the leather sliding free sending a shiver through the air.

"Sit in the chair. Don't move." Her tone remained calm, but the implication was clear. She looped the belt around his neck, every movement precise, as though it were part of a familiar routine. There was no need to speak further—in his dulled mind, he understood what was coming.

As her fingers tightened around the leather, a sudden flash of memory tore through her mind—her own breath coming in short gasps as hands closed around her throat. Her heartbeat quickened. Davyd's voice echoed faintly, distant. "— Stay focused, Liliya. You're in control." The trembling in her hands threatened to betray her, the belt suddenly feeling too heavy, too real. Her grip faltered. *No... not now.* She blinked hard, forcing the fragmented memories to the back of her mind, her breath shallow but steadying.

With deliberate focus, Liliya pushed the memories away, her hands once again steady on the belt. She tightened it, her gaze cold and detached. Aleekseev's gasps grew frantic, his body convulsing, but she didn't flinch. *This is now.*

Only when his body fell still did she allow herself a slow, quiet exhale. She stepped back, releasing the belt, her gaze sweeping the room as she began to prepare for the next phase. Each motion was fluid, controlled. There was no need for reflection—not yet. She had more work to do.

She dressed swiftly, mind running through the details. Keys, attire, room checked—every step bringing her closer to the exit. Aleekseev lay still, her focus already on the next objective.

The door clicked shut behind her as she slipped into the dim hallway, her heart racing beneath her cool exterior. Each step echoed through the corridor; the air heavy with her actions. The faint hum of the bar beyond, the murmur of voices—each sound grounded her, helping her maintain the appearance of calm.

It wasn't until she reached the bar and ordered her drink, blending into the surroundings, that she allowed a small moment of reflection. She couldn't afford to linger on Aleekseev's lifeless body. That part of the mission was done.

Liliya moved swiftly to a window in view of Davyd and Anatoli, signaling them. On cue, they jumped out, playing the part of two drunken friends. As they entered the door to the Loft, they loudly addressed the no-necks, while Liliya slowly moved through the curtain and glided to the door. She carefully opened it, slipped through a narrow opening. Her steps smooth, her demeanor steady, she exited and quietly closed the door behind her. The door clicked shut, and she moved down the stairs with control.

Once she slipped into the back of the car, the professional mask began to falter. The confined space felt suffocating. Her hands, resting on her lap, trembled almost imperceptibly. She clasped them tighter, willing them to still. But the control she had commanded so effortlessly inside the Loft began to fray.

She swallowed against the nausea rising in her throat, her pulse erratic despite her best efforts to control it. The tension coiled tight within her as the haunting image of Aleekseev's death clawed its way back into her consciousness. Her body felt cold, despite the warmth of the car. The weight of it all—the mission, the deaths—settled in, heavier than she anticipated.

"I'm supposed to save lives, not take them," she whispered, barely audible.

Liliya clenched her hands tighter, the knuckles white as the pressure built inside her, but she forced herself to keep it together—just a little longer. Davyd and Anatoli would be here any second. Then she could finally let go. But for now, she held on, barely. Liliya's hand tightened on her pistol, exhaling sharply as she steadied herself. Whatever came next, she was ready.

The car doors opened suddenly, jolting her from her thoughts. Davyd slipped into the backseat with her, and Anatoli into the driver's seat, their faces etched with the strain of the night's events. Davyd leaned over, his hand resting gently on her shoulder. Glancing at her, his eyes searching hers. Liliya's mind was a storm of conflicting emotions, yet she couldn't bring herself to meet Davyd's concerned gaze.

"It was necessary," Anatoli said softly from the driver's seat. "Aleekseev was a danger to many. You did what needed to be done."

Anatoli's words were meant to soothe, but they rang hollow. The logic was clear, the necessity undeniable, yet the weight on her conscience remained a heavy, unyielding burden.

The mission wasn't over, and she needed to stay focused. But as the car sped through the silent streets, Liliya couldn't shake the feeling that she was losing herself, one mission at a time.

"Just one more," Liliya whispered to herself, her voice a mix of determination and desperation. "One more mission."

Davyd reached over, his fingers grazing Liliya's hand in a brief touch, quickly withdrawing as if he'd surprised himself. She felt the warmth of his touch linger, a fleeting hint of something unsaid, unacknowledged.

She met Davyd's gaze, a single nod passing between them before the car sped away from the club. The city lights blurred through the windows, a silent testament to the night's success. Within moments, they slipped back into the maze of Moscow's quieter streets, leaving the Loft—and Aleekseev—far behind.

CHAPTER

TEN

Hiding in Plain Sight

At 5:00 AM, Anatoli strode in, a rare smile breaking his usual stoic demeanor. Davyd and Liliya, already dressed and seated, sipped coffee. "Nothing, absolutely nothing," Anatoli said, grinning. "Everything's a go. Yes?"

"Yes!" they replied in unison, rising to grab their gear. They slipped into the car, the Academy only minutes away. Silence filled the space, Liliya's gaze sharp on the approaching streets.

"Once we're in, no hesitation," Davyd reminded, his tone steady.

She nodded, forcing all distraction from her mind. There was only the mission ahead.

Dressed in Russian military uniforms as dawn broke, they pulled up to the Academy. They cut imposing figures, aided by the ID badges. Anatoli had secured. Their mission was bold: infiltrate the lab, secure Aleekseev's research, and exit unnoticed.

Davyd and Liliya moved in sync, grabbing their briefcases and the metal container. The Academy's cracked white facade, crowned by the infamous "Golden Brains," loomed overhead, but they barely glanced at it.

The cleaning staff's gaze flicked over their uniforms, his hand reaching mechanically for the glass door without a word. Inside, the Academy's cold fluorescent lights cast hard lines along the sterile, vacant corridors, each footstep absorbed by the polished floor. The hum of the building's systems throbbed low and steady, a metallic pulse beneath the surface. Every door they passed was closed, every window dark, leaving only their reflections sliding along the glass—two faceless figures moving through silent, unyielding walls.

Boots struck the marble—quick, unyielding. The faint antiseptic bite filled the air, catching in Liliya's throat. She forced her gaze forward, ignoring the tarnished bronze plaques that flickered past. Each step was a beat, a countdown.

As they approached the lab door, Davyd held back for half a second, just long enough to position himself slightly behind Liliya—an instinctive move to shield her from any sudden threat. His gaze swept the hallway, catching every flicker of movement, each shadow cast by the cold, fluorescent lights. He stayed close, his steps falling quietly in line with hers.

When Liliya moved her hand toward the briefcase, her grip too tight, Davyd's eyes drifted there briefly, his brow barely creasing before he looked ahead again, as though calculating their exit. But his hand remained close to her shoulder, hovering just out of sight.

A tall, thin blond man was exiting the lab just as they entered. His eyes widened slightly upon seeing them, and he faltered mid-step. Davyd's voice was cool, rehearsed. "Are you Alexei?" His gaze was fixed, firm.

Liliya watched Alexei's eyes shift nervously from Davyd to her. A beat too long. Her own voice was steady, but a momentary tightening in her chest reminded her of the lie. "Doctor Lebedev," she said, the title a foreign weight on her tongue. As she handed Alexei the ID badge, her fingers brushed his. She felt his hesitation—the cold, quick pressure of his grip, his pulse racing against her skin.

She pulled her hand back swiftly, averting her gaze before Alexei could see the flicker of discomfort. Her grip on the briefcase tightened.

"We need access to all bioweapon samples. You're in charge of the storage code, correct?" Davyd's voice was sharp, clipped.

Alexei's gaze dropped, his hands twisting. "Yes... but... shouldn't the doctor be—"

"Focus," Davyd cut him off, his eyes hard. "We spoke with Dr. Aleekseev yesterday," Davyd said smoothly, his voice steady as stone. "He's occupied preparing his data at his residence. We're here to ensure the transfer happens without delay."

"Strange he didn't come himself..." Alexei muttered, his voice barely a whisper.

Liliya stepped forward. "Relocation order. Samples, now," she said, her tone cold, unyielding. Alexei's breath hitched as he nodded, visibly shrinking.

His throat tightened as he swallowed again, his fingers flexing at his sides as though unsure of where to place them. "Right... right, of course. Procedure." His voice cracked once more as he turned, shoulders hunched slightly, to lead them towards the storage area.

Alexei picked up the pace, his shallow breaths rasping in the sterile lab. Liliya didn't let her stride falter. She tracked the quickening pulse at his throat. They couldn't afford a pause. "It's just... the doctor usually handles these things himself," he muttered, his voice barely a whisper. "I don't understand why he would—"

Davyd stepped closer to Liliya, his shoulder brushing against hers—just slightly. The physical proximity added weight to his next words. "The doctor's instructions," he said quietly, his voice cool, measured. His eyes flicked toward Liliya, not Alexei, as if waiting for her to back him up. She didn't move, her silence saying more than any words could.

The lights sputtered, plunging the hallway into darkness. Liliya's hand flew to her holster, instinct sharp as a blade. Breath held; she waited. The lights buzzed back to life, and her pulse hammered on. *No time for hesitation.*

"Without delay," Davyd added, his calm tone cutting through the silence.

Alexei flinched, the sound of his shoes squeaking on the polished floor the only sign of his misstep. A sheen of sweat formed on his temple, which he wiped hastily as they approached the keypad. His fingers hovered over the numbers, then hesitated.

Davyd moved closer, deliberate, cold. His hand hovered near Liliya's shoulder—a silent cue, a reminder. "Problem?" he asked, eyes fixed ahead. The question cut through the air, brittle and taut. Seconds thickened, weighed down by Alexei's silence.

She glanced at Alexei briefly, the corner of her mouth tightening in the slightest nod. It wasn't the question that mattered—it was the answer she was expecting. Alexei's breath hitched. "No... no problem," he stammered, his voice tight, barely above a whisper.

He hastily entered the code, but his fingers fumbled over the buttons, missing the first attempt. He tried again, the green light blinked on, and Alexei hesitated again before gripping the door handle too tightly. He glanced over his shoulder as if considering an escape route.

Liliya's cold stare bore into him. "Lead the way," she said, her voice sharp as ice.

The vacuum seal hissed softly as the door opened, the sterile scent of the storage room washing over them. Alexei's movements grew more deliberate, almost painfully slow, as he gestured towards the containers. His shoulders slumped forward as if the weight of the situation were pressing down on him. Liliya's gaze didn't waver, watching every twitch and shift.

Inside, Alexei gestured shakily to the containers.

Liliya noted the familiar symbol etched into the containers. Her pulse quickened. *Antiseptic.* Vials. Blood. Liliya's breath caught. *Not now.*

"This is all of it, right?" Her words were edged with suspicion, yet softer than she intended. Liliya's eyes lingered on Alexei's trembling hands, his uncertainty unmistakable. She held her breath for a second too long, gauging him.

When he nodded, the lie tightened around her like a steel band. This man wasn't an enemy, not in any way that felt real, but still she pressed him, her own doubts buried under the practiced authority in her tone. "Disinfect the containers and place them in the BSC," she said, forcing her focus back. Her voice felt hollow, but her body moved automatically, each gesture steady and precise.

He glanced toward the door, his eyes darting to the exit like a trapped animal. The sudden distant thud of a door slamming somewhere deep within the building sent a jolt of panic through Alexei, his body stiffening. Liliya's jaw clenched. She turned just enough to track the sound, her ears attuned to every creak and shuffle, but Davyd's silent stance at the entrance kept Alexei from bolting. The tension ratcheted higher with every passing second. When he finally spoke, his voice was deceptively calm. "We're running out of time." The message wasn't for Alexei. It was for her.

"Move," Davyd's voice cut through like a blade. He loomed just behind Alexei, watching his every move.

Alexei's hand trembled as he placed the containers in the BSC, the sound of the metal clinking unnervingly loud in the sterile silence.

Liliya watched him, her expression cool and detached, but internally, she was assessing every faltering movement. Alexei was unraveling, and they needed him to hold it together just long enough. "Once you're done, go to the BSC and prepare the samples for transfer," she said, her tone as sharp as a scalpel slicing through the tension.

Alexei's eyes widened, and his fingers fumbled as he wiped sweat from his brow once more. His gaze flicked nervously between the two of them, lingering on Liliya, as though searching for some sign of leniency that wasn't there. His breathing was erratic now, coming in short, shallow bursts, but he nodded quickly, too afraid to argue.

Liliya exchanged a glance with Davyd, both recognizing how fragile their cover truly was. They couldn't afford a slip—not now.

Liliya slid her arms into the BSC sleeves, her fingers pressing against the thin layer of fabric, the cold bite of the sterilized metal prickling through to her skin. The room's stillness amplified the soft rustle of her movements, each one precise, as if the walls themselves were listening. Across the room, Davyd's gaze remained fixed on the door, his stance taut, shadows sharpening along his jaw. As Liliya extracted the samples, her pulse echoed in her ears, steady but heavy—a quiet metronome against the sterile hum of the lab.

The sharp scent of antiseptic stung her nostrils—just for a moment, it was too familiar. Her fingers grazed the cold metal of the containers, and for a split second, the room seemed to tilt. *Gloved hands... tightening.* Liliya's vision blurred, the memory scratching at the edges of her mind. She blinked hard. The hum of the ventilation above twisted into something irregular, beating like a frantic pulse.

The sterile air thickened, pressing against her lungs. *Blood. Bleach.* It flickered—just a shadow, a static echo of something long buried. She swallowed, forcing the thought down, fingers tightening around the sample.

Blink. She steadied her breath, the past dissolving, the mission pulling her back to the present.

Liliya finished sealing the containers and removed her arms from the BSC, handing the metal container to Davyd. "Good work," she said flatly, but her eyes stayed on Alexei, gauging his reaction.

Davyd stepped closer; his voice low, almost polite. "Aleekseev will hear everything went smoothly, yes?"

Alexei's eyes widened, a bead of sweat sliding down his temple. "Of course. Smoothly," he whispered.

They moved toward the door in silence, Alexei's gaze heavy on them. As they passed, Liliya glanced over her shoulder, catching his wide-eyed look—a faint glimmer of desperation mixed with confusion.

She bit back the instinct to reassure him, to ease the worry written in his gaze. Instead, she straightened, her movements controlled. As the door closed behind them, she couldn't shake the tension that twisted in her chest, the faint dread that they'd left him with nothing but a question he'd never get answered.

At her side, Davyd was already focused on the next step, his footsteps quick and certain. But for Liliya, each step down the hallway felt heavier, the man's silent plea echoing in her mind.

Davyd shot a quick glance back. *Nothing.* Alexei hadn't followed. Another second bought. But the tension lingered, coiling tight beneath their every movement.

Davyd gave Liliya a quick nod, and she immediately reached into her pocket, pulling out the keys. The hallway stretched ahead, every second ticking by like a countdown. Liliya's fingers fumbled for a fraction of a second, the weight of the moment pressing down on her as she found the right key. She slid it into the lock, listening for the click.

The door creaked open. Without a word, Liliya slipped inside, the empty case in hand. She closed the door behind her, the soft thud of it shutting reverberating through the quiet. They couldn't afford a mistake now.

Remembering the combination, she positioned herself in front of the locked safe and entered '1917' and heard the electronic lock click.

Upon opening it, she came across reams of paper with numerous formulas and calculations on them. She opened the case and began scooping the papers into it. The amount of paper was almost more than it could hold but she was able to press down on the top with enough force to close the clasps.

As she was about to approach the door, Davyd appeared and rushed in. Alexei was on the move, and they needed to hide and wait for him to pass by. They flattened themselves against the door's wall and listened for Alexei's footsteps. As he approached his steps began to resound louder and then they stopped as he peered in the window of Aleekseev's office.

After a few seconds, the sound of steps continued, becoming softer as Alexei moved away from them. Davyd exhaled, the tension visibly easing from his shoulders, and they exchanged a glance before moving to the door. Liliya peered through the small window, scanning the dimly lit corridor. The coast was clear. They stepped out in unison, but as they made their way to the stairwell, Liliya's thoughts pulled her inward, the faint echo of Alexei's footsteps lingering in her mind.

At the stairwell, each step down the stairs felt heavier than the last. She hesitated, her eyes distant for a split second. The air in the tower felt colder now, pressing against her skin like the sterile chill of the labs she had tried so hard to forget. Davyd's hand brushed lightly against her shoulder as he moved forward, guiding her down. His touch was brief, steadying—gone in an instant but a quiet reminder that they were still on track. As they exited the tower, a thin layer of sweat clung to her back, though her face betrayed none of it.

As they reached the exit, Davyd slowed, his hand brushing her arm—a touch she barely acknowledged. "Let's keep moving," she murmured, her voice edged but steady.

Outside, the air was crisp, biting, yet her pulse still thrummed with the intensity of the lab. Davyd gave a nod, a silent affirmation, though his own gaze flicked back to the building, shadows lingering behind the glass. They were clear, no one on their heels, but he knew this wasn't over. Not for Liliya, and not for him.

A shadow passed over her mind—the sterile smell of the lab, the cold glass of the containers, the weight of past missions that never really ended. Her fingers twitched, remembering the feel of the BSC's sleeves, and the faint memory of gloved hands around her throat. It wasn't just Aleekseev's research that would remain buried; pieces of herself had been left behind as well.

She pulled in a deep breath, the cold air biting against her lungs, but the sensation of release never came. Instead, her heart thudded dully in her chest, a reminder that even when the mission was over, its echoes never truly faded.

As she reached the car, Anatoli clapped her on the back, his smile as wide as ever. "That's a win," he said, his voice brimming with pride. Liliya forced a smile, her lips tight, but her mind was elsewhere, deep in the recesses of what they had left behind.

"Yes," she muttered. But beneath her voice, Davyd caught it—the smallest crack. The mission was complete, but neither moved, as if waiting for the next step, the next signal. The shadows shifted outside, stretching toward them as dawn continued to rise.

CHAPTER

ELEVEN

Aftermath and Planning

The drive back to the Sky apartment was silent. Liliya caught Davyd's gaze in the rearview mirror, a shared glance that acknowledged the mission's success. Yet, behind her faint smile, Alexei's haunted look clung to her thoughts.

Davyd's voice broke the silence. "Still seeing his face?"

Liliya exhaled, eyes narrowing on the passing lights. "Yes... and wondering what he'd say if he knew."

"He won't. That's done," Davyd replied firmly, though his fingers tapped the wheel in restless beats. "It's tomorrow I'm more worried about."

Liliya nodded, shifting her focus back to the cityscape.

As they neared the apartment, Liliya's gaze caught on a street vendor unlocking his cart. For a moment, she saw the lives they disrupted, unseen in the shadows.

Davyd followed her gaze. "Easy to forget they're out there when everything feels like war," he murmured, then straightened, as if shrugging off a heavy coat.

"That's why we can't afford mistakes," Liliya replied, her voice a touch sharper than she intended.

Davyd offered a slight nod, and in his silence, she found an agreement. Their success meant little if they couldn't keep that world hidden and the real game was just beginning.

The quiet in the car grew heavier as the adrenaline ebbed, leaving only the cold reality of what lay ahead. The mission had been a success, but the danger hadn't passed—it was only the first move in a much larger game. She exhaled softly, her fingers tracing the edge of the armrest as they prepared to face the next phase.

They entered the Sky swiftly, eyes scanning for any signs of surveillance. The secure walls of the apartment gave them a moment's reprieve, but vigilance never left. The weight of tomorrow's challenges settled on their shoulders; victory overshadowed by the looming responsibilities ahead.

At the table, Liliya's fingers hovered over a map. "Do you ever wonder…" she trailed off, the words catching as she pictured a life that felt forever distant.

Davyd's hand lingered over the stack of documents. "Sometimes… but not now." He glanced at the clock, his expression hardening.

The clock barely moved. Liliya paced, fingers tracing the air, searching for answers. Davyd's foot tapped in rhythm, their eyes meeting briefly, an exchange of unspoken concerns.

Davyd busied himself folding documents, each movement precise. His jaw clenched as his fingers paused over a family photo. For a moment, he lingered, then placed it on the stack and shut the lid with a sigh that echoed in the stifling room.

He leaned against the wall, the cool surface a brief relief. His eyes drifted to the dimming light outside. 'Today was important,' he muttered, trying to fend off the creeping despair. One small victory in a war of shadows, yet the sacrifices lingered.

Every mission took a piece of him, lost to the abyss of necessary evils. He paced the room. 'Who will step in if we don't?' he whispered. His resolve hardened, ready for the next battle, carrying both hope and despair.

Hours passed with the soft rustle of papers and the scrape of chairs. Finally, Anatoli pushed back from the table, rubbing a hand over his face. Without a word, he drifted toward the kitchen, the faint clink of a mug filling the silence as he poured himself a drink. The faint memory of his sons' laughter flickered through his mind, a sharp reminder of all he'd sacrificed.

Davyd entered silently, his presence grounding amidst the thoughts swirling in Anatoli's mind. He settled across from him, searching Anatoli's face before speaking. "You okay?"

Anatoli's fingers tightened around his cup, his gaze drifting. "This war… my boys…" His voice faded, heavy with unspoken weight. "Every fight feels heavier. Like holding back the tide."

Davyd reached across the table, gripping Anatoli's arm. His eyes said what words couldn't—this was more than just survival.

Anatoli looked into Davyd's eyes, finding strength in his words. "I just want to see it… for once."

Davyd nodded; his expression resolute. "We'll see it." He paused, eyes narrowing. "We keep going. Together."

In that moment, Anatoli felt a renewed sense of purpose. Despite the personal conflicts and the ever-present pain, he knew he wasn't alone. With Davyd and Liliya by his side, he could face the darkness and continue the fight for a better future.

Anatoli pushed back from the table, rising with a determined set to his jaw. "We move forward," he said simply, already shifting into action.

Davyd nodded, crossing the room in quick strides. "Time to focus," he muttered, his hand already reaching for the documents on the table.

The plan for the next day was anything but clear: early in the morning, they would separate, but timing was crucial. Liliya and Anatoli had to reach Dmitryashevka without drawing attention, while Davyd's route to the underground drop-off was less certain. "The couriers haven't confirmed the handoff," Davyd muttered, glancing at his watch. "If they're late or compromised, we'll be stuck with the sample and data."

They reviewed the plan again, rehearsing each detail to exhaustion. Maps cluttered the table, the room thick with the unspoken weight of failure. Every word carried a layer of urgency, each second more critical than the last.

Liliya's finger tapped the blueprint. "Vault here. Plant the charges, set exits."

Anatoli studied it, jaw taut. "Guard rotation?"

"Standard. I'll work the gaps if they shift," Liliya replied.

They shared a look, the plan etched in their minds—no room for error. Davyd's voice broke in, tight with unease. "Liliya, how do you get in?"

She exhaled, glancing at the blueprints. "The night shift is the cleanest option... but if there's any shuffle in the roster, I'll need a fast plan B." Her finger hovered over an alternate entry point, though uncertainty flickered in her eyes.

"Then we'll have a plan B in place," Davyd replied, his tone hardening. "This time, there's no room for error."

The weight of his words hung between them, and Liliya's fingers resumed tracing the entry points, her focus sharpening.

"Okay. Hopefully it works because we will only have this one opportunity," Anatoli interjected

Liliya, clinching her fist replied, "I know. This is personal. One mistake… and it's over. I won't let that happen."

They fall back into silence, the weight of their mission hanging over them. Each team member lost in their thoughts; the room thick with unvoiced tension.

Anatoli's voice broke through the quiet. "How're you getting close?"

Liliya stepped forward, her tone sharp, leaving no room for doubt. "I'll pose as a local's relative. I'll get close."

Davyd leaned forward, his gaze steady. "And if they don't take the bait?"

Liliya's lips twitched into a faint smile, her eyes never leaving the map. "They will."

"It's dangerous. If they catch on?" Anatoli asked, his concern evident.

Liliya squared her shoulders. "We improvise." Her hand slid to the locket at her neck, fingers brushing it, her focus already back on the plan. She let go of the locket, her hand falling to the map before her. With a sharp inhale, Liliya traced the path, her fingers pressing harder against the paper as if forcing the uncertainty aside. "There's more riding on this than ever before," she murmured, her eyes fixed on the image, determination masking the fear that simmered beneath the surface.

Davyd's voice cut through her thoughts, pulling her fully back to the present. "I'll connect with our friends in the local resistance. They'll provide quiet support and protection," he said, his tone steady, drawing them back to the logistical framework.

Anatoli nodded, picking up the thread. "We'll be in position, maintaining oversight from our surveillance points." He turned toward her, his gaze firm. "Liliya, you won't be alone in this."

The brief silence that followed felt heavier, but it was clear—they were moving forward, with no room for hesitation.

Just then the apartment phone rang. Liliya answered it with a quick glance at Davyd and Anatoli before passing the receiver to Anatoli. His posture shifted as he listened, the tension melting away from his body. Anatoli's face softened. "Aleekseev's death... ruled an accident." Relief flickered briefly in the room, though for Liliya, it felt fleeting, like smoke dispersing too quickly.

With the immediate danger temporarily eased, they cautiously allowed themselves a brief respite. A dinner was planned, every detail of it measured, meant to preserve a sense of normalcy. They would walk around Patriarch's Ponds afterward, both to clear their minds and to complete the final dead drop in Moscow.

Anatoli noticed the subtle exchange of glances between Liliya and Davyd. "I'll give you two some space," he said with a nod, his knowing smile softening the words. "See you tomorrow."

After Anatoli left, Davyd turned to Liliya, his hand brushing her arm. "Shall we?"

Liliya smiled, but it barely reached her eyes. "If we must." As they stepped outside, the cool night air washed over them, sharp and crisp. Liliya inhaled deeply, exhaling slowly as she matched her steps with Davyd's. The antiseptic scent from earlier clung to her senses, a reminder of all the places she'd rather forget.

"You good?" Davyd's voice was low, almost drowned out by the rustle of leaves along the path.

She blinked, snapping back to Davyd's voice. "Yeah." The weight of the mission settled in again, and she focused on her footsteps, the cool air sharpening her senses.

The tree-lined paths brought a brief contrast to the tension. She glanced over her shoulder, aware that the peace was only an illusion.

They continued walking, the tranquility of the night doing little to quell the tension simmering beneath her skin. They fell into a comfortable silence, but for Liliya, the peacefulness only made her feel more aware of how temporary it was. The weight of their mission pressed down on her shoulders, even in this quiet, stolen moment.

The night paths, lined with trees, brought a contrast to their world. Liliya glanced over her shoulder, aware the peace was an illusion. Reaching the designated bench, Davyd crouched, fixing the final set of instructions to its underside, pulling her focus back.

The serenity of the park worked its slow magic, though a knot of unease remained in her chest. "It's beautiful here," she said softly, watching the reflection of the city lights ripple across the water.

Davyd squeezed her hand. "It is. We should enjoy moments like this whenever we can."

They walked in silence for a while, the quiet settling between them. After a few steps, Liliya's hand brushed against his, a small, unconscious gesture. 'This... this is why we fight, isn't it?' she murmured, her eyes scanning the horizon, searching for something beyond the shadows.

Davyd glanced at her, his gaze softening. He didn't answer right away, allowing the moment to stretch between them. 'For moments like this,' he finally said, though the weight in his voice hinted at the unspoken truth.

They fell into a comfortable silence, but for Liliya, the peacefulness only made her feel more aware of how temporary it was—they both knew how fleeting this peace was. The weight of their mission pressed down on her shoulders, even in this quiet, stolen moment.

On their way back, Liliya paused by a dress shop window, her eye catching on an elegant red gown. "I need this," she said, a playful smile tugging at her lips, though part of her wondered if she was pretending.

Davyd matched her grin. "Then I need something too." For a moment, they felt like ordinary people making ordinary choices, unburdened by secrets and danger.

Liliya changed into her gown, feeling an unfamiliar lightness even as it was tinged with bittersweet longing. Davyd emerged in a suit, adjusting his tie. "Feels right," he said quietly, his eyes lingering on his reflection as if to believe it.

Room service arrived, and he led her to the balcony. "Milady," he teased, pulling out her chair with a wink, almost dispelling the weight she carried.

Liliya laughed, the sound a little too carefree. "Thank you, kind sir," she replied, taking her seat. As they sat across from each other, the candlelight flickering between them, she felt the weight of the mission creeping back in, coiled beneath the surface.

They ate quietly, not for the food, but for the illusion it created. Every word, every gesture felt tentative, a fragile attempt at normalcy.

"Do you think we can ever... leave this behind?" Davyd's question hung in the air. She hesitated, her eyes fixed on the horizon.

"Sometimes," she murmured, "but then I remember why we fight. It's not just for us. It's for those who can't."

Davyd held her hand, anchoring her again. "Or are we destined to always look over our shoulders?" His voice was as heavy as the night air, drifting unanswered.

Liliya wanted to look at him, but her eyes were already scanning the room, calculating, planning. "We can't afford to slip, at any time." Her voice was low, her grip tightening as if she could hold onto their fragile reality.

Davyd squeezed her hand, but his gaze was distant. "We're still together," he murmured, though the weight of what they were about to face overshadowed any sense of comfort.

As they shared that moment, the shadows on the edge of Liliya's mind never truly left. Her mind wandered back to the mission—the danger still lurking just out of sight.

They got up and lingered on the balcony, hands entwined, the world below seemingly far away. Yet for Liliya, the tranquility of the moment felt fragile, as if the slightest shift could shatter the illusion. She stole a glance at Davyd, his features softened by the candlelight. He looked at ease, but she knew better—their lives never allowed for true relaxation.

As they turned back inside, the room's warmth greeted them, but the earlier tension lingered. Davyd picked up a plate, turning it over as if holding onto something simple. "Feels almost normal," he muttered.

Liliya nodded, her gaze drifting to the window where the city's shadows loomed. "It's nice, isn't it?" she replied, though her voice carried a quiet sadness.

They moved together, cleaning up the remnants of their dinner, but Liliya's thoughts were already elsewhere. She glanced at Davyd, sensing the same undercurrent in him—the knowledge that this brief respite would soon end. The routine of their normalcy felt almost rehearsed, each movement practiced, their harmony born out of necessity rather than ease.

As the night drew on, they prepared for bed, though each step carried the weight of tomorrow's burdens. The gentle clinking of dishes gave way to silence, and soon they were side by side in the dim light of the bedroom, the quiet pressing in on them. Liliya stared at the ceiling, feeling Davyd's presence beside her, yet unable to escape the gnawing anxiety that crept into her thoughts.

"Tomorrow, we go back to the fight," Davyd whispered into the darkness, his eyes on the mission folder resting on the nightstand. The map was still open, the lines and routes blurring in his mind. He rubbed his temples, his head too full of possibilities, of potential missteps.

Liliya placed a hand on his arm, but her mind was already on the explosives, the guard rotations, the escape routes. "We have to stay sharp," she muttered, pulling the blanket tighter as if shielding them from the mission looming over them. "There's no room for more nights like this... not yet."

As they lay there, the quiet between them grew heavier, and Liliya's mind drifted back to the mission—the constant, unrelenting presence of danger that lingered, even now. The thought of Aleekseev's death being declared accidental had eased the immediate threat, but it did little to quell the larger storm brewing around them. She closed her eyes, willing herself to relax, but the shadows of their world always seemed to creep in.

In the stillness of the night, Liliya allowed herself to dream for a moment—of a future where the weight of their lives didn't follow them so closely. A future filled with more nights like this, where the threat of tomorrow didn't hang over their heads. But even as she entertained the thought, a cold realization settled in her chest: it was just that—a dream. One that felt as distant as the stars flickering outside their window.

Finally, as sleep began to claim them, Davyd's voice broke through the darkness, soft and almost fragile. "Sweet dreams, Liliya. We'll make it through. Together."

Liliya squeezed his hand, her eyes still closed. "Together," she echoed, though the word felt like a quiet plea rather than a promise. Their shared vulnerability deepened their connection, the night a fragile bubble of peace in their turbulent lives. As they drifted into sleep, their hands still intertwined, Liliya couldn't shake the feeling that this brief reprieve would be short-lived. The shadows of their world always seemed to find a way in, no matter how tightly they tried to hold onto the light.

And in the depths of the night, with the mission looming ever closer, Liliya's dreams were restless—filled with the ghosts of battles yet to be fought and the weight of secrets too heavy to keep.

Davyd awoke early, the dawn light filtering through the curtains. He slipped out of bed, careful not to disturb Liliya, his mind was already on the mission ahead.

Moscow stretched out before him, indifferent to the lives hidden in its shadows. He thought of the life he sometimes dared to imagine in the quiet hours. Behind him, Liliya stirred, wrapping her arms around him, her head resting against his back. "You're awake early," she whispered, her voice still thick with sleep.

Davyd covered her hands with his, but he didn't turn. "Just thinking about what's next," he said, his voice low. He felt her tense slightly against him, and he knew she understood that it wasn't just the mission on his mind.

Liliya's grip tightened. "I know it's always there," she murmured, pressing her cheek into his back, as if her presence could shield him from the weight of the world outside. "But for now, we're still here."

He finally turned to face her, his eyes scanning her face. He could see the echoes of her own restless thoughts, the quiet turmoil she tried so hard to hide. "We've been through so much," Davyd said, his hand brushing a loose strand of hair from her face. "But sometimes, I wonder... if we'll ever truly leave it behind."

Liliya's eyes flickered with something he couldn't quite place—fear, maybe, or a resignation to the life they had chosen. "Maybe we don't," she replied quietly. "Maybe this is who we are now." Her voice was steady, but there was a trace of sadness there, a realization that their hopes for a different future might never materialize.

Davyd sighed, pulling her closer. "I don't want to believe that. Not yet."

Liliya looked away, her gaze drifting to the window, to the city beyond. "We fight for a future we might never see. But if we stop now, it's over. There's no room for anything else until it's done." She swallowed hard, the finality of her words hanging in the air between them.

He studied her for a long moment, his thumb tracing the back of her hand. She was right, of course, but it didn't make the truth any easier to accept. "I know," he said finally. "But there's a part of me that wishes we didn't have to carry so much."

Liliya's eyes softened, and for a brief second, the hardened walls she had built around herself seemed to crack. "So do I," she admitted, her voice barely above a whisper.

They stood there, wrapped in each other's embrace, the weight of their lives pressing in around them. The quiet morning felt fragile, like it could shatter at any moment, and both knew that this stillness wouldn't last.

Eventually, Liliya pulled away, her movements deliberate, as if she were slowly withdrawing back into the role she needed to play. "We should get ready," she said, her voice firm again, though a hint of weariness lingered. "We can't afford to lose focus now."

Davyd nodded, but before she could step away, he caught her hand, holding it tightly for just a moment longer. "Last night... it was a glimpse of something real," he said softly. "I won't forget that."

Liliya's lips curved into a small, almost imperceptible smile. "Neither will I," she whispered. Then, she gently pulled her hand free, the connection severed as they both turned back toward the reality that awaited them.

They dressed in silence, each movement quick, automatic. Liliya met his gaze with a firm nod. "We'll make it," she said, her voice steady, leaving no room for doubt.

He nodded, though a part of him clung to the moment of peace they'd shared, hoping that lightness wasn't entirely lost.

TWELVE

Dawn of Disguises

The morning sun sharpened their path, casting long shadows as Liliya and Anatoli prepared to head for Dmitryashevka. Their movements were brisk, focused. Davyd's plan was clear: meet the underground resistance, transfer the bioweapon, and Aleekseev's encrypted data—every minute counted. He would then head to Khlevnoe, just outside Dmitryashevka, to set up monitoring stations from two vantage points.

By early morning, Anatoli had coordinated and arrived with Davyd's driver, Yaroslav Kuznetsov, a middle-aged man with a face aged by life's challenges. Yaroslav forced a smile. "Good to meet you, Davyd."

"You ready?" Davyd asked, catching the tremor in Yaroslav's hand. Their handshake lingered a moment longer—just enough for Davyd to catch the tension behind the man's eyes.

Yaroslav nodded, avoiding Davyd's eyes.

After introductions, the Anatoli and Yaroslav began transferring luggage to the waiting cars below. Meanwhile, Davyd and Liliya took a brief walk around the apartment, their smiles reflecting their shared hope of a life beyond this mission.

A cool breeze slipped through the balcony door, brushing against Liliya's skin like an icy whisper. Red Square gleamed below, silent, the stone imposing under the pale morning light. Her gaze caught on the dark silhouette of the Kremlin. The sight tightened her chest.

In a flash, she was back in the alley with Ivan, the traitor, the heavy steps of Russian agents closing in. She gripped the window frame, forcing the image back. Her breath caught, the memory tightening its grip. She clenched the window frame, forcing the image away, the chill still clinging to her skin. With a final glance at the Kremlin's silhouette, she pushed the memory aside and turned for the door.

They left the apartment, their footsteps synchronized, echoing in the quiet hallway. The elevator doors slid open, releasing a cold draft mixed with the scent of damp pavement. Davyd's hand brushed Liliya's arm—a brief, caring touch. They shared a look—no words needed.

Outside, city sounds grew louder—distant horns, footsteps—jarring against the quiet apartment they'd left. Davyd's gaze lingered as Liliya opened the car door, the metal cold under her fingers.

Sliding into the seat beside Anatoli, she felt the stiffness of the fabric against her back, her muscles tightening instinctively. The door clicked shut, a sharp sound that cut through the morning air. She didn't turn, didn't need to—Davyd's presence weighed on her, but there was no time for second thoughts. The engine rumbled to life, and she fixed her eyes ahead, forcing her breath steady as the city began to blur into the distance. Liliya stared straight ahead, her thoughts already distant, on Dmitryashevka.

Davyd watched as she settled into her seat, then turned toward his own ride, the unspoken weight of their parting hanging in the air. He approached an older model Mercedes Benz, its gray exterior in excellent condition. Yaroslav loaded the car with sharp, deliberate movements, his focus unwavering.

Davyd, in a purposefully light tone, "You good? You seem a bit preoccupied."

Yaroslav hesitated, his fingers gripping the package tighter before setting it down. 'Everything's in place,' he muttered, his eyes darting to the backseat, scanning it as though expecting something—or someone—to be there. Yaroslav's eyes flicked to the backseat, tension knotting in his voice. "We're set," before settling in the driver's seat. "No room for slip-ups."

In the car, Davyd watched Yaroslav's jaw tighten, the tendons in his hands standing out as he gripped the wheel with rigid force. "Feels like one of those days," Davyd muttered, the tension thickening between them, as if waiting for something to break.

Yaroslav glanced at him, his body visibly tensing, then returned his focus to moving the car into traffic. The drive passed the silence stretching between them. As they approached the nondescript coffee shop, the mood shifted, and the air seemed to grow even heavier.

The tires crunched over the gravel, and Davyd stiffened, his fingers flexing near his holster. His eyes swept the surroundings—no movement, but something felt off, the stillness too perfect. He stepped out, the sudden change in light hitting him. The harsh morning sun reflecting off the glass windows of the coffee shop. The sharp scent of exhaust mixed with baked products drifted through the air, the low murmur of patrons blending with the distant city noise.

His eyes flicked toward the corner, where a shadow hesitated just a beat too long. Davyd glanced at the door, then back at Yaroslav, who remained in the car, posture rigid, eyes on the street. He didn't need to say anything; they both knew what was at stake. He grabbed the packages without a word and with a final look down the street, he moved toward the entrance.

The bell above the door chimed softly as he stepped inside. The coffee shop's warmth hit him like a wall, a sharp contrast to the chill outside. The air was thick, almost stifling, carrying the scent of burnt espresso and overheated machinery. The low murmur of conversation and the rhythmic hiss of steaming milk filled the space, while dim lights cast long shadows over the small tables, making the corners feel just a little too dark. A poorly hidden camera peeked out from behind a hanging plant, catching a brief glint of light.

At the counter, Kirill stood with a name tag pinned crookedly to his apron, his face calm but eyes darting to the door every few seconds. His fingers twitched as he wiped the counter, the movement quick and nervous. When he glanced up, there was a flicker of recognition, but it vanished almost as quickly as it appeared.

"I hear your caramel latte's the best in Moscow," Davyd said, his voice low, the weight of the code unmistakable.

Kirill's hand tightened on the rag, his fingers twitching slightly as he looked up. His reply, a second too late, was tense. 'We do what we can,' he said, his eyes drifting past Davyd to the door, scanning the shop's corners with barely concealed anxiety.

Davyd slid the packages across the counter. The rustle of the wrapping cut through the quiet, drawing a brief glance from Kirill, who swept them up swiftly, his fingers shaking as they brushed the counter. "It'll... find its way," he muttered under his breath, eyes flicking toward the back of the shop. His glance lingered there, as if waiting for something, or someone, unseen. Without another word, he disappeared into the back room.

Davyd glanced around. A man in a trench coat sat unnaturally still, staring into his untouched coffee. A woman by the window turned the pages of her newspaper too slowly, her eyes flicking up more often than necessary.

When Kirill returned, he carried a brown-wrapped box, the edges worn as if handled too many times. He slid it across the counter, avoiding Davyd's gaze. "This should cover everything," Kirill murmured, his voice barely audible, his hand trembling as it brushed the edge of the box. His eyes darted once more toward the back. "Watch yourself," he added, his tone tight, the words hanging in the air like a warning.

Davyd's hand hovered over the package for a moment before he gripped it tightly, his fingers brushing Kirill's for the briefest moment—cold, despite the warmth of the room. Kirill flinched at the touch but said nothing more, his gaze dropping to the floor.

With a curt nod, Davyd turned, his pulse quickening, though his expression remained unreadable. As he stepped outside, the bell chimed faintly behind him, but the quiet tension from the shop followed him into the cold air, heavier than before.

Yaroslav was waiting, engine idling, eyes sharp. Davyd slipped into the car without a word. Once inside the car, Davyd placed the package on the back seat, his gaze still scanning the sideview mirror for anything out of place. His eyes darted from shadow to shadow, his hand twitching near his holster, every passerby a potential threat.

Yaroslav wasted no time, the car's engine roaring to life as they merged back into the flow of traffic. They sped away, the coffee shop fading in the rearview, tension clinging to them like smoke.

The late morning sun cast long shadows across the bustling city. Pedestrians rushed by, taxis honked, and the air buzzed with energy. Yet inside the car, the tension was thick. Yaroslav's grip on the wheel was tight, his eyes flicking to the mirror. Davyd leaned forward; every muscle ready.

Moscow's busy streets thinned as they moved further out. The crowds faded, replaced by quieter, narrower roads. The towering buildings shrank into smaller homes as they cruised toward the outskirts, the hum of the city falling behind them.

As they left the city behind, the world seemed to expand. The claustrophobic press of traffic gave way to open fields stretching on either side of the highway. The wind rushed through the cracks of the windows, a constant hum as the engine and the tires as they rolled over the smooth asphalt. The sun hung higher now, its rays glaring off the windshield, painting the road ahead in a harsh, white light.

Davyd's eyes darted to the mirror, scanning the empty road behind them. The pulse of the city was gone, leaving only the long, empty stretch of highway ahead, drawing them deeper into isolation.

The silence grew heavier with each passing hour. Yaroslav's grip tight on the steering wheel. Davyd didn't push. Instead, he let the silence stretch. "Long day," Davyd murmured.

"Long few years," Yaroslav replied, his voice barely audible over the hum of the engine.

Davyd glanced at him, "You don't have to carry it alone," he said quietly.

Yaroslav exhaled, the tension in his shoulders easing slightly. "Some things... stick with you," he muttered, trailing off.

They continued down the road, the last afternoon sun yielding to dusk. Davyd's gaze flicked to the mirror. A pair of headlights gleamed in the distance, growing closer at an unsettling pace. "Yaroslav, something's off," Davyd muttered, eyes narrowing on the headlights that had drawn too close, too fast.

Yaroslav's knuckles tightened on the wheel. "What?" he asked, voice low.

"A possible tail," Davyd replied, his eyes locked on the rearview mirror. "They're closing in."

Yaroslav's foot hung over the brake as the car behind sped up, its headlights flooding the interior. Davyd's hand instinctively moved toward his holster, his pulse quickening. "Don't react yet," Davyd muttered. "Let them make the first move."

The car drew closer, too close now. "Keep steady," Davyd said. "No sudden moves."

The lights grew blinding, the engine's roar louder. Yaroslav's grip tightened; tension palpable. "They're too close," Yaroslav murmured.

"Don't brake," Davyd ordered. "If they want something, we'll know."

Then, without warning, the car swerved into the left lane, speeding past them. Davyd's breath hitched, ready for a threat that never came. The car vanished into the night.

"Clear," he muttered, though the tension didn't leave him.

Yaroslav released a breath he hadn't realized he was holding. "Thought that was it," he rasped, voice tight.

Davyd's eyes flicked back to the mirror. The road ahead was empty, but the unease lingered. "Keep an eye out," he said quietly. "Something's off."

Yaroslav shot him a glance. "You don't think it was nothing?"

"I don't believe in coincidences," Davyd replied, his tension unrelenting.

Yaroslav's grip on the wheel tightened again.

Davyd's expression hardened. "They're always watching," he muttered.

The silence settled again, heavier now. Yaroslav's gaze stayed fixed on the road, but Davyd's words transported his mind elsewhere. "I sent them," he whispered his voice trembling. "Many never came back."

Davyd remained quiet, the shared weight of guilt hanging between them.

"I thought I could outrun it," Yaroslav murmured. "But you can't."

Davyd rested a hand briefly on Yaroslav's shoulder, his touch light. "You made it this far." He paused, then added quietly, "That's enough... for now."

Yaroslav's nod was slight, but it was there. His posture eased a little. "Anatoli... pulled me in. Gave me a way out, a purpose." He glanced over at Davyd. "Feels like we've been at this forever," he muttered. Davyd nodded, feeling the weight of the unspoken truth—some battles you never left behind.

Davyd didn't need to hear the rest. The road unfolded ahead of them, their shared burden lightened by the silence, the understanding between them growing stronger in the dark.

As they moved south on the M-4, Davyd's thoughts drifted toward their next move. Somewhere up ahead, Liliya and Anatoli were already deep into their own leg of the mission, having arrived in Dmitryashevka.

Liliya's arrival had been seamless, the familiarity of the town working in her favor. Dmitryashevka, with its layered history—once a strategic site during the Russian Civil War—was a place where old stories lingered on every street. For Liliya, those streets were familiar territory, her cover as the niece of a local resident offering her the perfect camouflage. The military had hardly ever taken notice of her, apart from wolf whistles as she walked through the town.

Her network of contacts, scattered across the fifty-kilometer radius, was already waiting. The underground was prepared for her arrival, and her pseudo aunt and uncle were waiting with warm food and information about the commander in charge. As they drove into the town, it was as if the pieces of the mission were quietly falling into place.

Sergei and Nadya, an older couple, waited eagerly at the door, their faces worn by grief but resolute. Their losses had only deepened their commitment to the mission. As Liliya stepped out of the car, they embraced her warmly, their eyes glinting with hope. The familiar scent of Sergei—a sharp blend of tobacco and leather—hit her.

For a moment, it transported her back to Kursk, to that alley where Ivan had set her up. She could still see his face, hear his whispered promises of loyalty—until she caught his tell. The memory surged, vivid and raw. But she shoved it down, her jaw tightening as she forced herself to focus on the present. There was no time to dwell on the past.

The sting of the setup hit her again: his infiltration of the resistance, his carefully orchestrated trap that left her vulnerable, exposed, and almost captured. It also made her question how much she could trust those in the circle she had helped to create.

They quickly shared a hearty meal of borscht and lamb, turning the conversation to Commander Timofey Volkov, the strict overseer of the retrofit project. Volkov often frequented the Prestige, a popular haunt for military personnel, and a potential vulnerability. He had the habit of building himself up when talking about his previous escapades and his present role, especially when seducing local women. Sergei commented, "Liliya, you are just his type. As soon as he sees you, he will be like his name, a wolf going after its prey."

Though this would work well for Liliya, as Sergei spoke of Volkov's weakness for women, Liliya felt a familiar knot tighten in her chest. She knew what was expected of her—what the mission would demand. But the cost had always been higher than she let on.

However, by exploiting this weakness it allowed her to infiltrate the plant as a night shift cleaner and visit the Prestige to catch Volkov's attention. An underground member who already working as a cleaner had arranged for her cousin, Liliya, to cover for her while she traveled for medical reasons.

As supper ended, Anatoli said his goodbyes. He knew his wife was waiting at home and would not relax until he was there. Liliya excused herself for the night, she slipped into bed, her hand brushing the cool sheets. Her eyes flicked to the mission plan, her mind already on the next step.

While Liliya prepared for the night, Yaroslav navigated the M-4, they veered onto the A-133 toward Khlevnoe. After hours of traveling from Moscow the car came to a slow stop in front of Hotel Three, its modest facade blending into the quiet street. The town seemed asleep, the only sound the soft rustle of leaves in the wind and the distant call of a dog.

Yaroslav parked with precision, and Davyd stepped out, the crunch of gravel beneath his boots echoed in the stillness, and he took a moment to scan the narrow street, noting the dim, flickering light from a nearby lamppost.

While Davyd grabbed his bag. Yaroslav unloaded the box containing the operational equipment. They moved swiftly, no words needed.

Inside, Davyd secured the key. Together, they headed for the elevators, the quiet hum of the lobby undercut by the sharp focus of the moment. The elevator dinged, and they stepped in. As the doors slid open on the fourth floor, their footsteps echoed in the hallway, leading them straight to Room 410.

The hotel room was sparse, functional. The air was stale, with the faint smell of cleaning chemicals hanging in the air. The bedspread, stiff and uninviting, matched the cold tiles underfoot. It was nothing like the comfort of the Sky apartment, but it would do. The silence inside pressed down, broken only by the faint hum of the overhead light.

Yaroslav deposited the bags and extended his hand to Davyd. Davyd accepted, shaking it firmly. "I am privileged to know you," he remarked.

Yaroslav drew Davyd into an embrace, affirming, "No, it is I who am privileged. We'll reconvene first thing tomorrow. We have matters to attend to, don't we?"

"Yes, indeed, my friend. Rest well," Davyd replied. The next step of the mission was waiting.

With that, Yaroslav bid farewell and disappeared into the night, his footsteps fading down the dimly lit hallway. Davyd stood still for a moment, the quiet of the room settling over him like a thick blanket.

He stared out the window at the quiet street below, the flickering streetlight casting restless shadows over a parked car—the same one that had drawn his attention earlier. A passing vehicle's headlights swept through the alley, distorting the darkness.

Davyd's gut twisted, but was it instinct or paranoia?

His eyes lingered on the car. Nothing seemed out of place, yet something felt wrong. Just as he was about to turn away, he thought he saw movement—a figure? Or just a shadow?

CHAPTER

THIRTEEN

Shadows of the Plant

The following morning, Liliya tightened her fingers around Volkov's dossier. The sharp edges of the crinkling paper against her skin. Her eyes bore into Volkov's smirk, a haunting reminder. The ghost of a memory scraped against her senses—an icy grip, the weight of a mission. The harsh light of the photo twisted his smirk for a split second—until she saw the commander's face staring back.

Her breath stilled, the weight of memory pressing in, hard and unforgiving. The thumb drive, the bewildered look in his eyes as she struck, his hand heavy on her shoulder. She flattened the paper, her grip steady, her breaths shallow. *Not the commander. Not anymore.* Each shallow breath pulled her focus to the task—*just another mission, another mask.* The commander's shadow lingered, but her mind stayed on the here and now. She had a plan; Volkov was the target.

The thought snapped her back, her mind pivoting to the persona she'd need. Sergei's description—the arrogance, the indifference—gave her an angle to bait Volkov, to use his pride against him. She practiced his downfall in her mind, letting the tension in her hands ease as she reviewed each step, the plan now a steady rhythm.

Liliya moved through her quarters, her movements sharp, each item snapped into place without pause. Her fingers brushed against a tucked-away photograph—her parents, frozen in a moment of warmth. The cool edge of the frame bit into her fingers, sharpening her focus. "And for everyone else who's lost someone," she added, a solemn pledge that strengthened her resolve. The words echoed in her mind as she steadied her breath, holding onto the coldness of the metal handle.

Her gaze flicked to the window. Outside, the gray morning was cloaked in a stillness that belied the turmoil about to unfold. She lingered one last time on the photo, then slipped it back into her bag, releasing any trace of softness as she did. Her focus now needed to be absolute. *No weakness. Just the mission.*

The chill sliced through her as she stepped out, her breath visible in the early morning air. Across town, Davyd would be breathing in the same icy morning, bracing himself in parallel. He moved with practiced calm, each movement deliberate as he anticipated the day's first task. He felt the cold edge of the air sink into his skin as he stepped out, eyes scanning the quiet of the morning. The mission sharpened his focus as he joined Yaroslav, every movement purposeful. The stillness around them held an unspoken weight—one that would snap the moment they were in position.

Their first task was to survey the surveillance points they would utilize, beginning with the church. The Church of the Intercession of the Most Holy Theotokos, built in the early 17th century, stood proudly at 17 Sverdlova Street.

The Mercedes pulled up in front, its engine idling in the still morning. The cold clung to Davyd as he stepped out, his breath a faint mist in the early air. His fingers tingled from the frost, but he ignored it, his mind already on the mission.

Yaroslav moved up beside him, their boots making no more than a whisper against the cobblestones. Davyd's eyes swept the path ahead, tracking every shadow and angle. The church rose before them, its bell tower a perfect blind spot—a vantage point. The plan hinged on it.

Father Vitali stood in the doorway, his eyes scanning the street with practiced vigilance. His fingers twitched at his robe as he adjusted his grip on the doorframe, watching the quiet traffic of the morning. With a subtle nod, he stepped aside, silently ushering them in. The door clicked shut behind them, muffling the sounds of the city. Inside, the scent of incense mixed with the sharpness of cold stone, a quiet refuge for now.

"This place has always offered protection," Father Vitali murmured, his eyes sharp, taking in the stone around them. "Now, it guards more than souls."

Yaroslav, eager, broke the silence. "He's helped many escape."

"A priest does what must be done," Father Vitali replied, his gaze locking with Davyd's for a fleeting moment. "Sometimes, that means standing still. Sometimes, it means everything."

They reached a small, concealed room at the back of the church, the air thick with secrecy. Davyd noted the lines of worry etched into the Father's face. Here, the weight of his role was unmistakable.

"You've done more than most," Davyd said quietly, acknowledging the risk Father Vitali had taken for them.

The priest sat, his fingers tapping lightly on his knee. "We all have our burdens," he muttered, half to himself. "No one carries them alone."

Yaroslav leaned forward. "This place—it's more than a sanctuary."

Father Vitali's smile flickered. "Belief needs vigilance."

Silence settled over them. Father Vitali stood, his hand resting briefly on Davyd's shoulder. "Follow me. I'll show you what we've prepared."

They climbed the narrow steps of the bell tower in silence. At the top, Father Vitali pointed toward the reinforced plexiglass hidden behind the old stone façade. "You can see everything. They won't see you."

As Davyd examined the setup, his fingers hovered over the reinforced plexiglass, tracing its edges as if testing its strength against an unseen weight. A flicker of tension passed through his hand—a reflexive grip—before he forced it to ease. "You've thought of everything."

Father Vitali's voice was steady, though his words hung heavy. "It's enough... for now." He pressed a small signal amplifier into Davyd's hand—a slim device disguised as a prayer card. "Keep it near," he murmured. "If anything disrupts your signal, this will extend the radius. We can't risk a loss of contact at a critical moment." Davyd slid it into his pocket without a word, his thumb already resting on a button that would cue Yaroslav three blocks away.

As they prepared to leave, Father Vitali pulled Davyd aside. His voice dropped, the burden in his tone heavy. "How do you carry it?"

Davyd hesitated. "Sometimes, I don't know. I just keep going. People like Liliya... they help."

Father Vitali's expression hardened, a thin line forming at his lips. "Don't let your focus blind you. Hope is strong... until it isn't."

Davyd placed a hand on the priest's arm. "We'll be careful."

Father Vitali nodded, but his gaze was distant. "God willing... every step."

They got into the Mercedes and drove north on Sverdlova Street. A silent understanding passed between them as they veered southwest onto Dmitryahevka's main thoroughfare.

Yaroslav navigated the Mercedes past the plant's entrance, finding seclusion behind a grove of trees 600 meters away. They trekked southeast through dense foliage before turning west to their observation point, providing an unobstructed view of the plant. Equipped with their thermal scope, they stood poised to decipher the cryptic movements of Liliya and her Russian guardians from their clandestine perch.

Later, as they arrived back at the hotel, the cold air seemed to cling to Davyd, though he barely noticed it now. His thoughts were with Liliya, her steps mirrored in his mind as he adjusted the radio. The room around him buzzed with preparation, but his focus remained on the crackling sound of the radio, waiting for her voice to break through.

Davyd adjusted the radio, his fingers tense. "Do you ever think... what comes after this?" He didn't look up, the question hanging between them.

Yaroslav didn't meet his eyes. "I try not to." He paused, his jaw tightening. "But I do."

"We have to believe it's worth it," Davyd muttered, more to himself than Yaroslav. "Otherwise, none of this matters."

Yaroslav opened his mouth to speak again but was interrupted by a knock. Yaroslav moved to the door, hesitating for a second. He glanced back at Davyd, his voice quieter now. "We have to."

Anatoli entered, his presence solid and unhurried, as if no amount of tension could move him. The seasoned resistance fighter gave a curt nod, taking in the room with a sweep of his eyes. "On track." he said simply, his voice carrying the authority of experience. He wasn't one to waste words.

The clock struck twelve, and Davyd turned back to the radio, his fingers manipulating the transmitter with precision. Moments later, Liliya's voice crackled through the static. "What's your status?" Davyd's voice was direct.

"All stable. Starting tonight. Anatoli is briefed," Liliya responded. Anatoli's nod was barely perceptible.

"What time?" Davyd asked, his focus intense.

"Entering at 2130 hours, staying until 0600," came Liliya's clipped reply.

"Got it. Stay low. We've got you covered. Over and out." Davyd shut off the radio, the room falling into a silence thick with anticipation.

Anatoli sat at the table; his movements slow, deliberate. He tapped a spot on the map, his voice steady and seasoned, "Volkov's at The Prestige, 1600 hours. Arrogant bastard likes to brag."

Davyd leaned in, eyes narrowing, jaw tightened, "Liliya plans to feed that ego."

Anatoli's voice dropped. "She'll play him. His pride. Then she'll make her move."

Davyd sat back, arms crossed, tension visible, "I trust her, but we're watching. Every move."

"I'll take the first vigil at the church," Yaroslav offered, a touch of determination in his voice. "I can monitor The Prestige from there."

Anatoli chimed in without missing a beat, "I'll relieve you at 0400. Davyd, you take the forest watch at 2000 hours."

Davyd nodded slowly, his mind racing ahead to possible complications. His voice cut through the room like a command, "No gaps. Not one." He spread the surveillance schedule across the table, his fingers pressing each time slot with measured deliberation. "Let's make sure this is airtight," he said, his voice calm, though his jaw set tightly against a deeper concern. They huddled for the next hour, the air thick with the gravity of the mission. Anatoli's calm, methodical voice carried as they refined the details, "Shift rotations. We rest."

"We can't lose her." Yaroslav's words were soft but edged with tension, as if one wrong sound could shatter the fragile calm. Davyd tightened his grip, feeling the fabric beneath his fingers ground him, keep him steady. "We're not losing anyone," he replied, his voice a low, unwavering promise.

The silence hung, thick with unspoken resolve as they huddled over the schedule and map, its lines and pins a fragile barrier between them and the danger ahead. Davyd's hand pressed onto the map, his gaze piercing each critical point, as if willing it to hold under pressure. "Rest up. Long days ahead," he said, his voice a command more than a reminder. He met their eyes one by one, feeling the weight of the moment settle into their shared breaths. One by one, they nodded, each carrying that silence like armor.

They stood in silence, their postures straight, eyes hardened. Each knew their role, and each was prepared to face whatever came next. The air thrummed with a palpable energy, a silent understanding passing between them.

"Everyone knows their position. Let's get to work," Anatoli's voice cut through the silence like a blade, cool and certain.

"Stay sharp. No mistakes," Davyd added, his overseer's gaze sweeping over them one last time before they dispersed, the weight of their purpose driving them forward. As they spoke, Liliya was already slipping into her role, preparing for the night ahead, knowing she had a team counting on her.

Liliya's day began at 1900 hours, slipping into her undercover role with the practiced precision they had planned. Nadya served her a robust meal, the scent of hot stew grounding her briefly as she ate in silence. Dressing for the part, she chose a plain dress from Nadya's collection— neutral, unremarkable. The fabric brushed against her skin, soft but worn.

She tightened the handkerchief around her hair, its rough texture scraping her skin. A flicker of memory—*Mel'nyk's grip, icy and unrelenting.* Her throat tightened, a tremor racing through her fingers as if his shadow lingered just out of sight. She forced herself to breathe, to remember the simple fabric under her hands and ignore the ghostly chill pressing against her neck. She drew in a deep breath, forcing her fingers to steady as she adjusted the knot. *This isn't then. Focus. It's just fabric. Just a disguise.*

With one last glance in the mirror, Liliya adjusted her dress, her hands now steady. The ghosts faded into the background as she resumed her preparations, her mind pulling back to the task ahead. The mission was clear. Volkov was next.

Her go-bag held the essential tools—an earbud, a hidden camera, and a signal pen—everything needed to coordinate with her team.

Sergei and Nadya's modest home had become a refuge for Liliya. As she prepared for her mission, the couple watched her with quiet intensity, their unspoken concern hanging in the air.

Sergei leaned against the doorway, his eyes tracking her movements. "When you first came here, I wasn't sure about you."

Liliya paused, offering him a small smile. "I remember. You had that look."

Nadya, seated at the table with her knitting, glanced up. "And now look at you. You've done more than we imagined."

Liliya adjusted her clothes, her hands smoothing down the fabric to ensure everything was in place. Her belt concealed a low-frequency jammer, small enough to hide but strong enough to knock out any signal if things turned against her. She gave Sergei a nod, and he tapped his own watch twice in response, ready to activate the backup comms frequency if her earpiece went silent.

When she turned to them, her eyes were focused, but gratitude flickered in her gaze. "I couldn't have done this without your help."

Sergei stepped forward, placing a hand on her shoulder. "You've earned it," he said, his voice quiet but steady.

Nadya set her knitting aside and stood. She handed Liliya a thick scarf, tugging it tighter than necessary around her neck. "It's cold out there. Don't forget to breathe," she murmured, her hands lingering as if to shield her from more than the weather. Pulling Liliya into a firm embrace, she whispered, "Be careful."

Liliya nodded, holding her tightly for a moment. "I will."

Sergei joined the embrace briefly, then pulled back, his eyes meeting hers. "We're with you."

Liliya swallowed, the weight of their support settling on her. "Thank you," she said simply.

As she turned to leave, Nadya's voice followed her. "Come back."

Liliya smiled, her gaze sharpening with resolve. "I will."

She stepped out the door, the weight of their trust pressing on her with each step. As she moved into the night, her hand brushed the small earpiece hidden beneath her hair, tapping it twice. The signal sent a quiet confirmation to Davyd and Anatoli—she was on the move. Every signal tonight would guide them, feeding crucial details to map the plant. She trusted them to follow.

From his hidden perch, Davyd tracked her silhouette through the scope, watching as Liliya approached the plant. His breath slowed, syncing with her steady pace.

The hours of waiting melted away. The night wasn't just about gathering intel; it was about precision. No room for mistakes.

Anatoli's knock had broken the silence earlier. Together, they had prepared, slipping into the shadows toward the forest's edge. Their earpieces already buzzed with Liliya's faint signal. Anatoli had handed Davyd a lunch bag, his rare smile gone as he muttered, "Borscht. You'll need it."

Now, hunkered in the grove, Davyd tapped his earwig. "Leader to One. I see her."

Yaroslav's voice crackled in his ear. "All clear."

Davyd's grip tightened around the radio. Every second mattered now. The mission wasn't just about survival; it was about proving they could still fight back.

Davyd's scope followed Liliya's approach as she neared The Prestige, her movements precise, unhurried. His vision tunneled in the glass, framing her silhouette against the flickering neon sign, a flare that seemed to pulse with every quiet step she took toward the building.

The neon lights cast a staccato glow on Liliya's face as she moved closer to the entrance, each flash like a heartbeat counting down to the mission's start. She blinked, feeling the cold prickle at her skin, establishing herself in the here and now.

Liliya's faint tap echoed in his ear again—she was ready.

Liliya's steps were measured and silent as she skirted the south edge of the plant, the Prestige's neon sign flickering in the periphery of her vision. She could not afford a second glance; her role tonight was to be as invisible as the shadows that cloaked her. She noted that the place was already busy, with many of its patrons wearing Russian uniforms. She did not peer too long as she did not want to bring attention to herself. She turned west into the parking lot of the plant and began to pull her credentials out of her pocket, while approaching the entry checkpoint.

A stout young man stood at attention. "Your identification," he said as Liliya approached.

She handed over her documents. He scrutinized them. "You're new. What's your story?"

"Covering for my cousin. She's pregnant."

He raised an eyebrow. "That was fast."

"She knows a conscription officer."

"Lucky her. Go ahead."

Liliya moved through the plant, each click of the camera documenting its weaknesses. Her focus narrowed with every step; her movements as precise as the shutter's rhythm.

Each step on the hollow grates felt like a pulse beneath her feet, the hiss of steam slicing through her focus. *The alley—Kursk—Ivan's face, pale in moonlight. Wide, terrified eyes. Her hands, slick with blood.* Her hands twitched as if the warmth of it lingered, soaked through to her bones. She jerked back, biting down on the bile rising in her throat, and planted herself firmly in the now. *Focus.*

A guard shouted from the end of the row, breaking through the haze, snapping her back to the present. She blinked hard. *Steam. Just steam.* The plant, still in front of her.

With each step forward, the memory of Ivan slipped further into the shadows of her mind, but the weight of it lingered, like the steam rising from the grates. By the time she had to go to punch in, she had covered the plant from a macro perspective.

Throughout the night she focused on key areas and was more deliberate in what she captured with the camera, while Davyd, Anatoli and Yaroslav ensured her movements were shadowed with precision.

She was aware her work was essential to their planning the next morning, as she would be providing her oversight team with the internal image of a place they would only see through thermal imaging. The images Liliya captured were vital, slated for analysis by engineers and demolition experts to strategize the plant's destruction.

With her shift ending at 0600 hours, she felt the unforeseen stress leave her as she stepped out into the sun. Anatoli was parked a couple blocks away, where she would get in his car and be taken to the command center: Davyd's hotel room.

As dawn broke and Liliya exited the plant, Davyd breathed a quiet sigh of relief. He watched until he saw Liliya pass through the checkpoint and then he rushed to the entrance to the grove where he found Yaroslav waiting for him. He jumped in the Mercedes, and they were off. The first phase was over, but the hardest was yet to come.

The cold leather of Anatoli's car seat bit into her skin, bringing a sense of calm finality. She glanced through the fogged window, watching the plant fade into the distance. The weight of what they had seen and gathered pressed in, solid and undeniable.

Liliya exhaled, her breath fogging the glass, a single steadying moment before the storm. Her gaze lingered on the faint reflection—a shadowed figure in the glass, familiar but unrecognizable, dissolving in the fog.

Somewhere across town, the low hum of an engine stirred the early silence, just as the first lights flickered on. Yaroslav's gloved hands gripped the steering wheel of the Mercedes, while Davyd's gaze was fixed on the quiet street stretching ahead.

The hotel room transformed into a hive of activity as the four of them sifted through the digital photographs. Each image captured by Liliya was a puzzle piece revealing the intricate layout of the plant. The room buzzed with a sense of urgency and focus. Davyd pointed to a series of images on the screen, "Look at these. This is the manufacturing floor. You can see the assembly lines and the main office locations."

Anatoli leaned in to get a closer look, "We need to map out the security patrols. If we can predict their routes, we can find the gaps."

Davyd nodded thinking to himself. *Every detail matters. One mistake could mean the end.*

They marked the photos with notes and arrows, plotting their movements. The oversight from the forest's vantage point became crucial, providing a real-time canvas to adjust their strategy. Each observation was meticulously compared against Liliya's intelligence on the detailed floor plan.

Focusing on the screen, Liliya remarked, "I need to synchronize my timing perfectly. If I miss by even a few seconds, I risk exposure."

"Agreed. We'll coordinate from the forest. Yaroslav, you'll handle the entry point while Anatoli and I monitor the guards' movements."

It was a dance of shadows and light, where accuracy and anticipation hoped to outmaneuver the rigid predictability of their adversaries. With the foundation of their plan solidified through the photos' secrets, attention shifted towards the critical task of communication.

Davyd reached for the encrypted satellite phone. "We need to get this data to Kyiv. They'll distill it into our next steps."

In the dimly lit confines of their makeshift command center, Davyd's fingers danced over the encrypted satellite phone with the precision of a seasoned pianist. The weight of their mission was palpable in the air, dense with anticipation and the soft hum of computer screens. He dialed in the secure line to Kyiv, his movements deliberate, mirroring the ritualistic importance of the moment. "This is more than just data," he muttered under his breath, "it's our defiance, our fight."

As the connection beeped alive, signaling a link to their distant allies, a wave of resolve washed over him. Each photo he transmitted was not just an image; it was a whisper of defiance, a critical piece of the larger puzzle they were painstakingly assembling. "Data is incoming. Confirm receipt and begin analysis," Davyd spoke into the phone, his voice a calm command amid the storm of their clandestine operations.

Beside him, Yaroslav watched the data transfer, the glow from the screen casting sharp highlights on his concerned face. "Do you think they'll be able to use it effectively?" he asked, his voice tinged with the anxiety of reliance on unseen allies.

Davyd turned, meeting Yaroslav's gaze with a look of ironclad certainty. "They will," he affirmed without a hint of doubt. "We've done our part. Now it's up to them to make it count." His tone didn't just convey assurance; it was a testament to their unwavering commitment to the cause.

Meanwhile, Liliya stood slightly apart, her eyes scanning their secure perimeter through a nearby window. Her thoughts mirrored the gravity of their task. *We've laid the groundwork. Now we need to stay sharp and be ready for anything*, she reminded herself, her hand absentmindedly brushing the pistol holstered at her side.

As they finished their preparations, Liliya's jaw tightened and her eyes steeled, as if she willed the success of their mission through sheer resolve. Davyd's posture was equally telling; his shoulders squared and his stance firm, embodying a readiness to face whatever came next. Maps, photos, and digital displays surrounded them, each telling a part of a story that was still unfolding.

They had taken the first step in their mission, and now, the wait began for the next signal. Ready to execute their plan with the precision and resilience that defined their collective struggle, they stood together, a unit bound by a common cause and an unspoken promise to each other and their nation.

CHAPTER

FOURTEEN

The Dance of Deception

After the transfer, silence fell. Faces mirrored the same unspoken tension, awaiting Kyiv's blueprint. The operation was at a critical turning point. Anatoli broke the silence, rubbing the back of his neck, clearly feeling the weight of the situation. "We need to move quickly. Liliya, do you—"

"Yeah, I've got a plan," Liliya interrupted, her eyes scanning the room, waiting for everyone's attention before continuing. "It's not perfect," she added with a slight pause, as if bracing for any pushback, "but it's our best shot."

She stepped forward, sweeping her hand across the notes. "I'll head to The Prestige, blend in, catch his eye."

Davyd leaned forward, his fingers drumming against his knee as Liliya outlined her strategy.

Liliya paused, casting him a sidelong glance. "Do you have something to add?" Her tone dared him to question her.

His fingers stilled. "Not if you're sure."

Her eyes flashed, a hint of something unsaid. "I'm sure," she replied, but her fingers tightened on the edge of the table.

She's still pushing through, Davyd thought, feeling that old twist of unease coil in his gut. Liliya could handle pressure, always had, but he could sense it—this mission was different. She was running faster, leaning harder into the risk.

"So, how do you plan on making him trust you?" he asked, letting the silence stretch a moment longer than necessary.

Liliya's tone stayed level, almost clipped. "Subtlety. I'll play into his vanity."

Davyd's gaze didn't waver. He exhaled, nodding. *She was pushing the edge.* But she needed him steady, not doubting.

Yaroslav crossed his arms. "He's sharp, Liliya. Too sharp. What makes you think you'll be any different?"

Liliya's jaw tightened at the challenge, but she held her ground, meeting Yaroslav's gaze. "It's not just about his ego. It's about creating the right moment—making him feel like he's in control, like he's choosing to engage." Her voice dropped, her tone firm. "Volkov thrives on power, and I'll make him believe he's the one with it. Once he thinks that, he'll open up."

Davyd's fingers clenched against his knee, each second stretching thin between them. He met her gaze with a tight nod, the message clear.

Yaroslav's eyes narrowed, clearly unconvinced. "And what if he doesn't? What if he sees through it, realizes you're playing him?"

The room fell silent, the weight of the question hanging in the air. Liliya's finger traced the map's edge, her voice clipped. "If he catches on, we adapt. No mistakes." She flattened her palm against the table, feeling the grain under her skin. "I know how he operates. This will work."

Davyd's gaze was fixed on the dossier now, his lips pressed together. A slow exhale escaped him as he ran a hand through his hair, the silence between them thick with unspoken tension. His fingers paused, resting on the back of his neck, before he looked up, meeting her eyes with a wordless warning.

Liliya caught his look, her jaw setting for a moment before she nodded, her voice low. "I know. I'll be careful."

Anatoli sighed, looking between them. "Careful is one thing, but ... you could end up in a very dangerous position."

Liliya didn't blink, giving Anatoli a tight smile.

There was a heavy silence, the room thick with tension.

Yaroslav let out a low whistle, shaking his head. "What, no backup dancers? If I'd known it was this kind of operation, I'd have dressed up," he muttered with a grin, earning a faint, reluctant smile from Davyd.

"We can't afford to miss anything," Anatoli concluded while rubbing his temples.

Liliya, softening a little, added, "The resistance will cover me. I'm not going in unprotected."

Davyd didn't meet her gaze immediately. His focus drifted to the dossier on the table, fingers drumming softly against its edge. "You know when to pull out." The words were quiet, more question than statement.

Davyd's hand brushed hers, not meaning to linger. But when she met his gaze, he saw the exhaustion swimming just beneath her surface. Her assurance that she'd "be careful" rang hollow, and he could feel her steadying herself, as if to keep him from seeing the cracks.

You're slipping, Liliya, he thought, but he only tightened his grip. Out loud, he managed, "I know you've got it handled." But his jaw clenched as he looked away, fighting the urge to pull her out of the mission before it even began.

Roles established; the group dispersed. Davyd shared a look with Anatoli and nodded. "Get some rest," he said, his voice steady, though the concern it masked felt like a weight pressing on his ribs.

But Liliya only gave a tight smile, that hard edge of determination in her eyes, and went to gather her notes. Davyd's gaze lingered on her for a beat longer. The hard line of her jaw, that focused stare—like steel about to shatter.

"Liliya," he said, voice low as she passed. She paused, glancing up at him.

His hand flexed against his leg. For a moment, he wanted to tell her to walk away from this one, to let someone else step in. But instead, he said, "Be sharp."

Her lips curled in a faint smile, and she nodded, brushing past him. But as she went, he felt the weight of unspoken words settle on his shoulders. He'd been here before—watching her keep going when she had no business doing so.

Anatoli escorted Liliya to the safe house provided by Sergei and Nadya. As they walked, the gravity of the mission ahead pressed on them.

Anatoli broke the silence, "You know the risks, Liliya. Be careful."

Liliya nodded, her resolve clear in her voice, "I'm ready, Anatoli. Every step is calculated."

At Sergei and Nadya's, Liliya found a quiet corner to gather her thoughts and marshal her strength. The upcoming days would demand everything she had. Sergei handed her a cup of tea, "You look like you could use this."

"Thank you, Sergei," she said gratefully. "I just need a moment to clear my head."

She sat in the dim room, her fingers tracing the paper's edges. Her knee bounced under the table, tension rising as she muttered the plan. Doubt lingered, but she forced it aside, the cold tea forgotten. There wasn't room for fear.

With a deep breath, she set the cup down and stood, readying herself for her much-needed rest, not sure if she could face the challenges ahead. Liliya blinked hard, as if clearing the fog in her mind. The Prestige loomed in her thoughts, the web she had to weave. Volkov wouldn't see it. He couldn't. Her heart pounded, uncertain if it was fear or something darker.

In sleep, her dreams twisted into violence. *The knife. The commander's face. Ivan. Blood.* Even unconscious, her body remained on edge. She awoke at 1430 hours more tired than when she had gone to sleep. She dragged herself into a shower in hopes that the water would rejuvenate her and clear the fog in her mind.

Her reflection in the mirror flickered, eyes darkened by sleepless nights. The mission—her lifeline. Each breath anchored her, just barely. The nightmares? She pushed them back, drowning in the routine. A needed distraction that placed her in greater jeopardy, mentally and physically, with each passing moment.

Armed with Sergei's intel, she knew Volkov would be at The Prestige by 1530 hours. Her entrance would be calculated, every detail meant to dominate his field of vision. This wasn't just a walk into a bar; it was an invasion of his world.

Liliya dressed quickly, setting her focus with each movement. Outside, she braced against the biting wind, her jacket pulled tight as she neared the glow of The Prestige. Sergei and Nadya were already blending with the crowd, stationed within earshot of the commander's table. Positioned to intercept intel from inebriated soldiers, their presence was an invisible shield, ready to protect her if things went south.

The Prestige buzzed with quiet anticipation, a dimly lit cocoon of dark wood and velvet, where conversations floated in the smoky air. The scent of tobacco, whiskey, and sweat mingled in the background, a low hum from the flickering neon sign punctuated by the clink of glasses.

Liliya stepped inside, the door creaking softly as it closed behind her. The cool night air that had clung to her skin was replaced by the oppressive warmth of the bar, thick and suffocating, yet she moved through it with practiced ease. Her heart raced, but her gaze remained calm as she spotted Volkov's table, shadowed in the far corner.

The bar buzzed with activity; bodies pressed together in close quarters. Liliya's gaze slid past Volkov, her hand grazing the lapel of her coat where a tracker had been carefully sewn, invisible to all but her team.

Laughter rose sporadically, tension humming beneath the surface. The thrum of music vibrated through the floor, matching the beat of her pulse.

Sergei, seated at a table near the back, caught her eye with a subtle nod. To an outsider, it was casual, but to Liliya, it was the signal she'd been waiting for. She moved toward him, her steps deliberate, slipping through the crowded space.

As she reached the table, something shifted in the air. She felt it before she saw it—a pause, a lull in the room's atmosphere, like a predator's eyes narrowing in on its prey. The soft clink of a glass stilled, conversation to her left faded. Volkov had noticed her.

Liliya didn't need to look to know she had his attention. His gaze landed on her with the weight of scrutiny, predatory, assessing. She kept her movements steady, muscles tensing instinctively against the heat of his stare. He was watching her, testing her, waiting for her next move—like a lion eyeing its target, patient and calculating.

In the corner of her eye, she saw him. Volkov sat back in his chair, a cigarette dangling loosely between his fingers, exuding arrogance. His posture was deceptively relaxed, but his eyes told a different story—sharp, cold, taking in every detail. His head tilted slightly, the faintest twitch in his fingers as if deciding whether to pounce.

Their eyes met, and Liliya's breath hitched, but she held his gaze, steady, unflinching, with equal intensity. A challenge was issued, unspoken, but felt in the space between them.

Volkov's lips curled into a slight smirk, a flicker of amusement crossing his face as if recognizing her attempt to hide in plain sight. She had entered his web, and he knew it.

Liliya exhaled, feeling her muscles tighten as control slipped into place. With a practiced smile, she lifted her drink and leaned into the tension, letting Volkov's attention drift over her like smoke. She let her gaze slide past him as if distracted, then shifted just enough to catch his eye, her faint smile daring him to break the silence. It was a subtle dance, the flicker of her eyes and the tilt of her head speaking volumes where words wouldn't do.

Finally, Liliya made her move. She stood from the table, her departure timed perfectly to match Volkov's exit. They crossed paths near the door, the faint smell of his cigarette smoke already curling into the cool air of the night beyond the bar.

Volkov lit a cigarette, the glow casting a sharp edge across his face. With a raised brow, he offered her one without a word.

Liliya paused, feigning casual interest as she accepted it. "Thanks." Her voice was light as she brought it to her lips, trying to ignore the tightness in her chest.

Volkov's gaze stayed on her, assessing. "Not your usual scene, is it?" he asked, flicking ash onto the floor.

Liliya shrugged, her eyes sweeping the bar like she hadn't just walked into his line of sight. "Sometimes you need a change." She let her voice trail off, like she hadn't quite decided if he was worth talking to yet.

Volkov's lip curled in amusement. "So, you're here... just to people-watch?"

"Something like that," she replied, her tone breezy, almost disinterested. She gave him a sideways glance, letting a small smile creep in. "Or maybe just curious to see if all the talk about this place was true."

"Talk?" Volkov leaned in a little, his interest piqued. "And what did they say? You know curiosity can be dangerous."

Liliya laughed, soft but genuine. "Nothing I'd repeat to someone who actually knows the place. But finding out might be worth the risk."

The faintest flicker of a grin crossed his face as he relaxed, visibly intrigued now. "I suppose I could give you a proper tour, then."

She met his gaze directly for the first time, allowing a hint of challenge to flash in her eyes. "Depends," she said, leaning back with casual ease. "Would it be worth my time?"

Volkov's expression darkened slightly, his interest sharpening. "I think you'd find it... interesting."

She exhaled smoke slowly, giving him a cool, appraising look. "Then I guess I'll have to stick around, won't I?"

Liliya snubbed out the cigarette and bid Volkov goodnight. The night air around them crackled with unspoken challenges and hidden meanings, both aware that this was only the beginning of their intricate dance.

Their exchange was brief but charged, a spark igniting the tinderbox of their mutual intrigue.

Outside, the cool night air was a balm to Liliya's heightened senses, sharpening her focus as she replayed the moment. The street was quiet, shadows stretching like familiar ghosts along the sidewalk. Her breath misted, and she tightened her coat around herself, aware of the weight of her next step.

She kept a steady pace, instinctively adjusting her route through the dark streets. The shadows blended, swallowing the distant hum of Davyd's voice over her earwig, a faint crackle snapping her back to the task.

Meanwhile, in the shadows of the night, Davyd and Yaroslav maintained their vigil, their eyes and ears an extension of Liliya's presence within The Prestige. Through their earwigs, the communication lines buzzed with updates, a lifeline that connected the operatives in a network of shared purpose and resolve.

Back at the house, Liliya discarded her day's guise, the jeans and top giving way to the nondescript uniform of a night cleaner. As she changed, the events of the evening replayed in her mind. The initial phase of her mission was complete, the foundation laid for the next steps. The intelligence, freshly dispatched to Kyiv, shifted her mission's focus. Under the cover of insignificance, her task was to shadow the guards' patrols, a silent waltz of observation and stealth.

The challenges ahead were daunting, but Liliya's resolve was unshakeable. She was a woman on a mission, her heart and mind aligned with the cause that had brought them all together.

The night had ended, but the game was just beginning.

Her transformation, now a ritual, cloaked her in anonymity as she retraced her steps towards the industrial heart of their operation.

The checkpoint, a familiar hurdle, offered no resistance this time—just the guard's indifferent nod, a silent admission into the belly of the beast. Liliya felt a mix of relief and tension as she passed through, her heart pounding in her chest. She knew she had to remain calm, to blend in and not draw any attention to herself.

As Liliya edged closer to the plant's secluded rear, her cautious steps masked by the distant clatter of machinery, she paused. Her eyes narrowed as she took in the sight before her—workers, oblivious to her presence, were unloading large, ominous tanks from a heavy truck. The stark white lettering on the side read 'Acetylene' and 'Oxygen.' She counted quickly under her breath, "Forty-eight, forty-nine, fifty..." Fifty tanks in total.

The realization of what this could mean in the wrong hands caused a shiver to run down her spine. She knew too well the explosive potential when these gases were mixed with C4—a thought that both terrified and invigorated her. This could change everything. We could bring this place down in seconds, she thought, her mind racing with the possibilities and the massive responsibility now resting on her shoulders.

Confident she had all the information she needed, Liliya sought refuge behind a large, rusted shipping container to relay her findings. She tapped the comm in her ear. With a cautious glance around, she whispered into the mic, "Davyd, it's Liliya. I've seen fifty canisters— some marked for welding, some for breathing. It's more than enough to spark a big fire if needed. Over."

She waited, her heart still pounding, as the seconds stretched out. The weight of the information she had just shared hung heavy in the air. The realization of what they could achieve—and the risks involved—loomed over her.

Davyd's voice crackled through the earwig, his voice a steady anchor in the storm of her thoughts. "Understood, Liliya. That's crucial information. We'll coordinate the next steps. Stay safe. Over."

Liliya felt a surge of decisiveness wash over her. The discovery of the tanks not only solidified the importance of their mission but also fueled her resolve to see it through. *We can do this. We have to*, she reassured herself silently, the weight of their potential to change the course of the conflict pressing firmly upon her. With one last look at the hazardous tanks, she melded back into the shadows, her steps silent and purposeful.

She adjusted the volume on her earpiece, balancing sound clarity against ambient noise to reduce detection risk. "Ten paces east, past the security grid. No sound," Davyd instructed. She visualized the route, memorizing the turns and tracking the sound of her footsteps to match the nearest patrol's approach. Timing each breath to his words, she moved, tuning out distractions as she counted silently, preparing to stop on his next signal.

As dawn broke, Liliya shed her disguise, her findings pressing heavily on her mind.

Davyd watched as Liliya completed her mission and retreated to their temporary sanctuary. At their command center, he relayed the crucial information about the tanks to the engineers.

The whisper of a grander scheme soon reached Davyd, stirring the air with the promise of a decisive blow. A military strike against the steel heart of Lipetsk loomed on the horizon, a daring assault aimed at severing the sinews of the enemy's missile capabilities.

Davyd's pulse raced with the news, a torrent of adrenaline and anticipation coursing through him. Using the communication system, Davyd, the excitement evident in his voice, shared the news with everyone, "We've received word of a planned drone strike against the steel plant in Lipetsk. This could be the turning point we've been waiting for."

Liliya heard his voice, and her eyes widened, "A drone strike? That's bold. Are they really going to hit their missile production at its core?"

"Yes. This could cripple their operations. If we integrate this strategy with our own mission, we can maximize the impact," Davyd replied confirming the objective.

"What do we need to do to align our efforts with this strike?" Anatoli interjected.

"We gather intel, secure the blueprints, plant the charges—all timed with the Lipetsk strike." Davyd went into more detail of the dual strike.

The prospect of this coordinated effort ignited a shared sense of purpose within the group. Their vision for the path forward became unified, each member feeling the weight and significance of their roles.

Liliya speculated, "This could change everything. We need to be at our best."

Davyd felt the buzz of energy within him, a stark contrast to the exhaustion that usually followed such intense planning. He knew the importance of being mentally sharp for the challenges that awaited. Yet, amidst the whirlwind of excitement, he recognized the imperative of rest.

Taking a deep breath, Davyd calmed himself, " Rest up. We'll need to stay sharp for what's next."

Davyd was alone in the quiet of the apartment, his body buzzing with energy, resistant to the call of sleep. He moved to the window, gazing out at the city. The skyline, a tapestry of lights against the receding night, seemed to reflect his restless thoughts. *This is it. This could be the turning point. But I need to be sharp. I need to rest.*

With a disciplined effort, he tore himself away from the window and lay down, forcing his mind to calm. He knew that the effectiveness of their next moves depended on his ability to remain vigilant and focused.

Liliya, too, felt the surge of energy that defied the need for rest. The news had injected a dose of vitality into her veins, a restless anticipation for what lay ahead. Despite the exhilaration, she understood the necessity of mental clarity. The initial hours were restless, a struggle against the tide of thoughts and plans that flooded her mind. Eventually, the exhaustion of her body commanded a truce, and she succumbed to sleep, but the thoughts continued.

The game of deception she played with Volkov, a dance on the razor's edge of danger, had triggered her mind to replay the many times she had taken life. Her hand flexed involuntarily. *Blood. Eyes dimming. Pressure. Knife.* Images flickered, just out of reach but close enough to choke.

Liliya awoke, her body rigid from the restless sleep. The thrill of the previous night had been replaced by creeping doubt. A familiar tremor began in her hands, thoughts spinning into dark memories. *What if I can't keep control when it matters most?* The fear pressed in, cold and sharp, as she sank to the floor. Her breath caught; chest tight. *I can't keep running forever.*

In the stillness of the room, the ghosts of her past pressed harder. Fear nipped at her resolve, the weight of old failures threatening to pull her under again. But this time, she couldn't afford to let them win.

The door creaked open, and Nadya stepped inside, placing a tray of food on the bed. Her eyes fell on Liliya, crumpled on the floor. Without a word, she knelt beside her, pulling her into a quiet embrace. "You're safe, Liliya. Breathe," Nadya whispered.

Liliya clung to the warmth, the steady rhythm of Nadya's breathing settling her. "I can still see them," Liliya murmured, her voice shaky. "The faces... the blood. What if I can't hold it together?".

Nadya pulled back slightly, meeting Liliya's gaze. "You've been through hell, and you're still here. That strength? It's what will carry you through this."

Liliya's voice cracked. "But what if I lose control—when it matters most?"

Nadya cupped Liliya's face gently. "You won't. We're here. You're not doing this alone."

Liliya closed her eyes, Nadya's words sinking in. *I don't have to carry it all alone.*

Nadya's words slowly began to penetrate the fog of fear in Liliya's mind. She felt a small spark of assurance reignite within her. Talking a deep breath Liliya replied, "You're right. I can't let the past control me. I need to focus on the mission, on the future we're fighting for."

Nadya smiled, her eyes full of encouragement. "Exactly. And we're all here for you. You're not alone in this, Liliya."

With Nadya's help, Liliya stood up, still shaky but more resolute. She embraced Nadya tightly, drawing strength from her friend's unwavering support, "Thank you, Nadya. I don't know what I'd do without you."

Nadya pulled away slightly and smiled, "You don't have to find out. We'll get through this together."

As Liliya prepared to face the day, the specters of doubt and fear still lingered. She took a deep breath, forcing herself to focus. The stakes were too high for doubt to take hold. Each breath, she locked away the demons that sought to undo her, her resolve hardening.

Slipping into her carefully chosen disguise once more. The fabric of her costume was not just a cover but a mantle of resilience, each thread woven to fortify the resolve needed to face the impending night with unwavering courage. However, dressing, once mundane, now felt like a battle against her own body. Opting for the comfort and ease of a light sweater over the struggle with another button-down shirt, Liliya paused, caught in a moment of vulnerability.

As she stepped away from the mirror, Liliya left behind the moment of doubt. She was not just Liliya; she was the hope and the fury of those who fought silently in the shadows. And she would not falter.

Liliya slipped into The Prestige, the warmth of the bar enveloping her in an instant. The sharp contrast from the biting night air outside did little to ease the coil of tension tightening in her chest, but she held herself steady. One step at a time, she reminded herself. The familiar scent of cigarette smoke mingled with stale whiskey, filling the dimly lit space with a sense of gritty comfort. Her fingers flexed briefly at her sides as she took in the room.

The bar was crowded, busier than she'd expected. Patrons clustered in small groups, laughter rising sporadically, their conversations bubbling over each other. It was easy to get lost in the noise here—a part of what made The Prestige such an ideal meeting spot. But her attention wasn't on the hum of the crowd. It was on him. Somewhere in this room, Volkov was watching.

She inhaled deeply, feeling her heartbeat settle into a steady rhythm. Her eyes flicked over the crowd casually, avoiding any direct stares. She could feel it, though, even before she saw him—Volkov's gaze on her, heavy and assessing. She didn't look his way; there was no need to give him the satisfaction. Instead, she made her way toward Sergei and Nadya, their familiar faces a welcome sight in the crowded bar.

As she crossed the room, she felt the atmosphere shift around her. Conversations softened; bodies moved slightly out of her path. She could sense the subtle change in the bar's energy, like a ripple in still water. Volkov had noticed her.

Finally, she reached Sergei and Nadya's table, allowing herself to relax—just a fraction—as she took the seat Sergei offered. He gave her a slight nod, his expression casual, but the glint in his eyes told her he was ready. "Took your time," he murmured, barely glancing her way.

She let a faint smile tug at her lips. "Had to make an entrance," she replied, her tone light but layered with meaning. She picked up the drink he'd ordered for her, taking a slow sip, her fingers steady on the glass as the ice clinked. She needed to stay calm, look collected. Don't show any cracks. Volkov's gaze was still on her, sharp and unrelenting.

Out of the corner of her eye, she saw him: Volkov, in hi usual posture. He looked deceptively relaxed, but she didn't miss the way his eyes were fixed on her, narrowing slightly as he took her in. He was testing her, waiting for her to make a move.

She let her gaze sweep the room before resting briefly on him, acknowledging his presence with the barest flicker of eye contact. He straightened in his seat, tapping ash from his cigarette, a faint smirk touching his lips. Got you, she thought, forcing her pulse to slow. Her heart was pounding, but she masked it with a calm, almost bored expression, lifting her glass for another sip.

Then, just as she'd anticipated, Volkov stood up. He moved with that practiced ease, every step radiating control. She could feel the bar's energy shift again as he approached, patrons turning subtly in their seats, aware of his presence without needing to look directly. Volkov stopped in front of her, that familiar arrogance in his eyes.

Her stomach twisted as the sharp scent of smoke curled into her nose. She stared at her drink, willing her hands to stay steady as his shadow loomed, cold and suffocating.

"Well, well. What do we have here?" Volkov's voice oozed arrogance. "Back already? Must have made quite the impression."

Liliya took the drink with a faint smile, her voice smooth, almost lazy. "Seems I found exactly what I was looking for."

Volkov's smirk deepened, testing her with a slow, appraising look. "Did you?" he replied.

Liliya lifted her glass, holding his gaze as she sipped. "I don't leave things to chance."

Volkov's smile widened, basking in his own sense of importance. "Join me?" He didn't wait for an answer, waving his hand for his table to be cleared.

Liliya lowered herself into the chair, the velvet fabric prickling against her skin. "Why not?" she said, her voice smooth, though the heavy heat of the room pressed down on her, mixing with the sharp scent of vodka.

They moved to his table and took their seats. Volkov waved to the bar and their drinks arrived swiftly. Volkov raised his glass. "To new acquaintances."

Liliya lifted her glass, the soft clink of it meeting his instantly triggering a memory. *Vials. Shattering.* Her fingers trembled against the glass. *Cold. Metallic.* She forced a smile, but the lab lingered. "To new acquaintances," she echoed, taking a sip and steadying herself.

Volkov leaned back, his eyes trailing over her like a predator sizing up its prey. The smoke from his cigarette curled lazily between them, filling the space with a bitter scent. "So, what brought you to our small town? Not your usual scene, is it?"

Liliya's smile sharpened slightly. "Moscow's all show, too many people eager to impress." She let her gaze drift around the room before flicking back to him, voice lower. "Here, everything's... more intimate."

Volkov's smile twisted slightly, eyes narrowing. "Too many eyes, Moscow. A place like this... offers freedom, doesn't it?"

Liliya nodded, though his gaze—the way it lingered, cold and calculating like Ivan's—sent a shiver down her spine. Her fingers tightened on the glass, but her voice remained light. "Exactly." She paused, then added casually, "I'm sure you know a thing or two about pressure."

His ego flared. "You could say that. Comes with the job."

Liliya leaned in slightly, trying to keep her tone playful. "What kind of job is that?"

Volkov's eyes glimmered, savoring his control. "Oh, you know. The kind that keeps the world in check." He took a slow sip, relishing the moment.

"You must be used to... delicate matters." Liliya's voice was barely a whisper, eyes catching his. "Not many could manage it."

Volkov's eyes glinted with pride. Taking the bait, he replied, clearly savoring her approval, "It's not for the faint-hearted."

Liliya's smile tightened. "It's a skill—to handle so many things without slipping up."

Volkov raised an eyebrow, intrigued. "Yes, and Secrets... well, those come with the territory."

"And what kind of secrets?" Liliya's voice dropped, her words more suggestion than question.

Volkov chuckled, leaning back. "Let's just say not everything's as visible as it seems. Sometimes, the real power is the kind you never see coming." He took another sip, the sharp scent of vodka on his breath curling in the air.

Vodka. Sour. Blood. Knife. Her fingers twitched—remembering. It hit her like a jolt, tightening her chest. She blinked, suppressing the reflex to pull back. "That sounds... fascinating," she said, controlling her breath. "I suppose you've got ways to ensure those forces stay unseen."

Volkov tapped the edge of his glass, watching her closely. "We're working on things that will change the game. Undetectable. Revolutionary."

Liliya leaned forward just slightly, her focus sharpening. "Undetectable?" She let the word hang. "That must take precision."

Volkov leaned in, his chest puffing out with pride, "Staying ahead, yes... control is everything."

"That's quite impressive," she replied, lightening her tone. "I imagine you're the one making sure it all runs smoothly?"

Volkov's eyes glinted. "Of course. Someone has to keep things... secure."

Liliya caught the shift in his tone, seizing the opportunity. "I'd love to see how someone like you keeps everything so perfectly aligned and secure. It can't just be about planning... it's about placing the right pieces, isn't it?"

Volkov studied her for a moment, his smile widening. "Maybe you'll see for yourself. Dinner tomorrow?" He leaned in, lowering his voice. "I'll show you what I'm working on. You might appreciate it more up close."

Liliya leaned in, her heartbeat steadying as she slipped into character. Volkov's smirk widened, his arrogance sharpening the lines of his face. She held her gaze level with his. Her voice as soft as velvet. "Dinner, secrets..." She paused, watching him savor the mystery. "I'll bring an appetite." Her fingers tapped the glass in a steady rhythm, each pulse counting down. *One chance. No falter.*

Volkov grinned, clearly pleased with himself. "I'll have my driver pick you up. 1730. Wear something... fitting."

"Something memorable," Liliya replied, her smile widening, the moment of panic behind her as she refocused on the mission.

Liliya tilted her head, feigning a thoughtful pause. A coy smile played on her lips as she nodded. "Such an important place deserves a memorable evening. Maybe something special to mark the occasion?"

Volkov leaned in, intrigued. "What do you mean, something special?"

Liliya smiled softly, her eyes meeting his. "Oh, you know, just a little something to make the evening even more memorable. It's always nice when a gentleman adds a touch of charm."

Volkov's eyes lit up with understanding and eagerness. "How about roses? Would a dozen long-stem roses suffice?"

"A man with taste… rare these days." She paused, a faint smile in place. "Two dozen roses, perhaps? I like a bold gesture."

Volkov chuckled, visibly pleased, he nodded. "Only two dozen?" he teased.

Liliya's lips curved faintly. "I wouldn't want to ask too much… yet."

Their exchange, seemingly innocent to any onlooker, was a dance of strategy and subterfuge. Liliya's play to get Volkov to provide the roses was not just a whimsical desire but a carefully placed piece in the intricate chess game they were playing—a game where every move, every word, carried weight far beyond the surface.

She kept a steady pace, instinctively adjusting her route through the dark streets, her gaze shifting to check reflections in the shop windows. She could still feel Volkov's gaze like a distant, shadowed threat. In the silence, her footsteps softened, each step calculated. As she reached the alley, she crouched low, one hand on her pistol, and exhaled slowly. Time to disappear.

Her eyes narrowed as she scanned the deserted street. "*Curiosity can be dangerous,*" Volkov's voice echoed in her memory, but she wouldn't let his arrogance unsettle her. She smirked faintly, a flash of cold determination replacing any lingering doubt. He was right—curiosity *would* be dangerous, but only for him.

Without a second glance, she moved again, her pace unwavering, every step a reminder of the control she needed to maintain. The streets blurred behind her as she disappeared into the shadows, the night's events coiling tightly around her resolve.

CHAPTER

FIFTEEN

Preparations in the Shadows

While Liliya was with Volkov, Davyd's fingers moved over the rough schematics, marking potential entry points with quick strokes. The lamp's dim light barely pierced the gloom, casting long shadows across the paper—like the ones pressing at the edge of his thoughts.

The scratch of the pen seemed to echo in the silence. He paused. Voices from the hallway—muffled, but too close. Time was slipping.

His eyes darted to the window. Below, a car idled, its headlights cutting through the dark. The low hum seemed to burrow into his skull. In the shadows, a figure shifted just outside the light. Remembering the previous night. *Watching?* His body tensed, grip tightening around the pen.

A car horn blared, making him flinch. His heart pounded, gaze snapping back to the window. Was it a signal? The shadow remained still, blending with the night.

He stood, moving closer, palm pressing against the cold glass. The figure shifted again. Was someone there—*or his imagination?* His breath caught. *No time for this.*

The hum of the city droned on, indifferent. He stepped back, shoving the doubt down. He turned to the desk, his movements deliberate. *No more distractions.*

The earpiece crackled to life, startling him from his thoughts. He grabbed it, listening intently to the sharp voice on the other end. "We've got 36 hours. Drone strike hits just before dawn."

Davyd's mind whirred as he processed the new timeline. "Understood." He adjusted the plan in his head and packed his gear, moving with a fluid efficiency. Time to act.

He turned to his desk, eyes narrowing as he packed his gear with a quiet, unhurried efficiency. The weight of it—the familiar cold steel, the rough canvas—triggered an echo of that old weight he had carried on his back in the Carpathian Mountains. The chill of that endless trek, cold seeping through layers of wool, each step a measured risk. *Just like now*, he reminded himself. He drew in a sharp breath.

The cool night air hit Davyd's face as he stepped into the street. He climbed into the Mercedes, eyes flicking to the side mirror. The shadow by the car—gone. He pulled away, muscles tensing as the streetlights blurred past, their flickering glow fading as the city thinned.

Concrete shifted to gravel beneath the tires. The road narrowed. Trees loomed on either side, swallowing the last traces of light. He cut the engine, stepping out. Silence. The air, thick with damp earth and wet leaves, clung to his skin.

Boots hit the ground, soft but sure. The forest absorbed him—quiet, alive with rustling branches. The scent of moss and smoke filled his lungs, as he moved deeper into the dark.

Yaroslav stepped out of the shadows, his watch catching the moonlight. They locked eyes, a brief nod. "Resistance?" Yaroslav's voice was barely a whisper, blending into the quiet.

"Set for 2. Sync now. Strike in 36," Davyd's reply was clipped, sharp.

Yaroslav gave a short nod, nothing more. Then he slipped back into the shadows, his mission clear.

Alone, Davyd breathed in the damp air, centering himself. There was no room for hesitation. His movements were quick but controlled as he continued his own preparations. The night thrummed around him, the weight of what was to come settling on his shoulders. The forest was still, but the air vibrated with the unspoken promise of what lay ahead.

Through the binoculars, Davyd's hand held steady on the focus dial, but a faint tremor crept into his fingertips as Liliya's silhouette merged with the shadows. He tightened his hold on the binoculars, pressing them harder against his brow until the discomfort forced him to ease up. Only then did he breathe, his exhale quiet but hard, as he tracked her movements in silence. "Take it easy—easy," he muttered into the comms, his voice barely above a whisper. He scanned the streets, tension creeping into his muscles.

Liliya acknowledged briefly, just enough for Davyd to know she was fine and following the plan. She navigated the risks with the precision they had rehearsed.

Davyd's mind shifted gears, returning to the critical details of their future operation. He whispered into the comms, "Liliya, I need your input on the layout. What are you seeing inside?"

Liliya sank deeper into the shadows. Eyes darting. The plant floor, dim and endless. Machinery's hum drilled through her. Sharp. Cold. Her pulse jumped, chest tightening. Buzzing fluorescent light—blinding. She jerked back, spine hitting the column. *Hide.* Fingers twitched toward her knife, finding nothing.

The smell. Sterile, suffocating.

"Liliya!" Davyd's voice burst through the comms. The jolt shook her back to the present, the column biting into her spine.

"Copy," she breathed, voice thin, shaky.

"Liliya?" The hesitation in her voice sent a spark of alarm through him. He pressed harder on the comms, not waiting for a response. The last time he had heard a partner's voice like that, breath short, words cut off, it had been the last time he'd heard them at all. He forced his breath even, keeping his voice steady. "Focus on the supports. Time it right."

Her gaze locked on the supports. Solid. Weak spots. "Corner sectors," she murmured. "Central support. Hit them... it all goes down."

"Noted. What about the processing area?" Davyd's voice hummed in her ear.

Liliya crouched, narrowing her focus on the generators. *Tanks. Chain reaction.* "Weak spot-main generator," she whispered. Breath shallow. "Tanks below. Chain reaction. Generator first."

"Good. Keep moving."

Liliya pressed flat against the metal. Cold biting into her. Footsteps. Distant. Too close. Her pulse thundered, a rapid thud in her throat. Blinked. *Alley shadows. Footsteps, louder, closing in. Run.*

"What's happening?" Davyd's voice cut through again, static and sharp.

She blinked hard, vision swimming back into focus, the cold metal beneath her fingers steadying her. "... Heard something... The guards," she whispered, voice shaking. "They pass every twenty minutes. Near the central support." Her palm pressed harder into the wall. "I'll need to time it right for the charges."

"Understood. Just focus on the intel. No rush."

The silence of the plant weighed down on her as she moved. The hum of the machinery swallowed the world, amplifying each step, each breath. *In. Out.* Each movement calculated. *No mistakes. No rushing.*

But her body felt heavy, disconnected, like she was walking through water. The hum—it drilled into her head, too loud, pushing against her thoughts. *Not here. Not now.* Her breaths came faster, short, sharp bursts. *Focus. Just focus.*

The stairwell loomed ahead, and the air thickened, damp and stale, closing in around her. *Wet stone.* Her pulse raced; her vision blurred. *Flash of Light, Gunpowder. Blood. The stench.* Her knees buckled. *Not real. Not here.*

She gripped the railing, knuckles bone-white, forcing herself upright. The cold steel bit into her skin, anchoring her in the present. She forced her eyes to survey the layout below. "Looks like there's plenty of cover near the generator," she whispered into the comms, fighting to keep her voice even. "If we time it right, it'll give us the perfect spot to plant without being seen."

"Good to know. Anything else?" Davyd's voice was steady, but Liliya's mind was slipping.

Liliya responded, "No," but her voice faltered. Her mouth was dry, her head spinning, her breath refusing to come in full.

The air felt too thick. Each breath caught, heavy in her chest. Her limbs dragged, leaden. The hum—sharp, constant—pressed into her bones. Each step, a struggle. Dark spots edged her vision.

She pushed forward, muscles tight, vision narrowing. Cold air hit her like a slap as she stumbled outside. It grounded her—barely. She inhaled, sharp, but the tightness wouldn't ease. Her ribs felt caged, breath shallow. *Move. Just move.*

Her steps quickened, uneven, a tremor running through her legs. The hum still buzzed in her skull. *It's over. Get out.* The thought hammered in her mind. Her hands twitched, adrenaline spiking, pulse erratic.

The checkpoint loomed. She straightened, forced calm into her body. Tired. Just another worker. Her uniform sagged, wrinkled, but convincing enough. *Blend in. Don't think.* Her mind spun, fragments of sound and light—footsteps, the hum, the glare of machinery—clinging, choking.

The line of departing staff moved sluggishly forward, their tired expressions mirroring the early morning atmosphere. Liliya tried to blend in, forcing her steps to fall in sync with the rhythm of the other workers, but her heart still pounded, the adrenaline surging through her veins.

She walked toward the guard attempting to reflect confidence, her heart hammering in her throat. She gave him a brief nod, fingers fumbling slightly as she reached for her ID card. *Calm. Breathe.* But the ID felt heavy, the world teetering as she handed it to him.

The guard's gaze lingered, too long, too aware. "Rough night?" The guard's voice was casual, but his brow furrowed ever so slightly, his attention flicking to her trembling fingers.

Liliya forced a tight smile, her breath barely coming through her clenched throat. "Yeah... long one," she managed, her voice cracking slightly. She swallowed hard, steadying herself as best she could.

He hesitated, his eyes narrowing briefly before nodding slowly. "Right. Move along." His tone was dismissive, but the weight of his stare clung to her as she passed, her back rigid, every nerve in her body screaming to run.

She slipped out of the plant, pre-dawn air cutting sharp. Cold, biting through her. The panic clawed at her chest. *Too close.* Eyes on her back? She forced herself forward, resisting the urge to run.

189

Her legs trembled as she hurried down the street, her steps uneven. The shadows shifted. *Footsteps?* She glanced over her shoulder. *Empty.* She quickened her pace. *Move. Just move.*

The Mercedes loomed ahead, half-hidden in the dim light. *Almost there.* Her fingers fumbled with the door handle. A click. She slid into the backseat, shutting the door behind her. The air felt thick. Her breath shallow, rapid.

Davyd shifted in the passenger seat. He didn't say anything, but his eyes lingered, noting the pallor of her skin, the slight tremor in her hands. Yaroslav's gaze flicked to her through the rearview mirror, his brows knitting together in quiet concern. They exchanged a glance but remained silent. The hum of the engine filled the tense silence, but the unspoken worry hung heavy in the air.

Liliya stared out the window, her reflection fractured in the glass. *Keep it together. Don't fall apart.* But the cold grip of the lab, the relentless hum, and the sharp lights clung to her, tightening their hold with every passing second.

SIXTEEN

A Quiet Before the Storm

The drive blurred past, shadows slipping along the windshield as the city began to wake. Silence thickened in the car. Davyd's fingers tapped the armrest, Yaroslav's grip tightening on the wheel. Liliya barely moved, her gaze fixed out the window, jaw set, fingers clenched around the seatbelt. Words could wait.

Each turn stretched the silence, their breaths the only sound cutting through the hum of the engine. He kept his gaze forward, but the stillness between them seemed to tighten, the unspoken tension settling across the car like a thick fog. Davyd's fingers tapped faster, almost imperceptibly, each beat slipping past like a shadow. He stole a glance at her hand gripping the seatbelt, knuckles paling as her fingers tightened.

They passed the old stone church, a faint outline in the pre-dawn light. Anatoli's Lada rumbled into view, falling into line as the convoy slipped through the misted streets, headlights cutting a path toward their control center.

On arrival, Liliya moved ahead, slipping into the shadowed alley with practiced ease. Davyd got out across the street, watching as she disappeared from view. There were no words, no signals; just a nod—a brief exchange, the kind they'd perfected over the years. They split, each moving on their own, yet in perfect rhythm. The city sounds—the shuffle of vendors setting up, distant footsteps—filled the silence left between them. His gaze lingered on the corner where she vanished, waiting until her figure merged completely with the shadows before he moved. They'd meet soon enough; for now, silence was enough.

Anatoli and Yaroslav, parking in different spots, moved discreetly through the streets, blending into the early morning hustle as vendors began setting up and streetlights flickered off. The cobblestones echoed under their steps, a reminder of lurking danger.

In the hotel room, the low hum of the laptop joined the crackle of comms, filling the dim hotel room with quiet purpose. Maps sprawled across the table, pins marking critical points. Davyd's hand hovered over one, his focus on the shifting lines. Across the table, Liliya traced a route with the edge of her fingertip, her movements deliberate, precise. She didn't look up. No one did.

"Yaroslav, tower. Precise." Her voice low, sharp, and Davyd's eyes caught her hand—stilled for just a second too long. She was grounded, determined—yet a tension lingered, barely masked. He caught her eye for a moment, an exchange as quick as it was steady. Just enough.

As Anatoli shifted, adjusting a pin on the map, Davyd tracked each small sound—the scratch of metal on paper, the faint rustle of jackets as they leaned in closer. No one spoke beyond the necessary. Each glance, every tap of the map, tightened their focus. Words would only complicate things; this silence was more precise than anything spoken.

Davyd's fingers jabbed the map. "Explosives—where and how fast?"

Anatoli leaned forward, adjusting the pins on the map. "I'm on the work crew this afternoon. We'll use the truck to bring in the explosives. No one will notice." He slid a map toward Davyd, detailing weak points and showing micro-bursts from thermal imaging they'd mapped the previous night. "Thermal confirms minimal movement near the eastern wall at shift change," he murmured. Davyd noted the time, then tapped his watch's silent alarm—syncing their moves with a pulse code Yaroslav would receive through his earpiece across town.

Liliya's eyes narrowed, her focus slipping for a second as the hum grew louder in her ears. The hum burrowed under her skin, a reminder of electric wires buzzing in that sterile room, the world fading to a white glow. She gritted her teeth, pressing her fingers into the map. *Focus. Here, now.* "And... where will you ... hide them?" she asked, her voice thinner now, her fingers brushing the table absently.

Davyd's focus shifted to her hand; fingers clenched so tightly the knuckles had gone white. She was here in body, but something in her gaze seemed distant, like she was fighting a battle he couldn't see. His fingers brushed the table edge, feeling the rough wood beneath his fingertips, grounding him. He wanted to tell her to step back, catch her breath, but this was war—there was no stepping back. He kept silent, each beat of his pulse a reminder to stay in line, stay focused. Whatever was haunting her, she'd have to face it on her own terms.

Anatoli's finger stabbed at the map. "Storage area. Tanks. Access secure."

Liliya and Davyd leaned forward to see where Anatoli was pointing, nodding their heads in agreement. "Okay, once they're in, what's in place to coordinate the accident and block the access. No civilians get near the plant." Davyd asked.

Anatoli nodded. "Prestige—final coordination. Solid front. Everyone, lock roles."

As Anatoli spoke, Davyd's mind wandered briefly to past operations. *We have to get this right. No room for error.* His grip tightened around a marker, the click of the cap a reminder of the stakes.

Liliya met his gaze, her grip on the table firm. She forced herself to focus on Anatoli's directions, tracking the lines on the map—potential routes, potential fates. The press of Davyd's hand steadied her like a lifeline. They mapped out the diversion, shifting cars and roadblocks with precise hands. Liliya placed a roadblock, her focus unwavering as she set each piece in place.

The briefing wrapped; Davyd's gaze held each team member. He followed Liliya as she gathered her bag, noting the faint lines of strain around her eyes. His fingers tapped once against the edge of the table, stopping only when he caught himself. "You good?" he asked, keeping his tone even. Her pause, the slight falter in her smile, held him still. When she nodded, he managed a brief nod in return, but his hand hovered over the door handle, the cool metal biting against his palm. Vulnerability flickering in her gaze before she turned into the hall. The connection between them lingered, unspoken but understood.

Anatoli's jaw clenched as he shouldered the bag containing the C4 and components the resistance had provided, a deep breath escaping his lips. Yaroslav tightened the straps on his backpack, his movements precise and controlled, masking the underlying tension.

At the threshold of Sergei and Nadya's house, Liliya and Anatoli exchanged a glance, the weight of the mission pressing down. Anatoli dropped the bag on the table, its contents shifting with a soft clink of C4, detonators, and timers.

Anatoli placed the detonators in a neat line, each precisely spaced. He glanced at Liliya, brow raised. "We don't get second chances with these," he muttered, double-checking a wire connection before stepping back. "Let's make sure they're exactly where we need them."

Liliya leaned forward, her heart thudding harder than it should. She stared at the explosives, her pulse loud in her ears, drowning out everything else. She swallowed hard. "It's time," she whispered, half to herself, her voice tighter than intended.

Anatoli shot her a sharp look. "Let's sit. No mistakes." They settled at the kitchen table as he laid out the components with practiced hands. "Steady hands," Anatoli muttered, holding up the detonator. "One slip..."

Liliya nodded, trying to concentrate, but her mind flickered. The room seemed smaller. Hotter. Her fingers twitched as she watched him work, feeling the edges of her focus slip. *Just breathe.*

"Here," Anatoli muttered, moving his hands to the detonator. "C4. Timer. Wire. Fast."

The room blurred slightly as her vision faltered. Her head swam. Chest tightened. *Focus, dammit.*

Anatoli slid the timer across the table, his eyes sharp. "Your turn."

The detonator was cold in Liliya's hand, every part of it a step closer to finality. She adjusted the wires quickly, her fingers steady, movements sharp. Outside, the noise faded to nothing. Her focus was absolute, the task narrowing to a pinpoint. The last charge clicked into place, locking her into the moment. One second. One trigger. Everything they had planned hinged on this. A whisper of adrenaline coursed through her veins. One misstep, and it was over.

"Done," she muttered, voice flat but steady. She placed the detonator on the table, fingers briefly lingering on the rough surface before pulling away.

Anatoli nodded once, eyes on her hands. "Good. Now again. Faster."

She reset the charge, her fingers moving more fluidly this time. But the edges of her vision wavered again—too many thoughts, too many images flashing. The smell of antiseptic from the lab. The cold bite of metal. A jolt of panic surged through her. *Stop.* She clenched her jaw, forcing the thought away.

As she set down the completed charge, a dull thud sounded from the street outside—a trash bin overturned by some stray animal. Instinctively, she froze, her hand slipping to her sidearm. The silence tightened, stretched, every nerve attuned to the slightest sound.

Anatoli's eyes shifted to her hand, then back to her face. He gave a barely perceptible nod, a sign of trust but also a reminder to stay sharp. "False alarm," he murmured, his voice barely a whisper.

She forced her hand back to the table, the weight of her pulse steadying her. Anatoli's fingers closed around the last detonator as he began to re-pack the bag. His movements were controlled, assured. "Remember," he said, glancing at her one last time, "when this goes off, there's no time for error. Just stick to the plan."

Their eyes met, an unspoken understanding passing between them. The task loomed, heavy and uncompromising, as Anatoli shouldered the bag and moved toward the door. Liliya's gaze followed him, each step of his receding figure marked by the quiet promise of what lay ahead—a plan razor-thin, its outcome uncertain.

The table's cool surface steadied her, cutting through the buzz of adrenaline. Liliya's fingers traced the wood. Her breath held. She was ready.

SEUENTEEN

The Strike

Liliya closed her bedroom door, her outward calm slipping away as exhaustion finally took hold. The next twenty-three hours stretched before her, carrying a weight she hadn't felt in years. She sank onto the bed, eyes closing as sleep claimed her quickly, her mind too tired to grasp for comfort or dread.

She awoke abruptly at 1500 hours, her heart pounding hard in her chest. The air felt dense, pressing down on her as she got her bearings. Her bag waited on the dresser. Liliya's hand hovered over the silenced pistol on the dresser, her fingers grazing its cool metal surface before she tucked it into her bag. The weight of it felt steady, grounding, until her fingers brushed the edge of the barrel. Her chest tightened, and her thumb instinctively ran along the familiar grip, the memory creeping in, unbidden.

A different room, a different mission. She could almost feel the rough floor beneath her knees, hear the hiss of breath in the dark as her hand clenched around the weapon's handle, her pulse wild against her skin. The muffled scrape of boots on concrete had been the only sound, her whole body taut with the wait—until the door creaked open, her fingers already curling, tense, around the trigger.

She blinked, grounding herself in the present. That mission was behind her, but the adrenaline still lingered, a quiet hum under her skin. She placed the pistol firmly into her bag and flexed her fingers, one by one, until her pulse slowed. This time, she reminded herself, there was no room for hesitation.

In the shower, the hot water stung her skin, the steam thickening the air. Her throat tightened, chest heaving. The glass fogged over; shapes blurred behind the condensation. Steam curled thick around her, clouding the air. Her pulse quickened as smoke and the faint hum of machinery crept into her senses—a memory snapping in, unwelcome. She squeezed her eyes shut, gripping the handle, and opened them to nothing but steam.

Stepping out, her legs wobbled, knees giving way. She caught the edge of the vanity, her hand tightening around it, nails scraping against the cool surface. Her throat closed—something tight, rough against her skin. Air thinned. Then nothing—just a tangle of steam and her heartbeat pounding in her ears. Her chest heaved. The bathroom blurred around her, the fog creeping in again.

Her reflection in the mirror—half-covered in mist—stared back, blank-eyed. The grip on her throat loosened, replaced by the chill of the bathroom air. She took a deep breath, blinking away the lingering ghost of Mel'nyk's hands. *It was over.* She told herself that. But the pressure hadn't fully left her chest. Her fingers fumbled as she wrapped the towel around her. Her skin felt too raw, exposed, the heat of the shower now an uncomfortable itch.

She walked back to the room, each step automatic, the ground unsteady beneath her feet. Clothes waited. She pulled on her underwear, the fabric cool. She slid the garter belt around her waist. Her breath hitched as the garter belt cinched around her waist. For a split second, she felt pressure around her throat—hands tightening, unseen. She forced a breath, eyes flicking to her reflection to pull herself back. *Waist. Just fabric.*

Focus, damn it. Her hands shook as she reached for the stockings, securing them with quick, jerky movements. She dabbed on makeup with practiced strokes, the feel of the brush against her skin too light, too distant, as if her hands belonged to someone else.

She glanced in the mirror, her reflection wavering as she slipped into the red dress. It hugged her form, sequins catching the dim light, yet something was off, like she was only partially there. She blinked, pulling herself back to the present. *Focus,* she told herself. The mission awaited. She was prepared, armor in place, but pieces of her mind still lingered in shadows she couldn't fully banish.

Liliya joined Sergei and Nadya in the dimly lit living area, the worn map spread across the coffee table between them. Their faces were etched with focus as they plotted in hushed tones, sketching out the plan. Every move mattered; the lives of the unwitting workers depended on their timing. The quiet tick of the clock punctuated the tension that hung in the air.

Sergei's gaze lingered on Liliya as he traced a path on the map, his fingers trembling slightly. "The signal will be at 5:30. You need to be in place," he said, his voice low, betraying a hint of the unease he worked hard to hide.

Liliya met his eyes with a calm nod, her expression steady. "I will," she replied, her voice measured, but the weight of the mission pressed behind her composure.

Nadya reached out, her hand settling over Liliya's with a firm yet silent plea. The warmth of her touch contrasted with the chill creeping into Liliya's thoughts. Nadya squeezed once, her grip tightening as if to hold onto something more than just the moment.

Liliya returned the squeeze, her lips pressing into a faint, determined smile. No words were exchanged, only the quiet understanding of what was at stake. The ticking clock filled the silence, stretching each second until 1725 arrived.

Liliya stood, the movement quiet yet final. She glanced at Sergei and Nadya, their expressions revealing what their words could not. Sergei's hand tightened on her shoulder, a steady, anchoring grip.

The chill of the room seemed to thicken around her, pressing close. For a split second, the shadowed doorway seemed to narrow, like the long corridors of that basement cell in Lipetsk—dark, damp, closing in. Her pulse quickened, her hand hovering instinctively over her weapon.

The scent of Sergei's coat—a faint mix of cologne and machine oil—snapped her back. She forced a breath, shaking off the memory. *This isn't then*, she told herself. Eyes steady, she pulled away, her focus tightening as she fixed her gaze on the distant point just beyond the door.

As she stepped towards the door, she paused, casting a glance over her shoulder. Her gaze met theirs one last time, a fleeting smile crossing her lips. She nodded, a simple gesture of thanks, before disappearing into the shadows outside.

Just as Liliya prepared for her dinner with Volkov, Anatoli sat in the truck, surrounded by the work crew as the engine rumbled beneath them. The smell of oil and dust mingled with an undercurrent of fear that clung to the men. His fingers brushed the rough fabric of his trousers, his movements steady, controlled, as he mentally rehearsed each step. The hidden bag, only feet away, felt heavy in his thoughts.

The truck jolted through the plant gates, gravel crunching under its tires. The guard's indifferent glance barely brushed the vehicle, but the sound of his pen scratching against the clipboard felt louder than it should. A tiny victory, unnoticed but vital.

When the truck stopped, the quiet felt almost deafening. The crew moved as one, the sound of crates scraping metal mingling with the heavy thud of boots on the ground. His fingers slid over the cold metal handle of the hidden bag, the chill biting into his skin, a stark reminder of the danger lurking behind every gesture.

His breath tightened as he slipped the bag from its hiding place, each movement precise despite the tension in his chest. A low hum reverberated through the walls, the plant's lifeblood pulsing beneath his feet as the air thickened with each step. The stairwell yawned before him, the air cool and stale, carrying the faint scent of damp concrete. Each step down echoed, the dim light casting long, distorted shadows on the walls, making the narrow space feel suffocating.

Inside, Anatoli moved with deliberate care, retrieving the bag and making his way to the storage area. The tanks loomed in the dim light. He crouched, placing the bag with precision. His heartbeat quickened but his hands remained steady. As he left, the plant's hum faded, the faint scuffle of his crew's distraction echoed through the halls. The shouts and commotion were already dying down, and Anatoli smoothly rejoined the team, sliding back into place as if nothing had happened. The crates moved again, the rough wood scraping over the steel floor of the truck, the operation moving like clockwork.

As the truck rattled away from the plant, the guard's indifferent wave felt like the final exhale after holding their breath for too long. The truck's engine hummed in the background, the tension easing with every bump in the road, every meter that passed beneath them. Anatoli's voice crackled through the comms; the relief palpable in his tone as he delivered the simple, triumphant message:

At The Prestige, Liliya heard Anatoli's voice over her comm, a steady reminder of the plan. "Bag is in place. Good luck." She allowed herself a brief smile as she crossed to the main entrance, where a soldier waited beside a black Mercedes. "Commander Volkov requests your presence, Miss," he announced, the formality a thin veneer over his underlying tension.

With a nod, Liliya secured her handbag, with her silenced weapon, and waited for the soldier to open the back passenger door for her. She stepped inside the car and sat down; the door was closed behind her. As they departed, the car swallowed her into its depths, cruising towards a destination fraught with danger and deception.

The brief journey to the command center concluded with an air of expectancy as they pulled up to the grand facade. Commander Volkov, anticipation etched into his features, awaited on the veranda, cradling a sizable rectangular box. Its contents, two dozen roses sourced from the far reaches of Voronezh, were a vivid reminder of his intentions. As he approached, the car door was opened by the driver and Volkov presented the blossoms to Liliya with a flourish. Her response was a measured smile, the epitome of calculated gratitude, as she accepted the gift.

Volkov extended the bouquet slowly, his smile tightening as he held her gaze, his fingers lingering on the stems as if reluctant to let go. A muscle in his jaw flickered, almost daring her to question the gesture.

Liliya accepted the bouquet with a measured smile, the warmth and reservation finely tuned. "Thank you, Commander. They're beautiful." Her tone was steady, even as the scent of roses nudged something distant, a flicker of memory she swiftly buried.

When she expressed a desire to explore the premises, Volkov, captivated by her enigmatic charm, eagerly complied. He led her through the corridors, his voice echoing off the walls as he boasted about the house's secrets. Her heels clicked in sync with Volkov's voice, the sound off by half a beat. She kept pace, ignoring the hum in her ears. The rhythm belonged somewhere else—a hallway, a lab. The scent of oil mingled with roses, thick in the air. Volkov's words pulled her back. *Stay present. Move with him.*

Volkov pushed the door open, gesturing to the equipment inside. "This… is where everything flows," he said, his tone low and prideful, his eyes tracing the machines as if each piece reflected his own achievements.

Liliya nodded, her expression neutral. "Impressive. How many operators?" The words left her mouth automatically as she noted the equipment, the layout. The details blurred at the edges. The hum wavered, static curling through the air. A cabinet? Or just the radio—her head couldn't sort the difference. Her breath caught. She forced it out, returning her focus to the man beside her.

Volkov smiled proudly. "Just two operators, but they never miss a beat." Volkov's smile curved. "Nothing escapes us."

They moved on, Volkov's voice a steady stream of self-importance as they entered the interrogation suite. Her gaze snagged on the interrogation chair in the center of the room—reclined, waiting. For a heartbeat, the room shifted, sterile and stark. *Cold metal, light bearing down. Hands.* Liliya clenched her jaw and exhaled, bringing herself back in Volkov's smug presence beside her.

"I see. Quite comprehensive," she murmured, her voice betraying nothing.

She kept her face unreadable, but inside, the walls of the house seemed to shift unnervingly. Each room Volkov showed was another layer of his power, but with it came the fragmented echoes of her past, snapping at the edges of her focus. The ticking of a clock somewhere merged with the dull thud of a heartbeat—her heartbeat, too loud in her ears.

They then came to a solid oak door with finely chisels adornment. Volkov opened the door and stepped back to allow Liliya a better view. "This is my private study. A place for contemplation and strategy."

Liliya briefly scanned the room, "Quite the collection of books. You must spend a lot of time here."

"Indeed. Knowledge is power, after all," Volkov remarked with pride.

Liliya smiled faintly, "Yes, it certainly is."

When they returned to the main hall, Volkov was undeterred by her seemingly detached responses. His enthusiasm remained intact.

"Well, I hope you've enjoyed the tour. I'll make sure dinner is exceptional tonight," he said, stepping back with a flourish.

"I look forward to it, Commander. Thank you for showing me around." Her tone was polite, distant—barely holding together the cracks beneath. She felt the tremor in her fingers again, hidden as she clasped her hands together. As Volkov turned away, the chandelier above caught the light just so. Light flashed—too bright, too sharp. Her breath caught— *antiseptic? Not here. Not now.* She drew a quiet breath, her composure wavering, and followed Volkov toward the dining room.

They exchanged polite smiles, the unspoken dynamics of their interaction simmering beneath the surface. As they prepared for the evening's dinner, both were keenly aware of the delicate game being played, each move calculated, each reaction measured.

The dining room had become a battlefield, the roasted Peking Duck at the center like a forgotten relic. Volkov held court with an air of practiced ease, though Liliya could see the subtle falters beneath his charm—his laugh a beat too loud, his smile lingering a moment too long. Volkov raised his glass, his hand wobbled slightly before steadying itself midair. His eye s holding Liliya's with an unblinking intensity, "To power, my dear. Always best to know which side to favor, wouldn't you agree?"

The vodka's sharp scent hit her, cutting through the room's warmth. Shadows closed in—a different room, the eyes blank, blood drying on gloved hands. Liliya's grip tightened on her glass. She blinked, centering herself in Volkov's careless grin across the table. The chandelier glinted like a blade. She smiled, her voice steady, "To power and prosperity, indeed." Her gaze sharpened, locking onto Volkov's increasingly strained expression. *Let's see how long you can keep it together, Volkov.*

Volkov's eyes met hers, and for a fleeting second, the mask slipped—a flicker of weariness quickly smothered beneath another grin. She saw it then: the cracks forming, the bravado beginning to splinter under the weight of the evening.

The conversation drifted as the meal wore on, Volkov's hand returning to his glass with increasing frequency. His words softened around the edges, the polish dulling sip by sip. Liliya pressed forward, her voice light but sharp, cutting into him with precision.

"Quite the spread, Volkov. You must be proud. But tell me, is it all just for show?" The casual jab landed with precision. Volkov's fingers tightened on his glass, knuckles whitening as he forced a chuckle. His gaze shifted briefly, hardening as he took a measured sip, "I assure you, my dear, everything here is real. A testament to my success."

Liliya leaned forward slightly, a ghost of a smile playing on her lips. "Success, yes. But how much of that is really yours, and how much have you borrowed from others—those stronger than you?" Her voice dripped with mockery; each word designed to peel away his composure.

Volkov's smile slipped, only for a second, before he forced it back, too tight, too fixed. Volkov's face blurred—wrong somehow, familiar. *Mel'nyk? No. Commander.* She swallowed hard, shoving the thought away.

He leaned forward, pouring himself another drink. His hand jerked, spilling a few drops of vodka, but he didn't seem to notice. "Everything here is mine," he muttered, each word heavy and bitter as he raised the glass again, a thin veil over his annoyance.

Good, he's unraveling. She kept pushing, her words precise, cutting. " Funny. You almost sound like you believe it."

Volkov's hand lingered on his glass before he set it down with a deliberate thud, his gaze hardening. "Believe me proof isn't something I lack." His fingers drummed once against the table, a rhythm slow and measured. "I keep certain things close—where only I'd know to look."

Feigning disbelief, she tilted her head, her eyes widening just enough. "And where is this proof that only you can find it?" Her voice was light, but inside, she was already celebrating.

Volkov leaned forward, his breath heavy with alcohol and misplaced pride. "Everything that matters," he slurred, the words dragging through his throat, "is right where I keep it. Where no one else can touch it."

Liliya leaned back, a satisfied glint in her eye, "Really?" The challenge was sharp, cutting through the haze of his intoxication. She kept her face composed, masking the tension beneath her calm exterior. *He's taking the bait. Stay calm. You've got this.*

Volkov's jaw clenched, the tension in his expression now impossible to hide. His movements were growing sloppier, his bravado melting into something desperate. The trap had been set, and he was walking into it with every drink, every word.

The command to bring the car around came too quickly, the bark in his voice more of a plea than an order. "Driver! Bring the car! We're going to the plant!" His words blurred at the edges, pride and frustration bleeding together. Volkov stood unsteadily, his swagger diminished but still intact enough to mask his unraveling state.

Volkov leaned close, his voice dropping, almost a whisper meant for her alone. "Patience, my dear. When we arrive, I'll show you things worth waiting for." His gaze held hers a beat too long, something dark flickering behind his smile.

Liliya nodded, her smile feigned, hiding the tumultuous mix of fear and resolve within her. "I can't wait to see it, Volkov."

As they departed the opulent confines of the dining room, Liliya made a calculated gesture of normalcy, securing her shoulder bag and the box of roses under the guise of preserving their beauty.

Their brief journey to the plant mirrored their earlier drive and was marked by the ease with which they navigated the security checkpoint. The guards, recognizing Volkov, waved them through without a second glance. With a salute he greeted Volkov and Liliya, "Evening, Commander. Ma'am."

Volkov waved dismissively, a self-satisfied smirk on his face. "We're staying in my office tonight. No interruptions."

Liliya maintained a neutral expression, her face a mask of composure. Inside, her mind was a whirlwind of thoughts, each one a flicker of strategy and anticipation. As the car rolled smoothly towards the plant's main building, she mentally rehearsed every detail of the plan, her focus narrowing with each passing moment.

Upon arrival at the plant's entry doors, Volkov, visibly impaired, performed the gentlemanly act of opening the car door for Liliya, though his movements were shakey. "Allow me, my dear."

Liliya smiled, "Thank you, Volkov."

Dismissing the driver with a wave of his hand, Volkov led the way, his steps unsteady but determined. The plant's industrial expanse loomed like a behemoth in the twilight, casting long shadows over their path. Liliya, in her role as the unsuspecting guest, feigned awe at the monolithic structures around her. "This place is incredible, Volkov. You must be very proud."

"Oh, you have no idea. Let me show you inside," Volkov replied, puffing out his chest.

Inside, the cavernous space of the plant floor unfolded before them. Volkov, ever eager to impress, saluted the guards outside his office with a bravado that belied his diminishing coherence. "At ease, gentlemen. We're here for a private tour."

The guards nodded, allowing them to pass without question. Liliya followed Volkov into the office, her heart a battleground between fear and the unyielding resolve to see her mission through to its perilous end.

As the door closed behind them, Volkov turned to Liliya, a triumphant look in his eyes. " He glanced around, hands in his pockets as if he were merely introducing her to a rare work of art. "You see, Liliya, not many are invited here. Real power doesn't need to announce itself." His gaze slid to her, something knowing in his eyes.

Liliya nodded, her mind already calculating the next steps. The stage was set, and the night's clandestine activities were about to begin.

His voice, tinged with pride and alcohol-induced bravado, broke the industrial silence. "Well, there it is," he proclaimed, gesturing towards the safe with a flourish. "This hand is the only one that can open it."

Liliya, maintaining her composure despite the adrenaline coursing through her veins, challenged him. "Show me," she urged, her words laced with an implicit challenge.

As Volkov turned his attention to the safe, Liliya's battle with her own trembling resolve reached its zenith. Despite her quivering fingers, she found the cold grip of her pistol, drawing it with a silent promise of finality. Volkov, oblivious to the imminent betrayal, proudly presented the fruits of his vanity — the blueprints, a testament to his hubris.

In the moment that followed, time seemed to distill into a crystalline tableau; Volkov, turning with triumph in his eyes, met not admiration, but the cold gaze of retribution. Liliya, her resolve solidifying into action, aligned the silencer with a precision born of necessity. The silencer coughed. Volkov crumpled.

With the grim task completed, Liliya spared a moment to gaze upon the man who embodied the oppressive force she so vehemently opposed. Her disdain for him and all he represented fueled her actions as she confirmed his demise with two more calculated shots. The blueprints, now unguarded in his lax grip, were quickly appropriated and concealed among the innocuous roses—a stark contrast to the violence that had just unfolded.

Bag over one shoulder and plans securely stowed, Liliya made her exit, her facade of composure intact as she passed the unsuspecting guards. "He's passed out and is going to need the night, boys. I've locked the door, so that no one accidently wakes him. Make sure he isn't disturbed," Liliya advised the guards. "He really enjoyed himself tonight and had a little too much I think." The guards nodded, aware that the commander was clearly drunk when he arrived earlier.

Once past the guards' eyesight, Liliya veered off her projected route, slipping into the changing room. Inside, the air was heavy with sweat and cleaning chemicals, clinging to her skin like a second layer. The door shut behind her with a hollow clang, and she leaned against it, her pulse hammering against her ribs.

Her hands gripped the edge of the sink, knuckles pale under the fluorescent lights. Thoughts flickered—disjointed and intrusive. *What if the guards had stopped me? Missed something?* The scent of bleach pulled her back, sharp and acrid. She inhaled deeply—once, twice. *Get it together.*

Peeling off the sequined dress, Liliya slipped into the stiff fabric of the cleaner's uniform. It scratched at her skin, grounding her. The sound of zippers and Velcro sealed her back into her role, her mind narrowing to the task at hand.

"Moving toward the tanks," she whispered into her comms.

"Roger. Be careful," Davyd's voice buzzed in her ear, low and steady.

Navigating the plant's shadowed corridors, Liliya kept her steps soft and precise. The faint hum of machinery vibrated through the walls, matching the rhythm of her heartbeat. Down the stairwell she moved, the scent of metal and grease thickening with every step.

In the dim storage room, she crouched next to Anatoli's hidden bag. Cold metal bit into her fingers. *Focus.* She slipped the charge between tanks, thumb pressed firm on the timer. Click—0605. Each second ticked, steady as her heartbeat.

"Tanks charged, moving back to the locker room," Liliya reported.

"Be careful of the 2230 patrol moving towards you," Davyd advised.

She retraced her steps, each footfall light and deliberate, slipping into the locker room to store the explosives in her locker. Keeping a few of the devices in the bag, she adjusted her grip and moved into the plant's corridors towards the south support columns. The faint tang of oil lingered in the air, mixing with the metallic bite of tension. Every movement was calculated, part of a choreography she could not afford to miss. As she went about her nightly chores, she used this guise to locate the designated charge location for the south support columns, then placed and activated them.

At 0200 hours, returning to the change room she grabbed the remaining devices, placing them in the bag. Repeating the same choreography for the north support columns. With this completed she turned her attention the final charge for the generator in the center of the plant.

Near the generator a sound stopped her cold. Footsteps echoed. Close. She froze, breath shallow, hand flexed on the charge. *Move. One shot at this.* Her heart thudded, pulsing through her fingers.

She grabbed a trash bin and rummaged through it, her hands brushing discarded wrappers and tools. The guard's boots scuffed behind her, his shadow spilling long across the wall.

"What are you doing here?" His tone was sharp, suspicious.

"Taking out the trash," Liliya answered smoothly, her voice even. "They needed this area cleaned before shift's end."

The guard's gaze lingered, scrutinizing her. The smell of oil grew heavier in the confined space, mingling with the faint scent of her own sweat. *Keep steady. Let him buy it.*

The guard grunted. "Finish quickly. You're not supposed to be here."

Liliya nodded, offering a small, deferential smile. "Of course, sir."

His footsteps receded, echoing down the corridor. She exhaled slowly, letting the tension drain from her shoulders. *That was close. Too close.*

"Area clear," she whispered into the comms.

Yaroslav's voice buzzed through the line. "Everyone's in place. We're ready."

"Charges set," she whispered as she placed the last charge.

Davyd's voice broke through the tension. "Drone strike on Lipetsk was successful. Get out now."

Liliya returned to the locker room and opened her locker. Grabbing the blueprints from the box with the roses and her handbag, she stuffed them into the bag used for the explosives. She closed the door and made her way for the front exit.

The corridors twisted around her, familiar yet suddenly foreign, each step bringing her closer to the exit. Alarms blared from deep within the plant—sharp, jagged bursts—and the pounding of fists against Volkov's locked door echoed through the halls. Panic surged around her, but Liliya moved with purpose, her focus sharp.

She reached the threshold just as the first explosion shattered the night. A blast of heat hit her, throwing her off balance. She hit the ground hard, the impact jarring her bones. For a moment, everything blurred—flashes of fire and debris painting the sky, the air thick with dust and smoke. *Get up. Keep moving.*

She staggered to her feet, heart pounding as secondary detonations erupted behind her. Nadya and Sergei appeared ahead, silhouettes frozen against the firelight. Then, from somewhere nearby, a faint groan pierced the chaos.

"Wait!" Liliya called, pointing toward the sound.

"We don't have time!" Sergei barked, panic lacing his voice.

Ignoring him, Liliya sprinted toward the noise. She found a young worker slumped against the wall, blood soaking through his shirt. His eyes flickered open, glazed with pain.

"Help me," he whispered, his voice rasping like sandpaper.

Liliya knelt beside him, the scent of iron filling her nose. Her hands moved on instinct, searching for something—anything—to stop the bleeding.

"Liliya, we have to go!" Sergei shouted.

"He'll die if we leave him," she shot back, pressing fabric to the wound. Her pulse thundered in her ears, but her hands remained steady.

Sergei and Nadya hoisted the injured man between them, dragging him away from the blast zone. Liliya tore a strip from her shirt and bound the wound as another explosion rocked the ground beneath them. *Doctor or operative? Make a choice.* The thought flitted through her mind, fleeting but sharp.

When the bleeding slowed, Liliya stood, her hands slick with blood. "He's stable for now," she muttered, already moving toward the waiting Lada.

Anatoli stood at the driver's door just outside the perimeter gate, his eyes sharp as a young guard rounded the corner, gun drawn. "Stop! I'm detaining you!"

Without a sound, Anatoli moved. The guard dropped before he could react, Anatoli's hand over his mouth as the knife found its mark.

"Thanks," Liliya whispered, gratitude passing like a shadow across her face.

Anatoli gave a quick, tight nod, brushing his hand over her shoulder as if sealing an unspoken promise. His eyes flicked toward the road ahead. "Come on," he muttered, the weight of what wasn't said settling between them like smoke.

They reached the Lada just as a military SUV pulled up, its tires crunching against loose gravel. Two soldiers disembarked, their boots hitting the ground with a dull thud, rifles slung across their chests, blocking the road with practiced precision.

Behind them, the plant groaned, collapsing inward as flames roared into the night, turning the sky a bruised orange. Heat radiated from the inferno, a dry, searing wave that seemed to chase them even as the crumbling structure sagged further into ruin. Shadows danced along the empty road, flickering like ghosts, too fast to grasp, too close to ignore.

"Get in the Lada," Anatoli ordered, his voice low but firm. "I'll handle this."

Liliya's fingers hovered near the car door, her senses stretched thin, every sound and smell amplified. The acrid scent of burning chemicals stung her nostrils, mingling with the oily residue of smoke. It clung to her throat, thick and sour, making each breath feel like a fight for air. Heat was everywhere—oppressive and suffocating—clinging to her skin, causing sweat to trickle slowly down her spine, her shirt sticking to her back like a second skin. Her pulse thudded in her ears, the rapid beat out of sync with the mechanical creak of metal collapsing behind them, its dull groan echoing in the distance.

The soldiers stood rigid; their faces unreadable beneath the flickering light from the fire. Their silhouettes shifted, blurred in the haze, as if the heat warped the air between them. Time felt jagged, fractured—too slow and too fast all at once. *Too close... too close... Have to move. Can't stop.*

The air vibrated with tension, the moment stretched impossibly thin. Liliya's mouth was dry, the taste of ash bitter on her tongue. Her fingers twitched toward the car door, her body taut, ready to spring, but she held still. The silence between them grew heavy, too full of questions left unspoken. Every heartbeat felt like it might break the stillness.

Anatoli's steady steps to the car broke the fragile moment. The gravel crunched beneath his boots, each step deliberate, measured. His heartbeat hammered beneath his ribs, loud and insistent, almost drowning out the crackle of flames behind him. The weight of past choices hung heavy on his shoulders—the memory of his boys, their faces pale and small, flashed through his mind. It was a cold, sharp pain, cutting through the heat of the fire. He knew what it meant to sacrifice, and he'd do it again.

His voice came out steady, wrapped in calm deceit, as if the chaos around them had no hold on him. Anatoli adjusted his grip on the car door, as if testing its weight, his thumb flicking absently over the latch. "They're injured," he said, jerking his chin toward the car, his voice as smooth as oil. "Explosion caught them bad. I need to get them out." His hand drifted to his belt, brushing the worn leather, ready to move if the words didn't land.

The soldiers shifted; their movements slow, cautious. One rubbed his jaw, his eyes narrowing with suspicion, while the other exhaled through his nose, a low grunt of doubt. The road shimmered between them, a battlefield of silence and suspicion. Liliya's grip tightened on the car door handle, the metal hot against her skin, burning. Her breaths came shallow, her chest tightening under the weight of anticipation. The heat pressed against her, almost unbearable, the tension coiling tighter. *Don't shoot. Not yet. Not yet.*

The moment stretched long enough for second thoughts to crawl in like snakes in the grass. Anatoli's jaw clenched as a bead of sweat slipped down his temple, the revolver's handle a silent comfort against his palm. He caught the soldiers exchanging glances. His pulse thrummed in his throat. *Too close... just wait. Not yet.*

The air between them was thick, unmoving, the weight of what would come next pressing down like a vice. The soldiers hesitated, just long enough.

His grip on the revolver tightened, and in one fluid motion, it was drawn. The cold steel felt right in his hand, heavy with intent. Time snapped back into place, sharp and immediate. The revolver bucked twice in his hand, the report sharp and final. Smoke curled from the muzzle, lost in the roar of the fire. One breath, then two bodies fell, limbs folding awkwardly beneath them as if the strings holding them up had been cut. The shots were swallowed by the roar of the fire behind them, the heat intensifying as the flames licked higher into the night.

Anatoli didn't look back. He sprinted to the Lada, breath tight in his chest, heat clawing at his heels. "Get in!" Anatoli hissed, yanking the driver's door open with one hand while turning the ignition with the other. The engine coughed, then roared to life as flames clawed higher into the night. Gravel spat beneath the tires as the Lada lurched forward.

The journey to the safe house was a blur of motion and emotion, each block traversed a step further from the devastation behind them and a move closer to the uncertain future that awaited.

First, Anatoli dropped Sergei and Nadya at their home, then turned the car in the direction of the hotel room. As they drove to their rendezvous site, Liliya prepared for the next phase, their escape. However, in the aftermath of the plant's destruction, the plan for a swift and silent exfiltration began to unravel in her mind. The air was thick with tension, each passing moment amplifying the dread of uncertainty.

Liliya's mind raced with scenarios, each more dire than the last. She glanced at Anatoli, whose face was set in grim determination, his eyes scanning the road for any signs of pursuit. They had to reach the command center and regroup, but the clock was ticking, and the margins for error were vanishingly slim.

As they approached the hotel, Anatoli parked the car in a secluded spot. "Stay sharp," he said, his voice low and urgent. "We're not out of this yet."

They exited the car, moving swiftly but cautiously towards the hotel entrance. Inside, the atmosphere was tense, the usual bustle subdued by the undercurrent of fear and anticipation. They made their way to the room, where they would lay low until the next phase of their exfiltration could be put into action.

When they entered, the room, the former command center, was now clear of indications of their clandestine activities, bags packed with the equipment and documents sat by the door. Prior to taking his position in the forest, Davyd had prepared for a quick exit from the area. Liliya checked the windows and doors, ensuring everything was secure. Anatoli took a seat at the small table, his posture alert. The weight of their situation pressed down on them, but they knew they had to stay focused.

"Anatoli, they should be here by now. Yaroslav should have picked Davyd up right after the plant went up. What do we do??" Liliya asked, her voice steady despite the turmoil inside her.

"We wait for them for another forty minutes" Anatoli replied. "Then we move to our contingency plan, load up the equipment and get out of here."

Minutes passed with agonizing slowness. The tension in the room was palpable, each creak and whisper of the wind outside magnified in the silence. Liliya and Anatoli kept their vigil, their eyes betraying the weight of their thoughts.

Finally, a soft knock on the door broke the silence. Anatoli tensed, motioning for Liliya to stay back. He approached the door cautiously, peering through the peephole before unlocking it.

Yaroslav entered the room, his expression grave. Liliya, who had been pacing nervously, immediately stopped and turned to him. A surge of relief coursed through her at the sight of a familiar face, but it was quickly quenched by the dire look in his eyes. Liliya asked anxiously, "Yaroslav, what happened? Where's Davyd?"

Yaroslav took a deep breath, his hands trembling slightly as he removed his cap and held it tightly. Yaroslav, his voice heavy, answered, "Liliya, there's no easy way to say this. Davyd has been captured."

The room seemed to spin slightly as Yaroslav's words sank in. Liliya felt a momentary dizziness as if the ground beneath her had shifted. The shock was like a physical blow, leaving her momentarily breathless. Not Davyd. He was always so careful; she thought despairingly as a torrent of questions and fears began to crowd her mind.

Struggling to maintain her composure, Liliya inhaled sharply, her chest rising visibly with the effort. Her face, though pale, was set. She squared her shoulders, standing a bit straighter, as if bracing herself against the storm of emotions threatening to overwhelm her. Her eyes narrowed with a steely focus, and her brow furrowed, as she managed to steady her voice. "How did it happen? Where is he?" she asked, each word measured, barely louder than a whisper.

Yaroslav's eyes met hers, filled with sorrow and regret. "I was on my way to pick him up. And when I got there. a military transport truck was parked by the grove." Yaroslav began to walk them through the events, "I drove past and parked down the road and waited. After a while a saw soldiers drag Davyd out of the trees and throw him in the back of the truck."

Liliya's hands clenched into fists, her knuckles white with tension. "And then what? Did you follow them?" Liliya demanded.

Yaroslav nodded his head, "I followed the truck to the command center. They dragged him inside. He looked... he looked bad, Liliya."

217

Her knees buckled. The ground wasn't steady—it wavered, just like Yaroslav's voice. *Davyd... gone.* She pressed her hand to her chest, as if she couldn't hold herself together. The sight of Liliya, once the embodiment of stoic determination, now succumbing to the tempest of her fears, was a stark reminder of the personal stakes entwined in their collective endeavor.

Anatoli and Yaroslav looked down at Liliya unsure of what to do. Desperate to break the hold Liliya's fears now had, Anatoli stepped forward and gripped her shoulders, his voice a low rasp. "Pull yourself together, Liliya. Davyd needs you now more than ever." It was not just a call to arms but a lifeline, pulling her back from the brink of despair.

Liliya rose from the ground and walked to the bathroom. She splashed water over her face, her reflection fragmented in the cracked mirror. The coolness stung, but it pulled her back—away from Davyd's capture, away from fear. When she stepped out of the bathroom, Anatoli's eyes held the same urgency as hers. 'Forty minutes,' he reminded her. "Then we move."

EIGHTEEN

Captured

While Liliya grappled with the approaching guard, a local hunter moved quietly through the forest east of the plant, his steps assured. His routine was shattered when he spotted a figure through the trees—a man focused on a scope, murmuring into a hidden device. Lately, his hunts had been disrupted by strangers in the woods, but he'd dismissed them as fellow hunters. Today, the lone figure's intensity and secrecy set his instincts on edge.

Retracing his steps, a growing unease drove him home, where his resolve solidified. At the command center, his news stirred immediate alarm among the young sentries, who, with the commander absent, brought him to the lieutenant.

The hunter's earnest recounting of a lone figure surveying the plant cut through the room's tension. Sensing an opportunity, the lieutenant swiftly marshaled a squad of a dozen men and set out for the forest, resolve and apprehension mixed among them.

The lieutenant barked instructions; his gaze sharp as he adjusted a soldier's rifle strap with a quick, forceful tug. "We move as one," he said, his voice low but leaving no room for debate. The men nodded, their eyes a mix of apprehension and obedience. As they filed into formation, the lieutenant's glance flicked over each of them, his lips pressed tight as if weighing their readiness—and finding them just shy of his standard.

As sun was breaking the horizon and they approached their destination, a radio message heightened the tension: a drone strike had just demolished a steel mill in Lipetsk. Though miles away, this news confirmed the broader conflict's reach and the hunter's warning, added urgency to their mission. The unit moved stealthily through the forest, guided by the hunter's information. The trees, silent witnesses, seemed to hold their breath as the soldiers advanced.

In the dim light, Davyd's silhouette emerged, isolated and unaware. The lieutenant signaled his men to flank him, cutting off any escape. As they tightened the noose, Davyd's defiant voice rang out: "Drone strike on Lipetsk successful." The lieutenant stepped forward, pressing his revolver against Davyd's head.

As Davyd's hands rose, his gaze caught on his watch—0604 hours. That familiar tick grounded him, each second steady, unyielding, beyond the chaos. The first blast split the morning silence, fire slicing through dawn's chill. He braced himself, jaw set, his pulse matching the clock's rhythm. No matter what, he told himself, time would keep moving forward.

Subsequent explosions broke their stunned silence, each blast a death knell for the facility they swore to protect. Flames devoured the plant, reducing it to a smoldering graveyard. The realization hit them hard: many of their comrades, possibly including their commander, were buried beneath the rubble.

The plant's destruction ignited a brutal frenzy among the soldiers. Two stepped forward, raining vicious blows on Davyd, who crumpled, shielding his head. The lieutenant watched with dark satisfaction, allowing the violence to unfold as a grim assertion of his newfound authority. With the commander buried beneath the rubble, the lieutenant felt destined to fill the leadership void, his authority cemented by the violence he permitted.

The lieutenant watched in silence as the soldiers beat Davyd, his gaze cold, unmoving. He allowed the violence to stretch until Davyd's body slackened under the assault, consciousness slipping away like air from a punctured lung. Only then did he raise a hand, signaling for the blows to stop. The men stood back, panting and dazed, as if the brutality had drained something from them too.

"Enough," the lieutenant muttered, though the flicker of disappointment in his eyes betrayed his lingering thirst for control.

Minutes passed before he gave his next order. "Get him up."

The soldiers obeyed, dragging Davyd's limp body without care, his arms scraping over dirt and jagged stones. One soldier's jaw clenched as he pulled, the sharp grind of teeth barely audible over the shuffling steps. They weren't just following orders—they were trying to purge the tension thrumming in their bones. Each rough tug was more than an action; it was a release.

Davyd's body hit the ground hard, a silent rhythm in the soldiers' arms. They moved without a word, sweat and blood streaking their faces. With a grunt, they threw him into the truck bed. He landed with a dull thud.

The journey back to the command center was quiet at first—just the low rumble of the engine, the occasional jolt of the truck over ruts in the road. Then one of the soldiers nudged Davyd with his boot, testing for a reaction. When none came, another followed with a half-hearted kick.

"This one doesn't even feel it anymore," one muttered, his voice hollow. There was no triumph in his tone—just fatigue and something darker, unspoken.

They took turns, more out of habit than malice—punches, kicks, the occasional spit aimed at Davyd's battered face. With every blow, their actions seemed to weigh heavier, each strike dragging them further into the muck of their own cruelty. None of them stopped. To stop would be to think, and thinking was dangerous.

By the time the truck lurched to a halt at the command center, Davyd's body was a canvas of bruises—his skin swollen and marred in dark hues that mirrored the soldiers' inner turmoil. They hauled him out with little care, his body scraping over the truck's metal edges and crashing to the ground.

"Get him inside," the lieutenant barked, breaking the silence.

The soldiers moved without hesitation, but there was no joy in their movements, only a mechanical obedience. As they dragged Davyd through the hallways, his body thudded against door frames and furniture. One soldier winced at the sound, a flicker of discomfort flashing across his face, but he kept moving. There was no room for hesitation here.

Each impact dragged a groan from Davyd, but the soldiers kept silent, their expressions fixed. They couldn't afford to look—couldn't let themselves feel anything. They dumped Davyd into the interrogation chair without ceremony, their hands already reaching for the tools they knew they would need. One soldier hesitated, his fingers trembling as he gripped the back of the chair. For a moment, his eyes locked on Davyd's swollen face, and something flickered—guilt, maybe, or regret. It didn't matter.

"Keep going," the lieutenant ordered, his voice cutting through the tension. And just like that, the moment was gone. The soldier's grip firmed, and the routine began again. *Stay conscious. Feel the pain. It's a reminder you're still alive. Just hold on.* His thoughts drifted to his comrades. Liliya, Anatoli... *they're counting on me. I can't let them down.*

In the stark confines of the room, Davyd was forcibly bound to a chair with a back that could be reclined. *This isn't the first time. You've endured worse. Just breathe.* The shallow tub in the room caught his eye. *Waterboarding. They're going to try to drown you. Remember your training. Stay calm.*

The men readied the pails and towels without a word, their faces set. The lieutenant's eyes stayed fixed on him, each glare boring in like a blade. Davyd felt his skin prickle, the cold sweat seeping down his back as if the very walls were leeching warmth from his bones.

Ice-cold water slammed into Davyd's face, the shock pulling him to full awareness. He blinked hard, steadying his breath. He felt the lieutenant's stare, sharp and waiting. The questions began:

The lieutenant's eyes narrowed. "Lipetsk. What was your part?"

Davyd's jaw clenched; his glare fixed.

It'll get worse," the lieutenant warned, leaning in close enough for Davyd to catch the scent of vodka lingering on his breath. The weight of his promise hung heavy, and for a split second, Davyd wondered how much more he could take. Each pulse of pain chipped away at his resolve, but he latched onto a memory—Liliya, her voice low but firm, saying he'd make it back. She'd said it without hesitation. He focused on her words, wrapping himself in them like armor. Davyd stayed silent, defiance flickering in his eyes.

The lieutenant's scowl deepened. Good, Davyd thought. *Let him burn.*

The chair back was reclined, leaving Davyd at a precarious angle, vulnerable and exposed. A heavy, wet towel was draped over his face. In an attempt to control his reactions to what was about to happen.

Davyd clenched his fists, the coarse fabric digging into his wrists, burning like sandpaper against raw skin. He bit back the wince, focusing on the slight give in the chair's legs—counting seconds, feeling for weakness.

The first splash hit, ice-cold, driving every breath from his lungs. Water seeped into his nose, laced with the rank smell of mold, rotting concrete—a reminder of old basements, barely ventilated. He forced himself to hold steady, each breath stolen but measured, grounding him as the chill crept through his body.

When the chair snapped upright, Davyd sucked in cold air, steadying himself on each breath. He forced his mind back—cold nights in the field, crouched with his team, each breath a countdown until the next strike. *Keep breathing,* he reminded himself, placing each thought in the memory of that steady rhythm, unbreakable.

The world narrowed to the faint drip of water hitting the floor, each drop spreading a damp chill through the room, seeping into his bones. A shadow crossed his vision, flickering like the dim lights of a bunker from another life—small, concrete, and cold. The smell of mold clung to him.

Davyd forced a breath, teeth clenched, digging his nails into his palms, sealing himself in the sensation. His pulse hammered in his ears, drowning out the lieutenant's voice, yet every footstep echoed, heavy and deliberate, a countdown. The air felt thick, damp with decay, and the odor of old mildew clung to him, sharp in his lungs. He centered himself on the cold bite of the chair's metal, each jagged edge beneath his wrists reminding him he was still here, still resisting. "We're just getting started," the lieutenant murmured, calm as a blade's edge.

"Why did you target Lipetsk?" The lieutenant demanded, as if trying to reclaim his control. Davyd though struggling for breath remained in his silence, *Let them think you're broken, but don't give them anything.*

"Silent types don't last. Talk." The lieutenant's grip tightened, watching Davyd's resolve waver.

The lieutenant looked down at Davyd with an arrogant smirk, "You beginning to break. Everyone does." He then turned to his men and nodded, "Again," and the chair was again tilted back.

The interrogation spiraled into a relentless loop of torment. Water cascaded over the towel, hammering Davyd's senses, each droplet pounding like a clock ticking down. He focused on that rhythm—the only constant in the storm—trying to measure time. Tick. Tick. Tick.

Liliya squinted at the map, tracing a route through the narrow backstreets. Every second felt heavy, counting down the moments until Davyd's endurance reached its limit. "We have hours—at best—before reinforcements from Voronezh reach the plant," she said, her voice low.

Anatoli, standing beside her, glanced at his watch, impatience tightening his jaw. "Then we don't have a choice. It's now or never."

Yaroslav moved to the window, scanning the street with a soldier's practiced eye. "The commander's death left a vacuum. They're scrambling, but not for long. Let's move."

Liliya nodded, her shoulders taut. Davyd was running out of time.

Her mind flashed back to the facility—the scrape of boots on concrete, the rust on the door hinges, the disinfectant masking the rot underneath. The plan came together in her head, sharp and clear.

"We walk in under Yaroslav's cover. No hesitation," she said. "You flash your badge, I'm your assistant. We get Davyd. We leave."

Yaroslav gave a quick nod. "The soldiers will fall in line—they're desperate for direction."

"We switch cars at Sergei's, head for the border." Anatoli checked his revolver. The click of metal was the only sound in the room. "Fast in, fast out."

Liliya's fingers brushed the cold grip of her revolver, steadying her nerves. "No mistakes," she muttered, her gaze fixed on the route. The three of them exchanged a look—if Davyd was still breathing, this was their only shot. They had to make it count.

At the command headquarters

Davyd sagged in the chair, the weight of every blow reverberating through his bruised body. He heard the lieutenant's voice, sharp and relentless, demanding answers. The words washed over him like a distant echo. *Hold on*, he reminded himself, *every second they dragged this out brought his team closer.*

As they laid out their strategy, each member knew the stakes had never been higher. Failure was not an option, not with Davyd's life hanging in the balance and the imminent threat of their own capture. Their resolve hardened, they set about their preparations, each action a step towards the anticipation of a successful escape and a strike against the forces aligned against them.

With Yaroslav's description of Davyd's condition, the conversation moved to contingencies after the rescue. "Davyd's condition may require us to alter the original plan. There is a good chance we can't continue together." Yaroslav noted.

Anatoli, his face set in grim determination, glanced between Anatoli and Liliya. "You're right. We need to split up. Yaroslav, you know the border crossings and patrols. You should take Davyd to safety. Along with the plans."

"Yes, you're the best one to navigate through. Anatoli and I will move onto the next objective." Liliya said turning to Yaroslav.

Yaroslav's jaw clenched as he considered the options. "Alright. But if it comes to that be careful. Both of you."

Liliya turned to the satellite radio and confirming contact shared the situation with the operations center. "We need a site that is safe to transfer Davyd and allow Yaroslav to get back without detection."

"That's perfect, I will confirm that the package is coming." Armed with a plan, the group set their scheme into motion, quickly gathering their essentials into Anatoli's Lada before setting off. They then jumped in and made their way back to the town. Stopping at Sergei's and Nadya's, they parked the Lada, and in a swift change of vehicles, Anatoli took the helm of the Mercedes. Their destination was the grim site where Davyd was held, a house now marked by the echo of his torment.

Liliya's knowledge of the house's layout and the typical posts of the soldiers stationed there was invaluable. This insight, gained from a reconnaissance the previous night, became the linchpin of their strategy to infiltrate the building, rescue Davyd, and escape with minimal confrontation.

Upon arrival, Yaroslav and Liliya stepped out of the car, embodying the very essence of officialdom and authority so acutely missing among the ranks of the confused military. With confidence, Yaroslav presented his credentials to the sentries, his tone laced with a feigned severity that demanded immediate compliance.

"We're here to question the man responsible for the destruction at the plant," Yaroslav said, introducing Liliya as his assistant tasked with documenting the encounter.

The sentries, unmoored by the power vacuum and desperate for direction, hesitated only briefly before capitulating to Yaroslav's authoritative demand. The doors swung open, granting them entry.

The door clicked shut behind them. Liliya gave Yaroslav a brief nod, directing him toward the interrogation room.

"We need to see the prisoner," Yaroslav demanded, his voice cutting through the silence.

Moments later, the lieutenant stepped into the hallway, his eyes narrowing with suspicion. "What are you doing here, Kuznetsov?" His words dripped with contempt.

Yaroslav met the lieutenant's glare, keeping his voice steady. "Keeping this operation from going under." *Stay calm. Don't let him see the cracks. You've handled worse.*

The lieutenant's voice grated in the hallway, sharp and tense, clashing with Yaroslav's. Liliya's pulse pounded in her ears. *Not now. Keep it steady.* Composing herself she brushed her hand brushed against the cold metal of her revolver. She slipped to the interrogation room door, cracking it open just enough to peek inside.

Sweat. Blood. Antiseptic. The air reeked of it, making her stomach twist. Davyd sagged in the chair, his head drooping, his skin a patchwork of bruises. Two soldiers leaned against the walls, their blood-stained shirts clinging to their bodies, their exhaustion making them careless.

Move. No second chances.

Panic crept at the edges of her mind, but she squeezed her eyes shut—just for a second. The faint scrape of metal on concrete pulled her back. *Breathe.* She opened her eyes. *Just get him out.*

The revolver was in her hand before she realized it. Her grip tightened, finger brushing the trigger. A different memory flashed—her hands shaking as she held Ivan's lifeless body in the alley.

The door gave a quiet groan, but the soldiers didn't react. The sound of a distant gunshot—real or memory? —echoed through her mind.

She exhaled once, smooth and steady. *Now.*

Two shots muffled but sharp, and the soldiers dropped before they even registered the threat. The thud of bodies hitting the floor echoed, the scent of gunpowder mixing with the blood.

She turned. The lieutenant, mid-sentence in the hallway, froze at the sound. His eyes locked on hers, wide with disbelief.

"You—"

Liliya's third shot silenced him. He fell hard, body crumpling into the stillness.

The tension in the air broke like a snapped wire. She didn't wait to savor it. Yaroslav was at Davyd's side, checking for a pulse. "He's alive," he muttered, "but not by much."

Liliya knelt beside them, hands steady as she worked. Davyd's shallow breaths told her enough—there was still time. "Let's go," she whispered.

Yaroslav moved swiftly toward the communication room; revolver drawn. Liliya signaled to Anatoli outside. Two muffled shots later, the guards at the entrance collapsed.

Anatoli joined Liliya, and together they dragged the bodies inside. "We need to hurry," she whispered.

Yaroslav eased open the communication room door. Two officers sat with their backs to him, eyes glued to their screens. He hesitated, his gun lowering slightly. *They're just kids, like the ones I sent to the front.* His grip on his gun lessoned, his arm becoming limp as these were the same as those, he tried to save but couldn't.

One of the officers shifted, hand drifting toward his sidearm. Instinct took over. Yaroslav fired twice, each shot finding its mark. His chest tightened as he stared at the bodies. *What a waste.*

Without another thought, he turned the gun on the communication equipment, emptying the clip into the electronics until sparks flew. He backed out of the room, jaw tight.

Returning to the grim scene of Davyd's captivity, Yaroslav and Anatoli lifted Davyd carefully, his body limp and battered. They placed him gently into the backseat of the Mercedes.

"Let's get out of here," Liliya said, sliding into the driver's seat.

They drove swiftly to Sergei and Nadya's place. The Lada awaited them, packed and ready.

At Sergei's safehouse, Anatoli stood guard, his revolver steady in his hand. Liliya moved to the Lada and withdrew the bag holding the plans.

Yaroslav stood by the open car door, his gaze flicking between Davyd's limp form and the dark horizon ahead.

Anatoli's voice cut through the heavy night air. "We're out of time."

Liliya gave a sharp nod, crossing the gravel in quick, deliberate strides to the Lada. She yanked open the door, crouching low to reach beneath the driver's seat. Her hand brushed against the bag—leather cracked from years of use—and she pulled it free in one smooth motion.

Anatoli shifted behind her, glancing toward the road. "Liliya."

"I know," she snapped, slinging the satchel over her shoulder. The leather creaked, too loud in the stillness.

Liliya crossed back to the Mercedes, her steps quick and sure. she handed Yaroslav the satchel. "Get Davyd across the border," she said firmly. "And the plans. No mistakes."

Yaroslav nodded. "I'll get it done."

She gripped his arm once before stepping back. Without another word, Yaroslav got into the car and drove off into the night.

Yaroslav's eyes met hers for a moment longer than necessary, then he turned, looking at Davyd in the backseat. The car door shut with a soft click.

The Mercedes rumbled to life, engine vibrating beneath the weight of everything riding on its journey. Liliya stepped back, watching the taillights disappear into the night, swallowed by the narrow road.

Anatoli adjusted his revolver, the faint scrape of metal the only sound between them. "We should go."

Liliya nodded, pulling open the door of the Lada. The cold leather seat met her like an unwelcome reminder—not done yet. She settled in and exhaled slowly, gripping the passenger armrest as Anatoli started the engine. *One breath. One move. Just keep going.*

The tires crunched over the gravel as they rolled forward, the night stretching wide and uncertain ahead of them. Every second that passed pulled Davyd and the stolen plans further from danger—and pulled them closer to what came next.

The Lada slipped into the dark, its engine humming like a heartbeat, steady and relentless.

NINETEEN

Diverging Paths

The mission's final phase loomed: eliminate three crucial targets—Belyeyev, Ilyia, and Smirnov—key figures in the radar cloaking project, their fates sealed by Liliya and Anatoli as they left Dmitryashevka for Saint Petersburg.

Liliya's fingers danced a staccato beat on the armrest, her lips pressed into a thin line. Lines blurred—on the road, in her head. Precision was slipping through her grasp. A sharp pain throbbed in her temples, each pulse a reminder of the weight on her shoulders. Minutes passed. Closer to Saint Petersburg. Closer to the inevitable. She pressed her fingers to the dossier, the edges cutting into her skin. Just one mistake, one overlooked detail and the whole mission could collapse.

As the car advanced, she flipped through the dossiers, each face cold and still. These weren't just targets—they were linchpins. She gripped the file tightly, the edges biting into her fingers as she pushed the doubt away.

Northbound, the hum of the engine filled the silence. Westward, Yaroslav's tires crunched over gravel roads. Each turn was a gamble—camps and checkpoints lay scattered, every mile inching them closer to danger. He glanced at Davyd, knowing one wrong move could end it all.

His prior duties, which had him crisscrossing these very routes to monitor conscripted men, now served a purpose far removed from their original intent. Yaroslav used his knowledge of military movements to create a roadmap of evasion. Their journey was a delicate balance between urgency and the need for stealth, each turn and decision weighted with the potential for discovery.

Yaroslav took the back roads, his grip tightening on the wheel as they neared the military net. Soon, Davyd would need to hide in the trunk. Dodging checkpoints felt like threading a needle in the dark, every escape tightening the noose.

Every bump in the road sent fresh waves of pain through Davyd's battered body, each jolt drawing a grimace. His fists curled unconsciously, a fleeting tremor betraying his attempt to steady himself. Every breath fought against the ghosts lodged in his ribs. He was acutely aware of his precarious situation; his face was now known to security forces across the region and soon it would be matched to a dossier in the secret service halls of Moscow.

The knowledge that he was the subject of an intensive search cast a heavy shadow over his attempts to rest. Capture would not just mean imprisonment but likely a public demonstration of dissent's consequences. This threat served as a stark backdrop to his profound exhaustion, momentarily eclipsing the fear and resolve that had propelled him.

As he looked at Yaroslav in the rearview mirror, Davyd noticed a troubled expression. He set aside his pain and focused on his friend.

"Yaroslav, you seem troubled." Davyd began gently. "What's on your mind?"

Yaroslav's shoulders slumped; his eyes downcast. He ran a hand over his face, as if trying to wipe away the memories of the young men he had just killed. "The men I just killed, their faces are haunting me, Davyd," he murmured, his voice trembling.

Davyd looked away, fingers brushing the bruises on his wrists—a reminder of the men who had done the same to him. Anatoli's advice came to him in a sharp whisper, "Pain is a weapon; if you can endure it, you've already won half the fight." He breathed in, holding the words close. "They chose their path," Davyd muttered to Yaroslav, voice steady. "They knew the price."

Davyd shifted slightly and moaned due the pain but continued. "You saved my life. That's what matters." The car jolted over a bump, sending another wave of pain through his side, but he held still, bracing against the ache.

Yaroslav looked at him through the rearview mirror, gratitude and pain mingling in his eyes. "I hope it's enough. I can't forgive myself."

Davyd's voice, barely above a whisper, was filled with conviction. " Forgiveness is tough, but you're doing the right thing. We're in this together."

As sleep began to drag Davyd into its uneasy grasp, the ache in his body gave way to a numbness just shy of relief. Yet even in slumber, his mind offered no peace—his breath hitched, and his face twitched with lingering fear. The car hummed beneath them, a lullaby laced with exhaustion and unspoken promises. Yaroslav drove on, each mile both a step toward safety and a reminder of what they'd sacrificed to get this far.

In another car, farther north, Liliya pressed a finger to Ilya Belyeyev's photo, her touch light but deliberate. The cold, vacant eyes stared back at her from the page, waiting to be crossed off like a name on a list. Her jaw tightened as the car hit a pothole, and the jolt snapped her back to the present.

Three men. Three deaths. Clear. Clinical. Too easy.

She skimmed the edge of the file, her finger tracing its rough edge like an anchor. The plan was clear: eliminate them, neutralize the threat. *Why does this feel so... wrong?* It felt too smooth, too simple."

The same places. The same meetings. Over and over. Too perfect. Something's missing. Liliya flipped another page. *Too neat. Too predictable. What am I not seeing?* Patterns tangled, slipping through her grasp. There had to be more. Something—anything—to make this make sense. To justify what they were about to do. Or condemn it.

She could almost hear Davyd's voice reminding her to look closer, to avoid the easy answer. "A clean path can be a trap, Liliya. Take the extra step." A flicker of irritation ran through her. She was alone in this. And yet, the thought of his presence steadied her hands, the file held firm in her grip. If this was a trap, she would be ready.

She read through the details again, her mind churned with conflicting thoughts.

As Liliya and Anatoli trekked north on the freeway to Moscow, Yaroslav's journey with Davyd, marked by a blend of urgency and caution, and had them winding through the less-traveled paths for eight exhaustive hours. The transition from the backroads onto the R298 highway signified a shift towards more perilous terrain, bringing them closer to their destination yet also to the denser mesh of security that draped the border regions.

As the landscape darkened, Yaroslav's thoughts were with Davyd, whose resilience was a steady flame against the encroaching night. Yet, the closer they got to the border, the more tangible the tension became. Each kilometer traversed was a step into a territory where the stakes were life and death, where every decision could mean freedom or capture.

The encroaching dusk was a welcome ally for Yaroslav. He knew the cover of night would shield their movements from military eyes, but they both understood that darkness could just as easily turn against them. Davyd kept his breathing steady, repeating Liliya's words from months ago: "Don't focus on the fear—focus on the next step." His pulse quickened as a checkpoint loomed, his instincts tightening. One more obstacle. He turned his gaze toward Yaroslav, whose jaw was set in quiet resolve—a reminder that he wasn't facing this alone.

During their short time together, Yaroslav had come to respect and admire the man and was proud to call him a friend. Yaroslav's eyes darted to the rearview mirror, checking on him. He exhaled slowly, trying to steady his nerves. The darkness provided cover, but also heightened his anxiety. He tapped his fingers on the wheel, a nervous habit. The stealth needed to navigate checkpoints and slip past guards required strategy and a bit of fortune.

The night was their cover, but every bend in the road carried a silent threat. Yaroslav steered through the darkness; tension coiled in his muscles. Davyd's life hung on his every move.

While Yaroslav moved closer to the border with heightened vigilance, the rhythmic purr of the car became a metronome, marking time until their next move.

Liliya's mind churned as Moscow's outskirts faded into the long road ahead. Heightened security following the bombing and drone attack added tension to their journey, turning their escape to Saint Petersburg into a race against time and discovery.

The roads to Saint Petersburg stretched before Liliya. Three names burned in her mind. *Kill them. Move on. Simple.* But nothing about it felt simple. *Sanctity of life?* She almost laughed. *Service of a greater good? Another empty phrase.* She clenched the dossier tighter. No comfort. No clarity. Just three faces.

They weren't soldiers. Just men—thinkers. Scholars, twisted into weapons. Inquiry turned into war. Innovation into death. And they'd designed a system—something lethal. Something unstoppable. They had to be stopped. She knew that. But still... a question echoed in the quiet of her mind: What if this is the wrong path? Each decision felt like a blindfolded step into quicksand.

Anatoli glanced at her, noticing the tension in her posture—the way her shoulders curved inward, as if bracing for a blow. His hand left the steering wheel momentarily, brushing against her arm in a silent invitation to speak. "You seem troubled, Liliya. What's on your mind?"

Liliya's gaze lingered on the dashboard, her hand smoothing a crease in the dossier before she looked up to meet his eyes. She hesitated for a moment, her fingers tapping an erratic rhythm on the file's edge. "It's this plan. It's straightforward, effective. But..." she trailed off, unsure how to articulate her feelings.

Anatoli's grip tightened slightly on the wheel, the leather creaking under his fingers as he kept his focus on the road ahead. He could feel the hesitation in her voice, and he gave her the space to fill the silence. "But what? Talk to me."

Liliya whispered, almost to herself: "I keep reading it. It looks so... simple. Too simple. Kill them, save lives." She pressed her thumb into the page. "We pull the trigger, Anatoli, and they're gone. Just like that." She exhaled through her nose, her jaw tightening. "And who does that make us?"

Anatoli's hand briefly shifted on the wheel, his fingers drumming once against the rim, as if searching for the right words. He glanced at her sideways. "I get it. It's not easy. None of this is." A pause hung between them, thick and heavy, as if the truth had a physical weight. "But remember why we're doing it. Belyeyev and his team could be responsible for countless deaths. Stopping them is saving lives. Sometimes, the lines blur, but we have to trust our judgment."

Liliya exhaled sharply, her hand dragging across her face, pausing momentarily at her temple as if trying to wipe away the doubts swirling in her mind. "I know you're right. It's just..."

Her voice trailed off as she leaned back in her seat, folding her arms tightly across her chest. "The closer we get to carrying out this plan, the more I feel the weight of it all. The tactical ease of it makes it feel almost... too simple, too detached."

Anatoli gave a brief nod, his hands loose on the wheel now, as if relinquishing control would bring clarity. He stole another glance at her, catching the distant look in her eyes. "It's okay to feel conflicted. It means you haven't lost your humanity."

He adjusted his grip again, fingers tightening as he pressed forward through the dark highway. "We need that, especially in this line of work. But don't let it paralyze you. We have to act, for the greater good."

She took a deep breath, trying to steady her thoughts. "Your right, we have to move forward," Liliya acknowledged, but her conscious lingered. How do I reconcile these feelings? The car was silent as they both absorbed the gravity of their mission.

While Liliya was struggling with her thoughts about the plan, Yaroslav faced the enemy face to face. His encounter at the checkpoint was a dance of wits and will, balancing authority and urgency. As they approached, a grove of trees provided cover for concealing Davyd in the trunk. Despite the discomfort and indignity, both men understood the high stakes. The transition was executed efficiently and compassionately, guided by necessity and concern for Davyd's wellbeing.

Once Davyd was hidden, Yaroslav re-emerged onto the road, assuming the role of an authoritative government official with grim determination. The checkpoint loomed ahead, manned by guards whose scrutiny could unravel their plans.

The blinding flash of the guard's light seared Yaroslav's vision, but he didn't flinch. He leaned forward, narrowing his eyes.

"Lower that light, soldier, unless you want me filing a report with your name on it."

The guard hesitated but kept the beam steady.

"What's your destination, sir?"

Yaroslav exhaled sharply. "The front. It's in the paperwork. Checking on conscripts."

The guard shifted uneasily. "This is a restricted zone, sir."

Yaroslav shot him a flat look. "How else do you think I'll reach the front? Through a playground?"

The guard faltered, uncertainty creeping in. His beam then wavered— just enough. Yaroslav pushed forward before doubt returned. When the barrier finally lifted, Yaroslav continued to ease the car forward, muscles taut with restraint. Each kilometer ahead held its own threat— an unseen checkpoint, a patrol just beyond the bend. Relief flickered as the guard receded into the night, but the tension clung to Yaroslav, tightening around him like a second skin. The highway disappeared into the horizon, where certainty ended and peril began.

Miles away, Liliya's eyes flicked over the dossier again, every line of text a puzzle piece that refused to fit. She traced the patterns hidden in the scientists' lives, but the picture remained incomplete. Each new detail revealed another layer of control—a complex web binding them to their roles, trapping their families in silence and isolation. The scientists, much like Yaroslav at the checkpoint, operated under a thin veneer of choice.

In both places—one in motion, the other in thought—the same tension wound tighter. Lives hidden in plain sight. Choices shaped by coercion. Plans balancing on a knife's edge. Yaroslav gripped the wheel as the darkness deepened ahead, while Liliya and Anatoli switched places at the wheel. The engine thrummed beneath them, vibrating through the metal frame, and the weight of the dossiers mirrored the tension threading through every decision—whether at the checkpoint or in a moving car bound for St. Petersburg.

The parallel journeys continued, the line between control and freedom blurring. For Yaroslav, it meant slipping past guards without notice. For Liliya, it meant unraveling lives possibly shaped by coercion and deciding whether execution was the only way forward.

Speaking aloud but wanting his feedback, Liliya queried, "In noticed that two years ago, they had separate lives in Moscow. Now, in Saint Petersburg, they live in the same complex. Their kids are homeschooled, and their wives have stopped socializing."

Anatoli mulled over Liliya's observations. "From one perspective it could be they're being controlled." he finally responded; his voice laced with skepticism. "Isolated, watched, and pressured. But that doesn't mean they aren't willing participants. The same circumstances applied to the scientists of the Manhattan Project, and they all believed they were doing the right thing. However, I think we need to take our time and check things out before proceeding."

Liliya, her eyes on the road but her mind churning, became resolute. The easy path—clean and efficient—was no longer an option. The facts surrounding the scientists demanded a deeper understanding, and with it, the harder path. One that required time, care, and risk. She glanced at Anatoli, the unspoken agreement between them hanging in the still air. "We need a new plan. One that considers all possibilities," she said firmly.

Anatoli nodded. "It'll be risky, but it keeps us on the right side of this. No shortcuts."

The winding road twisted like a question, forcing them to navigate both danger and doubt. Every turn, every decision could take them further from the clarity they sought—or plunge them deeper into compromise. The mission demanded precision, not just in action but in judgment. "We'll take the harder path," Liliya whispered, "if it means staying true to our values."

The hum of the Lada's engine carried them forward, each mile marked by the weight of decisions still to come. The way ahead was tangled in complexities, where lives and integrity were interwoven in a precarious dance. But Liliya knew they had to find a way through it—without becoming the very thing they fought against.

Miles away, Yaroslav's car glided through the darkness, just as burdened with uncertainty. Every checkpoint was a test, every encounter a gamble. He kept his hands steady on the wheel, each forged document, each sharp word a tool to slip past suspicion. His mission, too, carried no room for shortcuts

As the border drew nearer, the stakes sharpened. One wrong move could unravel everything—just as easily as one flawed assumption could shatter Liliya and Anatoli's new plan. Both journeys shared the same thread: the choice between convenience and conviction. And in both, the weight of responsibility pressed heavy, demanding they remain on the narrow path between survival and compromise.

Yaroslav adjusted the rearview mirror, checking the outline of Davyd curled in the backseat. Every action hinged on deception, but beneath it, loyalty and purpose held him steady. Just as Liliya kept their car moving toward St. Petersburg, Yaroslav steered deeper into the night, where a moment of hesitation could cost everything.

After a short drive through contested territory, they finally crossed into the relative safety of Ukraine, nearing the outskirts of Kharkiv. The tension that had been their constant companion began to ebb, giving way to cautious optimism. Yaroslav's turn off the E105 and into the quiet town of Pytomnyk marking the final leg of their arduous journey. The town, with its unassuming streets and the cloak of nightfall, served as the perfect backdrop for the clandestine exchange that was about to take place.

The road eastward, leading them away from the populated areas and into the secluded embrace of the forest, was a path to a new beginning. This large, forested area, away from prying eyes and the ever-looming threat of discovery, was the chosen spot for Davyd to be safely transferred to the care of anothermember of their covert network.

Darkness closed in around the forest road, shadows thickening under the trees. Yaroslav's grip tightened on the wheel, each turn a gamble in the night. Every minute dragged, their escape feeling just out of reach. Each turn into the forest felt like slipping deeper into enemy territory, the road narrowing with every second. The dense canopy overhead absorbed the light, stretching time until minutes blurred into hours. The lack of visibility, with no natural light to guide their way or reveal potential dangers ahead, added to the oppressive atmosphere of their journey.

However, as they emerged from the forest's grip, the sight of the headlight beams cutting through the darkness was akin to a lighthouse beacon for a ship lost at sea. The flash of the passcode, a pre-arranged signal understood only by those within their trusted circle, was a moment of profound relief and reassurance. It represented a brief respite in the storm, a sign that they were not alone in the darkness and that, for the moment, they were safe.

"My friend, we're here and you are going to get back to Kyiv. I promise you that I will see this mission and those to come, through to completion. For you, my friend, and everyone else that we fight with and fight for." Yaroslav vowed to Davyd.

"How is our friend doing?" came the voice from the figure standing in the shadows by a Land Rover.

"He's in rough shape but I think he'll make it," Yaroslav responded.

With that the figure stepped forward, opened the back door, and peered in. "He better, because I didn't drive him from Kyiv to Serindina-Buda just to drive his dead body back to Kyiv," and with that Rostyslav smiled at Davyd.

Yaroslav steadied his grip on Davyd as Rostyslav glanced at him, eyebrows raised. "Next time," Rostyslav quipped, "try to get out of here without making me carry you."

A faint smile tugged at Davyd's lips, and he shook his head. "I'll remember that. Just focus on getting us out without extra trouble."

They moved carefully, they guiding Davyd out of the Mercedes and toward the Land Rover with calculated precision. Each step was slow, deliberate, as they worked to keep Davyd steady, the weight of his injuries clear in every grimace.

Rostyslav adjusted his grip, his tone turning serious. "I know a safe route back to Kyiv—less traffic, and no checkpoints. We'll make it."

Yaroslav nodded, glancing over his shoulder as he settled Davyd into the back seat, adjusting him with care. "Let's move. Before someone notices us."

As the Land Rover rolled into the shadows, Yaroslav watched them disappear, a chill settling over him. Their mission was more than survival; it was a vow, a bond of loyalty that kept them moving forward, even as the odds stacked higher.

TWENTY

Shadows of Saint Petersburg

The New Holland Hotel rose through the mist like a watchful sentinel. As Liliya stepped out, her boots met the damp cobblestones, the chill of Saint Petersburg's late autumn air sinking into her collar. A low fog rolled from the canal, wrapping around the hotel's timeworn stones. She let her gaze rest briefly on the darkened windows, knowing they might conceal more than they revealed.

The faint scent of varnish and damp leather trailed through the lobby, mixing with the earthy tang of wet stone. Liliya's boots whispered across the polished marble, each step swallowed by the thick silence that seemed to settle here like dust. She scanned the walls—ornate but sparse, and just restrained enough to be unassuming. The hotel wore its elegance like a mask, hiding the secrets lurking behind each door.

Shadows pooled in the corners, thick and silent. Liliya moved, steps sharp. She scanned the room—angles, exits, shadows. Everything noted, cataloged. Years of watching. Waiting. She could feel Saint Petersburg's weight, the city's tension bleeding through the thick walls, seeping into the silence around her.

Liliya's fingers gripped the satellite phone, dialing without thinking. Static buzzed. Her stomach clenched. Kyiv came through, Sanenko's voice sharp, pulling her back. Her shoulders dropped slightly, but each second felt stretched, fragile—anything could shatter it.

"Commander, any word on Davyd?" Liliya's voice stayed steady, even as her fingers tapped against the table with sharp, rhythmic precision.

Sanenko's voice crackled. "He's safe, resting in the medical wing."

Her hand froze mid-tap. Pulse hammering, then slowing. Steady. She pressed her fist into the table, the edge biting her palm. Her mind snapped back, here, now.

A steady drizzle pattered against the thick glass, a sound that echoed faintly through the walls, grounding her in the moment. Anatoli's gaze flicked toward her, the faintest nod—a silent assurance that, for now, they were invisible. Liliya's fingers drummed absently on the desk, in rhythm with the city's muted pulse, reminding her they'd be at its mercy if they weren't careful.

Anatoli, sensing her concern, turned from the window and walked over, offering a reassuring smile. "He's tough, Liliya. Davyd will be back on his feet in no time."

Liliya's shoulders eased, and the sound of rain on the window seeped back into her awareness. She blinked once, exhaling slowly. The mission wasn't over, not by a long shot. Anatoli turned from the window, sensing her relief.

The static buzzed faintly again, snapping her back into the moment. The phone felt cold and heavy in her grip, a tether to command. "Are we clear to proceed?" Sanenko's voice was steady, authoritative. Liliya's grip tightened, her pause stretched into an eternity, while her stomach knotted tighter with each second.

Words hovered on the tip of her tongue, weighted by the risk they carried. Were they enemies—or just men trapped like everyone else? Not like Aleekseev or Volkov... or are they? "Not exactly, sir. I checked their files.

Something's off. We are not sure what exactly are the circumstances here," she replied, her voice firm despite the turmoil inside her.

"No, eliminate them. We can't take that risk," Sanenko's words clipped through the line, harsh and final.

Liliya felt her chest tighten, the hum of the static loud in her ear. She shifted, barely noticing the chair's edge pressing into her leg. "Sir, with respect…we're not sure. If they aren't what we think, we have time." Her hand closed around the phone, knuckles white. "Just… give us that."

Sanenko's silence lingered, hard and unyielding. In the window, her reflection flickered. Harder, sharper. Her hand rubbed her wrist absently, the watch metal cold against her skin. She took a breath, steadying the knot in her chest.

Accept the job. Finish it. The words were her own, yet they grated as she repeated them, barely above a whisper.

"You sound sure. What's your plan?" Sanenko relented.

Relief flooded her, but she kept her voice steady. "Starting tomorrow, give us a few days to watch them. We'll use the time to plan the executions— or figure out if we're making a mistake." Liliya's jaw clenched. What if they were never meant to be killed at all? "If things are different, we'll come up with a new plan."

"Alright, a few days of surveillance. A van will be ready at the hotel. Keys will be at the desk under your cover name," the commander committed.

"Thank you, sir," Liliya said, her voice a mix of gratitude and resolve. The authorization for surveillance and the possibility of defection offered a glimmer of hope, a chance to avert unnecessary bloodshed.

The commander's tone softened. "Anything else?"

Liliya's thoughts turned to Davyd. She felt a lump form in her throat, a mixture of relief and longing. She hesitated, gripping the phone tightly before quietly saying, "No. That's all."

Anatoli, having approached silently, caught the tail end of her emotional moment. He observed as Liliya quickly wiped a stray tear and straightened up, her face morphing back into the mask of determination that she wore so well. The depth of her resolve, tinged with a palpable strain, didn't go unnoticed by him.

"Liliya, you did the right thing," Anatoli spoke with gentle firmness, his voice a soft echo in the room. He watched as she nodded, her hands steadying as she took a deep, resolute breath.

Liliya gave a brief nod, eyes sharp again. "Thank you." Her jaw clenched. Losing humanity? That wasn't an option. Not yet.

Recognizing the need for solitude after such a heavy exchange, Anatoli picked up his bag, giving Liliya a reassuring nod. "I'll give you some space. Call me if you need anything," he offered, his tone imbued with respect and an unspoken promise of unwavering support.

As Anatoli left the room, Liliya sat down, the quiet hum of the satellite phone filling the silence. The connection they had maintained, despite the physical distance, was a lifeline that brought a sense of relief and renewed purpose. Her shoulders eased, and the sound of rain on the window seeped back into her awareness. She blinked once, exhaling slowly. The mission wasn't over, not by a long shot.

She picked up the room phone and dialed Anatoli's room number. "We need to get some rest. We'll get down to business at 1430 hours."

Liliya hung up the phone, directive set, resolve firm. The brief pause she proposed wasn't idle rest—it was a calculated regroup, a moment to fortify for the critical phase ahead. They would meet again only when every edge was sharpened, their minds focused, ready for what lay ahead.

Anatoli's pen tapped against the map, punctuating the silence, mingling with the hum of the coffee machine. Liliya leaned over the table, tracing routes with a steady finger, eyes narrowed. At precisely 1430, she glanced up, time to lock in the plan.

Together, they mapped out the surveillance points, their movements precise. "Our cover has to hold. Zero margin for error," Liliya said, her voice low. She drove a red pin into a rooftop location, holding it steady a moment before letting it go. "These marks are lives, Anatoli." Her finger paused on one of the red pins, a thin line pressing into her skin. "If we miss something, we're as exposed as they are."

Anatoli nodded. "Agreed. We have to cover all angles without drawing attention. Multiple surveillance points are crucial." He leaned further over the table, his finger tracing potential escape routes.

Liliya bent over the map, marking each spot with swift, practiced gestures. "You've got the day shift—compound during peak hours," she said, pinning down the last point with a firm press. "I'll take nights, tail them to the university, track every move." Her voice was low, barely a murmur over the scratching of the pencil on paper, the plan unfolding with the quiet force of necessity.

"We'll need to overlap for debriefings. Continuous communication and quick adjustments are key." Anatoli noted. His role in this partnership was clear. He was not just a participant but a pillar on which Liliya could lean, a co-strategist in their shared endeavor. His presence offered not just operational support but a reminder of the shared burden of their mission. "You'll also need to recon the university. We need precise data on the scientists' work location."

"It's risky, but essential. Mapping ingress and egress routes will be critical," Liliya agreed. "I'll make a quick tour of the place, after our first night of surveillance."

They finalized the surveillance plan, balancing risk with necessity. As they marked the final observation point, Liliya's pen tapped lightly on the paper—three times, a habit she'd picked up in Kyiv. She glanced at Anatoli, and their unspoken understanding hung in the stillness between them, sharper than words.

"We're ready. Let's get some rest and be prepared for what's ahead," Liliya ordered.

Anatoli paused at the door before leaving, "Remember, we're in this together. Trust in our plan and in each other."

"I know. Thank you, Anatoli. We'll get through this," Liliya replied smiling.

With a final nod, Anatoli left the room, leaving Liliya to her thoughts. The connection they shared, built on trust and a common goal, was the anchor that kept them steady amidst the turbulent seas of their mission.

In the late afternoon, they slipped into Saint Petersburg's shadows, eyes locked on the compound—their mission's prize. With practiced precision, Anatoli transported the surveillance gear while Liliya retrieved the keys from the hotel desk. They met outside, the air smelled faintly of coffee and grease from the nearby café. They then moved toward their vehicle: a UAZ-452 van, chosen for its reliability and nondescript appearance.

The van's stale, metallic scent—tinged with oil and rust—clung to her senses. Liliya adjusted the equipment in the back, her movements precise, the cramped space echoing with the city's distant hum. She glanced through the cracked windshield at the maze of damp streets ahead, her mind already marking routes and escape points.

Unseen among other cars, they loaded the equipment without a word. Liliya tossed the keys to Anatoli, and with a quick nod, crossed to retrieve the Lada parked nearby.

Crossing the street, Liliya's step faltered as the sharp tang of gasoline sliced through the damp air. Her pulse kicked up, the scent too close, too familiar, stirring an image. Gasoline. Ivan's hand—cold and limp—her fingers stained. She forced herself forward, her jaw tightening against the memory.

Anatoli noticing her pause, shouted out, dragging her back. She turned and acknowledged him and then continued to retrieve the Lada. It was the final, critical piece of their logistical setup, ensuring they had a surveillance base and a mobile unit ready for immediate deployment.

They navigated Saint Petersburg's maze-like streets, the van's engine a low rumble beneath the rain-soaked hum of streetcars. Liliya, following Anatoli, scanned the passing storefronts, her fingers drumming the wheel, each reflection slipping away in the slick pavement.

Their movements were calculated and quiet, blending seamlessly into the cityscape. Every glance in the rearview mirror, each subtle nod, carried the silent language of shared purpose and resolve. The city streets weren't just roads—they were conduits to critical intel.

The Lada's windows fogged slightly from the cold. Liliya ran a hand over the glass, clearing just enough to see the compound across the street. Each shift change, each flicker of movement—they all led somewhere.

Near Perevoznaya Street, they settled into their surveillance point, targeting a nondescript apartment complex that concealed their objective. Posing as an ordinary building, the complex held the lives of three scientists and their families under tight control, masked by a tan and white facade. The garrison, characterized by its tan and white facade, stood as a silent sentinel in the otherwise unremarkable neighborhood, its appearance belying the significance it held for their mission.

Anatoli parked the van. Liliya slipped out of the Lada parked down the block, tight to the curb. Wind pressed cold against her neck. She ducked into the shadows, collar pulled high, then entered the van from the door opposite the compound. Quiet filled the van, every sound magnified. She moved with practiced, silent precision, her fingers ghosting over her equipment. The faint scent of wet asphalt filtered through the cracked window, as Anatoli's steady breathing behind her filled the quiet space.

The entrance loomed under a wrought-iron fence, its weight more prison than protection. Two sentries stood rigid by the gate, their eyes flat and empty, guarding the quiet lives trapped within. Liliya shifted behind the scope, counting seconds between glances, each beat a reminder of just how tightly these people were held.

This fortified entrance, coupled with the limited traffic of vehicles belonging to the scientists and the rotating shifts of guards, painted a picture of a location under strict surveillance and control, effectively isolated despite its urban setting.

As the days would stretch ahead, Liliya and Anatoli prepared for a slow, careful reveal. Every movement inside the compound—each guard rotation, each flicker of light—fed into their strategy. Liliya focused the thermal scope, confirming the scientists' presence. The varied heat signatures told a silent story: families clustered; guards stationed. She tapped her pen against the notebook in her lap. Their plan would unfold step by step, each action refining the picture. Just a matter of time.

Anatoli shifted by the window, frowning as he watched the compound. "They move freely enough, but something's off." He gestured toward the apartments. "No families leaving, no visitors. They're boxed in."

Liliya's eyes narrowed. "Control through fear. Or resignation." She tossed the dossier to him, voice tight. "What if they're not collaborators? What if they're just... trapped?"

Anatoli shrugged, still watching the street. "Does it matter? Either way, they're doing the work."

Liliya leaned back, jaw tight, steadying her gaze on the compound across the street. "If they're forced, we're no different from the ones with their hands around their throats."

Anatoli glanced over, eyes dark with understanding. "Maybe that's the job."

The van's heater hummed—a steady backdrop to the tension building around them. Intelligence was in place; the next steps were clear. Stationed inconspicuously, the surveillance van was more than a hiding spot. It was a launch point for Liliya and Anatoli, poised to expose the truth within the compound.

The interior was thick with the smell of stale coffee and warm metal—a reminder of countless hours and sharpened focus. The silence breaking only with the faint stir of leaves and the distant pulse of the city. Liliya steadied her grip on the thermal scope, the compound's lights flickering in it. Liliya blinked, her eyes gritty from hours on duty. Eyes trained on the compound, she scanned for any movement.

Anatoli approached quietly, "How's it looking?"

"Quiet. Just the usual patrols. Go back to sleep, Anatoli. I'll wake you if anything changes," Liliya whispered.

"You sure you're okay? You've been up for a while," Anatoli whispered.

Liliya smiled reassuringly, "I'm fine. I've got this."

Anatoli returned to his makeshift bed, trusting Liliya to keep watch. He knew her well enough to understand that her determination was as much a shield as it was a strength.

At 0700 hours, they gathered for their early morning debrief, a crucial touchpoint in their operations. "After the 2000 hour shift it appears that the families remain in their apartments," Liliya noted as she handed over her notes. "There wasn't any movement between the residences."

Handing the surveillance over to Anatoli, she moved out of the van and back to the Lada. She heard the gates groaned open just as the first light spread across the street. Liliya's hand hovered over the ignition—waiting, watching. The black SUV rolled out, tires crunching against wet gravel. The Lada hummed to life beneath her touch, and she slipped into traffic, the chase unfolding with quiet care.

Liliya moved through the streets of Saint Petersburg with sharp precision, blending seamlessly into the morning traffic as she trailed her target. Eyes fixed on the SUV ahead, her mind cut through any distractions. Each turn, each street was a tactical decision.

The serene beauty of the city, with its vibrant flower beds and majestic trees lining Dekabristov Street, offered a stark contrast to the turmoil brewing within her. The sight of the Mariinsky Theatre, a jewel of cultural heritage, momentarily distracted her from her mission, a reminder of the profound dichotomy between the city's outward splendor and the dark undercurrents she was there to confront.

When her target veered toward the university on Glinski Street, she closed in, her focus tightening. The SUV halted at the university's yellow-tan facade, signaling her cue. Liliya exited her car, her boots striking the pavement with purpose. She approached the entrance, one hand skimming the cool metal of a nearby car, every movement calculated. She slipped into the stream of students and faculty, unnoticed, her mission advancing from surveillance to direct observation.

Inside, the historic university bustled around her—a backdrop of knowledge and innovation, now tinged with coercion and manipulation. As the scientists moved deeper into the building, Liliya followed from a careful distance, scanning for every detail.

As Belyeyev opened the door to the lab, her eyes captured the its contents: charts, models, and machinery. This was no ordinary research, it held potential for something far larger, something twisted by unseen forces.

A soft clink echoed as the lab door clicked shut. Liliya pressed against the wall, forcing her breathing to slow, ignoring the faint smell of antiseptic that stirred old memories. This was her moment to map escape routes, entry points, and potential vulnerabilities. The mission's demands were immense, and Liliya knew rest would soon be crucial to maintain her edge.

As she returned to the Lada, the weight of the day's intel settled over her. The lab's contents confirmed the scientists' involvement, and her course was set. Hands tense on the steering wheel, she scanned the rearview mirror, her gaze bright, prepared for what lay ahead.

Armed with new knowledge and fortified by a brief respite, she and Anatoli were poised to continue their vigil. Each shift mapped. Every guard counted. The compound unfolded, piece by piece, under their watchful eyes. This relentless accumulation of data, hour by hour, revealed not just the physical layout but also the routines that governed life within the compound.

At the 1900 debrief, Liliya reviewed the compound's security data while Anatoli studied the guard schedules. The sound of his pen tapping against the notebook reminded her of the ticking of a biological safety cabinet—steady, relentless. The rhythm burrowed into her thoughts. Lab. Antiseptic. Vials. She took a breath, forcing the images back before they could take hold. Returning her focus to the task at hand. The schedules of the guards, observed and recorded with precision, highlighted a rigorous and methodical system designed to ensure constant surveillance. "The guards rotate every eight hours—no deviations," Liliya said, tapping the map.

Anatoli added, "I noticed something else. The wives and children... they never left the apartments." Anatoli's words lingered in the air, and Liliya's thoughts raced. Were they afraid? Or were they being controlled? If this wasn't by choice—what did that make us?

"That is strange or just something that happened," Liliya nodding took in his observation. "Hold on, I remember something," and with that Liliya pulled out the dossier for each family.

Liliya flipped through the dossiers, her finger tapping on an old address. "Two years ago, separate homes in Moscow. Now? One compound. Kids homeschooled, wives off the grid."

Anatoli grunted, arms folded. "They're locked down. Either they're too dangerous to trust or they've lost all choices."

Liliya set the file down slowly. "Victims, maybe. But that complicates things." Anatoli's quiet patience, a steady reminder, echoed faintly as she met his gaze. She thought back to one of Davyd's favorite sayings — "Complicated just means you're asking the right questions."

A breath eased out of her, settling her focus. She didn't need all the answers. Just enough to know the next step. With a short nod, she pressed the folder shut and looked at Anatoli, as if finally seeing the path between question and certainty. Liliya nodded, absorbing Anatoli's insights.

"For today, let's continue to focus on what is happening with the families. Let's try to get a picture of their lives here."

"You're watching them during the day and keeping a close eye on the scientists' movements outside the compound to see if there are any possible locations to eliminate them," Anatoli noted. "It may also provide potential weaknesses in security and open up opportunities to get to them,"

"Belyeyev and the others left the university at around 1300 hours without anyone following them," Liliya replied. "I followed him to a coffee shop and shortly after that the other two arrived. They returned by 1400."

"No tails. No guards. That doesn't sit right." Anatoli noted.

"Your right," Liliya acknowledged. "If they're controlling the families, why follow them?"

Anatoli nodded, tapping his pen against the table. "No one gets away clean from something like this."

Liliya didn't respond right away, her gaze on the street outside. "Tomorrow, I'll head to the coffee shop early. If they're hiding something, we'll find it."

For Liliya and Anatoli, these revelations were more than operational wins; they were moral directives. Each surveillance session wasn't just target tracking—it was gathering the intel that would drive their next moves. The weight of their discoveries would shape their strategy ahead.

CHAPTER

TWENTY-ONE

The Covenant

The New Holland Surf Coffee, nestled along the canal's edge, hummed with quiet activity. Liliya's gaze drifted over the brick walls and polished wood, the room dimmed by the afternoon shadows pooling in corners. Her gaze swept the room. To an observer, she was just another patron, face neutral, gaze indifferent. But her eyes cataloged angles, reflections, and clear sightlines to the hallway.

Near the restroom, a man sat with a book open on the table, shoulders hunched and posture lazy. But the angle of his head, the way his gaze skimmed past the page, triggered her focus. Something in the rigid set of his hands or the stillness of his posture felt calculated. Too familiar. She shifted slightly, enough to keep him in her peripheral vision. If he was here for her, she'd see his first move.

Her mind traced options: hallway to restroom, tables by the exit, the alcove near the counter. A faint gleam from the espresso machine mirrored her, distorting her reflection just enough to prick at her nerves. For a split second, a flicker of Nikolai's face, shadowed and faint, flashed beside her own.

Her fingers brushed the cold metal at her side, grounding her. Belyeyev and Ilyia's taut forms mirrored the anxiety humming beneath her skin.

Then, Smirnov slipped in, lingering a second too long when he met her gaze in the mirror. A chill coiled up her spine—a warning.

Her eyes flicked to the mirror again, catching the silent exchange among the scientists. Smirnov's fingers tapped against his cup, Ilyia leaned in close, their whispers barely contained. She studied their faces, scanning for any cracks in composure. Every darting glance, every tense murmur only reinforced one thing, they were scared.

The scientists' tension was thick, marked by restless gestures and hurried whispers. Smirnov's hand twitched on his coffee cup. Every look over their shoulders made her stomach tighten. Something was haunting them.

She forced herself to sip her coffee, though it had long gone cold and bitter. Her gaze drifted again to the man by the restroom, his slouched pose edged with tension—too deliberate, too practiced. Her heel tapped softly against the hardwood, matching the faint smell of cold metal lingering in her mind. She'd last sensed it the night she'd waited for Nikolai's release that never came. Her pulse quickened, heel pressing firmer to the floor. Coincidence? No chance. She tapped her foot against the floor in a slow rhythm, a focus point to stay calm. He wasn't a guard, but he was watching. Waiting.

Behind her laptop screen, her fingers drummed against the keys. The steam from her refilled coffee curled upward, stinging her nose as her gaze drifted—divided between the scientists' strained voices and the man's unmoving figure. A glance back at the scientists showed her the same: their pale knuckles, taut expressions, words hushed as if spoken through gritted teeth. Someone was closing in on them—or they already knew the walls were tightening.

Her heel tapped against the floor, a quiet rhythm matching the thrum of her pulse. When her foot slipped out of sync, she caught herself, easing into stillness. The shadowy corners of the café pressed in, and she reminded herself: Stay still, stay invisible. She adjusted her laptop, angling it toward the mirror on the far wall. From there, she had a clear view of Dr. Belyeyev.

At their secluded corner, Dr. Belyeyev leaned in closer, his voice dropping to a barely audible murmur, his expression taut. "Did you hear what was said yesterday?" His gaze flicked around the room, careful, almost paranoid, before settling on his colleagues.

Dr. Ilyia, his face drained of color, gave a small nod, his lips pressing into a thin line. "I heard. The warning was... clear." He hesitated, his fingers fidgeting with the edge of his sleeve. "It's not just us anymore." His words hung in the air, heavy with implication, though unsaid names and threats hovered in the spaces between.

Dr. Smirnov joined the huddle, his knuckles white against his coffee cup, which trembled slightly in his grip. "We're running out of time. They're going to figure it out." His tone was strained but vague, the details left unspoken, though the underlying threat was unmistakable.

Liliya shifted in her seat, trying to ignore the way her pulse sped up. Her training warned her to stick to the mission: Observe, gather intelligence, stay detached. That was the plan. But her fingers stalled on the keyboard. The tension at the scientists' table tightened around her like a noose. She couldn't shake the feeling: These men aren't going to make it.

Liliya caught fragments of their cryptic conversation, barely enough to piece together. A phrase slipped through the tense silence—"like prisoners," muttered by Dr. Ilyia, his voice a whisper carried on the edge of panic. The weight of their predicament pressed down on them all.

Her foot tapped again, harder this time, the old habit pulling her back to nights when that rhythm was her only comfort in the waiting. How many times had she kept herself still, waiting for a signal that never came? She flattened her heel to the floor, jaw tightening. If she acted now—if she stepped in—there was no telling how things would unravel.

Blow the mission, and they were all as good as dead. But if she did nothing… the odds weren't much better.

Each word was a calculated risk, clinging to her thoughts with the weight of consequence. Compassion was a liability, a weakness she couldn't afford. But beneath the surface, her resolve hardened—steel, not sentiment. In this line of work, there was no room for hesitation.

The café was steeped in history, but Liliya ignored the nostalgia and focused on her mission. Her mind turned to the scientists' families— their vulnerability sharpened her focus. Strategy demanded precision; empathy was a dangerous indulgence.

Each scrap of intelligence confirmed the stakes. The scientists' fear was palpable, their desperation a reminder of the grim reality she sought to disrupt. Liliya's plan had to be tight, every risk calculated. There was no room for error—only the slimmest chance to alter their fate.

Liliya slid into the van without a word, closing the door with a quiet click. Anatoli glanced over, his brow lifting slightly—a silent invitation to speak. She gave him a quick rundown: the tension at the café, snippets of the scientists' conversation, and the guarded movements she'd tracked.

"They've got the wives and kids under lock and key. Guards run errands, deliver groceries," Anatoli muttered, piecing it together aloud. "No one moves unless they say so."

"That fits," Liliya settled into the passenger seat, her gaze flickering toward the windshield, lost in thought. "One family member always stays inside the compound when the others leave."

Anatoli nodded, already following her line of thinking. "Control."

"Leverage," she corrected, her voice clipped.

He drummed his fingers against the steering wheel. "So, what's your read?"

"Not hostages exactly—but close enough." She leaned back, chewing on the implications.

Anatoli's gaze stayed on her, waiting.

"We use that," she said after a beat. "Flip it. If we can make them think there's a way out, we might turn them without a fight."

He gave a slow nod, the gears turning behind his steady expression. "Extraction?"

Liliya's hand tapped the dash once, absently. "Could work. They aren't followed when they go to the café. The guards know their families keep them in line. That's our gap."

Anatoli's jaw shifted, a signal he was considering every angle. "We need to approach Belyeyev. Quietly. See if he's ready."

Liliya glanced over, her lips pressing into a thin line. "He's ready," she said, certainty threading through her voice.

Anatoli gave a faint grunt of approval, the corners of his mouth tightening—a near-smile in their world. "Then we move."

Her fingers flexed once, then stilled. "We move fast."

Anatoli started the engine, no further discussion needed. Their plans were already taking shape, a silent agreement formed in the unspoken spaces between words.

Their arrival at the shop before the scientists, securing the table nearest to the hallway leading to the bathrooms, was the final piece in setting the stage for a direct encounter. Liliya's attention to Belyeyev's habitual bathroom visits represented a keen understanding of human patterns, turning routine into opportunity.

The arrival of the three men, each taking their usual seats and delving into a conversation marred by visible distress and anxiety, underscored the gravity of their situation. The metaphorical maze they found themselves in, with freedom and safety just out of reach, painted a vivid picture of their desperation. This backdrop of hopelessness made Belyeyev's predictable departure to the bathroom even more critical to the success of Liliya's plan.

The moment Belyeyev excused himself from the table, Liliya was already on his trail, her steps silent, hand hovering near her concealed revolver. The stakes pounded in her chest as they approached the bathroom door. She slid close enough to him to murmur, "Inside. Now."

He hesitated, a slight tremor in his shoulders as he processed her command, then pushed open the door with a shaking hand. She followed, nudging him farther in and letting her fingers brush the weapon—a quiet but clear signal of control.

Inside, the dim, flickering light threw shadows that sharpened Belyeyev's features, his eyes darting to her gun, then to the bathroom door—a twitch of a glance, a calculation. He took a breath, low and unsteady, but stayed silent, his posture edged in hesitation.

"I need answers," she murmured, her grip on the weapon firm but her tone softening by a fraction. "How secure is the compound?"

Belyeyev's fingers tensed around his sleeve, then released, as if he were pulling himself together piece by piece. His eyes flickered back to her, holding her gaze for a heartbeat longer than she expected. "Eight-hour shifts. Guards at every entrance." His voice was low, steady now, but the set of his jaw hinted at barely held resolve.

"Always watching?" she pressed.

He gave a jerky nod. "Yes. Always." His voice cracked. "If we try to…"

"Don't." Her hand stayed loose near the gun, her eyes steady. "You're not trying anything. Not without me."

His breathing slowed, but his eyes, flickering with panic, never left her face. A muscle worked in his jaw as he held her gaze, words balancing on the edge of his tongue. "If they find out—"

"Stop." She raised her hand, just slightly, the movement controlled. "Focus. Look at me." The weight of her gaze held him there, his own breath catching, her words pushing through his resistance with quiet authority. "I can get you out, but only if you trust me. We follow my plan. No second-guessing."

His eyes flicked between her face and the gun. "Out?" The word came out like a breath, laced with disbelief.

"Yes." Liliya's grip tightened on the revolver, then loosened, signaling a sliver of trust. "You and your family. But you have to work with me. Can you do that?"

For a second, hope flickered in his eyes—fragile, barely there. "I—" He swallowed. "Yes… I'll try." But fear dragged at the edges of his words. "You don't know what they'll do if—"

"I know exactly what they'll do." She cut him off again, her tone sharpening like a blade. "That's why we move first."

Belyeyev's shoulders sagged, the controlled composure slipping just enough to show the weight pressing on him. "What do you need from me?" The words were rough, ground out between breaths, but he held his posture steady, his eyes never leaving hers.

Liliya's own pulse quickened, the unguarded question hitting harder than expected. His face, lined with exhaustion, mirrored a resolve that felt brittle and raw, the last grip of a man caught in a silent war.

She looked away for a brief second, torn. Liliya's jaw clenched. She shifted her stance, the familiar weight of her gun pressing against her side—a reminder of what mattered. Assets, not people. But the tremor stayed with her, threading through her thoughts like a loose wire sparking just out of reach. She exhaled slowly, steadying herself. No room for hesitation. Not now.

"Where's the data?" she pressed, her voice softer, almost kind.

Belyeyev's gaze came up, his shoulders lifted. "Did… did you destroy the missile plant?" he asked, his voice barely more than a whisper. "If you did… thank you." His eyes met hers, a flicker of gratitude breaking through the fear. "You saved us."

Her breath caught. She had, but not for him. Not for them. It had been a target, a mission. Nothing more.

"What do you mean, I saved you?" she asked, keeping her voice low, steady.

His gaze dropped to the cracked tiles on the floor. "The radar…" he began, but his voice faltered. "It's… a sham. The whole system. We knew it wouldn't work."

Belyeyev rubbed his face, hands shaking. "If they'd launched… they would've killed us all." He shook his head, the weight of it pressing down on his narrow shoulders. "They never trusted us. We knew that. But we thought… maybe we'd buy enough time. Enough to get out."

Liliya's jaw tightened. Damn it.

Belyeyev shook his head, gaze flicking toward the door again. His voice broke, and his hands trembled at his sides. "We had no way out. Not with the families."

Liliya's grip on the gun slackened slightly, her pulse kicking up as his words hit harder than she wanted to admit. "So you're trapped," she murmured, half to herself.

She'd seen it before—the slow erosion of people caught between power and fear. Men trying to survive in a game where the rules shifted too fast to follow. It gnawed at her now, threatening to uncoil the tight knot of control she held over herself.

She should walk away. Keep the mission intact. But the look in his eyes—something brittle and broken—pressed against her like a hand on her chest. This isn't about you. This is no longer about the job.

"Do you want out or not?" she asked, voice clipped, controlled. He took a shaky breath, clenching his fists as if to steady himself.

Belyeyev blinked at her, then nodded, slow and deliberate, as if the word itself might break him. "Yes," he whispered. "We all do. But..." His voice trailed off into silence, his hands twisting together.

Liliya exhaled slowly, her focus narrowing to the task in front of her. No room for doubt now. No space for second-guessing.

She leaned in, close enough that her voice dropped to a whisper. "Stay calm. Follow my lead. Do exactly what I say."

His eyes stayed locked on hers. "And if they catch us?"

"They won't." Her voice hardened, a thread of steel running through it. "Because we'll be gone before they know what hit them."

Belyeyev's breath hitched, his fists clenching as if he could grip onto the thin thread of hope she offered.

"Let's move." Her voice was low, steady, and final. "We don't have much time."

Belyeyev nodded once, shaky but resolved.

A faint shuffle outside the door made them both freeze. Her instincts kicked in, and she pressed a finger to her lips, signaling him to remain silent. They stood in tense silence, each breath stretching out, their gazes locked. The voices outside grew louder, a murmur of footsteps inching down the hall, then silence.

Liliya let out a quiet exhale, her pulse still racing. She glanced back at Belyeyev, his face drained of all color, his eyes wide with barely contained terror. She didn't need to say it, but she leaned close anyway, her voice barely a whisper.

"It's only the beginning. Keep it together."

He nodded, his voice thin as a whisper. "I'll try."

Liliya turned toward the door, but the heaviness stayed with her—a knot pulling tighter in her chest. She hadn't planned for this. Her grip on the mission was slipping, the line between duty and instinct blurring in ways she couldn't afford.

She slipped back into the café, her senses sharp as she scanned the room. Every glance, every shadow became a threat to track. Her pulse hummed steadily beneath it all, fueling the tight rhythm of her movements.

Outside, the cold night hit like a slap, but she welcomed it. Her feet moved automatically, melting her back into the city's flow. Yet her thoughts refused to fall into neat lines—contingencies and outcomes tangled like static. The mission had shifted beneath her feet, and there was no going back.

Each step forward felt heavier, her gaze scanning for threats in every alley and reflection. This was no longer surveillance, it was survival, and the stakes pressed harder with every breath. But that ember of resolve remained—small, steady, and impossible to extinguish.

She would find a way. She had to.

CHAPTER

TWENTY-TWO

Veil of Night

The moment Belyeyev revealed the scientists' dire situation, Liliya's apartment transformed into a hub of frantic activity.

"Anatoli! Sat phone—now!" Liliya's voice sliced through the chaos, sharp and clipped.

"On it!" Anatoli replied, his fingers flying over the keyboard as he initiated the connection.

In Kyiv, the operations room hummed. Maps rustled, markers clicked against the board, while the hotel command center, Liliya scanned the blueprints, her fingers tracing the compound's tight corridors and blind corners, her senses attuned to the tight, charged atmosphere around her. This wasn't planning—it was the final breath before impact. "What's the latest on the guards?" Liliya's voice cut through the tense quiet.

Sanenko circled a spot on the map. "Eight-hour shifts. Tight changeovers—barely a gap."

"Noted. Ivanko, safe havens?"

"Latvia's green-lit asylum. Estonia's still pending." Ivanko's fingers flew over his laptop. "Border crossing's the hurdle."

"Get diplomacy on it. Now."

An operative entered the room, carrying a stack of documents. "Commander Sanenko additional authorized resources," he announced, handing the papers to Yankovic. "We've got tactical extraction specialists on standby to evaluate."

Yankovic scanned the documents and gave a curt nod. "Extraction specialists are here to advise."

"Timeline?" Liliya asked.

"Seventy-two hours for prep and diplomacy," Ivanko replied.

"Make it two. We deploy, then extract on day three. Move."

Ivanko, visibly anxious, approached Yankovic. "I've never been on a mission this critical," he admitted, his voice trembling slightly.

Yankovic placed a reassuring hand on his shoulder. "You've trained for this. Trust your instincts and stay focused. We're all in this together."

Ivanko nodded, taking a deep breath as he returned to his station.

"We're going to pull this off," Liliya said, her voice filled with unwavering resolve. "For the scientists, for their families, and for everyone depending on us. Let's get to work."

Liliya paced in front of the map-covered table, her steps sharp, gaze tracing every possible escape route. She saw the red marks—exits, patrols, blind spots. She could hear Nikolai's voice, his laugh, light and reckless. But she blinked, straightened. No time for ghosts. Her eyes hardened as she turned back to the team. "This isn't just an extraction. We get them out, no slips. Clean exits, every step."

Anatoli adjusted the comm link in his ear, his tone sharp. "We need the extraction teams synchronized to the second. No slip-ups. We can't afford loose ends—not with three families involved."

Ivanko leaned over his laptop, tapping furiously. "Getting them across the border is going to be the real challenge. Crossing without raising alarms? That's going to take more than just fast cars."

"Then we make it happen," Liliya snapped. "We've pulled off tighter missions before. Get the transport ready. We're moving fast—no room for errors."

The low, constant hum of voices was punctuated by the rapid taps of fingers on keyboards, blending with the swift, controlled shuffle of papers. Overhead, a fluorescent light buzzed faintly, its sterile glow casting harsh shadows across the map as Commander Sanenko leaned in, marking the infiltration points with the tip of his pen. "Extraction teams hit all points simultaneously. Silent, precise."

"Diplomats are in play," Yankovic confirmed, flipping a dossier. "Timing's everything—one team falls behind, the whole mission's blown."

Liliya absorbed the details, already mapping the next step in her mind. This wasn't theory anymore—it was execution. Soon, they'd be out there, slipping past those guards and moving fast, unseen.

The van jerked to a stop, shadows swallowing its form. Crouched in the back, Liliya heard boots grinding outside, each step syncing with her pulse. She held her breath, binoculars pressed to her face, senses sharp. No room for error.

Liliya beside Anatoli, the tight space pressing the scent of gun oil and damp metal into her senses. Through the scope, a guard shifted, his face sharpening into focus—and for a heartbeat, that focus twisted, revealing her brother's face, wide-eyed and fading fast. Her grip tightened on the metal, her knuckles pale as she forced herself to breathe through it, the cold weight familiar. *Focus. He's not here.* She forced her jaw to relax, the metallic taste fading as her pulse steadied. "Shift change in five," she muttered, recalibrating her focus. Her eyes settled back on the guard, only a threat, nothing more.

"Everything okay?" Anatoli asked, glancing sideways at her.

Liliya gave a sharp nod, her gaze fixed on the guards. "Fine," she muttered, though the pounding in her chest said otherwise.

"Shift change soon," Anatoli muttered, scribbling down notes.

Liliya barely registered his words. She shifted to stretch her legs, the long hours of surveillance sinking deep into her muscles. The ache gnawed at her, but the strain in her mind weighed heavier.

Liliya's hand drifted into her jacket, fingers brushing against the worn edge of a photo. She pulled it out, eyes skimming over her brother Nikolai's frozen smile, bright and unaffected by the weight of war. The faint paper smell—familiar, bittersweet—anchored her, pulling her into the present. The chaos around her faded for a beat, replaced by the muted thud of her heart as she stared down at his carefree face. A shadow stirred in her chest; it had been Two years since the Russians took him.

Every shift of the guards—every flicker of movement—became a potential thread to unravel. Yet as Anatoli cataloged their patterns, the familiar weight of dread pressed against her ribs, unwelcome and relentless. She forced the thought down, but it clung to her mind like damp cloth. *Don't think about Nikolai. Not now. Focus.*

But it was no use. The memory uncoiled from the shadows, creeping through her mind. Nikolai's face, frozen in time. *Gone. Just like that.*

The guards in her scope blurred for a moment, transforming into faces from the past. *The ones who took him. Hands dragging him. His face---lost. How could you not stop them?* She blinked hard, forcing the memory away. The guards snapped back into focus.

271

Anatoli noticed her looking at the photo and placed a reassuring hand on her shoulder. "We're doing this for them," he said softly. "For everyone who can't fight back."

Liliya nodded, slipping the photo back into her pocket. "I know. And we will succeed."

"They switch shifts at 0400, 1200, and 2000 hours. We'll have a window during the evening change," Anatoli noted as he looked over his notes.

Liliya nodded, barely hearing him. Her pulse pounded in her ears. His voice continued muffled by her thoughts, "After the 2000 hour shift it appears that the families remain in their apartments. There wasn't any movement between the residences."

He handed her his neatly scrawled notes, which she absently took. The weight of the slip of paper felt suddenly unbearable. It wasn't just paper and ink—it was responsibility. *What if I fail again? What if this mission ends like ...?*

She clenched the paper tighter, as if that alone could push the thoughts back into the dark.

"Good," she said absently. "... These windows? They work. We can build the plan from this."

Their exchanges were efficient, each piece of information building on the last. The foundation for their next steps was laid in these quiet moments of collaboration.

"What about the cameras?" Anatoli asked.

Liliya scanned her notes. "Yeah, some dead zones. Not enough, though. We'll need to jam the wireless cams —disrupt their signal to render them temporarily blind without triggering alerts. Use the blind spots— west wall, east, near the gate. The back section might allow an aerial entry—we can work with that."

Liliya adjusted the van's night-vision binoculars, tracking a guard pacing along the compound's west wall. The steady thud of his boots punctuated the silence.

Beside her, Anatoli scribbled down timings, every mark on the page another piece of their plan falling into place.

Anatoli's pen scratched the paper, punctuating the silence. Liliya felt a prickle at her neck. She glanced over her shoulder, searching the shadows.

"Relax," Anatoli muttered, sensing her tension without looking up.

"You hear that?" she whispered, her heart hammering.

Anatoli stopped writing, the pen hovering in the air. 'Hear what?'

There it was again—a soft scrape, like a boot dragging over pavement. Liliya's eyes darted to the side mirror. Nothing. But her pulse stayed elevated, and the uneasy sensation lingered, clinging to her like smoke.

"How's it look?" he muttered without looking up.

"Same shift, same window." Liliya's voice was clipped, her focus locked on the patrol. But the knot in her stomach tightened. "This one's all on us, Anatoli."

Anatoli shot her a quick glance, sensing the tension beneath her words. "That's why we won't screw it up."

He flicked through the pages of their notes. "We move fast, stick to the plan, and stay sharp.""

"It's the first mission without Davyd... No backup. It's all on us. You ever think—" Liliya hesitated. "What if we fail?"

Anatoli paused, his pen hovering over the notebook. He turned to look at her, his eyes serious. "Every day. But that's why we won't fail. We have to trust our training and each other."

Liliya nodded, drawing strength from his resolve. She scanned the compound, each flicker a threat waiting to surface. A prickle traced her spine, tightening with each breath—paranoia came with the job, but tonight, it felt personal.

"How are you holding up?" Anatoli asked quietly, breaking the silence.

Liliya smiled faintly. "It's a lot to take in. I've never been on a mission that personally means this much."

"Neither have I," Anatoli admitted, his voice steady. "But we have each other's backs. We'll get through this."

As the extraction hour neared, anticipation and responsibility weighed heavily on the team, prompting reviews of their strategies and mental preparations for the high-stakes mission. Liliya's stomach churned with a mix of anxiety and determination, fully aware of the stakes. She and Anatoli prepared themselves mentally and physically for the challenges ahead. Her hands trembled slightly as she adjusted her equipment, a silent testament to the pressure they were under

Liliya and Anatoli's strategic presence at the coffee shop during their daily visits served dual purposes, both of which were crucial to the overarching mission. The aroma of freshly brewed coffee mingled with the hum of conversations around them. Their regular interactions with Belyeyev provided subtle yet crucial reassurance. In the high-stakes world of covert operations, where trust is both scarce and sacred, these casual encounters became vital touchpoints.

For Belyeyev, the sight of Liliya and Anatoli amidst the café's hustle and bustle was a reminder that he was not forgotten, that plans were actively being woven to secure his and his family's escape. This reassurance was essential, providing a sense of solidarity in what had been a bleak and isolating ordeal.

Secondly, their regular presence aimed at embedding themselves into the fabric of daily life within the café, transforming from outliers into familiar faces. The clinking of cups and murmur of voices became a backdrop to their silent vigil. By establishing a routine that mirrored that of the scientists, Liliya and Anatoli minimized their chances of arousing suspicion. In doing so, they crafted an image of normalcy, blending into the background noise of the coffee shop's environment. This tactic of hiding in plain sight was a classic espionage maneuver, leveraging the human tendency to overlook that which becomes routine.

Their warm reception by the café staff and the other regulars played into this strategy, reinforcing their perceived role as just another couple enjoying their daily ritual. The barista's friendly smile and the familiar nods from other patrons became small but significant elements of their cover. This perception was critical, as any deviation from what was considered "normal" could potentially raise alarms and jeopardize not only their mission but also the safety of the scientists and their families.

This balancing act—between maintaining a visible presence for Belyeyev's reassurance and cultivating an aura of inconspicuousness—was a delicate one. Liliya and Anatoli's ability to navigate this duality showcased their adaptability and deep understanding of human psychology. Each visit to the coffee shop, each shared glance with Belyeyev, was a step towards building the trust and predictability necessary for the mission's success.

Each night's surveillance sharpened their understanding of the guards' rhythms, turning every pattern, habit, and lapse into potential leverage. The cataloging of guard movements, shift changes, and periodic lapses in coverage formed the backbone of their strategic planning. However, identifying the slightest inconsistency, habit, or gap in the guards' patrol patterns was critical, as it could provide the slim margin needed for a successful extraction operation.

As the second night ended, Liliya and Anatoli reviewed their notes, cross-referencing times and movements. "One more day," Liliya said, her voice tinged with exhaustion but also determination. "We have 24 hours to get everything in place."

"We'll be ready," Anatoli affirmed. "We have to be."

"We need to be in and out in a matter of minutes and give ourselves a large enough window to get to the border before they discover the situation and shut it down."

Armed with the information they had passed on to the operations room, Liliya picked up the satellite phone. The room was buzzing with a renewed sense of urgency. Commander Sanenko, Ivanko, and Yankovic were gathered around the large table, covered with maps and blueprints of the compound.

Liliya advised over the phone, her voice tight, almost mechanical. "We need to move swiftly. Eight-hour shifts. 2000—best shot. They're the most tired then." As she spoke, as her jaw clenched.

"Understood. Timing is everything. We hit them hard and fast. The element of surprise is crucial. No delays. None." Sanenko confirmed.

She barely registered the voice on the other end—her mind was elsewhere, trapped in the past. The silence on the other end jolted her back to the present.

"Liliya?" Anatoli called softly from beside her, his gaze cautious.

"Keep going," she hissed, gripping the phone tighter. "We don't have time for mistakes."

"Extraction routes?" Ivanko asked.

"Plotted. Direct path to the border," Yankovic confirmed.

"Good. Everyone stays on task—no deviations unless critical," Liliya ordered. Her thoughts drifted to the scientists and their families. They were counting on her.

After the briefing, Liliya and Anatoli sat in the van, reviewing the final details transmitted by the satellite phone.

Liliya taking in the information turned to Anatoli, "This has to work. It has to. We can't—can't let them down."

Anatoli placed a reassuring hand on her shoulder. "We'll get them out, Liliya. No other choice."

Liliya nodded, her mind pressing against the weight of each person who counted on them. She couldn't afford even a second of doubt. The van door slid shut with a sharp, definitive thud, muffling the ambient hum of the city outside. As the interior light blinked off, she settled into the dimness, her fingers flexing over the worn grip of her weapon, letting the cold weight pull her focus into a fine, taut line.

Anatoli's eyes caught hers in the rearview mirror, a fleeting moment of silent understanding before he turned his attention to the road.

As they watched the convoy taking the scientists to the university they readied themselves to slip back into the shadows.

The morning of the third day dawned with a crisp chill in the air. The operational planning session was a collaborative effort. It was a process marked by the pooling of expertise, the sharing of intelligence, and the collective commitment to a cause greater than any individual role. Sweat beaded on Anatoli's brow as he traced escape routes on the map, his focus unwavering. The operation room, linked to Liliya and Anatoli's hotel room via satellite, became a conduit for this shared purpose, bridging distances and uniting a diverse team towards a common goal.

Liliya and Anatoli, huddled around their satellite phone, were connected to their counterparts in Kyiv. The static on the line buzzed like the nerves in Liliya's veins. The enormity of their task loomed over them, a shadow of precision and stealth. Every detail, from the timing of the extraction to the silent choreography of their movements, demanded flawless execution. The city's maze-like streets and hidden corners were both ally and adversary in their high-stakes dance.

Ivanko, on the other end in Kyiv, responded with a tone of authority. "Understood. The key is exploiting their shift changes. We have a narrow window of eight hours where we need to get in, get out and make it to the border."

Liliya interjected, her voice steady but urgent. " Blitz. Hard, fast—before they even know what hit them. Teams move like clockwork. The element of surprise is our greatest asset."

Sanenko's voice came through, calm and reassuring. "Liliya is right. This operation is a blitz—a swift, overwhelming attack designed to incapacitate the enemy before they can react, minimizing resistance and confusion. Our movements need to be coordinated down to the second. No room for error."

To mitigate these risks, meticulous coordination was paramount. Anatoli would take on the role of overwatch from the van and move each team through the different phases of the plan. Each team's movements, entry points, and actions needed to be synchronized to the second, with contingency plans in place should any aspect not proceed as anticipated. This required not only technical skill and tactical acumen but also a deep trust among the teams and their coordinator.

Anatoli's voice cut through the tension. "We need to coordinate the teams to ensure simultaneous action. If one team falls behind, the whole mission could be compromised."

Yankovic, the tech specialist, added, "We've synchronized our watches. The guards' routines show a vulnerability at precisely 2100 hours. All teams must be in position by 2050 hours. Liliya, you'll lead the ground team."

Liliya's mind raced through contingency plans, each more complex than the last. " Primary target—the scientists. Anatoli, you're in the van. Watch the guards, move us through the plan. I will accompany one of the ground teams and handle the extraction of the families."

The decision to involve at least three additional specialized teams underscored the complexity of the extraction. "Two ground teams will approach the security gate from blind spots on the east and west. A third team will take positions on the rooftops to surprise and eliminate the interior guards," Liliya detailed.

"Silencers. Secure the perimeter, then signal the rooftop team to take out interior guards," Anatoli said, eyes scanning the map.

"Three SUVs will handle transport," Ivanko added. "Once the families are out, we move. Timing's tight—seconds will make or break us."

Liliya could almost hear the ticking of an invisible clock, each second slipping away like grains of sand. "Remember," she said, her voice firm, " Even a second off, and it all falls apart. Precision. That's all that matters."

"Radio silence unless critical," Sanenko's voice was cold and precise. "No detours, no hesitation."

Each escape route was a lifeline. Anatoli's fingers traced one last map overlay. He adjusted his headset, his voice clear and authoritative as he coordinated with the team in Kyiv. "Auto shop on Myasnaya—geared and ready by sixteen hundred hours."

Liliya nodded, one swift, determined motion. Every exit mapped, every second accounted for.

Sanenko, managing the operations center in Kyiv, ensured nothing was overlooked. "Let's go over the equipment checklist again," his voice firm through the speakers. "We can't afford to miss anything. Each

SUV needs to be equipped with medical kits, weapons, and secure communication devices."

As the meeting ended, the pieces of the plan had begun to coalesce into a coherent strategy. Equipment lists were finalized, and the sequence of actions confirmed. The weight of the impending operation pressed down on Liliya, a tangible force that tightened her chest. As the satellite phones clicked off, and the planning room fell silent, the resolve of Liliya, Anatoli, and their unseen allies remained firm.

With a determined glance at Anatoli, she reaffirmed their commitment. "This is more than just a mission," she reflected aloud, her tone resolute despite the distance from their team. "It's a statement. We can't afford to fail these people, not when they've placed their trust in us."

Anatoli nodded in agreement, his eyes meeting hers. "We're ready," he said, turning off the satellite communication device. " We need rest. Prepare for what's coming."

Hours later, the satellite phone buzzed—a coded message confirming everything they needed: manpower, equipment, and transport were in place at the staging point. This was the green light, the shift from planning to action. Liliya rolled her shoulders, each breath sharpening as the weight of waiting evaporated, replaced by the biting clarity of the task at hand.

The familiar scent of gun oil lingered as they loaded into the van, a subtle reminder of every mission before this one. She adjusted her seatbelt, feeling the cold press of metal against her side, grounding her in the movement. With each passing moment, the van's low rumble thrummed through her boots, syncing with the beat of her pulse, narrowing her focus as they slipped onto the road toward the cafe. The operation was no longer a blueprint; it was real, ready to unfold.

Heading to the coffee shop, their steps were measured, their minds occupied with the magnitude of what was to come. The familiar sound of their footsteps on the cobblestone streets seemed louder, each step a countdown to the impending mission. This visit was different from the ones before. It was no longer about maintaining a routine or ensuring their presence was noted by Belyeyev for reassurance. This time, they carried the weight of imminent action and the fulfillment of the promise.

Liliya tapped her finger against the coffee cup, the rhythm syncing with the ticking clock in her mind. Across the room, a familiar face slipped through the door—first Mikhail, then Matvey, each arriving from different directions.

Anatoli gave her a subtle nod. "Right on schedule."

Liliya shifted in her seat, but her gaze drifted to the café door, her breath hitching. For a split second, *Door. Nikolai!* The air in her chest locked tight, and the soft clink of a cup set down nearby jolted her, nearly spilling the espresso across the table.

Anatoli's eyes flicked to her. "Liliya?"

She inhaled sharply, forcing herself to sit back. Her hand shook as she gripped the cup tighter, the porcelain cool against her burning palms. "Just... tired," she whispered, though the knot in her stomach tightened with every passing second. If she couldn't keep it together now, there wouldn't be another chance.

She met Anatoli's gaze, and his steady look was all the reassurance she allowed herself. As Belyeyev entered his gaze hovered on the couple by the bathroom hallway, the flicker of recognition quickly masked briefly. It was a silent nod of recognition.

He trusts you. Don't let him down. Don't let any of them down.

Inside the coffee shop, the atmosphere was tense. Liliya sipped her espresso, the bitter taste grounding her. The scientists gathered in hushed conversation at the far table, unaware of the silent war playing out in her mind. She glanced at Anatoli, who was pretending to read the newspaper. The familiarity of their routine felt thin, a fragile disguise that could shatter at any moment. We can't screw this up. They're depending on us. We don't get second chances.

Each nod from the Belyeyev, each overheard snippet of their fraught conversations, was a reminder of what was at stake: not just the success of the mission, but the lives and futures of those they had pledged to save.

"Belyeyev's keeping it together," Liliya murmured, her voice barely audible over the low hum of conversation and the clinking of cups.

Anatoli nodded, his eyes never leaving the scientists. "He's doing well. The others have no idea."

At the scientists' table, the men spoke in hushed tones, their words just out of reach. Liliya focused, using her lip-reading skills to catch snippets of their conversation. Words like "trapped," "fear," and "no escape" drifted to her, painting a picture of their desperate situation.

The clink of cups on saucers jolted her, the sound twisting into something darker—a memory. Her brother's chains scraping across the concrete floor. His muffled cries as he was dragged into the darkness. She couldn't see more from the drone footage, as pushed into a makeshift pen by smirking guards. *Not your mission. Just collateral damage.*

Her hand shook slightly as she set her coffee cup down. *You won't lose them like you lost him. Not this time.*

"We can't keep living like this," Mikhail said, his voice trembling. "The constant threats, the pressure... it's unbearable."

Matvey, the youngest of the group, looked around nervously. "Do you think anyone suspects anything?"

Belyeyev shook his head, his expression grim. "No, we've been careful. But we have to stay vigilant. One mistake and we're all dead."

As the scientists continued their conversation, Liliya turned her attention back to Anatoli. "We need to be ready. Any sign of change, and we pull them out immediately."

Anatoli folded his newspaper and set it on the table. "Agreed. We can't afford any mistakes."

Liliya watched the scientists for a moment longer, her mind racing through contingency plans. She knew the risks, understood the stakes. But seeing their faces, hearing their fear, made it even more real. They were more than just assets; they were people whose lives depended on her.

Anatoli leaned closer, his voice barely a whisper. "This is it, Liliya. We're ready."

Liliya nodded, her eyes fixed on the scientists. "Yes, we are. For them, and for us."

This subtle exchange between Liliya and Belyeyev in the coffee shop marked a critical moment in the orchestration of the operation. Belyeyev's occasional glances towards Liliya, laden with expectation and a hint of urgency, signaled his anticipation for any updates or instructions. These looks were a silent query, a search for reassurance or news that could signal the next steps in their meticulously planned escape.

The nod from Liliya and her discreet motion towards the bathroom hallway was the cue bringing about Belyeyev's response, a casual excuse to visit the bathroom.

Belyeyev shuffled toward the restroom, passing close enough for the briefest exchange—a brush of hands as she slipped the note into his palm. The touch lasted less than a second, but it sent a jolt through her.

Anatoli noticed the tremor in her hand. He leaned closer, his voice barely audible over the café's background noise. "You good?"

Liliya gave a curt nod, her face blank. *Keep it together. One more day.*

Belyeyev's fingers trembled as he unfolded the note. His eyes scanned the hurried script, each word sinking in with a mix of relief and urgency. "We move tonight. No time for second thoughts.' The message was simple, but the weight it carried was immense. The plan required them to be prepared to leave at a moment's notice, underscoring that hesitation or delay could jeopardize the entire operation. There was no room for second-guessing. The reality that any misstep could lead to capture and imprisonment was a sobering thought, bringing home the risks involved for Belyeyev and his fellow scientists.

Belyeyev, faced with the immediacy of the situation, absorbed the information with a mix of apprehension and resolve. The prospect of finally escaping the oppressive grip of the authorities that had manipulated and threatened them was both a lifeline in the storm and a plunge into the unknown. Yet, the assurance from Liliya and Anatoli that the plan was in place and the support was ready offered a semblance of comfort amid the uncertainty.

The brief exchange in the coffee shop was a testament to the operation's delicate ballet of signals, trust, and silent communication. It highlighted the operatives' ability to adapt and communicate under the watchful eyes of potential adversaries. For Belyeyev, the note represented a tangible piece of the hope and plan that Liliya, and her team were offering. For Liliya, it was a reaffirmation of her role not just as a strategist or a fighter, but as a lifeline to those ensnared in a situation far beyond their control.

As Liliya exited the washroom and she and Anatoli left the coffee shop, the weight of what had just transpired hung in the air. The operation was now in motion.

Stepping out of the coffee shop, Liliya felt the cool night air settle around her, dense and heavy. Each step on the cobblestones seemed amplified, reverberating into the shadows stretching out behind them. Her gaze drifted back every few paces, catching only flickers of movement as the city lay quiet. Yet the feeling lingered—a subtle, prickling awareness that they weren't quite alone. She told herself it was nothing—just the lingering stress of the mission.

But as they crossed the cobblestone street, she thought she heard a clink of a lighter and spotted a shadow flicker just beyond the corner. Had someone—or something—been following them?

"Anatoli," she whispered, her breath hitching. "Don't look back,"

He gave her a quick glance, recognizing the look of panic rising. "Just keep moving," he said, under his breath, his jaw tight.

Her heart pounded against her ribs as they reached the van. She slid inside, but the feeling lingered—she was sure someone was watching, waiting, just out of reach.

As the van rumbled to life and pulled away from the curb, Liliya leaned her head against the cold window, her breath fogging the glass. Every flicker of passing streetlights set her nerves on edge, feeding the gnawing sense that something—or someone—was trailing them just out of sight. She crossed her arms, rubbing her hands against her sleeves, but the unease clung to her like a second skin. Beside her, Anatoli kept his eyes on the road, his jaw set, but his hands tightened around the steering wheel—not from fear, but frustration. He knew the signs. The glances over her shoulder, the shallow breaths, the way her fingers twitched against her thighs. She was slipping, the pressure eating away at her focus.

"Liliya," he muttered, eyes fixed ahead. "No one's there."

She gave him a sidelong glance, her expression tense, as if weighing whether to believe him. "You didn't see—"

"No one's following us," he cut in gently but firmly. "It's just the mission playing tricks on you."

Liliya pressed her lips into a thin line, her hands curling into fists in her lap. She wanted to believe him—needed to—but the feeling wouldn't loosen its grip. The shadows around them felt too thick, too patient, like they knew something neither of them did.

The engine hummed steadily as the van weaved through narrow alleys and side streets, avoiding the main roads. Anatoli kept his hands light on the wheel, eyes flicking between the windshield and the side mirrors. The mission was already in motion, and Liliya needed to be sharp. If she unraveled now, they were done.

A glint in the mirror caught his eye—a shape moving in sync, silent as a shadow. His grip tightened.

"That's odd," Anatoli muttered, more to himself than to her.

Liliya stirred, glancing toward him. "What?"

"Nothing," he said, forcing a shrug. "Just a car."

He tried to let it go, but the thought festered. The streets were practically deserted at this hour—anyone else out here was either lost or had a reason to be. The car stayed two turns back, its headlights steady, neither falling behind nor closing in.

He forced himself to focus on the road ahead, but his fingers tapped lightly against the steering wheel. Stay cool. It's probably nothing.

At the next intersection, he took a sudden right without signaling, easing the van into another narrow street. His eyes flicked to the mirror.

The car appeared again, rounding the corner a moment later. Same pace. Same distance.

Anatoli exhaled slowly through his nose, adjusting his grip on the wheel. "Could be nothing," he murmured, though his pulse was starting to quicken.

The city lights blurred past, flickering through the windows as the van slipped deeper into the maze of streets. Another glance. Still there. Just far enough back to stay out of reach, but close enough to feel deliberate.

Liliya shifted beside him, her gaze scanning the side streets as if she could sense his unease. "What is it?" she asked quietly.

"Nothing," he repeated, his voice too even.

He took one more hard turn—through a narrow lane tucked between two buildings—and checked the mirror again. The headlights were gone. Just the empty stretch of asphalt behind them, washed in amber light.

Anatoli forced a breath, trying to ease the knot tightening in his chest. "See?" he said lightly. "Nothing."

But the tension stayed, prickling at the back of his neck like a warning.

TWENTY-THREE

Bridge to Freedom

At 1600 hours, Liliya and Anatoli slipped into an unassuming auto shop on Myasnaya Street. The city noise dulled behind them, giving way to the muted hum of their nerve center. Behind the cluttered workbenches and tires, a back room held their mission's heart: a sprawling map of the compound, escape routes, and guard rotations, every line and mark carved out with precision. This unadorned space pulsed with purpose—their nerve center.

Liliya's eyes locked on the diagram pinned to the wall, maps layered with guard rotations and escape paths. Her team filtered in, silent, forming a tight circle around her. Liliya stepped into the center of the team, her voice low and steady. "We don't have much time."

Her gaze swept across the faces in the circle, lingering briefly on each before turning to the sprawling blueprint pinned on the wall.

Anatoli's pen tapped once against the map, a barely-there flicker of a grin as his finger circled the guard station. "Guard's always on his phone at 21:00. He won't see us coming."

The quick glance from Liliya stilled his hand; he slipped the pen into his pocket, the grin fading. She turned back to the map, the circle around the guard's station holding her gaze for a beat. "This window is thin. We move the moment his attention slips." Her tone sharpened, a finality to her words that left no room for error.

"What if he changes routine?" a team member muttered.

"We adjust," Liliya replied, voice crisp. "Our focus is that gap. We use it."

"Routes and timing," Anatoli's gaze was sharp. "Clear?"

Silent nods all around.

"One shot," he muttered. "Don't miss."

At her command, the team gathered around, each member equipped with a digital device or a set of notes. They watched as Liliya illustrated their approach, highlighting the guard rotations and the moments when their paths would be clear.

Liliya's finger hovered briefly over the map before tracing each line, her grip steady but taut, as if holding back something unseen. With every sharp turn on the escape routes, a slight hesitation flickered in her movements. Her breaths deepened as she forced each inhale to steady her pulse. She clenched her jaw, tapped the map, and moved on, eyes sharper, more focused. "Entry sequence. Again," she commanded, her voice cold, controlled. She had to keep them safe. This time, no one would be left behind.

"Sync watches. To the second," Liliya commanded. "Precision. Unity. That guard at the north gate? He's our moment."

As Anatoli and Liliya led the discussion, their strategic expertise evident, Sanenko's voice crackled in over the comms from Kyiv. "Drone confirms guard shifts easing by evening. You've got a slim window."

Anatoli watched Liliya make the last adjustment to the timeline. "That works," he murmured, nodding once before glancing toward the SUVs lined up in the corner. "Let's position the SUVs and do a final gear check."

The team broke off, quiet and swift, each movement practiced but tense. Liliya pulled her gear bag closer. Her fingers tightened around the straps, checking, re-checking each piece. Every item, every tool— she felt their weight, knew their purpose. One mistake and the whole mission could unravel.

The SUVs were packed, the night unfolding around them in cold silence as they gathered under the moon's dim light, faces streaked with paint, weapons checked with a final click. Night goggles snapped into place. Radios, silent. Every breath muffled in the tension that swelled with each passing second.

At 2030 hours, Liliya shifted back from the team, gripping the satellite phone with a quiet ferocity. Davyd's calm and steady response provided a momentary solace. "We're here, Liliya. We're with you."

Her thumb pressed against the cold plastic, tension coiling in her hand like a silent anchor. The dim garage light caught the set of her jaw as she steadied her breath, absorbing the weight of Davyd's voice on the other end, settling herself for a second, then releasing a barely noticeable exhale.

"I know. Just... hearing your voice makes this easier."

The name Davyd drifted through the static, low but distinct. Anatoli shifted his weight, pretending to concentrate on the teams in the shop, though the sound stuck with him.

He watched from the SUV, saw her shoulders drop slightly, voice low as she murmured into the phone. He looked away, catching the shift as she straightened, unreadable, when she returned.

She'll keep it together. She always has.

She pressed her lips together, steadying herself. "Copy that," she whispered, wiping a hand quickly across her face. She clenched her fists, placing herself in the resolve that had brought her this far. Turning back to the teams, she drew in a final, steadying breath. The moment of vulnerability passed, leaving behind a desire to see the mission through.

Anatoli exhaled slowly, tapping the toe of his boot against the asphalt. Not my business. And it wasn't. But even as he turned toward the group, he couldn't quite shake the feeling that this time might be different.

"It's time." Liliya's voice was low, steady. She glanced at the team, barely nodding. A breath—sharp, bracing. "Let's go."

The night swallowed them whole as they slipped toward the SUVs, boots clicking softly on concrete. No wasted movements. Just silence and shadows.

The convoy turned north, headlights cutting the wet asphalt on a bridge. Liliya's gaze flicked to her team—grim, focused. She tightened her grip on the holster, breath matching the steady beat of her pulse. Steady. Ready.

The bridge dropped away behind them, the road straightening as the convoy picked up speed. Liliya's battle with her inner demons intensified, a silent struggle that threatened to undermine her composure.

She stared out the window. The landscape bled into a blur—faces. People I couldn't save. The weight of the commander's death clawed at her—that knife, that night... Too close. Almost lost everything. Liliya forced the memories down, pressing them into the pit of her mind. The compound loomed ahead.

Her pulse quickened, a telltale hitch in her breath. A flicker of tension traced her limbs, her fingers pressing against her leg as she braced against the rush. She rubbed her arm briefly, letting the cool air slip over her skin to steady her focus. This was a point of balance—control hard-fought and kept in check, one heartbeat at a time. Inhale. Her shoulders dropped slightly with each exhale, the movement barely visible but deliberate. The physical act helped to ground her, pulling her out of the spiraling thoughts.

A quick look back again—sharp eyes met hers, ready. No hesitation. She couldn't slip. Her fingers pressed into her palms. Steady. This is what you trained for.

As they sped through the city's darkened streets, Liliya leaned closer to the windshield, her breaths pacing with the rhythmic hum of the road beneath. Her fingers flexed against her thigh, each tightening pulse an attempt to keep focus. Her eyes narrowed, dismissing the nagging flickers of doubt in her periphery as she fixed herself on the road stretching ahead.

The SUVs, nondescript and silent, navigated through the darkness, each movement calculated, each turn a step closer to the compound that held the scientists and their families. The convoy slowed.

The meticulously planned operation began to unfold as the teams approached their target. The darkened streets of Perevoznaya Street, lined with the shadows that would serve as their allies, whispered of the impending action.

Meanwhile, in a nearby building, Belyeyev climbed the stairwell two steps at a time, his breath tight in his chest. Every creak of the wooden steps felt amplified, every shadow a threat. He stopped at Dr. Ilyin's door, pressing an ear to the frame. No noise from inside, but his skin prickled with the awareness that the guards were always listening.

His knock was a whisper against the heavy wood. The door opened a crack, revealing Dr. Ilyin's face—pale, with eyes wide and sunken from sleepless nights.

"Belyeyev, what's going on?" Ilyin whispered, his voice barely audible, glancing nervously around as if the walls themselves might be listening.

"We move tonight. Be ready to leave everything. It's risky, but it's our chance," Belyeyev murmured, passing the paper like a clandestine token of rebellion. His voice was steady, a stark contrast to the tremor he felt inside.

Ilyin's hands trembled as he took the paper, his eyes scanning the message quickly. "I understand," he replied, his throat tightening. "I'll prepare my family."

As Belyeyev turned toward the next apartment, the weight on his shoulders grew heavier. Every family carried their hope like fragile glass, and it was his job to keep it from shattering.

The compound emerged through gaps in the buildings, a looming silhouette against the dark sky. The operation now split into synchronized, strategic movements. The front-running SUV was the first to arrive and turned onto the street, traveling 50 meters past the gate.

Memories and fears that had threatened to overwhelm her were gradually replaced by a steely resolve. This transformation was not born of denial or suppression but of acceptance and determination. The time for doubt was over.

The second set of vehicles discreetly positioned themselves on the cross street to the compound, parking along the walkway near the Buckles River. A strategic location that offered both cover and an advantageous approach. As the SUVs came to a stop and the team prepared to disembark, Liliya took a deep breath, steadying herself. She cast one last glance at the compound, a silhouette against the night sky, then turned to her team, her eyes reflecting the unwavering tenacity that had brought them to this moment.

Anatoli emerged first from the first SUV, the shadows welcomed him, concealing his movements as he made his way to the parked van. Slipping into position in the van, he adjusted his night vision, breath measured, muscles coiled with intent.

"Anatoli, are you in position?" Liliya's voice crackled softly in his earpiece.

"Copy that, Liliya. I've got eyes on the gate and surrounding areas," he replied, his voice calm and controlled. He scanned the perimeter, noting the positions of the guards. "Everything's clear for now."

She flicked her gaze to the guard post ahead. "Ninety seconds," she muttered to her team. "We move on my mark."

"Team One go!" Anatoli's voice cracked over the comms. They exited the vehicle and moved, shadows against the darkness, reaching the wall.

Back in the van, Anatoli monitored their progress, "You're clear to proceed to point two."

They reached the wall by the gate, pausing to listen for any signs of detection. The lead signaled, receiving a nod. They scaled the wall, landing silently. The guard shifted, unaware. Heartbeats steady, breaths tight.

Anatoli's voice came through the comms, steady. "Clear. Move on Leader's signal."

Anatoli watched vigilantly through the scope. "Everything looks clear for now," he muttered, his voice steady but his mind whirling with scenarios and contingencies. He keyed his mic, "Team Two and Three, you're clear to proceed. Remember, no mistakes."

Liliya's hand hovered over the door handle, breath steady. "This is it," she muttered, eyes sweeping over her team—silent, sharp, ready. "Stay close. Stay sharp," Liliya whispered. "We move as one."

Together, they stepped out into the night, moving towards the compound with a silent and coordinated precision that belied the tumultuous journey that had led them here. Liliya's mind raced with memories of past missions, each success and failure acting as a possible trigger or fortifier. This operation was not just a mission; it was a step towards reconciliation with her past, a chance to channel her experiences into a force for change.

Liliya moved forward, carrying the team's hopes—and her own. Her breaths, controlled. Each step: resolve.

The team assigned to neutralize the inner courtyard guards demonstrated their readiness and skill, launching grappling hooks with accuracy. The sound of metal biting into the rooftop was barely audible. As they ascended, they resembled specters climbing towards their targets, invisible to all but the most vigilant observer.

"Keep it steady," whispered the lead climbers, his voice barely audible. He glanced at his fellow team member, a silent nod confirming their synchronization.

Meanwhile, Liliya's team, operating under the cover of the building's shadow, advanced with deliberate caution towards the gate. Liliya, despite the tremors and weakness that betrayed her inner turmoil, moved with purpose, her resolve steeling her against the physical manifestation of her stress. She clenched her fists. Her eyes locked on the guard. Almost there. Don't miss it.

Across the courtyard, Dr. Smirnov stood by the window, his silhouette hidden behind heavy curtains. His wife clutched their daughter, her fingers white against the child's arm.

"They'll come for us, right?" her voice trembled, but she kept it low.

Smirnov placed a hand on her shoulder, squeezing tighter than he meant to. "Yes," he whispered, more for himself than for her. "They will."

He checked his watch. Seconds stretched into eternity. His stomach twisted, every sound from the street setting his nerves on edge. Somewhere out there, his fate—and the future of his family—rested in the hands of strangers dressed in black.

The guard stood at the gate, bathed in the faint blue glow of his phone. Liliya's breath sharpened, her shoulders setting as the guard shifted, oblivious to their movement. This is it—no room for error. She tightened her grip, her pulse keeping time with the seconds ticking down, her movements crisp and silent.

"Team Two, prepare to move," Anatoli's voice whispered through the comms.

Liliya gritted her teeth, watching the guard scroll lazily through his phone. Move now. Before he looks up. Her chest tightened, the weight of every failure pressing against her ribs. You can't fail now.

"Guards still distracted." Anatoli's voice crackled.

Liliya's nod was sharp, her mind focused. Now, before anything goes wrong.

The operation reached its peak at exactly 2100 hours. With a terse "Go, go, go," from Liliya over the comms, they sprang forward, moving as a single, silent force into the night.

The stillness fractured as teams slipped into their assigned positions, each movement sharp and deliberate. Shadows among shadows, they advanced, weapons raised, eyes keen. The ground teams moved from their cover, closing in on their unsuspecting targets. Silencers hissed in unison, sharp and final. Without a sound, the bodies dropped, disappearing as swiftly as they'd come.

They lifted the bodies, stowing them in the shadows they'd just emerged from. By the time the night fell silent once more, there was no trace of the chaos that had punctuated it—only the faint echo of their swift, deadly precision.

In Smirnov's apartment, Smirnov's wife clutched her daughter close, her gaze snapping to Liliya. "Are we safe?" she whispered.

Liliya held her gaze, unflinching. "We will be."

The operation unfolded in precise, silent movements. The third team, perched atop the building, melted into the shadows, slipping over the edge with practiced ease. Dark figures against a darker sky, they moved in sync, the roof fading behind them as they descended, each motion calculated to avoid detection.

Below, two guards paced the courtyard, oblivious to the shifting shadows above. A flash of movement—a muffled step, a quick, quiet strike. The guards barely registered the threat before they fell, silence swallowing the brief scuffle.

A low crackle in Liliya's earpiece broke the stillness. "Liliya," Anatoli's voice came, calm but taut. "Inner courtyard is clear. Move to the next waypoint."

She gave a curt nod, the sound barely a whisper. "Roger," she murmured, gesturing her team forward with a quick hand signal. They moved as one, slipping into the shadows ahead, the weight of the mission pressing in on every step.

Liliya felt a moment of doubt creep in. What if something goes wrong? She pushed the thought away, concentrating on the mission. No room for errors now, she reminded herself, her grip tightening on her weapon. She glanced at her team; their faces were set. They were ready.

As the last guard slumped silently to the ground, Liliya signaled to the teams. Phase one was complete. The tempo quickened, the operation's rhythm shifting to match their precise, practiced coordination. Moving like shadows, they pressed deeper into the compound's heart, their steps precise, each movement fluid and silent.

Liliya and Teams One and Two hugged the perimeter wall, slipping eastward past the scientist's building. Every glance shared between team members was brief but loaded with intent. Across the compound, Team Three advanced, weaving southward before veering east, positioning themselves at the building's south entrance. The compound's tight grip loosened with each step forward, its secrecy unraveling under the team's relentless push.

The night, once cloaking the compound in silence, now pulsed with the silent beat of a mission well underway.

They paused at each waypoint. Liliya's pulse pounded, every step tightening the grip on her chest. Each step, one closer to the edge. Don't falter.

"Two guards. North entrance," Anatoli's voice crackled through the comms. "Move now."

Belyeyev reached his own apartment, where his wife and children sat waiting in the dark. He knelt by his children. "We're going on a trip," he murmured, brushing a lock from his daughter's face. "Stay close."

His son nodded solemnly. They didn't ask questions. They'd learned that much.

Liliya raised her hand, fingers stiff, each knuckle tight under her skin. Her hand hovered, poised like a drawn wire ready to snap. Beneath the surface, her muscles ached, a reminder of the one chance they had. Keep it together. No sound. No hesitation.

"Stay close. Quiet." Liliya's voice was a whisper, her thoughts focused. Almost there. No mistakes. Almost there. Just a little further. No mistakes.

She could almost feel the cold press of metal, hear the faint murmur of mocking voices, dark rooms and shadows waiting to close in. The guards shifted, oblivious, as her hand tightened around her weapon. She forced a calm breath. This was her move now, her rules. "Mark." She moved, swift and silent, reclaiming control with each step.

With the guards down, Liliya gave the signal. "Go, go, go," she whispered.

The teams slipped inside—silent, precise. Liliya crouched low in the dim hallway. Two guards stood by Belyeyev's door, their backs to her. The muffled thud of her pulse filled her head, a thick drumming that blurred the sharp edges of her surroundings. Each tick of the second hand grated against her focus, stretching into minutes.

Anatoli's voice crackled in her ear. "Ready on my mark. Three... two... one. Go."

Liliya moved. Fast. Fluid. Her silenced pistol slid up as if on its own, her fingers cold and automatic around the grip. A single shot, no more than a whisper, yet the recoil shot through her arm and reverberated in her teeth. One guard folded: the second slumped in a silent ripple. She caught the man's weight before he hit the ground, easing him down. No sound. No trace.

Her eyes swept the hallway. Clear. She gave a quick nod—keep moving.

Simultaneously, other teams struck. Shadows in motion. Silenced shots whispered through the night. One by one, guards fell—without a cry, without warning. Their bodies folded, then quickly moved out of camera sight.

Through her earpiece: "Team One, secure."

Another voice: "Team Two, secure."

The third: "Team Three, secure."

Liliya's breath steadied, but her mind stayed sharp. No time to pause. Keep pushing.

She and her partner reached the next door. Quick glance. Clear path. Liliya's thoughts flickered to Davyd—so close now. Just one more step.

"Proceed as planned," Anatoli ordered, his voice calm, controlled.

Liliya gave the nod. The teams pressed forward, swift and soundless. Each step was a heartbeat in the mission's rhythm. No hesitation. No mistakes.

TWENTY-FOUR

Chase Through Shadows

With all hostiles down, the team slipped back toward the SUVs in tight formation, movements sharp and silent. The vehicles were their lifeline; there was no room for error. Shadows swallowed their approach as they moved, each step calculated, each breath held steady.

The SUVs rolled in, engines purring low, vibrations thrumming through the ground like a heartbeat. High walls of the compound loomed dark and empty, a silent witness to the bodies left behind. Doors opened and slammed shut in quick succession, each one a signal, crisp and final. In unison, they pressed forward into the night, leaving only silence in their wake.

Liliya's fingers skimmed the cold metal, a sharp anchor against the dread threatening her focus. She knocked once, crisp and quick. Belyeyev's wary gaze met hers as the door swung open. "It's time," she murmured, voice steady despite the flicker of dread creeping up her spine. "We need to move quickly."

Belyeyev glanced at the fallen guards, his relief barely a whisper. "Thank you," he murmured, urgency thick in his voice. "We'll move quickly."

"Neither did I," Liliya replied, managing a small smile. "But we're here now. Let's get you and your family to safety."

His smile, wide and genuine, was a testament to the depth of his despair and the height of his newfound hope. With a nod, Liliya beckoned him and his family to follow, leading them from the darkness of captivity into the light of potential freedom.

As Belyeyev knocked on his colleagues' doors, Liliya scanned the dimly lit hall, her fingers curling into fists at her sides, knuckles white with tension. The faint murmur of children's voices seeped through the walls; small, uncertain sounds that made her jaw tighten reflexively. Her gaze flicked back to the corridor, sharpening with a silent vow she couldn't voice. No one was getting left behind this time.

He called out, "Move now. Bring only what you need."

As each door opened, Liliya gave a sharp nod, answering the unspoken question in their eyes. "It's happening. Now, stay close."

As Liliya ushered each family member toward the SUVs, her hands found familiar places on their shoulders, guiding them firmly but gently. Her grip hardened unconsciously on the shoulder of a teenage girl, who glanced up with a questioning look. Liliya quickly softened her hold, shifting her gaze forward, swallowing against the tightness in her throat. Her jaw clenched at the sight of their hopeful faces, the weight of each life pressing against her chest like armor she couldn't remove.

As they approached the waiting SUVs, Anatoli's earpiece crackled with sudden static—a garbled frequency cutting through the night.

"Open line," Liliya whispered, tension sharpening her voice. "One of the guards' radios is still live."

Andrei muttered a curse, already sprinting toward the nearest body. He reached the guard just as the radio crackled, "Unit four, report!"

The team went still. Liliya's pulse pounded in her ears, each beat ticking too fast. Andrei grabbed the radio, pressed the button, and forced out a calm, "All clear. Quiet here."

A pause. Silence stretched, pulling every nerve taut.

"Copy that," came the reply. "Next check-in in ninety."

Andrei dropped the radio and exhaled, sharp.

Andrei ripped the radio from the guard's belt, brought it to his mouth, and forced his voice into calm. "All clear. It's quiet here."

There was a brief, tense pause before the reply crackled through the static. "Copy that. Don't miss your next check-in. Over and out."

Andrei clicked the radio off and tossed it aside, exhaling slowly.

Liliya was already moving. "Now. No time to second-guess. Get to the SUVs," she ordered, her voice sharp with urgency. She gave Belyeyev a nudge, spurring him forward. "Now." Liliya's hand moved to the handle, a silent directive.

The scientist's grip tightened around his child's hand as he paused at the SUV door, his gaze flitting between Liliya and the dark compound. She gave a quick nod. "Keep moving. We're getting out."

The man hesitated, then gave a reluctant nod and hurried his child into the vehicle. Liliya lingered for half a second longer, her grip on the handle tightening as the scent of gasoline and the distant hum of an engine coiled around her senses. A flicker of doubt brushed against her resolve, light as a breath.

Liliya exhaled, forcing the air out as she shut the SUV door with a solid, final snap. "Move," she ordered, her voice clipped as she spun toward the others. Behind her, the rumble of engines filled the air, growing louder, more urgent, like a heartbeat driving them into the dark.

Engines idled, their vibrations humming beneath her feet. The team moved fast, securing scientists and families, working silently in the dark.

Andrei dragged a limp body by the wrists, the man's boots scraping over concrete, leaving faint trails in the dust. The faint stench of blood mingled with motor oil and exhaust, souring the night air. He grunted, shifting his grip. "I hate this part," he muttered, his voice tight with disgust.

Daria knelt beside the open van; her hands slick with sweat beneath her gloves as she hauled another body into position. "We all do," she replied, her tone flat but resolute. "But it has to be done."

Andrei's arm cut across his face, smearing sweat that stung like salt in his eyes. "I know." His shoulders sagged under the weight of the task. "Still doesn't make it any easier." He kept his movements quick, precise, as if any wasted motion might draw attention. Even the night air, thick with gasoline and the bite of motor oil, pressed in close, sharpening his senses against any lapse

Daria straightened, the leather of her gloves creaking as she adjusted them. She rested a hand on his shoulder, the gesture brief but deliberate. "Focus on the goal," she said, her voice low. "We're almost there."

Andrei gave a curt nod, the faint scent of gasoline thickening as he swung the van's door shut with a dull thud. The sound echoed in the quiet, heavy as the knowledge of what lay behind it.

The hum of the engines grew louder, more insistent, pulling them forward. Time pressed down on them like a vice, each second ticking away too fast. They couldn't leave any trace behind—not if they wanted to cross the border before the alarm was raised.

Daria glanced toward Liliya, who stood by the lead SUV, her expression unreadable beneath the shadows that stretched across the lot. The cold night air clung to them all, thick with unspoken urgency.

"Let's finish this," Daria murmured, turning back to Andrei.

The two of them moved with grim efficiency, the scent of motor oil and cold metal trailing in their wake as they secured the scene. Every action—every drag of a body, every turn of a key—was measured against the ticking clock in their minds.

The anticipation of reaching the border and successfully completing their mission was tempered by the knowledge that their safety was not yet assured. The final leg of their journey was fraught with the potential for discovery. However, the resolve that had brought them this far fueled their dedication to see their charge to safety.

Liliya and Anatoli's positions in the front seats of the first SUVs underscored their leadership roles, ensuring oversight and readiness to respond to any unforeseen complications. As they led their charge out of the compound, the route plotted to avoid detection and maximize speed.

Liliya's gaze flicked to the sideview mirror, where the boy in the back seat clutched his father's sleeve. Her grip tightened on the armrest, heart pounding. Keep your eyes forward, she told herself. This isn't the past.

She forced her gaze back to the road, swallowing hard. There was no room for ghosts here, not with so much at stake.

From the backseat, a small voice broke the silence. "Are we safe?" a child's voice whispered.

Liliya couldn't answer. Not with the checkpoint ahead, and shadows pressing in from every side. But Anatoli's steady reply filled the silence: "Yes. Almost there. Just hold tight."

Liliya glanced at him, grateful for the lie she couldn't bring herself to tell. But she watched the road ahead stretching into darkness, hands clenched tight. She knew too well that promises like that were made to be broken.

The night wrapped tightly around the convoy; every kilometer covered pulling them closer to safety but with no guarantees. The dim headlights cut through the darkness, catching glimpses of wary faces, each jolt over rough pavement reminding them that freedom was not yet won. The team, aware of the stakes, navigated the route with a keen awareness of their surroundings, prepared for any contingencies that might arise.

The first turn came fast—a hard left north toward Bannyy Bridge. Anatoli's hands tightened on the wheel, knuckles pale against the leather as he guided the convoy onto the slick road. Liliya's eyes flicked to the rearview mirror, watching their tail, her fingers tapping a silent rhythm against her thigh.

"Clear behind," she murmured, but her gaze didn't leave the mirror.

The convoy moved with precision, rolling through the darkened streets toward Staro-Petergofskiy Avenue. Anatoli navigated each intersection, skirting puddles that could betray their path with splashes. Streetlamps loomed overhead, casting long shadows that twisted across the road like silent watchers.

"Turn ahead," Liliya said, voice low, fingers braced against the dashboard as he swung them onto the Obvodniy Channel embankment. The river's inky black water mirrored the tension pressing down on them, the steady hum of the tires the only sound breaking the silence.

They followed the Ekateringofka River, sliding onto the Western High-Speed Diameter. Each turn felt like a step closer to freedom, yet every stretch of road stretched longer than the last. Ahead lay the E-20—their final path toward the border.

"Almost there," Anatoli muttered, eyes scanning the road, his jaw set.

"Stay sharp," Liliya replied, her voice tight, almost a whisper. Her fingers gripped the edge of her seat as another streetlamp passed, its light flashing briefly across her face. They shared a look, a silent acknowledgment of the risk hanging over them like a blade.

Liliya gripped the door handle, her fingers numb against the cold metal. Every bump in the road sent vibrations through her arm, each jolt pulling her back to a dozen other rides, each one a reminder: don't look back. Her voice came out low, pressed. "We don't stop. Not for anything."

In the back seat, a child's small voice wavered. "Are we going to make it?"

Anatoli met the child's gaze in the rearview mirror, a quick nod. "Almost there."

Liliya turned her gaze to the window, her breath fogging the glass for an instant. Her reflection stared back—pale, ghostlike. She exhaled slowly and whispered, almost to herself, "We have to."

She keyed the radio and spoke into the handset. "We're on the final stretch. Stay sharp. Report status."

The second SUV's response came through first, Andrei's voice low and clipped. "Checkpoint at Kilometer 8 just came online. They're stopping vehicles. We need to avoid the main route."

Liliya stiffened. "Take the detour. If we hit that checkpoint, we're done."

Daria's voice followed from the third SUV, laced with static. "Copy that. Signal's breaking up—stay close, or we'll lose comms."

Anatoli's hands tightened on the wheel; his knuckles white against the leather. "The alternate route takes us near the industrial yard," he muttered. "There might be cameras."

Liliya adjusted her grip on the radio. "We'll handle it if we have to. Just keep moving."

The convoy veered onto a side road, engines rumbling low, slipping into the thick of night. Shadows spilled over the path, rusted machines jutting out like sentries from a forgotten war, watching them pass. Every gear shift and turn felt like a gamble, each shadow a reminder of the eyes they knew they were leaving behind. Beyond, the checkpoint's lights flickered faintly, a reminder of what lay behind.

They pushed past the industrial yard, avoiding cameras where they could. Back on the E-20, the hum of the tires felt deafening, each kilometer dragging them closer to the border and the heightened risk of discovery. It was a race against time, precision their only ally.

The city lights vanished. Darkness stretched ahead, each turn sharpening the line between safety and danger. Liliya's grip loosened on the radio, her voice barely a murmur: "We might just make it."

Line's breaking up," Anatoli muttered, tapping his earpiece with a grim expression.

Liliya glanced sharply at him, a sense of dread pooling in her gut. "How bad?"

A crackle of static cut through the line, then Andrei's voice came through, tight with urgency. "Signal's compromised. I'm picking up an external frequency."

The interference grew, a sharp, electric hiss filling the line. Liliya clenched the armrest, her pulse hammering as her eyes flicked between the dark road and the sideview mirror. The weight of every second stretched her nerves taut as wire.

"Someone's on us," she muttered, voice a low, tight thread. Her hand curled, nails pressing into her palm, anchoring her to the present. "We can't afford to slow. We keep moving."

With a quick, decisive motion, she switched to the convoy's private line. "Switch to the detour now," she commanded, voice cold with urgency. Her eyes flicked to the sideview mirror, catching a faint glint in the distance—a flash of light reflecting off something metallic.

"Everyone, move. Fast."

A final look at the sideview mirror revealed a faint light far behind, hovering just at the edge of visibility. It flickered once, twice, and then dimmed, leaving her pulse thrumming with unspoken tension. Liliya narrowed her eyes, every nerve alert to the darkness beyond. This wasn't over—not yet.

CHAPTER

TWENTY-FIVE

Dawn of a New Day

The convoy lurched sharply, tires biting gravel, the jolt snapping Liliya back against the seat—a shock that echoed the bruising weight of old, steel restraints. Shadows thickened, swallowing them whole, engines dying to a soft, steady pulse, barely audible under the sharp crunch of tires on dirt. Each bounce jarred her spine, pressing her deeper into the seat, body braced against the cold bite of metal as the trees tightened around them. Liliya's grip on the radio tightened again, her thoughts racing even as her voice remained steady.

It took a long stretch of miles before the static in the radio cleared. Gradually, the tension in the car settled, the passengers lulled by the rhythm of the road. Liliya's pulse steadied as the convoy pressed through the dense forest, each vehicle slipping like shadows into the dark. She glanced back—children bundled close to their parents, clinging to any hint of safety they could find. The flicker of relief in their tired faces was brief, easily overtaken by fear as the vehicle bounced over another rough patch. Liliya tightened her grip on the radio, her focus sharpening with every mile they cleared.

As the convoy returned to the E-20, a tentative calm took hold. As she adjusted her grip on the radio, her thumb traced the smooth, worn edge—a practiced gesture that steadied her breath, just enough to ease her pulse. Her gaze drifted back to the families, the soft laughter almost blurring in her ears, replaced by the echo of her own harsh breathing in the tight, empty spaces of past missions. A muscle in her jaw clenched, pulling her back to the present, to her resolve.

Liliya's journey felt like walking two tightropes: one leading her through the mission's dangers, the other through her tangled emotions. The stark contrast between her experience and the budding relief visible among the other occupants of the vehicle underscored the solitude of her struggle.

Liliya's gaze drifted over the huddled families. Her fingers tapped twice on the radio, a habit she hadn't noticed until now. The children's laughter, tentative and fleeting, brushed against the silence like a soft breeze—momentary relief in a heavy air that refused to lift. She felt a tightness in her chest ease, just a bit, as she absorbed the simple joy of that moment.

Anatoli's hands tightened on the steering wheel, his knuckles whitening. A slight, nearly imperceptible frown creased his brow as he scanned the road ahead, glancing at Liliya's fingers as they gripped the radio. Without taking his eyes off the road, he muttered, "Think they're ready for this?"

Liliya's gaze shifted to the families behind them, her mind cataloging every vulnerable face, every clutched child. No one's ever ready. Her hand flexed around the seat handle, her thumb grazing over a small ridge in the metal as if tracing out an old scar. For a second, she let her eyes close, the faint echo of that first day of training—rigid hours and aching muscles—settling over her. When she opened them, her hand held the handle tighter, her jaw set. She glanced over to Anatoli, "They don't have a choice."

His fingers relaxed on the wheel for just a moment, then tightened again. "Guess neither do we." His tone was casual, almost light, but a flicker of something crossed his face—there, then gone, like the brief reflection of sunlight in the rearview mirror.

Liliya's mind was a whirlwind of thoughts and fears. She turned her gaze to the passing landscape, trying to anchor herself. The memories of past missions, the faces of those she couldn't save, and the constant threat of failure loomed large in her mind. Her pulse quickened, and she had to remind herself to breathe.

She wiped her eyes with the back of her hand, the tears hidden beneath her hair. Her jaw clenched as she fought to keep her emotions in check, not wanting to show any sign of weakness. She glanced at Anatoli, his concentration unwavering, and felt a pang of gratitude for his steadiness.

You can't afford to break down now. Not when we're so close.

Liliya traced the ridges of her radio's antenna with her thumb, the familiar sensation grounding her momentarily, though not enough to steady the unease curling in her chest. The air inside the vehicle was thick with gasoline and the stale scent of leather seats, but as she shifted her weight, a hint of pine drifted in through the cracked window. It was faint, carried by the cool breeze, but it tugged at a memory.

Her hand instinctively brushed over her shoulder, feeling for a weight that wasn't there, a phantom press of his hand that would usually steady her in times like this. She swallowed, her fingers curling into the fabric of her own jacket, drawing a deep breath as she forced herself to focus on the road ahead.

Her breath hitched, a flicker of warmth sparking in her chest. She could almost feel Davyd's hand press between her shoulder blades, steady and firm. But the warmth twisted, bringing the chill of another hand—the weight of cold fingers against her neck, forcing her still. Liliya jerked her head, snapping herself back to the present, her fingers twitching around the radio's antenna. Davyd. Focus on Davyd. He was here, in the edges of her thoughts, a lifeline she couldn't afford to lose. She exhaled slowly, her grip on the radio easing as the thought flickered, warming her from within.

Anatoli glanced her way from the driver's seat. "You okay?"

Liliya gave a small nod. "Yeah. Just thinking." They were approaching the next turn, the border receding behind them like a memory best left unvisited. She refocused, forcing her mind to the convoy's progress, counting the distance markers as they passed in a blur.

She closed her eyes briefly, letting the hum of the engine beneath them mimic the steady rhythm of his heartbeat when she rested her head against his chest. For just a second, her breath slowed, as if the idea of that future could make the tightness in her chest bearable.

I'm coming back to you. Just hold on a little longer.

Her fingers twitched, and she tightened her grip on the doorhandle. She blinked hard, forcing herself to concentrate on the road ahead as the tires thumped over a crack in the asphalt.

"One thing at a time," she reminded herself, releasing the door handle, unaware of how tightly she had been gripping it. The ache in her fingers told her just how deep the tension ran—so constant she no longer noticed until she tried to let it go.

Outside, the wind whispered through the cracked window, carrying hints of damp earth and diesel. Liliya inhaled sharply, the scent biting at her senses, and for a moment, she wondered what it would feel like to breathe air that wasn't saturated with fear.

"When we cross the border," she murmured to herself, "that's when it ends." She imagined the moment—crisp, neutral air filling her lungs, free of gasoline and control. She'd let the mission go, finally. But not yet. First, she needed to get them there. One more time. One last time.

Engines hummed beneath them, steady and deliberate, as the convoy pushed toward the border. Liliya's eyes flicked to the side mirror, tracking the other vehicle. A sharp, unbidden thought sliced through her focus—if these families didn't make it to NATO soil, everything they risked would be for nothing.

"Stay close," Liliya murmured into the radio, her tone sharp. "If we lose anyone, the whole operation unravels." She'd seen the unraveling before—the slow bleed of hope, the fraying of lives when a single hand slipped, and then another. She knew how even a moment of hesitation could leave fractures in a mission that would never heal.

She pressed the radio closer, as if that alone could reach every car in the convoy, her will clamping around them like an iron band. Not one slip. Her voice hardened, her entire being narrowing to the conviction that they'd make it through, that she wouldn't let history repeat itself. "One shot at this," she whispered, her words swallowed by the engine's low rumble. "No second chances."

Liliya's resolve to complete the mission became intertwined with her resolve to embark on this personal journey of healing. The path to recovery would likely be long and fraught with its challenges, mirroring the complexities of the operations she had led. Yet, the promise of a future with Davyd, of a life reclaimed from the depths of her profession's demands, offered a compelling incentive.

We're doing this for them, too. For their chance at a new life.

The bridge loomed ahead. Its concrete frame stood stark, an indifferent divider between captivity and freedom. Liliya's pulse steadied, her mind narrowing to the familiar rhythm of high-stakes operations. Every second felt thin, every movement honed. The guards moved like clockwork—rigid patterns drilled into muscle memory. Soldiers trained to guard what was never truly theirs.

The scent of pine clung to her memory, a fragile tether to Davyd. But now wasn't the time to linger on ghosts. Her eyes caught a large amount of movement at the crossing. They darted from guard to guard. Sandbags dropped. Wooden beams clattered into place. Every gesture was hastened as they were in the process of shutting the crossing down.

"Floor it on my signal," she bark into the radio, voice low and steady. Her grip on the radio was firm, any trace of doubt smothered by the looming countdown. She surveyed the road, calculating the exact moment they'd need to break for it.

The guard at the checkpoint took a step forward, squinting into the distance as if catching movement. His hand rose toward his radio. Liliya's pulse quickened.

Liliya's thumb hovered over the transmit button, pulse thrumming in her wrist as her other hand clenched around the cold metal of the door. Her eyes narrowed on the silhouettes of the guards, muscles coiling as if bracing for impact. She could almost feel the weight of the mission pressing against her shoulders, the faint clink of shifting rifles breaking through the silence. One heartbeat, then two, then— "Go! Hit it now!"

Engines snarled to life, tires screeching as the convoy launched forward, her spine slamming back—a hard, unforgiving impact like the crack of bone against concrete, the grind of grit biting her skin. Headlights bore down on the guards, cutting through the darkness like blades. The guards hesitated, momentarily frozen by the sudden burst of speed. Her breath turned shallow, heartbeat rapid and uneven, matching the relentless churn of tires clawing for purchase, pulling them past shadows of waiting rifles.

A shout cut the night. Rifles jerked upward as the guards dove aside, sandbags crashing down around them. One stumbled, his weapon clattering against the pavement as he scrambled for cover.

Liliya's SUV hurtled forward, tires clawing at loose gravel. The next two clung close, the engines snarling as one. Her fingers clenched around the armrest as they barreled forward, every nerve on edge.

Headlights flashed over another guard. He dove behind a sandbag as the convoy tore through, gravel spitting up in clouds. A bullet pinged off the trailing SUV, but they kept pushing.

Her pulse matched the tires' rhythm as they hit Estonian asphalt. Behind them, the dark swallowed up the Russian side. But relief wouldn't come yet—the adrenaline stuck, cold and heavy. She gripped the armrest, fingers curling into it as if that tension alone would hold her steady. The Russian checkpoint melted into the night behind them, but the weight in her chest stayed lodged, heavy and unmoving.

Her breath stuttered, every inhale sharp and jagged, the ache rising through her ribs, tight as the first time she'd been trapped under the glare of interrogation lights, unable to exhale fully until the threat was a shadow fading behind her.

Her gaze flicked to the side mirror, tracking the dark ribbon of road unspooling behind them. Fence posts whipped by in a blur, shadows stretching long and thin—each one a potential hiding place. What if they following? The thought coiled tight, knotting her stomach. Her thumb tapped twice against the cold door frame—a habit, a tether to keep her in the moment—but the pulse of fear refused to release its grip.

Even as the border disappeared behind them, her mind stayed locked on the possibility: What if they come?

The convoy slipped into Estonian territory. Fifty meters in, they slowed—then stopped. Engines cut, leaving a silence that rang sharp. Liliya sat still, fingers hovering over the door handle, calculating next moves out of instinct—because even here, she knew how quickly safety could unravel.

Not yet. Not until they were further away. Not until there was no chance of pursuit.

Anatoli let out a low breath, more exhale than words. His shoulders sagged slightly, but only for a second before he squared them again, the practiced resilience settling back in place. "We made it," he said, his voice steady.

Liliya caught the slight tremor in his hand as he adjusted his grip on the wheel, but she said nothing. Instead, Liliya nodded but didn't answer. We made it. The words sounded distant, as if they belonged to someone else. Anatoli met her gaze for just a moment, a shared, unspoken acknowledgment of the toll. "You hold up okay?" he asked, his voice low.

"Long as you do," she replied.

He grunted, a flicker of a grin pulling at his lips

She opened the door and stepped out, her boots landing softly on the pavement. The cold air bit at her skin, sharp enough to sting but not enough to clear the lingering fog from her mind. She inhaled deeply, testing the air, and scanned the treeline again, her gaze sharp and restless. Every sound—the rustling of leaves, the distant hum of power lines—felt amplified, too close.

Behind her, the scientists began unloading their children from the vehicles. The murmur of cautious laughter drifted through the air, fragile and hesitant, like the first thaw of spring. Liliya allowed herself a glance in their direction. A small girl clung to her father's hand, her wide eyes reflecting something Liliya hadn't dared to feel yet: hope.

Anatoli's voice broke her reverie. "You can stop now, you know."

She gave him a tight smile, though it didn't quite reach her eyes. "Not just yet."

She turned her attention back to the empty road, her gaze lingering on the dark ribbon of asphalt stretching toward the horizon. The mission was over. They were safe. And yet, her muscles refused to relax, as though her body knew something her mind hadn't caught up to yet. Safety felt like a temporary illusion—a trick of geography. She rolled her shoulders again, forcing herself to stand straighter, to appear steady, even if she wasn't.

"You good?" Anatoli asked, as he stepped beside her.

"Yeah," she replied, her voice steady. "Just a few more steps."

Estonian border guards spun toward them, rifles snapping up, quick and ready.

"Hands up!" the lead guard barked, his stance rigid as others fanned out, blocking the road with a hasty line of bodies and weapons.

Liliya raised her hands slowly, palms out. "We mean no harm," she said calmly, her eyes locking with the lead guard's.

Anatoli whispered under his breath, "Easy."

"State your purpose!" the guard demanded, his rifle aimed squarely at Liliya.

Liliya held her ground, her voice low but unwavering. "We are refugees fleeing persecution. We're seeking asylum in Estonia. These families—" she gestured subtly toward those behind her— "are running for their lives."

The guard hesitated, glancing at his comrades, doubt flickering in his eyes. "Asylum seekers, huh?" His gaze shifted to the weary faces inside the vehicles, suspicion tightening his jaw. "And who exactly are you?"

"Liliya. I'm leading this group to safety," she answered with careful precision.

"You expect us to take your word for it?" another guard muttered, his grip tightening on his rifle.

Before Liliya could respond, the screech of tires broke the tension. A sleek gray sedan rolled to a stop behind the guards. A man in a tailored suit emerged, his commanding presence turning heads.

"Lower your weapons," the man ordered, cutting through the tension like a knife. The guards hesitated, glancing between each other, reluctant to obey.

"Now," the man snapped, and the rifles lowered in unison.

He approached the convoy, his sharp gaze landing on Liliya. "I am Mihkel Saar, with the Estonian Ministry of Foreign Affairs." His tone carried the weight of authority, but there was an edge of curiosity beneath it. "And you are?"

"Liliya," she said firmly. "These people have been living under constant threat. I have documented evidence of the danger they face." She stepped closer, her voice measured. "All we ask is safe passage and asylum."

Saar's eyes flicked to the families huddled behind her. The sight of frightened children peeking over their mothers' shoulders seemed to shift something in his expression.

He gave a curt nod, then turned back to the guards. "At ease," he ordered. "We've been expecting them."

As the guards relaxed, a palpable sense of relief washed over the group. Liliya exhaled slowly, grateful for the official's swift intervention.

Anatoli let out a breath he hadn't realized he was holding, his fists tight, knuckles white. "That was close."

Liliya shot him a quick glance. "Not out of the woods yet."

Saar's attention returned to her, his tone softening slightly. "Follow me. We'll handle the documentation and provide an escort through Estonia and Latvia."

"Thank you," Liliya replied, meaning it. The words came out quieter than she intended, the adrenaline finally draining from her system.

Anatoli leaned over, his voice low. "We good?"

"Good enough," she whispered back, offering him the barest hint of a smile.

In the distance, the checkpoint glowed faintly, its watchtowers reduced to dots of light. Liliya watched it, as if waiting for movement, a shadow slipping free of the darkness. But there was nothing. The border lay quiet.

As they followed Minister Saar, the scent of woodsmoke clung faintly to the wind. Liliya paused, inhaling sharply as the scent mixed with the crisp autumn air, stirring another memory—Davyd's laugh, low and rare, shared over a campfire on a cold night. She remembered the way his eyes crinkled when he smiled, the flicker of warmth that felt, if only for a moment, like safety.

Anatoli brushed past her, muttering, "Let's move," and the spell broke. Liliya swallowed hard, the cold air sharp against her lungs.

As she followed Minister Saar toward the checkpoint, her thoughts strayed, drawn not by longing but by habit—Davyd's steady presence had been her anchor through every mission, every storm. He wasn't just someone to return to, he was the reason she kept going. When everything frayed at the edges, it was the thought of his touch—a quiet hand on her back, or the way his fingers trailed down her arm—that kept her upright.

Saar's brisk voice cut through her reverie. "This way."

Liliya adjusted her jacket, the weight of the fabric settling over her shoulders like Davyd's embrace. It was a small comfort, but enough to keep her moving forward. She could almost hear his voice: Almost there, Liliya. Just hold on a little longer.

She glanced back at the families, now beginning to exchange relieved glances and even share a few smiles. The moment of shared laughter among the children offered a glimpse of the normalcy they so desperately sought.

"Stay strong," she told herself, feeling the weight of her silent tears masked by the veil of her hair. "We're almost there."

Minister Saar's swift validation of their claims and assurance of safe passage underscored the significance of their mission. It was not just a rescue operation; it was a testament to renewal and international cooperation, highlighting the profound changes since the collapse of the Soviet Union.

Liliya exchanged a brief, relieved smile with Anatoli, the weight of their journey momentarily lifting.

As Liliya relayed the official's assurances to her team and the families they had spirited away from under the nose of Russian authorities, a collective breath of relief was palpable. The mention of Ukrainian officials awaiting their arrival in Riga to commence the asylum process was a stark reminder of the bureaucratic hurdles that lay ahead. Yet, for the moment, the promise of sanctuary within any NATO pact country shone as a beacon of hope, a tangible reward for the risks they had taken.

The final leg of their journey, a six-hour drive to Riga, had an air of tentative celebration tempered with reflection. Laughter and shared stories of relief filled the vehicle, a stark contrast to the tense silence of their escape.

As the SUVs sped towards their final destination, the landscape around them a blur of night and motion, the occupants were united not just by their shared escape but by the anticipation of the new lives that awaited them. For the scientists and their families, the end of the mission was the first chapter in a story of rebirth and resilience. For Liliya, it was a poignant conclusion to a chapter of her life defined by duty, courage, and the shadows of covert operations.

The mission's success highlighted the bravery and expertise of the team, while also underscoring the broader geopolitical tensions and personal sacrifices inherent in international espionage. The arrival in Riga would mark the end of their immediate journey but the beginning of a new chapter, filled with the challenges of integration, the bureaucratic maze of asylum proceedings, and the construction of new identities in a foreign land.

For now, though, the road to Riga was a corridor to the future, a bridge between the life they had left behind and the promise of a new beginning. The mission's conclusion was a rare moment of unequivocal success in the murky world of intelligence and defection, a beacon of hope in a realm often overshadowed by compromise and sacrifice.

TWENTY-SIX

Epilogue

Davyd opened his eyes and the fluorescent glare sharp and intrusive, blurred Commander Sanenko's face at first. The steady beep of the heart monitor pulsed beside him, yet he couldn't shake the low thrumming from the fluorescent light overhead, like a drill boring into his skull. The noise swelled, layering with phantom echoes of distant shouts, footsteps echoing down concrete halls. Instinctively, his shoulders tensed as his eyes flicked to the corners of the room, half-expecting to see a guard stationed there, waiting in the shadows.

Exhaustion pulsed through him, weighted like the pressure of an unseen hand on his chest. In the situation room, he'd kept his voice steady, a lifeline for Liliya and the team. Now, his hands twitched against the sheets, his fingers curling involuntarily as though seeking the grip of a radio mic.

Mere moments after signing off, his strength failed. He collapsed from the strain and was swiftly carried to the medical wing, sedated and spared from witnessing the convoy's harrowing dash through the Russian picket line.

Sanenko's voice was distant, tinny, as if coming through water, and Davyd's hands curled tightly into the stiff, sterile sheets, his knuckles whitening with the effort to steady himself. "We did it, Davyd," the commander said, voice low and triumphant, yet the words felt hollow, barely grounding him. "They're all on their way back to Kyiv."

Davyd forced a nod, his fingers digging into the sheet's coarse fabric. The rough weave scraped his skin, a tether to the room and the empty, cold feeling that lingered in his chest, as if waiting for something to unravel. His grip on the sheet tightened, the faint pinch of pain a grounding sensation.

Each breath felt deliberate, sharp against his ribcage. The ache in his muscles pulsed in time with his thoughts, demanding that he push harder, move faster. He clenched his fists, feeling the strain press into his tendons—tangible proof of the progress he needed to make. Yet his mind slipped to Liliya, to the bruises he knew she carried, to her eyes that had seemed darker each time he'd looked. A future—fleeting as his grip on strength—lay somewhere beyond all this. He wouldn't reach it alone.

Liliya slipped into the room, her movements almost soundless, deliberate, her steps so light they barely scuffed the floor. Davyd's pulse quickened, his hand tightening briefly on the edge of the bed before loosening. When she reached him, her fingers brushed his arm, and he exhaled, his hand rising to meet hers—a brief, careful pressure, as if testing the reality of her presence. Davyd exhaled through his nose, pulling the scent of her in. The kiss they shared wasn't deep—a silent confirmation, a signal exchanged in the quiet space between them.

"You made it back," Davyd murmured, his arms wrapping around her, holding her as if to keep the world out.

"I always do," Liliya whispered, her forehead resting against his for a moment, the way a soldier takes a breath between skirmishes. There was no need for more words—her being here was enough. They didn't dwell on relief; there wasn't time. They both knew how brief these moments could be.

As he looked at her across the room, a soft smile playing on her lips as she read, Davyd knew with certainty. This—this feeling, this moment, this woman—was what he had been fighting for all along.

Liliya's presence was a balm to his soul, and the kiss they had shared was filled with a promise of the future. Later, as she rested her head on his shoulder, Davyd's thoughts raced. The missions, the dangers, the sacrifices—they all led to this moment, to the love they shared.

"We need to find a way out of this life," Liliya whispered, her voice tinged with both hope and fear. "We can't keep living like this, always on the edge."

Davyd nodded, his hand gently stroking her hair. "I know. We'll figure it out together. We'll find a way to have a normal life."

Liliya's eyes shone with unshed tears, but she smiled. "I believe you, Davyd. I really do."

As they held each other, the room around them seemed to fade away, leaving only the two of them, united by their love and their shared promise to carve out a future free from the shadows of their past.

Davyd pushed through another stretch the strain flaring up his arms like a warning signal. Each motion was a fight, muscles tense, and the stiffness scraped at his nerves. His gaze flicked to the window—too many shadows shifting outside. He flexed his grip on the resistance band, the tension biting into his palm. They'd be watching. Waiting.

He increased the resistance on the band, his fingers tightening until his knuckles paled, every inch of movement like a tether holding him to the present. "No room for weakness," he muttered, the words as much a command as an anchor. The strain in his muscles grounded him, kept his thoughts steady as he pushed against the burn, refusing to let the echoes of the past cloud his vision. Not now.

He moved deliberately, pushing through the ache, knowing every movement brought him closer to the field and further from the confinement of this guarded room. His captivity had made him enemy number one, and every day spent in recovery only increased the risk to Liliya.

Surveillance cameras tracked his every move, their lenses cold and unblinking. Guards stood at attention just beyond the door, and Davyd couldn't shake the feeling that their vigilance was too perfect, too staged. Every muscle stretched brought a flicker of unease—had the Russians already planted eyes inside this facility? He'd survived captivity, but paranoia clung to him like a second skin.

Davyd glanced toward the window; its curtains drawn tight to block any sniper's view. The isolation clawed at him, a necessary prison. "Better here than dragging her down," he thought grimly.

The commander's last words echoed in his mind: "You're staying until you can defend yourself." A cold, tactical truth that left no room for negotiation. Each hour in this room gave his enemies time to tighten their grip—but it also gave him time to prepare.

He shifted position, jaw tight against the strain. I need to be ready. For both of us. The resistance band stretched, burning through his muscles, but the discomfort grounded him. He wasn't just rebuilding his strength—he was taking back control.

As the clock ticked steadily onward, Davyd's resolve hardened. The fight wasn't over. This hospital room wasn't just a place of healing—it was a battlefield, and every grueling second was another step toward reclaiming the life stolen from him.

Weeks of therapy stripped Liliya to her core. Each session dredged up memories she had buried—faces of the dead, the conflict between healing and killing—and forced her to confront them head-on. Some days, she teetered on the edge of collapse, her identity unraveling under the weight of guilt and survival.

Alone in her apartment one night, she stared at her hands, imagining the blood still there. No mission could justify the lives she'd taken, not when she had sworn an oath to save. The contradiction twisted in her gut.

"I'm a doctor, not a killer," she whispered to Davyd the next morning, tears in her eyes.

"You're both," he said gently. "And you protect people by stopping those who hurt them. It's not easy, but you'll find a way."

Wrapped in his arms, Liliya let the sobs come, raw and silent. For the first time, she realized the conflict within her might never fade, but with Davyd beside her, she could learn to live with it.

Therapy pushed deeper, bringing breakthroughs she hadn't thought possible. With each EMDR session, painful memories lost their grip— Dr. Mel'nyk lunging at her, the glass in her hand sharp and cold, Ivan's face that haunted her dreams. Slowly, the intensity of the triggers ebbed.

"I used to see their faces every night," she admitted during one session. "Now... they're fading." The guilt remained, but its suffocating hold loosened.

By the end of her leave, Liliya had built more than resilience—she had learned to live with the duality within her. Armed with new coping strategies and a clearer sense of purpose, she was ready to embrace the life waiting with Davyd.

The day Davyd packed his bags to leave the hospital, Liliya was already there, folding his belongings with a quiet smile. Hand in hand, they stepped into the corridor, the weight of past dangers easing with every step toward the exit. But as they neared the facility's door, Davyd's eyes scanned the shadows instinctively, his grip tightening on Liliya's hand. He tried to dismiss the chill that ran down his spine—just an old habit, he told himself. But old habits were the reason he was still alive.

They walked toward a future unknown but filled with hope. For the first time, Davyd felt the clarity he had longed for—after decades of service, he could finally choose happiness. His loyalty now belonged to Liliya, not the shadows that had governed his life.

Beside him, Liliya's decision was just as resolute. Medicine was her calling, not espionage. With Davyd as her anchor, she was ready to reclaim that part of herself, to build something real. Together, they faced a future no longer defined by duty alone, but by the promise of a life worth living.

As they stepped out of the complex, the afternoon sunbathed them in its warm glow. They made their way to Liliya's sleek, gray BMW parked nearby. Davyd's gaze swept the parking lot, catching on a dark sedan at the far end. No movement, no sign of a threat—but he instinctively noted the model, the plates, even the dust settled on its hood, calculating how quickly he could shield her if anyone emerged. In the few seconds it took him to brush away the suspicion, he felt the familiar, restless awareness settle over him. As they got into the car, his shoulder eased against the seat only to tense at the faint glint of a side mirror angled too sharply. Just old habits, he told himself. Still, his hand hovered near his waistband, fingers twitching once before he closed them.

Turning towards each other, they shared a look of mutual understanding and affection. To punctuate their new beginning, they embraced tightly and sealed their commitment with a kiss, unconcerned by the possibility of onlookers. Their kiss was not just an affirmation of their love but a defiant declaration of their independence from the shadows that had once controlled their lives.

With a swift motion, Liliya engaged the gear, and they sped off toward Davyd's apartment. The car's smooth acceleration mirrored the rush of freedom and anticipation they both felt, driving away from their past and toward a future they would now write together.

That evening, after an afternoon of reacquainting themselves with Davyd's apartment and setting everything in order following his extended absence, they arranged a simple yet intimate candlelight dinner. It was a stark contrast to the lavish affair they had experienced in Moscow two months earlier, but this dinner was imbued with a deeper significance for both of them.

As they sat across from each other, the flickering candlelight casting soft shadows around the room, they shared not only a meal but also their dreams for the future. For the first time, they allowed themselves to consider possibilities that had once seemed off-limits. "Remember that mission in Vienna?" Davyd began, a nostalgic smile on his face. "We were supposed to extract the asset from the gala, but everything went sideways."

Liliya laughed softly, the memory vivid. "Oh yes, you ended up charming the ambassador's wife while I had to sneak out through the kitchen with the asset. The look on your face when she wouldn't let you leave her side was priceless."

"I thought I was going to be stuck there forever," Davyd chuckled, shaking his head. "But we made it out, like we always do." His expression turned serious as he reached across the table to take her hand. "We've been through so much, Liliya. Sometimes, I can't believe we're here, together, planning a future."

Liliya squeezed his hand, her eyes reflecting the candlelight. "I know. It feels surreal. There were times I didn't think we'd make it. Especially after that night in Moscow." She paused, taking a deep breath. "I was so scared, Davyd. Scared of losing you, scared of what might happen if we were found out."

"I was scared too," Davyd admitted, his voice low. "But being with you, it made everything worth it. And now, we have a chance to build something real. Something that's just ours."

Throughout the meal, they laid the foundation for their future, discussing plans and making decisions with a newfound freedom. "I've been thinking about going back to medicine full-time," Liliya said, her voice filled with determination. "I want to help people in a different way. No more missions, no more killing. Just healing."

Davyd smiled; his eyes full of pride. "I think that's a wonderful idea. You're an incredible doctor, Liliya. And I want to support you in every way I can."

"And what about you?" Liliya asked, her curiosity piqued. "What do you want to do?"

"I've been considering teaching," Davyd replied thoughtfully. "Training the next generation of operatives, sharing what I've learned. But with more focus on ethics, on the human side of espionage. Maybe we can make it a little less dark." He hesitated for a moment, then added, "Especially now that there's a price on my head. Being Russia's number one enemy agent doesn't exactly make life easy."

Liliya's eyes widened, the gravity of his words sinking in. "I know the danger is real, but we're stronger together, Davyd. We'll face whatever comes our way."

Davyd nodded, his resolve firm. "Yes, together. No matter what."

Silence settled between them, heavy with unspoken fears. Davyd's gaze drifted to the patio window, the glow of candlelight casting flickering shadows across the glass. Despite the warmth in Liliya's gaze, he felt an itch between his shoulder blades, a nagging sense that something— someone—was watching. He forced himself to focus on her laughter, to drown out the instinct to check every exit.

Liliya noticed his distraction, raising an eyebrow. "You're looking for someone?"

He gave her a small smile, brushing it off. "Old habit," he said, though his fingers tapped once on the table, a reflexive count of the steps to the door. Liliya's hand covered his, her touch warm, grounding him momentarily in the present. But when her eyes shifted back to her glass, his gaze returned to the shadows stretching across the room.

Their lives had always been fraught with danger, but now, with a target on Davyd's back, the threat felt even more palpable. "What about our safety, Davyd? What if they find us? We can never truly be at peace."

Davyd squeezed her hand, his eyes intense. "We'll take precautions. We'll stay under the radar, change identities if we have to. I've been doing this for years. We can manage."

Liliya nodded slowly, trying to absorb his confidence. "I just want us to be safe. I want a life where we don't have to constantly look over our shoulders."

"I want that too, Liliya. More than anything. But we have to be realistic. My past, our past, it will always be there. We just have to be smarter, more vigilant. We can build a future, but we'll have to be cautious. Always."

The reality of their situation weighed heavily on both of them. The flickering candlelight cast long shadows, mirroring the uncertainty that lay ahead. But amidst the darkness, there was a flicker of hope, a promise that together, they could overcome any obstacle.

"Imagine," Liliya said softly, "a place where we can finally breathe freely, where we can wake up each day without the fear of being hunted. It's a beautiful dream, isn't it?"

Davyd's smile held a flicker of something unspoken, a softness in his eyes. "It is. And we're going to make it happen, Liliya. We'll find our place—somewhere we're finally free."

Her gaze lingered on him, and for a moment, silence filled the space between them. She nodded, her fingers brushing his, anchoring herself in the touch. "We'll get there," she said softly, as if the words themselves could shield them from the uncertainty ahead.

As they began to clear the table, their movements grew slower, each shared task drawn out in a quiet ritual. When their hands met in the soapy water, neither pulled away, the warmth between them tangible. "Do you remember the first time we did this?" Liliya asked, a hint of mischief in her voice. "After Saint Petersburg, pretending to be... just a couple."

Davyd chuckled, eyes crinkling with amusement. "I remember," he said, his hand lingering over hers as he passed her a dish. "We broke half of them because you kept distracting me."

She smirked, nudging him lightly. "You were the one who couldn't focus."

Their laughter was soft, but every brush of their hands, every glance held, was loaded with an intensity that went beyond words. They moved in sync, sharing touches that lingered, a silent exchange of promises. As they finished the last dish, he turned, catching her hand as she dried it. Neither spoke, but the look they shared said everything.

In the quiet that followed, he pulled her close, his fingers tracing gentle circles along her back. She exhaled, sinking into his arms, letting the tension fall away as they stood together. When he finally leaned in, their kiss was slow, deliberate, a long-awaited answer to everything left unsaid. They made their way to the bedroom, each step an unspoken vow, each embrace a quiet reckoning of the time they'd spent apart.

In that moment, duty faded. Their reunion was fierce and tender, every touch a release of the months of waiting, every whisper a promise of nights beyond the shadows. Together, they reclaimed the sanctuary they'd dreamed of, holding onto each other as if the world couldn't pull them apart again.

The next morning, Davyd awoke to the low hum of running water, steady and faint. He watched Liliya's silhouette blur behind the steam, the soft rhythm pattering against the tile. His fingers twitched reflexively, as if grasping for his sidearm—a habit that even the quiet moments couldn't

332

erase. The steady stream of water, almost hypnotic, grounded him, if only for a beat, but shadows clung stubbornly to the edges of his vision. In this calm, the urge to move, to react, was hard to silence.

He joined her without a word, their movements slow and deliberate, not out of luxury but necessity—the kind of closeness born from shared danger, where even mundane moments held weight.

Their touches were brief—a hand lingering on a shoulder, a kiss pressed to damp skin—not indulgent, but caring. Each touch was a reassurance, a reminder: We're still here.

When they stepped out and wrapped themselves in towels, the world outside felt no less dangerous, but for now, they had each other, and that was enough.

They moved through the kitchen with practiced ease, the kind of coordination born from missions rather than routine. Liliya passed him the skillet without a word, and Davyd cracked the eggs with a precise motion, the yolks bubbling in the pan. Their touches were quick, efficient—hands brushing, a small nudge at the hip—reminders that they were still here, still together.

The aroma of toast and bacon mingled with the early sunlight streaming through the window. For a fleeting moment, the room felt like neutral ground, a brief ceasefire in a war that never really ended.

Liliya leaned into Davyd's side, her shoulder pressing against his, grounding him. "Almost feels normal," she murmured. Davyd's fingers tightened reflexively on her shoulder, his gaze flicking to the small reflection in the darkened window.

He smiled, returning his gaze on the skillet. "Almost," he agreed. He forced himself to let her presence settle over him, but each murmur in the apartment below set his jaw tight. He listened, attuning to footsteps, plumbing, the faintest drone of traffic. The silence felt stretched, the calm a fragile thread. He let her warmth anchor him, but in his mind, he still mapped every possible escape.

For the first time in months, it felt like they had escaped the shadows that haunted them—like a new beginning. Liliya nestled closer, her laughter soft and unguarded as she brushed a kiss along his jaw.

Yet, despite the lightness of the moment, something lingered beneath Davyd's surface, a shadow trailing the edges of his thoughts.

"It's too quiet," he murmured, almost to himself.

Liliya, sensing his hesitation, teased him lightly, "Almost too quiet." She kissed his cheek, lingering just long enough to coax him back into the moment.

He glanced at the window. A glint flickered across the glass—a sharp, fleeting shimmer that caught his attention. He stiffened, his breath pausing mid-inhale. A reflection? No, just sunlight playing tricks. He blinked, forcing himself to release the tension knotting in his chest. "Relax," he told himself. "Not here. Not now."

Davyd chuckled under his breath, trying to shake the unease still clinging to him. Yet the playful warmth between them remained, wrapping them in a cocoon, as if they were untouched by the dangers that once felt so close. The light shifted as Liliya leaned closer, tilting her head to meet his kiss. The shadows along the walls stretched with the slow rise of morning, casting long fingers across the room. Then, the glimmer returned—this time sharper, brighter.

Davyd stiffened. Scope flare. The realization struck, but too late.

The window shattered, splintering into a thousand shards that caught the sunlight like jagged mirrors, scattering fragments of light and shadow across the kitchen. A deafening crack split the air, and the warmth that had filled the room evaporated in an instant.

Liliya gasped as the glass exploded past her. Time fractured with the impact—hope dissolving into chaos. She turned just as Davyd staggered back, a red stain blooming across his chest, darkening the bright white of his shirt.

"Davyd!" Her scream tore through the silence.

The sun's rays, now broken by the shattered glass, painted uneven patterns across his collapsing form—light catching on the blood, shadows stretching across his body as he faltered in her arms. The promise of their future together faded with the dimming light in his eyes.

Liliya cradled him, pressing her hands desperately over the wound, but the sunlight, once so warm, now felt cold as it filtered through the ruined window. Every sliver of brightness on the walls seemed like a cruel reminder of the life slipping away from her grasp.

"Stay with me, Davyd," she whispered, her voice trembling but fierce. Yet even as she worked to save him, the light outside dimmed, clouds gathering to swallow the morning sun. The room grew darker, shadows thickening as if mourning what was already lost.

In that fleeting moment, as Davyd's life seemed to slip away, Liliya's world collapsed into ruin around her. But her training kicked in, overriding her despair. She quickly assessed his condition, her hands moving with practiced precision.

"Liliya, focus," she muttered to herself, wiping away her tears with the back of her hand. She checked his pulse—weak and thready—and noted the shallow rise and fall of his chest. Her mind raced through the possibilities: internal bleeding, a punctured lung, shock.

She tore open his shirt, exposing a wound that was already beginning to seep blood. "Damn it," she hissed, applying pressure with her hands. She glanced around, desperate for anything that could help. Her eyes landed on a nearby first aid kit, and she reached for it, her movements swift and deliberate.

With shaking hands, she pulled out gauze and antiseptic. "Stay with me, Davyd," she repeated, her voice a mix of command and plea. She cleaned the wound as best as she could, her mind a whirlwind of medical terms and procedures. She knew she needed to stop the bleeding and stabilize him, but out here, with limited supplies, it felt like an insurmountable task.

She placed a pressure bandage over the wound, her fingers deftly securing it in place. "You're going to be okay," she whispered, though she wasn't sure if she was convincing him or herself. She needed to get him to a hospital, somewhere with the right equipment and personnel. But the nearest one was miles away, and she didn't know if he had that much time.

Davyd's eyes fluttered open, and he looked at her with a mixture of pain and determination. "Liliya..." he gasped, his voice barely audible. "You need to go... leave me..."

"Not a chance," she snapped, her tone fierce. "I'm not leaving you. Not now, not ever." She checked his pulse again, relieved to feel it still there, even if faint. She leaned down, pressing her forehead to his, drawing strength from the contact. "Hold on, Davyd. Just hold on."

In that harrowing moment, as she held Davyd in her arms, Liliya was struck by a cruel revelation. Despite all her planning and the dreams, she had dared to nurture for their future together, fate had cruelly intervened. The stark reality settled heavily upon her: no matter how carefully she charted her path or how deeply she loved, some forces remained beyond her control. This truth, revealed amid tragedy, reshaped her understanding of life and its unpredictable nature.

With that stark realization, Liliya's resolve hardened. As she cradled Davyd, feeling the weight of their shattered future together, she understood that her path remained with the service—not out of a sense of duty to her country, but as a tribute to Davyd. Her mission would no longer be for national pride or strategic gains but a personal crusade in the name of the man who had changed her life. She knew she had to follow up on the intel they had intercepted last month, the hints of a new threat rising in the east. In the face of fate's cruel twist, this was how she would fight back, how she would honor the love and dreams they had shared.

OPERATION RETRIBUTION
(SNEAK PEEK)

CHAPTER

ONE

Winter Cabin

The sky stretched above them, a dazzling blue contrasting with the freshly blanketed snow on the mountain peaks. The untouched expanse of crystalline snow lay before them, pristine and inviting. A waterfall's steady cadence mingled with birdsong, creating a symphony of natural sounds. It was a blissful scene, just as the couple had imagined when planning their winter escape.

As the sun began its descent, painting the sky in hues of orange and pink, the couple started to feel the chill of the evening air setting in—a familiar sensation for them. Despite intending only brief strolls, they lost track of time in deep conversation, walking arm in arm. Their closeness was not just for warmth but to feel each other's presence and confirm their bond.

The deep, resonant fire of their love for one another fueled their discussions, which often ventured into the realm of dreams and aspirations. They found themselves walking through a forest path, the snow crunching under their boots. The moonlight filtered through the trees, casting a soft glow on the path ahead. Davyd squeezed Liliya's hand, his eyes reflecting the pale light. "I've been thinking about what you said, about going back to medicine full-time. It's a wonderful idea," he said, his voice warm with encouragement.

Liliya smiled, her cheeks flushed from the cold and the warmth of his words. "And I've been thinking about your idea of teaching. Training the next generation with a focus on ethics and the human side of espionage—it's something that could make a real difference."

Their eyes rarely strayed from one another, locked in a gaze filled with affection and longing. Only brief, necessary glances were spared to navigate the snow-covered path beneath their feet.

They continued walking, their steps in sync, the forest around them silent except for the sound of their voices and the occasional rustle of the wind through the trees. Suddenly, Liliya mis stepped, her foot catching on a hidden root. She stumbled, pulling Davyd with her, and they both tumbled into a snowbank. The impact caused a nearby branch to shake, releasing a shower of snow onto them.

Liliya gasped as the cold snow landed on her, but her gasp quickly turned into laughter. Davyd joined in, his deep chuckles resonating through the forest. They lay in the snow for a moment, catching their breath and savoring the pure joy of the moment.

"Alright, you got me good this time," Davyd said, still laughing as he helped Liliya to her feet.

"Let's call it even then," Liliya replied with a grin, brushing the snow from her coat.

They stood close, the laughter fading into a comfortable silence. Davyd wrapped his arms around Liliya, pulling her into a warm embrace. She leaned into him, feeling the steady beat of his heart against her own. "I love these moments with you," she whispered, her breath visible in the cold air.

"Me too," he replied, his voice filled with sincerity. "I wish they could last forever."

For a moment, they stood there, wrapped in each other's arms, the world around them falling away. In that embrace, they found not just the warmth of contact but the promise of all the nights to come, now free from the shadows of duty that had once kept them apart.

As they continued their walk, their conversations flowed naturally, each word weaving a tapestry of shared hopes and dreams. They spoke of a future where they could wake up each day without the weight of the world on their shoulders, where they could simply be together.

"It's so quiet today," Liliya remarked, her voice soft and content.

"Almost too quiet," Davyd responded, his tone light but with a hint of underlying tension. He glanced around, ever vigilant, but quickly refocused on Liliya, his loving smile reassuring her. Just a few yards away awaited the comforting warmth of a roaring fire and the promise of hot drinks. The knowledge of this near respite added a sweet anticipation to their journey, making each snowy challenge along the way a delightful interlude in their winter adventure.

The couple's serene walk belied the vigilance always simmering beneath the surface. Even in their blissful escape, an undercurrent of caution remained—a silent acknowledgment of the threats that lurked beyond their sanctuary.

Eager for the warmth that awaited them both inside and out, they stepped into the cabin and shed their coats. The fireplace, once blazing, now held only glowing embers. Davyd immediately set to work, skillfully stoking the coals and adding fresh logs to resurrect the fire. Soon, cheerful flames crackled anew, spreading warmth through the room.

Meanwhile, Liliya headed to the kitchen to prepare a comforting treat. She filled a pot with water and set it to boil for hot chocolate, the perfect remedy to the day's chill. As the fire roared, Davyd joined her in the kitchen. Together, they stood by the stove, stirring the simmering cocoa, synchronized in the cozy warmth. Preparing hot drinks became another shared moment, strengthening their bond against the cold outside.

Davyd carefully picked up the steaming mugs of hot chocolate and returned to the fireside, where Liliya was already nestled on the plush rug, mesmerized by the dance of the flickering flames. He handed her the cups, then settled down behind her, wrapping his arms and legs around her in a warm embrace. She passed back his mug, and together, they sank into a comfortable silence, each sip of the rich cocoa enhancing the cozy warmth enveloping them.

The gentle crackle of the fire provided a soothing soundtrack to their quiet contemplation. As the flames cast playful shadows around the room, they both relished the comforting heat that radiated from the hearth. It was moments like these—simple, serene, and shared—that deepened their bond and made the cabin a haven from the world outside.

Four months had passed since an assassin's bullet nearly took Davyd from her. As they sat by the fire, the crackling flames seemed to echo that morning's chaos. A simple breakfast had shattered into terror when the window broke, glass splintering, blood staining his white shirt.

Liliya's fingers tightened around the mug, its warmth grounding her against the cold dread that still lurked. She'd held his weight in her arms, the silence after the shot deafening. She'd been thrust into a role she hadn't prepared for—protector, lifesaver. Without the swift response from Commander Sanenko's team, he wouldn't have made it. That gratitude, mixed with the fear, sat like a stone in her chest.

Now, she looked at Davyd in the firelight, his face softened by the glow but shadowed with resilience. They'd survived, yet the attack left them changed. Every quiet moment together felt more precious—and more fragile. How would they balance love with the danger always close behind? The questions lingered, the answers still out of reach.

With a deep sigh, Liliya turned her gaze back to Davyd, his features softened by the firelight. In his eyes, she saw not just the reflection of the flames, but the steady glow of resilience and love. Whatever challenges lay ahead, they would face them together, fortified by the trials they had already overcome. This, she realized, was the true foundation of their life together — not the absence of danger, but the presence of an unbreakable bond.

www.ingramcontent.com/pod-product-compliance
Lightning Source LLC
Chambersburg PA
CBHW020826180626
46814CB00001B/122